ARCTIC CHILL

Arnaldur Indriðason worked for many years as a journalist and critic before he began writing novels. His crime novels featuring Erlendur and Sigurdur Óli are consistent bestsellers across Europe. The series has won numerous awards, including the Nordic Glass Key (both for *Jar City* and *Silence of the Grave*) and the CWA Gold Dagger (for *Silence of the Grave*). His most recent novel is *Hypothermia*.

ARNALDUR INDRIÐASON

Arctic Chill

TRANSLATED FROM THE ICELANDIC BY
Bernard Scudder and Victoria Cribb

VINTAGE BOOKS
London

Published by Vintage 2009

Copyright © Arnaldur Indriðason 2005
English translation copyright © Bernard Scudder and Victoria Cribb 2008

Arnaldur Indriðason has asserted his right under the Copyright, Designs
and Patents Act 1988 to be identified as the author of this work

First published with the title *Vetrarborgin* by
Vaka-Helgafell, Reykjavík in 2005

First published in Great Britain in 2008 by
Harvill Secker

Vintage
Random House, 20 Vauxhall Bridge Road,
London SW1V 2SA

www.vintage-books.co.uk

Addresses for companies within The Random House Group Limited
can be found at: www.randomhouse.co.uk/offices.htm

The Random House Group Limited Reg. No. 954009

A CIP catalogue record for this book
is available from the British Library

The Random House Group Limited supports The Forest
Stewardship Council (FSC), the leading international forest
certification organisation. All our titles that are printed on
Greenpeace approved FSC certified paper carry the FSC logo.
Our paper procurement policy can be found at:
www.rbooks.co.uk/environment

Mixed Sources
Product group from well-managed
forests and other controlled sources
www.fsc.org Cert no. TT-COC-2139
© 1996 Forest Stewardship Council

Printed and bound in Great Britain by
Clays Ltd, St Ives plc

In memory of Bernard Scudder

*Am I the one, who lives on,
or the other, who died?*
Steinn Steinarr, *In a Cemetery*

1

They were able to guess his age, but had more trouble determining which part of the world he came from.

They thought he was about ten years old. He was wearing a grey anorak, unzipped, with a hood, and military-style camouflage trousers. His school bag was on his back. One of his boots had come off and there was a hole in his sock. One toe poked through. The boy was not wearing gloves or a hat. His black hair was already frozen to the ice. He lay on his stomach with one cheek turned up towards them, and they saw his broken eyes staring along the frozen earth. The puddle of blood underneath him had started to freeze.

Elínborg knelt down beside the body.

'Oh my God,' she groaned. 'What on earth is happening?'

She held out her hand, as though she wanted to touch the body. The boy looked as if he had lain down to take a rest. She had difficulty controlling herself, did not want to believe what she saw.

'Don't move him,' Erlendur said calmly. He was standing by the body with Sigurdur Óli.

'He must have been cold,' Elínborg muttered, withdrawing her hand and slowly getting to her feet.

It was the middle of January. The winter had been reasonable until the New Year, when the temperature dropped sharply. The ground was now covered in a solid coating of ice and the north wind howled and sang around the blocks of flats. Rippling sheets of snow swept along the ground. They collected into little drifts here and there and fine powder snow swirled away from them. Straight from the Arctic, the wind bit their faces and penetrated their clothes, cutting to the bone. Erlendur thrust his hands deep into the pockets of his winter coat and shuddered. The sky was heavy with cloud and it was dark, although it had only just turned four o'clock.

'Why do they make military trousers like that for children?' he asked.

The three of them stood hunched over the boy's body. The blue flashing lights of the police cars bounced off the surrounding houses and blocks of flats. A few passers-by had gathered by the cars. The first reporters had arrived. Forensics were photographing the scene, their flashes vying with the blue lights. They sketched the layout of the area where the boy was lying and the immediate surroundings. The forensic investigation was in its initial stages.

'Those trousers are in fashion,' Elínborg said.

'Do you think there's something wrong with that?' Sigurdur Óli asked. 'Kids wearing trousers like those?'

'I don't know,' Erlendur said. 'Yes, I find it odd,' he added after a pause.

He looked up at the block of flats. People were outside on the balconies watching, in spite of the cold. Others stayed indoors and made do with the view through the window. But most were still at work and their windows were dark. The officers would have to go to all the apartments and talk to the residents. The witness who had found the boy said that he lived there. Perhaps he had been alone and had fallen off the balcony, in which case this could be recorded as a nonsensical accident. Erlendur preferred that theory to the idea of the boy having been murdered. He could not pursue that thought through to the end.

He scrutinised the surroundings. The garden behind the flats did not seem well kept. In the middle was a patch of gravel that served as a little playground. There were two swings, one broken so that the seat hung down to ground level and spun around in the wind; a battered slide that had originally been painted red but was now patchy and rusty, and a simple see-saw with two little seats made from bits of wood, one end frozen solid to the ground and the other standing up in the air like the barrel of a large gun.

'We need to find his boot,' Sigurdur Óli said.

They all looked at the sock with the hole in it.

'This can't be happening,' Elínborg sighed.

Detectives were searching for footprints in the garden but darkness was falling and they couldn't see much on the frozen ground. The garden was covered with a coat of slippery ice, occasional clusters of grass poking through it. The district medical officer had confirmed the death and was standing where he thought he would be sheltered from the gale, trying to light a cigarette. He was uncertain about the time of death. Somewhere in the past hour, he thought. He had explained that the forensic pathologist would calculate the exact time of death by correlating the degrees of frost with the body temperature. On first impression the doctor could not identify a cause of death. Possibly a fall, he said, looking up at the gloomy block.

The body had not been disturbed. The pathologist was on his way. If possible he preferred to visit the crime scene and examine the surroundings with the police. Erlendur was concerned at the ever-growing crowd gathering at the corner of the block, who could see the body lit up by the flashing cameras. Cars cruised slowly past, their passengers absorbing the scene. A small floodlight was being erected to enable a closer examination of the site. Erlendur told a policeman to cordon off the area.

From the garden, none of the doors appeared to open out onto a balcony from which the boy might have fallen. The windows were all shut. This was a large block of flats by Icelandic standards, six storeys high with four stairwells. It was in a poor state of repair. The iron railings round the balconies were rusty. The paint was faded and in some places it had flaked off the concrete. Two sitting-room windows with a single large crack in each were visible from where Erlendur stood. No one had bothered to replace them.

'Do you suppose it's racially motivated?' Sigurdur Óli said, looking down at the boy's body.

'I don't think we should jump to conclusions,' Erlendur said.

'Could he have been climbing up the wall?' Elínborg asked as she, too, looked up at the apartment block.

'Kids do the unlikeliest things,' Sigurdur Óli remarked.

'We need to establish whether he might have been climbing up between the balconies,' Erlendur said.

'Where do you think he's from?' Sigurdur Óli wondered.

'He looks Asian to me,' Elínborg said.

'Could be Thai, Filipino, Vietnamese, Korean, Japanese, Chinese,' Sigurdur Óli reeled off.

'Shouldn't we say he's an Icelander until we find out otherwise?' Erlendur said.

They stood in silence in the cold, watching the drifting snow

4

pile up around the boy. Erlendur looked at the curious bystanders at the corner where the police cars were parked. Then he took off his coat and draped it over the body.

'Is it safe doing that?' Elínborg asked with a glance in the direction of the forensics team. According to procedure they were not even supposed to stand over the body until forensics had granted permission.

'I don't know,' Erlendur said.

'Not very professional,' Sigurdur Óli said.

'Has no one reported the boy missing?' Erlendur asked, ignoring his remark. 'No enquiries about a lost boy of this age?'

'I checked that on the way here,' Elínborg said. 'The police haven't been notified of any.'

Erlendur glanced down at his coat. He was cold.

'Where's the person who found him?'

'We've got him in one of the stairwells,' Sigurdur Óli said. 'He waited for us. Called from his mobile. Every kid carries a mobile phone these days. He said he'd taken a shortcut through the garden on his way home from school and stumbled across the body.'

'I'll talk to him,' Erlendur said. 'You check whether they can find the boy's tracks through the garden. If he was bleeding he might have left a trail. Maybe he didn't fall.'

'Shouldn't forensics handle that?' Sigurdur Óli mumbled to deaf ears.

'He doesn't appear to have been attacked here in the garden,' Elínborg said.

'And for God's sake, try to find his boot,' Erlendur said as he walked off.

'The boy who found him . . .' Sigurdur Óli began.

'Yes,' Erlendur said, turning round.

'He's also col . . .' Sigurdur Óli hesitated.

'What?'

'An immigrant kid,' Sigurdur Óli said.

The boy sat on a step in one of the stairwells of the block of flats, a policewoman sat with him. He had his sports kit wrapped up in a yellow plastic bag and eyed Erlendur with suspicion. They had not wanted to make him sit in a police car. That could have led people to conclude that he was implicated in the boy's death, so someone had suggested that he wait in the stairwell instead.

The corridor was dirty. An unhygienic odour pervaded the air, mingling with cigarette smoke and cooking smells from the flats. The floor was covered in worn linoleum and the graffiti on the wall seemed illegible to Erlendur. The boy's parents were still at work. They had been notified. He was dark-skinned with straight jet-black hair that was still damp after his shower, and big white teeth. He was dressed in an anorak and jeans, and holding a woollen hat in his hands.

'It's awfully cold,' Erlendur said, rubbing his hands.

The boy was silent.

Erlendur sat down beside him. The boy said that his name was Stefán and he was thirteen. He lived in the next block of flats up from this one and had done so for as long as he could remember. His mother was from the Philippines, he said.

'You must have been shocked when you found him,' Erlendur said after a lengthy silence.

'Yes.'

'And you recognised him? You knew him?'

Stefán had told the police the boy's name and where he lived. It was in this block but on another staircase and the police were trying to locate his parents. All Stefán knew about the boy was that his mother made chocolate and he had one brother. He said he had not known him particularly well, nor his brother. They had only quite recently moved to the area.

'He was called Elli,' the boy said. 'His name was Elías.'

'Was he dead when you found him?'

'Yes, I think so. I shook him but nothing happened.'

'And you phoned us?' Erlendur said, feeling he ought to try to cheer the lad up. 'That was a good thing to do. Absolutely the right thing. What did you mean when you said his mother makes chocolate?'

'She works in a chocolate factory.'

'Do you know what could have happened to Elli?'

'No.'

'Do you know any of his friends?'

'Not really.'

'What did you do after you shook him?'

'Nothing,' the boy said. 'I just called the cops.'

'You know the cops' number?'

'Yes. I come home from school on my own and Mum likes to keep an eye on me. She . . .'

'She what?'

'She always tells me to phone the police immediately if . . .'

'If what?'

'If anything happens.'

'What do you think happened to Elli?'

'I don't know.'

'Were you born in Iceland?'

'Yes.'

'Elli too, do you know?'

The boy had been staring down at the linoleum on the stairwell floor all the time, but now he looked Erlendur in the face.

7

'Yes,' he answered.

The front door swung open and Elínborg was blown indoors. A thin sheet of glass separated the stairwell from the entrance and Erlendur saw that she was carrying his overcoat. With a smile he told the boy he might talk to him again later, then stood up and walked over to Elínborg.

'You know you must only interrogate children in the presence of a parent or guardian or child welfare officer and all that,' she snapped as she handed him his coat.

'I wasn't interrogating him,' Erlendur said. 'Just asking about things in general.' He looked at his overcoat. 'Has the body been removed?'

'It's on its way to the morgue. He didn't fall. They found a trail.'

Erlendur grimaced.

'The boy entered the garden from the west side,' Elínborg said. 'There's a path there. It's supposed to be lit but one of the residents told us there's only one lamp-post and the bulbs are always getting smashed. He got into the garden by climbing over the fence. We found blood on it. He lost his boot there, probably when he was clambering over.'

Elínborg took a deep breath.

'Someone stabbed him,' she said. 'He probably died from a knife wound to the stomach. There was a pool of blood underneath him that froze more or less directly it formed.'

Elínborg fell silent.

'He was probably going home,' she said eventually.

'Can we trace where he was stabbed?'

'We're working on it.'

'Have his parents been contacted?'

'His mother's on the way. Her name's Sunee. She's Thai. We

haven't told her what's happened yet. That'll be terrible.'

'You go and be with her,' Erlendur said. 'What about the father?'

'I don't know. There are three names on the entryphone. One looked something like Niran.'

'I understand he has a brother,' Erlendur said.

He opened the door for her and they went out into the howling north wind. Elínborg waited for the mother. She would go to the morgue with her. A policeman accompanied Stefán home; they would take a statement from him there. Erlendur went back into the garden. He put on his overcoat. The grass was dark where the boy had been lying.

I am felled to the ground.

A snatch of old verse entered Erlendur's mind as he stood, silent and deep in thought, looking down at the patch where the boy had been lying. He took a last glance up the length of the gloomy block of flats, then carefully picked his way over the icy ground towards the playground, where he grasped the cold steel of the slide with one hand. He felt the piercing cold crawl up his arm.

I am felled to the ground,
frozen and cannot be freed . . .

2

Elínborg accompanied the boy's mother to the morgue on Barónsstígur. She was a short, petite woman, in her mid-thirties and tired after a long day at work. Her thick, dark hair was tied in a ponytail, her face round and friendly. The police had found out where she worked and two men were sent to collect her. It took them some time to explain to her what had happened and that she had to go with them. They drove up to the flats where Elínborg joined them in the car and realised that they needed an interpreter. One of the policemen contacted the Multicultural Centre, which sent a woman to meet them at the morgue.

The interpreter had not yet turned up when Elínborg arrived with the mother. She accompanied the woman straight into the morgue where the pathologist was waiting for them. When the mother saw her son she let out a piercing howl and slumped into Elínborg's arms. She screamed something in her own language. At that moment the interpreter walked in, an Icelandic woman about the same age as the mother, and together she and Elínborg tried to comfort her. Elínborg got the impression that the two women were acquainted. The interpreter tried to talk to the mother in a soothing tone but, out of her wits with grief and helplessness, she tore herself loose, threw herself onto the boy and cried at the top of her voice.

Eventually they managed to get her out of the morgue and into a police car, which drove her straight home. Elínborg told the interpreter that the mother ought to ask a member of her family or a friend to be with her during this painful ordeal, someone close to her, someone she trusted. The interpreter passed on the message but the mother showed no response.

Elínborg explained to the interpreter how Elías had been found lying in the garden behind the block of flats. She described the police investigation and asked her to inform the mother.

'She has a brother in Iceland,' the interpreter said. 'I'll contact him.'

'Do you know this woman?' Elínborg asked.

The interpreter nodded.

'Have you lived in Thailand?'

'Yes, for several years,' the interpreter said. 'I first went there as an exchange student.'

She said her name was Gudný, and she was slender and quite short, with dark hair and large glasses. She wore a thick woollen sweater and jeans under a black coat, and had a white woollen shawl over her shoulders.

When they arrived back at the flats, the woman asked to be shown where her son was found and they took her into the garden. It was pitch dark by now but the forensics team had set up lights and cordoned off the area. News of the murder had spread rapidly. Elínborg noticed two bouquets of flowers laid against the wall of the block of flats, where a growing crowd was gathering by the police cars, looking on in silence.

The mother went through the police cordon. Forensics technicians in white overalls stopped their work and watched her. She was soon standing alone but for the interpreter at the place where her son had been found dead. She knelt down, placed the palm of her hand on the ground and wept.

Erlendur emerged from the darkness and watched her.

'We ought to go up to her flat,' he said to Elínborg, who nodded in reply.

They stood in the cold for some time, waiting for the two women to come back. Eventually, the detectives followed them out of the garden and into the stairwell in the part of the block where the mother lived. Elínborg introduced Erlendur to her as a detective who would be taking part in the investigation into her son's death.

'Perhaps you'd prefer to talk to us later,' Erlendur said. 'But the fact is that the sooner we receive information, the better, and the more time that passes after the deed, the more difficult it might be to find the person who did it.'

Erlendur stopped talking to allow the interpreter to translate what he had said. He was about to continue when the mother looked at him and said something in Thai.

'Who did it?' the interpreter said at once.

'We don't know,' Erlendur said. 'We'll find out.'

The mother turned to the interpreter and spoke again, a look of acute anxiety on her face.

'She has another son and she's worried about him,' the interpreter said.

'Does she have any idea where he might be?' Erlendur asked.

'No,' the interpreter said. 'He should have left school around the same time as his brother.'

'Is he older?'

'Five years older,' the interpreter said.

'So that makes him . . . ?'

'Fifteen.'

The mother hurried up the stairs in front of them until they reached the fourth floor, the second-highest. Erlendur was surprised that there was no lift in such a tall building.

Sunee unlocked the flat, shouting something before the door was even open. Erlendur thought it was the name of her other son. She ran around the flat but, seeing that no one was home, stood helpless and strangely alone in front of them until the interpreter put an arm around her, led her into the sitting room and sat down on the sofa with her. Erlendur and Elínborg followed, and they were joined by a thin man who had come running up the stairs and introduced himself as the vicar of the local church and an experienced trauma counsellor.

'We have to find his brother,' Elínborg said. 'Let's hope nothing's happened to him.'

'Let's hope it wasn't him who did this,' Erlendur said.

Elínborg looked at him in astonishment.

'The things you think of!'

She looked around her. Sunee lived in a small two-bedroom flat. The front door opened straight onto the sitting room, while to one side was a small corridor leading to a bathroom and two bedrooms. The kitchen was beside the sitting room. A strong aroma of oriental spices and exotic cuisine filled the flat, which was spotlessly tidy and decorated with ornaments from Thailand. All over the walls and tables were photographs that Elínborg imagined showed the mother's relatives on the other side of the globe.

Erlendur was standing beneath a red paper parasol with a picture of a yellow dragon on it, which served as a lampshade. When the interpreter said she was going to make tea, Elínborg followed her into the kitchen. Sunee remained on the sofa and the vicar sat down beside her. Erlendur said nothing and waited for the interpreter to come back.

Gudný knew a little about Sunee's background and recounted it to Elínborg in the kitchen in half-whispers. She was from a village about two hundred kilometres from Bangkok and had been brought up in a household where three generations lived together in straitened circumstances. There were many children and Sunee had moved to the capital with two of her brothers when she was fifteen. She did manual labour, mainly in laundries, and lived in poor, cramped conditions with her brothers until she was twenty. After that she had described herself as being alone, working in a large textile factory manufacturing cheap clothing for western markets. Only women worked there and the wages were low. Around that time she met a man from a far-away country, an Icelander, at a popular nightclub in Bangkok. He was several years older than her. She had never heard of Iceland.

While the interpreter told Elínborg this story and the vicar consoled Sunee, Erlendur walked around the sitting room. There was an oriental charm about the flat. A small altar stood halfway along the wall with cut flowers, incense and a bowl of water, and a beautiful picture from rural Thailand. He perused the cheap ornaments, souvenirs and framed photographs, some of them showing two boys at different ages. Erlendur presumed these were the deceased and his brother. He picked up from the table what he took to be a photograph of the elder boy and asked Sunee whether it was him. She nodded. He asked to borrow it and took it to the front door, where he gave it to the policeman who was standing there and told him to distribute it at the police station and to start looking for the lad.

Erlendur was holding his mobile in his hand when it began to ring. It was Sigurdur Óli.

He had traced the boy's tracks from the garden, to a narrow path and down it across a quiet road, past houses and gardens until it stopped beneath the wall of a small electricity utility building or substation that was covered in graffiti. The substation was about five hundred metres from the boy's home and not far from the local school. On first impression, Sigurdur Óli could see no signs of a struggle. More policemen descended on the scene and began searching with flashlights for the murder weapon in nearby gardens and on paths, streets and in the school yard.

'Keep me informed,' Erlendur said. 'Is it far from this place to the school, did you say?'

'It's really next door. But that doesn't mean the boy was stabbed here, even if this is where the tracks stop.'

'I know,' Erlendur said. 'Talk to people at the school, the principal, the staff. We need to interview the boy's teachers and classmates. His friends in the neighbourhood too. Everyone who knew him or can tell us anything about him.'

'That's my old school,' Sigurdur Óli mumbled.

'Really?' Erlendur said. Sigurdur Óli rarely talked about himself. 'Are you from this part of town?'

'I've hardly been to the place since,' Sigurdur Óli said. 'We lived here for two years. Then we moved again.'

'And?'

'And nothing.'

'Do you think they'll remember you, your old teachers?'

'I hope not,' Sigurdur Óli said. 'What class was the boy in?'

Erlendur went into the kitchen.

'We need to know what class the boy was in,' he said to the interpreter.

Gudný went into the sitting room, spoke with Sunee and came back with the information.

'Have there been any racial clashes in this area?' Erlendur asked her.

'Nothing that's reached our desk at the Multicultural Centre.'

'What about racial prejudice? Have you been aware of that?'

'I don't think so, no more than the usual.'

'We need to look into any ethnic violence in this part of town, find out if there have been any clashes,' Erlendur said over the phone to Sigurdur Óli, once he had given him the details of Elías's class. 'Also where they've occurred in other districts. I remember some trouble not so long ago: someone pulled a knife. We need to check that out.'

The tea was ready and Elínborg and the interpreter went into the sitting room with Erlendur. The vicar left and Gudný sat down beside Sunee. Elínborg had brought a chair with her from the kitchen. Gudný talked to Sunee, who nodded. Erlendur hoped she was telling the mother that the sooner the police received precise information about the boy's movements that day, the better it would be for the investigation.

Erlendur was still holding his mobile and was about to put it in his pocket, but hesitated and stared at it. His thoughts turned to the young witness who carried a mobile phone because his mother was worried about him being alone after school.

'Did her son have a mobile phone?' he asked the interpreter.

She translated what he said.

'No,' she said then.

'What about his brother?'

'No,' Gudný said. 'None of this family has a mobile phone. She can't afford one. Not everyone can afford those phones,' she added, and Erlendur had the feeling she was expressing her own thoughts.

'Doesn't he go to school near the block here?' he said.

'Yes. Both her boys attend that school.'

'What time does Elías finish?'

'His timetable's on the fridge door,' the interpreter said. 'He finishes around two on Tuesdays,' she said with a glance at her watch, 'so it's three hours since he left for home.'

'What does he generally do after school? Does he go straight home?'

'As far as she knows,' the interpreter said after consulting Sunee. 'She doesn't know exactly. Sometimes he plays football in the school playground. Then he generally comes home by himself.'

'What about the boy's father?'

'He's a carpenter. Lives here in Reykjavík. They got divorced last year.'

'Yes, his name's Ódinn, isn't it?' Erlendur said. He knew that the police were trying to contact Elías's father, who had still not heard the news of the boy's death.

'He and Sunee don't have much contact these days. Elías sometimes stays with him at weekends.'

'Is there a stepfather?'

'No,' the interpreter said. 'Sunee lives alone with her two sons.'

'Is the elder son usually back at this time of day, in normal circumstances?' Erlendur asked.

'The time they come home varies,' the interpreter quoted Sunee.

'Isn't there any rule?' Elínborg asked.

Gudný turned to Sunee and they talked together for some

17

time. Erlendur could see what a good support the interpreter was to her. Gudný had told the detectives that Sunee understood most of what was said to her in Icelandic and could express herself fairly well, but was very precise, so when she felt the need she called in Gudný to help her.

'She's not entirely sure where they go during the day,' the interpreter said finally, turning back to Erlendur and Elínborg. 'They both have keys to the flat. If she does overtime she doesn't finish at the chocolate factory until six o'clock, and then she has to get home, and often do the shopping. Sometimes she has the chance of more overtime and then she comes home even later. She has to work as much as she can. She's the only breadwinner.'

'Aren't they supposed to tell her where they go after school, where they are?' Elínborg asked. 'Aren't they supposed to let her know at work?'

'She can't hang around on the phone all the time at work,' the interpreter said after consulting Sunee.

'So she doesn't know their whereabouts when school's over?' Erlendur said.

'Oh yes, she knows what they're doing. They tell her, but not until after they meet up in the evening.'

'Do they play football or do any sports? Do they train or take classes in anything?'

'Elías plays football but he didn't have training today,' the interpreter said. 'Surely you see how tough this is for her, being a single mother with two boys,' she added as a comment of her own. 'It's not exactly child's play. There's no money for courses. Or mobile phones.'

Erlendur nodded.

'You said she has a brother who lives in Iceland,' he commented.

'Yes, I contacted him and he's on his way.'

'Are there any other relatives or in-laws that Sunee can talk to? On the boy's father's side? Could the elder boy be with them? Are their grandparents alive?'

'Elías sees his grandmother sometimes. His Icelandic grandfather's dead. Sunee is in close touch with the grandmother. She lives here in the city. You ought to let her know. Her name's Sigrídur.'

The interpreter asked Sunee for her number and gave it to Elínborg, who took out her mobile.

'Shouldn't the grandmother come over and be with her?' she asked the interpreter.

Sunee listened to the interpreter and nodded.

'We'll ask her to come,' the interpreter said.

A man appeared in the doorway and Sunee leapt to her feet and ran over to him. It turned out to be her brother. They hugged each other and the brother tried to console Sunee, who slumped weeping into his arms. His name was Virote, and he was several years younger than Sunee. Erlendur and Elínborg exchanged glances as they watched the sorrow cocoon itself around the siblings. A reporter came puffing up the stairs but Elínborg turned him away and escorted him out. Only Erlendur and Gudný were left in the flat with the sister and brother. The interpreter and brother helped Sunee back to the sofa and sat down beside her.

Erlendur went into the little corridor leading to the bedrooms. One was larger, clearly used by the mother. The other contained bunk-beds. The boys slept there. He was greeted by a large poster showing an English football team, which he recognised from the newspapers. There was a smaller poster of a pretty Icelandic singer. An old Apple computer stood

19

on a small desk. Schoolbooks, computer games and toys lay scattered across the floor, rifles and dinosaurs and swords. The bunk-beds were unmade. Boys' dirty clothes lay on a chair.

A typical boys' room, Erlendur thought, prodding at a sock with his foot. The interpreter appeared at the door.

'What kind of people are they?' Erlendur asked.

Gudný shrugged. 'Very ordinary people,' she said. 'People like you and me. Poor people.'

'Can you tell me whether they ever felt themselves the victims of prejudice?'

'I don't think there's been much of that sort of thing. Actually, I'm not quite sure about Niran but Sunee has settled into the neighbourhood well. Prejudices always come out and obviously they've been aware of them. Experience shows that the greatest prejudices are held by those who lack self-confidence and have had a bad upbringing, who have first-hand experience of negligence and apathy.'

'What about her brother? Has he lived here long?'

'Yes, a few years. He's a labourer. Used to work up north, in Akureyri, but he came back to Reykjavík recently.'

'Are he and Sunee close?'

'Yes. Very. They're great friends.'

'What can you tell me about Sunee?'

'She came to Iceland about ten years ago,' Gudný said. 'She really likes it here.'

Sunee had once told her she could hardly believe how desolate and chilly the country was when she took the shuttle from Keflavík airport to Reykjavík. It was rainy and overcast and all she could see through the coach window was flat lava fields and distant blue mountains. There was nothing growing anywhere, no trees and not even a blue sky. When she disembarked from the plane and walked down the gangway she felt the Arctic air hit her, like walking into a cold wall. She got goose-flesh. The temperature was three degrees Celsius. It was the middle of October. It had been thirty degrees Celsius at home when she left.

She had married the Icelander she met in Bangkok. He had courted her, repeatedly invited her out and acted courteously, and told her about Iceland in English, which she hardly spoke and did not understand particularly well. He seemed to have plenty of money and bought little things for her, clothes and trinkets.

He went back to Iceland after they met but they decided to stay in touch. Her friend, who had a better command of English, wrote him a few lines. He returned to Thailand six months later and spent three weeks there. They were together the whole time. She was impressed by him and everything he told her about Iceland. Even though it was small, remote and cold, with a tiny population, it was one of the wealthiest nations in the world. He told her about the wages, which were astronomical compared to the norm in Bangkok. If she moved there and worked hard she could easily support her family back home in Thailand.

He carried her over the threshold of their home, a one-bedroom flat that he owned on Snorrabraut. They had walked there from the shuttle terminal at Hotel Loftleidir. They crossed a busy road, which she later found out was called Miklabraut, and walked down Snorrabraut against the icy north wind. She was wearing Thai summer clothes, thin silk trousers that he had bought for her, a pretty blouse and a light summer jacket. On her feet she wore plastic sandals. Her new husband had not prepared her in any way for her arrival in Iceland.

The flat was fine once she had put it in order. She got a job at a chocolate factory. Their relationship went well at first, but eventually it transpired that they had lied to each other.

'How?' Erlendur asked the interpreter. 'What had they lied about?'

'He'd done it before,' Gudný said. 'Once.'

'Done what before?'

'Been to Thailand to get himself a wife.'

'He'd done that before?'

'Some men have done it several times.'

'And is it . . . is it legal?'

'There's nothing to stop it.'

'But what about Sunee? What lies had she told him?'

'After they'd been together for some time she sent for her son.'

Erlendur stared at the interpreter.

'It turned out that she had a son in Thailand who she'd never told him about.'

'Is that Niran?'

'Yes, Niran. He has an Icelandic name too but calls himself Niran and so does everyone else.'

'So he's . . .'

'Elías's half-brother. He's a Thai through and through and has had trouble finding his feet in Iceland, like some other kids in the same position.'

'What about her husband?'

'They got divorced in the end,' Gudný said.

'Niran,' Erlendur said to himself, as if to hear how the name sounded. 'Does that mean anything in particular?'

'It means eternal,' the interpreter said.

'Eternal?'

'Thai names have literal meanings, just like Icelandic ones.'

'And Sunee? What does that mean?'

'Something good,' Gudný said. 'A good thing.'

'Did Elías have a Thai name?'

'Yes: Aran. I'm not sure exactly what that means. I must ask Sunee.'

'Is there any tradition behind such names?'

'Thais use nicknames to confuse evil spirits. It's one of their superstitions. Children are baptised with their real names, but the nicknames are used to lead astray evil spirits that could harm the children. They mustn't find out the real name.'

Music came from the sitting room and Erlendur and the interpreter went back in there from the bedroom. Sunee's brother had put some gentle Thai music on the CD player. Sunee was huddled up on the sofa and now started talking to herself in whispers.

Erlendur looked at the interpreter.

'She's talking about her other son. Niran.'

'We're looking for him,' Erlendur said. 'We'll find him. Tell her that. We'll find him.'

Sunee shook her head and stared into space.

'She thinks he's dead too,' the interpreter said.

3

Sigurdur Óli hurried towards the school. Three other policemen had accompanied him and now spread out across the school grounds and vicinity in search of the murder weapon. Teaching was over and the building was gloomy and lifeless in the winter darkness. Lights were on in the occasional window, but the main entrance was locked. Sigurdur Óli knocked on the door. It was a grey, three-storey monstrosity, with annexes housing a small indoor swimming pool and carpentry workshop. Memories of cold winter mornings came into Sigurdur Óli's mind: children standing in double rows in the yard, quarrelling and teasing, sometimes fights that the teachers broke up. Rain and snow and darkness for most of the autumn and all winter until spring came, the days grew lighter, the weather improved and the sun started shining. Sigurdur Óli looked across the asphalt playground, the basketball court and football pitch, and could almost hear the old shouts of the kids.

He started kicking at the door and eventually the caretaker appeared, a woman of about fifty who opened up and asked what all the row was about. Sigurdur Óli introduced himself and asked if the form teacher of 5D was still in the school.

'What's going on?' the woman asked.

'Nothing,' Sigurdur Óli said. 'The teacher? Do you know if he's still here?'

'5D? That's room 304. It's on the second floor. I don't know if Agnes has left yet, I'll check.'

Sigurdur Óli had already set off. He knew where the stairs were and took them several steps at a time. The fifth form had been on the second floor in the old days as well, if he remembered correctly. Perhaps the same system was in operation as when he had been a pupil there at the end of the 1970s. In the last century. He felt ten heavy years older when that damn phrase went through his mind. Last century.

All the classrooms on the floor were locked and he bounded back down the stairs. In the meantime, the caretaker had been to the staff room and was waiting in the corridor to tell him that 5D's teacher had gone home.

'Agnes? Is that her name?'

'Yes,' the woman said.

'Is the principal in?'

'Yes. He's in his office.'

Sigurdur Óli almost barged the caretaker out of his way when he strode past her towards the staff room. In his day it had led to the principal's office, he remembered that much. The door was open and he went straight in. He was in a tearing hurry. He noticed that his old principal was still at the school. He was getting ready to go home, knotting a scarf around his neck, when Sigurdur Óli disturbed him.

'What do you want?' the principal asked, startled by the intrusion.

Sigurdur Óli hesitated for a moment, uncertain whether the principal recognised him.

'Can I help you at all?' the principal asked.

'It's about 5D,' Sigurdur Óli said.

'Oh yes?'

'Something's happened.'

'Do you have a child in that class?'

'No. I'm from the police. A pupil from 5D was found dead outside his home. He'd been stabbed and died of the wound. We need to talk to all the teachers in the school, especially those who can tell us anything about this boy, we need to . . .'

'What are you . . . ?' the principal gasped, and Sigurdur Óli saw him turn pale.

'. . . talk to his classmates, the school staff, other people who knew him. We think he was murdered. A single stab wound to the stomach.'

The caretaker had followed Sigurdur Óli into the office. She stood in the doorway, gasping and instinctively covering her mouth, staring at the detective as if unable to believe her ears.

'He was half-Thai, the boy,' Sigurdur Óli continued. 'Are there many of them at this school?'

'Many of them . . . ?' the principal said vacantly, sinking slowly into his chair. He was almost seventy, had been a teacher all his life, but was quite looking forward to retirement. He could not comprehend what had happened and there was no mistaking the look of disbelief on his face.

'Who is it?' the caretaker said behind Sigurdur Óli. 'Who's dead?'

Sigurdur Óli turned round.

'Sorry, maybe we can talk to you later,' he said as he shut the door.

'I need registers with the names and addresses of the parents,' he said, turning back to the principal. 'I need a list of all the boy's teachers. I need details of any friction within the school, gangs if there are any, race relations, anything that could explain what's happened. Is there anything that springs to mind?'

'I . . . I can't think of a thing. I don't believe what you're saying! Is it true? Can such a thing happen?'

'Unfortunately. We need to speed this up. The more time that passes from—'

'Which boy is it?' the principal interrupted him.

Sigurdur Óli told him Elías's name. The principal turned to his computer, went to the school intranet and found the class and a photograph of the boy.

'Before, I used to know every single pupil by name. Now there are just so many. This is him, isn't it?'

'Yes, that's him,' Sigurdur Óli said, peering at the picture. He told the principal about Elías's brother and they found Niran's class and photograph. The brothers were not unalike, both with jet-black hair down over their eyes, dark skin and brown eyes. They emailed Niran's photograph to the police. Sigurdur Óli phoned the station to explain and it was distributed at once, along with the one Erlendur had provided.

'Have there been any clashes between gangs in the school?' Sigurdur Óli asked when he had finished his telephone call.

'Do you think it's connected with the school?' the principal asked, his eyes glued to the computer monitor. Elías's photograph filled the screen, smiling at them. It was a shy smile and instead of looking straight into the camera he was looking just above it, as if the photographer had told him to look up or something had disturbed him. He had symmetrical features with a high forehead and inquisitive, candid eyes.

'We're investigating all the possibilities,' Sigurdur Óli said. 'I can't say any more.'

27

'Does it have something to do with racism? What were you saying?'

'Only that the boy's mother is from Thailand,' Sigurdur Óli said. 'Nothing else. We don't know what's happened.'

Sigurdur Óli was relieved that the principal did not remember him from his days as a pupil at the school. He did not want to get into a conversation about the old days and old teachers, what had happened to his class and all that crap.

'Nothing's been reported to me,' the principal said, 'or at least nothing serious, and it's out of the question that it could have resulted in this tragedy. I just can't believe what has happened!'

'You'd better believe it,' Sigurdur Óli said.

The principal printed out a list of Elías's classmates. It included the addresses, telephone numbers and names of the parents or guardians. He handed the list to Sigurdur Óli.

'They started here this autumn, the brothers. Shouldn't I email it to the address you gave me too?' he asked. 'This is terrible,' he groaned, staring at his desk as if paralysed.

'Definitely,' Sigurdur Óli said. 'I also need the address and phone number of his form teacher. What happened?'

The principal looked at him.

'What do you mean?'

'You talked about something that wasn't anything serious,' Sigurdur Óli said, 'and it was out of the question that it could have resulted in this tragedy. What was it?'

The principal hesitated.

'What was it?' Sigurdur Óli repeated.

'One of the teachers here has expressed a strong dislike of immigration.'

'By women from Thailand?'

'Those too. People from Asia. The Philippines. Vietnam.

Those places. He has very strong views on the matter. But of course they're just his opinions. He would never do anything like this. Never.'

'But he crossed your mind. What's his name?'

'That would be absurd!'

'We need to talk to him,' Sigurdur Óli said.

'He has a good grip on the kids,' the principal said. 'He's like that. He comes across as brash and surly but he gets through to the kids.'

'Did he teach Elías?'

'At some point, naturally. He teaches Icelandic but does a lot of substitution and has taught almost all the children in the school.'

The principal told him the teacher's name and Sigurdur Óli wrote it down.

'I cautioned him once. We accept no racial prejudice at this school,' the principal said firmly. 'Don't imagine that. We don't tolerate it. People discuss racial issues here like everywhere else, especially from the perspective of immigrants. There is absolute equality here, neither the teachers nor the pupils would put up with anything else.'

Sigurdur Óli could tell the principal was still holding back.

'What happened?' he said.

'They almost got into a fight,' the principal said. 'Him and another teacher – Finnur. In the staff room. They had to be separated. He made some remarks that annoyed Finnur. It turned into a kind of cockfight.'

'What remarks?'

'Finnur wouldn't say.'

'Is there anyone else we need to talk to?' Sigurdur Óli asked.

'I can't inform on people just because of their views.'

'You're not informing on people,' Sigurdur Óli said. 'Just because the boy was attacked, it doesn't have to be connected with people's opinions. Far from it. This is a police investigation and we need information. We need to talk to people. We need to map what's going on. It's nothing to do with what views people have.'

'Egill, the woodwork teacher, he got into an argument here the other day. It was a discussion about multiculturalism or something like that, I don't know. He's rather tetchy. He keeps himself well informed. Perhaps you ought to talk to him.'

'How many children of foreign origin are there at this school?' Sigurdur Óli asked as he wrote down the woodwork teacher's name.

'I suppose there are more than thirty in all. It's a big school.'

'And no particular problems have arisen because of it?'

'Of course we are aware of incidents, but none of them serious.'

'So what are we talking about then?'

'Nicknames, scrapping. Nothing that's been reported to me, but the teachers talk about it. Of course, they keep a close eye on what goes on and intervene. We don't want any kind of discrimination in this school and the children know that. The children are very aware of it themselves and notify us immediately, and then we intervene.'

'There are problems in all schools, I imagine,' Sigurdur Óli said. 'Troublemakers. Boys and girls who cause nothing but bother.'

'There are children like that in all schools.'

The principal stared thoughtfully at Sigurdur Óli.

'I have the feeling I recognise you,' he said suddenly. 'What did you say your name was?'

Sigurdur Óli heaved a silent groan. Such a small country. So few people.

'Sigurdur Óli,' he said.

'Sigurdur Óli,' the principal repeated pensively. 'Sigurdur Óli? Did you attend this school?'

'A long time ago. Before 1980. For a very short while.'

Sigurdur Óli could see the principal trying to recall him and could tell that it would not be long before the penny dropped. So he took a very hasty leave. The police would go back to the school and talk to the pupils and teachers and other staff. He was at the door when the principal finally began to get warm.

'Weren't you in the riot in seventy—'

Sigurdur Óli did not hear the end of the question. He strode out of the staff room. The caretaker was nowhere to be seen. The building was deserted this late in the day. About to head back out into the cold, he suddenly stopped and looked up at the ceiling. He dithered for a moment, then headed back up the stairs and was on the second floor before he knew it. On the walls were old class photographs, labelled with the names of the forms and the year. He found the photograph he was looking for, stood in front of it and looked at himself, a twelve-year-old pupil at the school. The children were arranged in three rows in the picture and he was standing in the back row staring straight into the camera, serious, wearing a thin shirt with a wide collar and a bizarre pattern on it, and with the latest disco haircut.

Sigurdur Óli took a long look at the photograph.

'How pathetic,' he said with a sigh.

4

Erlendur's mobile rang incessantly. Sigurdur Óli gave him a report about his meeting with the principal and said he was on his way to meet the boy's teacher and another member of staff who had spoken out against immigration. Elínborg called to tell him that a witness who lived on the same staircase as Sunee thought she had seen the elder brother earlier that day. The head of forensics quoted the pathologist as saying that the child had been stabbed once, presumably with a fairly sharp instrument, probably a knife.

'What kind of knife?' Erlendur asked.

'The blade would have been quite broad and even thick, but particularly sharp,' the head of forensics said. 'The stabbing need not have required much effort. The boy could have been lying on the ground when he was stabbed. His anorak is dirty on the back and torn too. It looks fairly new, so he may have been involved in a fight. He would have tried to defend himself, as is only to be expected, but the only wound is from the knife, which the pathologist said penetrated his liver. He died from loss of blood.'

'You mean that it didn't take much force for the knife to go in that deep?'

'Conceivably.'

'Even a child or a young person could have done it, for instance? Someone of his own age?'

'It's difficult to say. But it looks as if it was inflicted by a very sharp instrument.'

'And the time of death?'

'Judging from the temperature, he would have died about an hour before he was found. You can discuss that with the pathologist.'

'He seems to have been coming straight home from school.'

'It looks that way.'

Erlendur sat down in his chair and faced the brother and sister from Thailand. Gudný, the interpreter, sat down on the sofa with them. She translated the information Erlendur had received and Sunee listened in silence. She had stopped crying. Her brother chipped in and they talked together in half-whispers for a while.

'What are they saying?' Erlendur asked.

'His anorak wasn't torn when he left home this morning,' the interpreter said. 'It wasn't new, but it was in good condition.'

'Obviously there was a fight,' Erlendur said. 'I can't say whether the attack on Elías was racially motivated. I understand there are thirty children of foreign origin at his school. We need to talk to his friends, people who were in contact with him. The same goes for his brother. I know it's difficult, but it would help us if Sunee could give us a list of names. If she can't remember the names she can provide some details about his friends, their age and the like, where they live. Time is of the essence. Hopefully she realises that.'

'Do you have any idea how she feels?' the interpreter asked coldly.

'I can only imagine,' Erlendur said.

Elínborg knocked on the door. She was on the first-floor corridor off the stairwell. The door opened and a uniformed policeman greeted her. A new witness had come forward and talked to him, and was now waiting for Elínborg in the sitting room. She was a woman by the name of Fanney, a sixty-five-year-old widow with three grown-up children. She had made coffee for the policeman, who left as soon as Elínborg appeared. The two women sat down with a cup each.

'How awful,' the woman said with a sigh. 'This happening in our flats! I just don't know what the world's coming to.'

The flat was dark apart from a light in the kitchen and a small lamp in the sitting room. It was a mirror image of Sunee's flat, with a thick carpet on the floor and green wallpaper in the hallway and sitting room.

'Do you know the boys at all?' Elínborg asked. 'The two brothers?'

She had to get a move on, obtain vital information and keep going. Hurry without missing anything.

'Yes, a little,' Fanney said. 'Elías was a lovely boy. His brother took rather longer to get to know but he's a fine lad too.'

'You said you saw him earlier today,' Elínborg said, trying not to sound tired. Her daughter was at home ill with vomiting and a fever, and she had slept little last night. She had intended only to look in at work but that had changed when the report came in about the boy.

'I sometimes chat with Sunee out in the corridor,' Fanney said, as if she had not heard Elínborg's remark. 'They haven't lived here long. It's bound to be difficult for her to be alone like that. Sunee must work her fingers to the bone; wages aren't so high for factory workers.'

'Where was Niran the last time you saw him?' Elínborg asked.

'He was behind the chemist's.'

'What time was that?' Elínborg asked. 'Was he alone? Did he go into the chemist's?'

'I was getting off the bus from town at about two o'clock,' Fanney said. 'I always walk past the chemist's and that's when I saw him. He wasn't alone and he wasn't going into the chemist's. He was with some friends, schoolmates I assume.'

'And what were they doing?'

'Nothing. Just hanging around behind the chemist's.'

'Behind it?'

'Yes, you can see into the yard when you turn the corner there.'

'How many were there?'

'Five or six. I don't know who they were. I hadn't seen any of them before.'

'Are you sure?'

'Not that I noticed anyway,' Fanney said, putting down her empty coffee cup.

'Were they the same age as Niran?'

'Yes, I suppose they were around the same age. Coloured.'

'But you didn't recognise them?'

'No.'

'You say you chat to Sunee.'

'Yes.'

'Have you spoken to her recently?'

'Yes, a few days ago. I met her outside. She was coming home from work and was terribly tired. She's told me a lot about Thailand in her broken Icelandic. She speaks simply. That's fine.'

'What sort of thing has she told you?'

'Once I asked her what was the most difficult thing about living in Iceland or moving to Iceland from Thailand and she talked about how Icelanders were a bit reserved compared to the Thais. She said personal contact was more open over there. Everyone talks to everyone else, complete strangers will discuss anything quite happily. If you're sitting out on the pavement having a meal you're not shy about inviting passers-by to join you.'

'And the weather's not quite the same,' Elínborg said.

'No. People stay outside in all that good weather, of course. We spend most of the year indoors and everyone here lives in his own private world. You run into closed doors everywhere. Just look at this corridor. I'm not saying it's better or worse, but it's different. It's two different worlds. When you get to know Sunee you have the feeling that life in Thailand is much calmer and more relaxed. Do you think it would be all right for me to drop in on her?'

'Perhaps you should wait a day or two, she's under a lot of strain.'

'The poor woman,' Fanney said. 'It's not *sanuk sanuk* any more.'

'What do you mean?'

'She's tried to teach me a few words of Thai. Like *sanuk sanuk*. She said that's typical of all Thais. It means simply enjoying life, doing something nice and fun. Enjoy life! And she taught me *pay nay*. That's the usual greeting in Thailand, like we say hello. But it means something completely different. *Pay nay* means "where are you going?" It's a friendly question and a greeting at the same time. It conveys respect. Thais have great respect for the individual.'

'So you're good friends?'

36

'You could say that. But she doesn't tell me everything, the dear little thing.'

'Really?'

'I shouldn't be gossiping like this but . . .'

'But what?'

'She's definitely been having a visitor.'

'We all have visitors,' Elínborg said.

'Of course, no, it just occurred to me that it might be a boyfriend or something like that. I sort of have that feeling.'

'Have you seen him?'

'No, but I started suspecting it in the summer and again this winter. There was just the sound of people moving about. Quite late at night.'

'And nothing else?'

'No, that was all there was to it. I've never asked her.'

'So you're not talking about her ex?'

'No,' Fanney said. 'He comes round at different times.'

Elínborg thanked her for her help and took her leave. She called a number on her mobile and was out in the corridor by the time she got through to Sigurdur Óli. She told him about the group of lads by the chemist's.

'They could be his schoolmates,' Elínborg said as she hurried down the stairs. 'He could have gone home with one of them. They seemed to be about his age.'

'I think Erlendur's been making a list of the two boys' friends,' Sigurdur Óli said. 'I'm going to meet Elías's teacher, Agnes. I'll ask her about the chemist's. The question is whether we ought to phone the chemist's too and find out if the boys were hanging around there.'

'It might still be open,' Elínborg said. 'I'll check that out.'

*

Sigurdur Óli rang off and ran up the steps to a house divided into three flats, in the vicinity of the school. Elías's teacher lived on the first floor and came downstairs to open the door. He recognised her from one of the photographs he had seen at the school. She took one look at Sigurdur Óli, with his short, precise haircut, tidily knotted tie, white shirt and black raincoat over a dark suit, and interrupted before he could even introduce himself.

'No thanks.' She smiled. 'I don't even believe in God.'

Then she closed the door in his face.

Sigurdur Óli stood thoughtfully for a while then rang the bell again.

'You haven't heard the news, have you?' he said in a serious tone when the woman opened the door again.

'What news?'

'I'm from the police. One of your pupils has been found dead near his home. It looks as if he's been stabbed with a knife.'

The woman's expression became one big question mark.

'What?' she groaned. 'Dead? Who?'

'Elías,' Sigurdur Óli said.

'*Elías?*'

Sigurdur Óli nodded.

'I don't believe you! How? Why? What . . . what on earth are you saying?'

'Perhaps you'd let me come inside,' Sigurdur Óli said. 'We need information about his class, his friends, who he went around with, whether he'd been in trouble at school, whether he had enemies. It would be great if you could assist us. We're short of time. The sooner we can gather information, the better. It's terrible to have to call on people like this but . . .'

'I . . . I thought you were from one of those religious sects,' Agnes sighed. 'You're so . . .'

'May I come in and sit down with you for a moment?'

'Sorry,' Agnes said. 'Please do.'

As he entered the flat through a small hallway with a mirror, Sigurdur Óli could see the teacher's family eating dinner in the kitchen. Three children – two boys and a girl – eyed him curiously and their father stood up to shake his hand. Agnes took her husband to one side and in a low voice explained the unexpected visit to him, then showed Sigurdur Óli into their study.

'What happened?' she asked once they had closed the door. 'Was the boy attacked?'

'It looks that way.'

'My God, that's . . . the poor kid. Who could have done a thing like that?'

'Can you imagine that anyone at school or in his class would have wanted to do him harm?'

'Not at all,' Agnes said. 'Elías was a very sweet boy, always trying to please everyone. And he was a good pupil. Why do you want to link this to the school? Do you have any concrete lead?'

'No, nothing,' Sigurdur Óli said firmly. 'We have to begin somewhere. You haven't noticed him being hassled in particular? No incident that could be linked to the attack? Nothing you've been worried about?'

'Nothing,' Agnes said. 'As far as I know, nothing's happened at the school that could end like this. Nothing.'

She gave a deep groan.

'Do you know about a group of children who hang around by the local chemist's? Friends of the brothers, immigrants perhaps?'

'No, I don't know of any such group. How is his mother taking it, the poor woman? I must call on her. Though I don't know what to say to her.'

'I think she's bearing up, considering the circumstances,' Sigurdur Óli said. 'Do you know her at all?'

'I can't really say I do,' Agnes replied. 'She's had trouble with speaking Icelandic so a supervisor was appointed for the brothers, a kind of liaison between the family and the school, a lovely woman called Gudný. That's not uncommon when we want greater contact with the pupils and their parents. Some come from Croatia, others from Vietnam, the Philippines or Poland. There are Catholics, Buddhists, Muslims. I've met Elías's mother a few times and she seems very nice. Things must be difficult for her, being single like that.'

'How are the immigrants regarded?' Sigurdur Óli said. 'How well do they fit in?'

'Actually, these days we try to talk about ethnic minorities,' Agnes said. 'Some take longer than others to adjust. The most successful ones are those who speak and understand Icelandic, who were born here and are, of course, just Icelanders as well. Like Elías. Niran was a different matter. You know that they're half-brothers?'

'Yes,' Sigurdur Óli said. Erlendur had told him about his conversation with the interpreter. 'What about Niran?'

'You should really talk to his form teacher about this,' Agnes said. 'They sometimes find it difficult, the children who come here when they're already quite old and know nothing of the language.'

'And Niran was like that?' Sigurdur Óli said.

'Well, I shouldn't really talk about individual pupils but of course this is a special case. He doesn't seem interested in learning the language. Can hardly read Icelandic. Doesn't understand it too well. It's difficult for those poor kids when the languages are so different. They speak a tonal language and the meaning of words changes with the pitch. Icelandic's completely different, of course.'

'You say Elías was a good pupil,' Sigurdur Óli said.

'He was,' Agnes said. 'His mother clearly knows what she wants. She wants her sons to get an education and they are sharp, despite being different in many ways.'

'Different how?'

'I know Elías much better,' Agnes said, 'but I've taught his brother a bit as well. Elías is charming and tries to please everyone, he's always smiling and friendly, although I don't feel he has many friends, poor boy.'

'They've just moved into this neighbourhood,' Sigurdur Óli said.

'His brother's quite different,' Agnes said.

'How?'

'I don't know him that well, like I said, but I get the impression that he's much tougher. He's not afraid to stand up for himself and he's proud of his origins, proud of being Thai. You don't find that among the children very often, not among any of them really; they seem to know precious little about their origins. I noticed that about him once when he was talking about his great-grandfather. Niran had great respect for him. And for his other relatives in Thailand.'

Sunee's next-door neighbour was a man of about seventy who lived alone. He had not heard the news and said he was shocked to see the police cars and people milling around the block of flats when he came home. He wrangled with the police officers at the entrance when they wanted to know who he was and where he lived, because he did not like that kind of interrogation. The police would not tell him what had happened. So he was rather distraught when Erlendur greeted him on the landing below the top floor and introduced himself as a detective with the Reykjavík CID.

'What's going on here?' the man asked, short of breath from climbing the stairs. He held a plastic bag in one hand, was of average height and wore a shabby suit and a tie that did not match, underneath a green anorak. Erlendur thought he looked haggard, like many of the solitary individuals he encountered. The man was thin, with a receding hairline, fairly large protruding eyes and delicate eyebrows below a high, intelligent forehead.

Erlendur explained the situation to him and saw that he took the news badly.

'Elías!' he groaned, looking over at the door to Sunee's flat. 'What are you saying? The poor child! Who did it? Have you found the person who did it?'

Erlendur shook his head. 'Do you know the family?' he asked.

'I don't believe it. All those police cars . . . because of Elías . . . What does his mother say, the poor woman? She must be devastated.'

'They've been your next-door neighbours for . . . ?' Erlendur began.

'Who could do a thing like that?'

'You must have got to know them,' Erlendur said.

'Eh? Oh yes, I've got to know them. Elías sometimes pops out to the shop for me, such a dear boy. He's up and down these stairs in a flash. I just can't believe this.'

'I need to ask you a couple of questions, if you don't mind,' Erlendur said. 'As their neighbour.'

'Me?'

'It won't take a moment.'

'Come in then,' the man said, taking out a bunch of keys. He switched on the light inside his flat. Erlendur noticed a large bookcase, an old three-piece suite and a worn carpet. Two walls of the sitting room were decorated with white ribbed wallpaper, which was swollen in places and beginning to turn very yellow. The man, whose name was Gestur according to the small copper plate on the door, closed the door behind them and offered Erlendur a seat on the sofa. He sat down in the chair facing him. He had taken off his thick green anorak, put the plastic bag in the kitchen and turned on the coffee maker.

'What can you tell me about Sunee and her boys?' Erlendur asked.

'I have nothing but good to say of them. She works hard, their mother, she has to, being on her own like that. The boys have been nothing but polite to me. Elías has run errands and Niran . . . Where's Niran? How's he taking this?' Gestur asked with apparent concern.

Erlendur hesitated.

'Surely he hasn't been attacked too?' Gestur groaned.

'No,' Erlendur said, 'but we don't know where he is. Do you have any ideas?'

'About where he could be? No, I don't have a clue.'

Erlendur was deeply concerned about the victim's brother but could only hope that he would come home or be found as soon as possible. He felt it was premature to put his photograph on television.

'Hopefully he's just hanging around somewhere,' he said. 'What kind of relationship did the two brothers have?'

'He really looked up to Niran – Elías, I mean. I think he

43

worshipped his brother. He was always talking about him. What Niran said and did. How Niran won computer games and how good he was at football and how he took him to the cinema with his friends even though they were all older. Niran knew everything and could do anything in Elías's eyes. They're like chalk and cheese, the way brothers can be. Elías is quick to make friends but Niran is slower to get to know and more wary of people. Sharp as a knife. On the ball and quick to learn. He doesn't trust everything he sees and hears, plays it cautiously.'

'You seem to know them very well.'

'Elías is a bit lonely, the poor lad. He preferred living where they were before. Their mother often gets home late from work and Elías has been hanging around by himself in the corridor or down in the storage rooms and passages in the basement.'

'What about Sunee?'

'There ought to be more people who work as hard as she does. Sunee provides for herself and her sons through sheer hard graft. I admire her.'

'Is she completely on her own?'

'As far as I know. I understand her ex-husband has little to do with her.'

'Did Elías have any contact with anyone else on this staircase?'

'I don't think so. There isn't much contact between the tenants. These are all rented flats and you know the kind of people who are in the rental market. Always coming and going, individuals and couples and single mothers like Sunee, even single fathers, students. Some get evicted. Others pay their rent on time.'

'So does someone own the entire block?'

'All the flats on this floor at least, some speculator I imagine. I've never seen him. When I moved in a woman from the rental agency handled the paperwork and gave me an account number. If anything crops up I get in touch with the agency.'

'And the rent, is it high?'

'I could well imagine it is for Sunee. Unless she's got a different deal from mine.'

Erlendur stood up. The coffee was untouched in the coffee maker in the kitchen. The aroma filled the whole flat. Gestur stood up as well. He had not offered Erlendur any coffee. Erlendur peered into the dim hallway entrance. There was a peephole in the door, just above the nameplate. Looking through it, he could see the entrance to Sunee and the boys' flat. Erlendur looked Gestur in the eye and thanked him.

5

Erlendur's mobile rang yet again. He did not recognise the number but he knew at once who was calling when he heard the voice.

'Is it a bad moment?' Eva Lind asked.

'No,' said Erlendur, who had not heard from his daughter for some time.

'I saw about that kid on TV,' Eva said. 'Are you on that case?'

'Yes, me and other people. All of us, I think.'

'Do you know what happened?'

'No. We know very little.'

'It's . . . it's horrific.'

'Yes.'

Eva paused.

'You all right?' Erlendur said after a while.

'I want to see you.'

'Do. Come home.'

Eva paused again.

'Isn't she always there?'

'Who?'

'That woman you're with.'

'Valgerdur? No. Sometimes.'

'I don't want to interrupt anything.'

'You won't.'

'Are you together?'

'We're good friends.'

'Is she all right?'

'Valgerdur is very . . .' Erlendur hesitated. 'What do you mean, "all right"?'

'Not as bad as Mum?'

'I think . . .'

'She can't be as bad as Mum or you wouldn't bother to be with her. And definitely not as bad as me.'

'She's no better than anyone else,' Erlendur said. 'I'm not comparing you. You shouldn't either.'

'Isn't she the first woman you've been with since you left us? She must have something.'

'You ought to meet her.'

'I want to see you.'

'Do, then.'

'Bye.'

Eva rang off and Erlendur put his mobile in his pocket.

He had seen Valgerdur two days before. She came round to his flat in the evening when her shift was over and he gave her a glass of Chartreuse. She told him she had applied formally for a divorce from her husband, the doctor, and had appointed a lawyer.

Valgerdur was a biotechnician at the National Hospital. Erlendur had met her by chance during a murder investigation and found out that she was having problems in her private life. She was married but her husband had repeatedly cheated on her and she had eventually left him. She and Erlendur decided to take things slowly. They did not live together. Valgerdur wanted to live by herself for a while after her long marriage and

Erlendur had not lived with a woman for decades. Nor was there any hurry. Erlendur liked being alone. Sometimes she telephoned him, wanting to visit. Sometimes they went out for a meal together. Once she had succeeded in dragging him along to the theatre, to see Ibsen. He had nodded off fifteen minutes into the play. In vain she tried to nudge him awake but he slept most of the time until the interval when they decided to go home. 'All that artificial drama,' he had said by way of an apology, 'it does nothing for me.'

'Theatre is reality too,' she'd protested.

'Not like this,' he'd said, handing her volume two of *Stories of Rural Postmen*.

Erlendur had lent her some of his books that described ordeals in the wilderness and how people had frozen to death outdoors in Iceland in the old days, and others about death and destruction caused by avalanches. Although apprehensive at first, the more accounts she read, the more her interest had become aroused. Erlendur's interest in the topic was unquenchable.

'The lawyer thinks we can divide everything up more or less equally,' she said, sipping her liqueur.

'That's good,' Erlendur said. He knew they had lived in a large detached house close to the old children's hospital and wondered which of them would get the house. He asked whether it was important to her.

'No,' she said. 'He was always much fonder of the house. Apparently he's found himself a new woman.'

'Really?'

'Someone from the hospital. A young nurse.'

'Do you think anyone can create a good relationship when both parties have been unfaithful?' he asked, thinking about a missing-person case he was investigating. 'Do you think anyone can create a good, solid relationship if they've both cheated before?'

'I didn't,' Valgerdur said. 'He repeatedly cheated on me with any woman who would stand still long enough.'

'I'm not talking about you, but about a case I'm dealing with.'

'The missing woman?'

'Yes.'

'Do you think they both cheated before they got together?'

Erlendur nodded. He rarely discussed the cases he was handling with anyone else. Valgerdur was an exception. So was Eva.

'I don't know,' Valgerdur said. 'Obviously it can be difficult if both parties have left their spouses under circumstances like that. There are bound to be repercussions.'

'Why shouldn't it happen again?' Erlendur asked.

'You shouldn't forget about love though.'

'Love?'

'You shouldn't underestimate love. Sometimes two people are prepared to sacrifice everything for a new relationship. Maybe that's true love.'

'Yes, but what if one of them finds this true love at regular intervals?' Erlendur said.

'Did she leave on account of his cheating? Had he started again?'

'I don't know,' Erlendur said.

'Were you cheating when you got divorced?'

Surprised at the question, he smiled.

'No,' he said. 'I have no idea how to go about that sort of thing. In Icelandic, we talk about practising adultery. Like a hobby or a sport.'

'So you're wondering whether the man betrayed this woman's trust?'

Erlendur shrugged.

'Why did she disappear?'

'That's the question.'

'You don't know any more than that?'

'Not really.'

Valgerdur paused.

'How can you drink this Chartreuse?' she asked with a grimace.

'I happen to like it,' Erlendur smiled.

When Erlendur went back to Sunee's flat her ex-mother-in-law had arrived, a fairly slim, intense woman aged about sixty. She had rushed up the stairs and hugged Sunee, who was waiting for her on the landing. Sunee seemed relieved to have Elías's grandmother with her. Erlendur sensed that their relationship was warm. They had not yet been able to contact Elías's father. He was not at home and his mobile was switched off. Sunee thought he had recently changed jobs and did not know the name of the company he worked for.

The grandmother talked to Sunee in half-whispers. Her brother and the interpreter stood a little way off, to give them space. Erlendur looked up at the red lampshade with the yellow dragon on it. The dragon seemed to be curled around a little dog, but he could not work out whether it was to protect or to curse the dog.

'Such a terrible tragedy!' The woman sighed and looked at the interpreter, whom she seemed to recognise. 'Who could have done such a thing?'

Sunee said something to her brother and they went into the kitchen with Gudný.

The grandmother looked over and noticed Erlendur.

'And who are you?' she asked.

Erlendur explained his involvement in the case. The woman introduced herself as Sigrídur. She asked Erlendur to tell her exactly what had happened, what the police were doing, what hypotheses were being put forward and whether any clues had been found. Erlendur answered her as best he could, but he had very little concrete information. This seemed to irritate her, as if he were withholding details. She told him as much. He assured her that this was not the case, the investigation was just beginning and they did not have much to go on as yet.

'Not much to go on! A ten-year-old boy is stabbed and you claim you don't have much to go on?'

'My condolences about the boy,' Erlendur said. 'Of course we're doing everything in our power to work out what happened and find the culprit.'

He had been in this position before, standing in the homes of people who were paralysed by grief over something incomprehensible and unbearable. He knew the denial and anger. The incident was so overwhelming that it was impossible to face up to and the mind seized on anything to ease the pain, as if the situation could still somehow be put right.

Erlendur knew this sensation, had felt it since he was ten years old and he and his younger brother Bergur had got lost in a storm. For a while there was a genuine hope that his brother would be found alive after burying himself in the snow as Erlendur had done, and it was this hope that drove people on to search for him, long after his brother's fate had been sealed. The body was never found. When the hope began to wane by the day and then vanished by the week and month and year, it was replaced by a feeling of numbness towards life. Some people managed to keep it at bay. Others, like Erlendur, nurtured it and made the pain their lifelong companion.

He knew that it was crucial to find Elías's half-brother Niran. He hoped that the boy would return home as soon as possible and be able to shed light on what had happened. The more time that elapsed without him turning up, the more Erlendur felt that his disappearance was somehow connected with the boy's death. In the worst-case scenario, something had happened to Niran too, but he did not want to pursue that train of thought.

'Is there anything I can help you with?' Sigrídur asked.

'Have you heard from his brother?' Erlendur asked.

'Niran? No, Sunee's so worried about him.'

'We're doing everything we can,' Erlendur said.

'Do you think something's happened to him as well?' Sigrídur asked in horror.

'I doubt it,' Erlendur said.

'He must come home,' Sigrídur said. 'Sunee must get him back home.'

'He'll be back,' Erlendur said calmly. 'Can you imagine where he might be? He should have got back from school a long time ago. His mother said he's not supposed to be at any extra courses or football practice or anything like that.'

'I don't have the faintest idea where he could be,' Sigrídur said. 'I don't have much contact with him.'

'What about their old friends from when they lived on Snorrabraut?' Erlendur asked. 'Could he be with them?'

'I have no idea.'

'The boys haven't been living here long?'

'No. They moved from Snorrabraut in the spring. The boys

had to change schools this autumn. I think it's been terribly difficult for them, first the divorce, then moving to a new part of town and starting at a new school.'

'I need to speak to your son,' Erlendur said.

'Me too,' Sigrídur said. 'He's working for a new firm of contractors and I don't know the name.'

'I understand that Sunee wasn't his first foreign wife.'

'I can't understand the boy,' Sigrídur said. 'I've never been able to figure him out. And you're right. Sunee was his second wife from Thailand.'

'Did the brothers get on well?' Erlendur asked cautiously. She could sense his hesitation.

'Get on well? Of course. What do you mean? Of course they got on well.'

She moved a step closer to Erlendur.

'You think he did it, do you?' she whispered. 'You think Niran attacked his own brother? Are you crazy?'

'Not at all,' Erlendur said. 'I—'

'Wouldn't that be an easy solution?' Sigrídur said sarcastically.

'You mustn't misunderstand me,' Erlendur said.

'Misunderstand? I'm not misunderstanding anything,' Sigrídur hissed between clenched teeth. 'You think this is just a case of Thais killing each other, don't you? Wouldn't that be convenient for you and for the rest of us? They're just Thais! None of our business. Is that what you're saying?'

Erlendur hesitated. Maybe it was too early to ask the closest relatives about the boys' relationship. He should not be sowing suspicion with his tentative questions, causing even more anger and bewilderment.

'I'm sorry if I implied anything of the kind,' Erlendur said calmly. 'But we have to look for information, no matter how uncomfortable it might be. It's never crossed my mind that the elder boy had anything to do with this, but I think the sooner we find him, the better for everyone concerned.'

'Niran will come home soon,' Sigrídur said.

'Could he have gone to see his stepfather? Ódinn?'

'I doubt it. They don't get on. My son . . .'

Sigrídur hesitated now. Erlendur waited patiently.

'Oh, I don't know,' she sighed.

Sigrídur explained that she had lived in the countryside until recently and had only been to Reykjavík a couple of times a year for short visits. She always visited her son's family and sometimes stayed with them, although the flat on Snorrabraut was small. She had the impression that her son was not particularly happy, and even though Sunee never complained she could tell that all was not well with their marriage. This was around the time Sunee told him she had another son in Thailand who she wanted to send for.

Ódinn had not told his mother about Sunee when he met her. He had had another wife from Thailand before Sunee came on the scene. She had left him after three years. When he sent for her he had never seen her face to face, only in photographs. She was granted a month's visa to stay in Iceland. They got married two weeks after she arrived. She had brought all the necessary papers with her from Thailand in order to make the marriage legal.

'She moved to Denmark later,' Sigrídur said. 'Probably only came here to get an Icelandic passport.'

The next thing Sigrídur knew was that Ódinn had met Sunee and married her. The two women hit it off straight away. Sigrídur had been apprehensive about meeting her new daughter-in-law after what had happened before and was

54

anxious about the new relationship. She tried not to display any prejudice and was relieved when she shook Sunee's hand. She could tell at once that she had character. The first thing she noticed was how Sunee had transformed the squalid flat on Snorrabraut into a beautiful, tidy home with a strong Asian ambience. She had brought along or sent for objects from Thailand to decorate the home: statues of Buddha, pictures and various pretty ornaments.

Although she only visited Reykjavík intermittently at that time, Sigrídur tried to make life in Iceland easier for Sunee. Her daughter-in-law did not understand the language and had great difficulty in picking it up. She spoke little English, and Sigrídur knew anyway that her son had never been the sociable type and had few friends who could help Sunee adapt to a new lifestyle and a completely different society. Gradually Sunee got to know other Thai women who helped her to find her feet, but she had no Icelandic friends with the possible exception of her mother-in-law.

Sigrídur admired Sunee's readiness to accept the darkness and cold of her strange new environment. 'Just dress better warm,' Sunee would say, smiling and positive. Ódinn was not always happy with his mother's interference. They had argued after she found out that he was annoyed when Sunee spoke Thai to the boy. By that time she had begun to speak a little Icelandic. 'I don't know what she's telling the kid,' Ódinn complained to his mother. 'He should speak Icelandic. He's an Icelander! It's what's best for him. For the future.'

Sigrídur described how she had subsequently found out that her son was not alone in that opinion. In some cases, Icelandic husbands forbade their Asian wives from speaking their native tongue to the children, because they could not understand it themselves. When the mother spoke poor Icelandic or none at all, it hampered the child's linguistic development, which could affect its entire schooling. To some extent this was true of Elías, who excelled at mathematics but was weaker at subjects like Icelandic and spelling.

Ódinn refused to discuss their divorce and would not listen to his mother when she talked about his obligations.

'It was a mistake,' he said. 'I should never have married her!'

By now, Sigrídur had moved to Reykjavík and kept in close touch with Sunee and Elías, whom she regarded as family. Even Niran, who was unhappy with his lot, was on good terms with her, the little he had to do with her. She tried to make her son pay Sunee what he owed her after the divorce, including her share in the flat, but he flatly refused on the grounds that he had owned the property before Sunee came along. Elías sometimes visited his grandmother and stayed with her; a good, kind boy who would do anything for her.

Niran had been at odds with his stepfather from the outset and had trouble adapting to Icelandic society. He was nine years old when he arrived in the country accompanied by Sunee's younger brother Virote. Virote had stayed, found a job in a fish factory and dreamed of opening a Thai restaurant.

'Niran never regarded Ódinn as his father, understandably,' Sigrídur said. 'They had nothing in common.'

'Who is Niran's father?' Erlendur interjected.

Sigrídur shrugged. 'I've never asked,' she said.

'It must be tough for a boy like him to come to this country at that age and under those circumstances.'

'Naturally it was very difficult,' Sigrídur said. 'And still is. He's not doing well at school and he's something of an outsider in the community.'

'There are more like him,' Erlendur said. 'They take refuge in each other, they have a common background. There have been clashes between them and the Icelandic kids, but not many and not serious either. Though maybe we're seeing more weapons than before. Knuckledusters. Knives.'

'Niran isn't a bad lad,' Sigrídur said, 'but I know Sunee's worried about him. He always treated his brother kindly. Their relationship was rather special. They got on well together, I think, considering the circumstances. Sunee made sure of that.'

Gudný came in from the kitchen.

'Sunee wants to go out and look for Niran,' she said. 'I'm going with her.'

'Of course,' Erlendur said. 'But I think it would be better to wait here for a while in case he turns up.'

'I'll stay here in case he comes back,' Sigrídur said.

'Sunee can't just sit here and wait,' the interpreter said. 'She has to get out. She has to do something.'

'I can perfectly understand that,' Erlendur said.

Sunee was in the hallway, putting on her anorak. The door to the boys' room was open and she looked inside. She went to the door and started speaking. The interpreter and Erlendur moved closer.

'He dreamed something,' the interpreter said. 'When Elías woke up this morning he told her about a dream he had last night. A little bird came to him and Elías made a bird-house for it and they became friends, Elías and the bird.'

Sunee stood at the door to the boys' room and talked to the interpreter.

'He was a bit annoyed with his mother,' the interpreter said.

Sunee looked at Erlendur and continued with her account.

'He felt happy in the dream: he'd made a friend,' the

57

interpreter said. 'He was annoyed because she woke him up. Elías would have liked to stay in the dream for longer.'

Sunee recalled Elías on that last morning. He was lying in bed, trying to hold on to the dream about the bird; snuggled up under his too-small duvet in his too-small pyjamas. His skinny legs protruded a long way out of the bottoms. He was lying on his side, staring at the wall in the dark. She had turned on the light in the room but he reached over for the switch and turned it off again. His brother was already up. Sunee was late for work and could not find her purse. She called to Elías to get out of bed. She knew that he liked lying under the warm duvet, especially on cold, dark mornings with a long day ahead at school.

'We need to talk to his friends,' Erlendur said when the interpreter had finished translating her words.

Sunee looked back into the boys' room.

'Does he have many friends?' Erlendur asked, and the interpreter repeated his words in Thai.

'I don't think he had many friends in this new part of town,' Sunee said.

'That's what he was dreaming about,' Erlendur said.

'He dreamed of making a good friend,' Sunee said through the interpreter. 'I woke him up and he lay in bed for a long time before he came through to the kitchen. I was running out when he finally appeared. I'd called to him to hurry up. Niran had had breakfast and was waiting for him. They generally went to school together. Then Niran couldn't be bothered to wait any more and I had to leave.'

Sunee steeled herself.

' "I couldn't even say goodbye to him properly." That was the last thing I heard him say.'

'What?' Erlendur asked, staring at the interpreter.

Sunee said something. She spoke in such a low voice that the interpreter had to bend to hear. When she straightened up again she told Erlendur in Icelandic the last words that Elías had spoken to his mother before she hurried off to work.

'I wish I hadn't woken up.'

6

Elías's father had finally been located. He had asked to see his son's body at the morgue on Barónsstígur and was now sitting waiting in Erlendur's office at the police station on Hverfisgata. Erlendur left Sunee, her brother and the interpreter outside the block of flats where she lived. Two police officers intended to accompany them on their search for Niran. Sigríður stayed at the flat. Erlendur felt he had obtained all the information that Elías's mother could provide at this time. It was obvious that she had no idea why her son had been attacked or why Niran had not come home. She could not imagine where he was. Since they had only recently moved to the district, she did not know his friends very well and had only a vague idea of where they lived. Erlendur could well understand how she could not stay quietly at home, waiting for news. The entire police force was looking for Niran. His photograph had been distributed to all the stations. He could be in danger. He could also be in hiding. What mattered most was to find him as quickly as possible.

Elínborg contacted Erlendur to say that she had spoken to the staff at the chemist's shop where the witness had seen Niran and his friends hanging around. The staff did not remember any of the boys actually going inside the shop. Nor had they noticed any particular group of teenagers behind the building that day and so were surprised when Elínborg began asking detailed questions about them; schoolchildren were always loitering there. Graffiti was scrawled over the walls and cigarette butts had been stubbed out on the pavement in the little back yard. Elínborg said she would continue talking to Elías's classmates.

'Sunee's neighbour, Fanney her name is, mentioned that Sunee might have been receiving visits from someone.'

'What kind of visits?'

'It was all very vague. She thought someone was calling on her – you know, a man.'

'A boyfriend?'

'Possibly. She didn't know. She didn't actually see anyone. But she thought so. It had been going on since the summer.'

'We'll need to ask Sunee about that,' Erlendur said. 'Have her phone checked: who's called her and who she's been calling.'

'Okay.'

His mobile rang again when Erlendur was pulling up outside the police station. It was Valgerdur. She had heard about the murder and was surprised and horrified. They had arranged to meet that evening but Erlendur said it might not work out. She told him that it didn't matter.

'Do you have any idea what happened?' she asked anxiously.

'None,' Erlendur said.

'I don't want to hold you up. Let's talk later,' she said and they rang off.

Erlendur pulled his overcoat tight as he hurried into the police station, and it suddenly struck him that Niran could hardly be outdoors in such a raging northerly. The freezing, dry wind bit his face. When he looked up, the moon was barely visible, pale as frost.

At the reception desk an agitated middle-aged man was

telling the duty officer that his car had been vandalised. The man ranted at the police for their indifference, as if there were nothing criminal about causing damage worth tens of thousands of krónur. In his haste, Erlendur did not quite catch what the crime was, but he thought it sounded as if the man's car had been badly scratched.

Elías's father was sitting in Erlendur's office, head bowed. He was a skinny man in his forties, with a bald patch, wisps of straggly hair over his forehead and several days' growth of beard. He had a very small mouth but large, projecting teeth, which gave him a rather coarse look. He stood up when Erlendur entered and they exchanged greetings.

'Ódinn,' the man introduced himself in a low voice. His eyes were red from weeping.

Erlendur put his overcoat on a hanger and sat down behind the desk.

'My condolences about your son,' he said. 'Of course, this is too horrific for words.'

He allowed a short pause to follow his words as he looked the man over. Ódinn was wearing scruffy jeans and a thin, light-coloured windcheater with an old red scarf round his neck bearing the logo of a foreign football club. He lived alone in the flat on Snorrabraut, according to what he had told the police. On the way to his office, Erlendur was told that Ódinn had been very upset by the visit from the police and the news about Elías.

'Do you have any idea where your stepson might be?' Erlendur asked.

'Niran? What about him?'

'We can't find him. He hasn't been home.'

'I have no idea,' the man said. 'I have—' He stopped.

'Yes?' Erlendur said.

'Nothing,' the man said.

'When were you last in touch with your family?'

'It's always an on-and-off thing. We got divorced. You probably know that.'

'You've no idea what happened to the boys today?'

'I . . . it's terrible, absolutely terrible . . . I would never have believed this kind of thing could happen in this country. Attacking a child like that!'

'What do you think happened?'

'Isn't it obvious? Isn't it racism? Is there any other reason for attacking a child? What can a child do to anyone?'

'We still don't know what happened,' Erlendur said. 'You haven't phoned the boys recently or seen them?'

'No. I took Elías to the cinema a while back. I never had much contact with Niran.'

'And you can't imagine what could have happened?'

Ódinn shook his head.

'Do you think something's happened to Niran as well?'

'We don't know. There's a search under way for him. Do you have any ideas?'

'About his whereabouts? No, none. I have no idea.'

'Sunee moved out when you got divorced,' Erlendur said. 'The boys don't appear to have adjusted particularly well to their new neighbourhood. Did you take an interest in that at all?'

Ódinn did not answer immediately.

'Did you never hear about any trouble?'

'I wasn't in touch with Sunee much,' Ódinn said eventually. 'It was over.'

'I'm really asking more about the two boys,' Erlendur said. 'Your son in particular, perhaps.'

Ódinn did not reply.

'Elías was always more attached to his mother,' he said at last. 'We often argued about his upbringing. She had her own way entirely in bringing him up. She even called him by a Thai name. She rarely called him Elías.'

'She's a long way from home. She wants to hold on to something connected with her past in a new country,' Erlendur said.

Ódinn looked at him without saying a word.

'Your mother speaks highly of her,' Erlendur said. 'I gather that they're good friends. She hurried over to Sunee's flat as soon as she heard the news.'

'They've always got on well together.'

'I understand Sunee's your second wife from Thailand.'

'Yes,' Ódinn said.

'I also understand you were not very pleased when Sunee told you she had an older son and wanted to send for him,' Erlendur said.

'I suspected as much,' Ódinn said. 'It was nothing new. She'd told me she was single, then she wanted to bring Niran over.'

'What did you think about that?'

'I wasn't pleased about having the boy. But I stayed out of the matter, left it entirely up to her. I had no say in it.'

'So you didn't want to divorce her immediately then?'

'Sunee was okay,' Ódinn said.

'She hasn't learned much Icelandic in the time she's lived here,' Erlendur said.

'No,' Ódinn said.

'Did you help her with it at all?'

'What are you asking about that for? What's that got to do with anything? Shouldn't you be catching the person who did this instead of asking me stupid irrelevant questions? What kind of questions are these anyway?'

'Your son was probably attacked in the afternoon,' Erlendur said. 'Where were you then?'

'At work,' Ódinn said. 'I was at work when you lot came. Do you think I killed my son? Are you mad?'

He said this without raising his voice and without becoming worked up, as if the notion were simply too ludicrous to get angry about.

'We know from experience that such matters are often family-related,' Erlendur said without changing his expression. 'There's nothing unnatural about me asking where you spent the day.'

Ódinn remained silent.

'Is there anyone at work who could confirm your whereabouts?'

'Yes, a couple of blokes. I can't believe you think I'm implicated in this!'

'It's part of the job,' Erlendur said. 'A lot of what I get involved with is more far-fetched than that.'

'Are you telling me that I attacked the boy to get my own back on Sunee?'

Erlendur shrugged.

'Are you out of your mind?'

'Stay where you are,' Erlendur said when Ódinn rose to his feet. 'What we need to do is to examine all the possibilities. Why should you want to get your own back on Sunee?'

'What do you mean? I don't want to get my own back on her!'

'I didn't mention any reason,' Erlendur said. 'You yourself did. Those were your own words.'

'I didn't say a thing.'

Erlendur sat in silence.

'You're confusing me,' Ódinn said, agitated by now. 'You're

trying to make me say something I shouldn't. You're playing with me!'

'It was what you said.'

'Fucking hell!' Ódinn shouted, kicking the desk. Erlendur sat in his chair and looked up at him without moving. He leaned back, arms folded over his chest. The man looked as if he was about to attack him.

'I would never do anything to my son!' he yelled. 'Never!'

Erlendur remained unruffled.

'Have you talked to her boyfriend?' Ódinn asked.

'Her boyfriend?'

'Hasn't she told you about him?'

'Who is he? Who is Sunee's boyfriend?'

Ódinn did not reply. He stared at Erlendur, who was leaning forward in his chair.

'Is he the reason you got divorced?' Erlendur asked cautiously.

'No. I only heard recently.'

'What?'

'That she was seeing someone.'

Elínborg was standing in the home of one of Elías's classmates. She had not been offered a seat. They were in the kitchen and the boy's father was sitting beside him. His sister and younger brother were also sitting at the table. It was a small town house not far from the block of flats where Elías and Niran lived. Elínborg had disturbed them at dinnertime. Other police officers were simultaneously in the same position, visiting the homes of children who might conceivably be linked to Elías.

She apologised repeatedly. The boy's mother said she had seen the television news and was shocked to hear about it. The father showed no particular reaction. Neither did the children.

Elínborg looked at their food: spaghetti with mince. The smell of frying filled the house, mingled with basil and boiled tomato. Her thoughts flew home. She had not managed to shop for days and there was nothing in the refrigerator.

'He came here for Biggi's birthday party,' the mother said, also standing beside the table. 'We wanted to invite the whole class. I thought he was a particularly delightful boy. I just can't understand what could have happened. They said he'd been stabbed. As if anyone could have wanted to harm him. They implied he'd been attacked, like it was premeditated. Is that true?'

'We have no idea,' Elínborg said. 'The investigation is just beginning. I haven't seen the news but I doubt the reporters got that information from the police. We know very little at the moment. That's why I'd like to have a little chat with you, Biggi,' she said, addressing her words to the boy.

Biggi looked at her, wide-eyed.

'You were his friend, weren't you?' Elínborg said.

'Not really,' Biggi said. 'He was in my class but—'

'Biggi doesn't know him very well,' his mother interrupted with an embarrassed smile.

'No, I see,' Elínborg said.

The father sat in silence at the kitchen table. The food was on his plate but he had no intention of eating it in front of a police officer. All three children were tucking into their spaghetti. When Elínborg had rung the doorbell, the mother had answered and hesitantly let her in. Elínborg had a strong sense that she was disturbing the peace of their home.

'Do you sometimes play with him?' Elínborg asked.

'I don't think Biggi plays with him much,' the father said.

The man was slim and drawn-looking, with bags under his eyes and several days' worth of stubble. He was wearing blue overalls, which he had unbuttoned to the waist when he sat down at the table. His hands were worn from manual labour. His face and hair were covered in a grey substance that Elínborg thought might be cement dust. Instinctively she assumed that he was a plasterer.

'I wanted to—' Elínborg said.

'I'd like some peace to eat with my family,' the man said. 'If you don't mind.'

'I know,' Elínborg said, 'and my apologies once again for disturbing you. I just wanted to ask Biggi a few questions because we need to gather information as quickly as possible. It won't take a moment.'

'You can do that later,' the man said.

He stared at Elínborg. His wife stood beside the table and said nothing. The children wolfed down their food. Biggi looked at Elínborg as he sucked up a piece of spaghetti. He had tomato sauce all round his mouth.

'Do you know whether Elías was on his own when he went home from school today?' Elínborg asked.

Biggi shook his head, his mouth full of spaghetti.

The man looked at his wife.

'I don't think that has anything to do with Biggi,' he said.

'He was really sweet, that boy, polite and well brought-up,' the woman said. 'He was the only one who thanked us for inviting him to the birthday party and he wasn't noisy like the other kids.'

As she said this she looked at her husband, as if justifying having invited Elías to their son's birthday party. Elínborg looked at the parents in turn and then at the children, who had stopped eating and were watching the adults apprehensively. They sensed that an argument was brewing.

'When was this birthday party?' Elínborg asked, looking at the mother.

'Three weeks ago.'

'Around Christmas? And everything went well?'

'Yes, very well. Don't you think so, Biggi?' she asked with a glance at her son. She avoided looking at her husband.

Biggi nodded. He looked at his father, uncertain whether he ought to say what he wanted to say.

'Will you please leave us in peace now?' the man said, standing up. 'We'd like to eat.'

'Did you see Elías when he came to the birthday party?'

'I work eighteen hours a day,' the man said.

'He's never home,' the woman said. 'There's no need to be so rude to her,' she added, darting a look at her husband.

'Do immigrants get on your nerves?' Elínborg asked.

'I've got nothing against those people,' the man said. 'Biggi doesn't know that kid in the slightest. They weren't friends. We can't help you with anything. Now will you please leave us alone!'

'Of course,' Elínborg said, looking down at the plates of spaghetti. She pondered for a moment, then gave up and left.

'It was a very ordinary day at school,' Agnes, Elías's form teacher, told Sigurdur Óli. 'I think I can say that. Except that I moved the boy to a different seat in the classroom. I'd been meaning to for some time and I finally did it this morning.'

They were sitting in the study at Agnes's house. She had produced a cigarette from a drawer. Sigurdur Óli watched her cast a surreptitious glance at the door, then sit down by the window, light the cigarette and blow the smoke outside. He could not understand people who wanted to kill themselves by smoking. He was convinced that smoking caused more harm than any other single factor in the world, and sometimes lectured on the subject at work. Erlendur, a smoker, paid no heed and once answered that he was convinced that what caused more harm than any other single factor in the world was dyed-in-the-wool killjoys like Sigurdur Óli.

'Elías was a bit late,' Agnes continued. 'He wasn't usually, although he used to dawdle a bit. He was often the last to leave the class, the last to get his books out and that sort of thing. He would be thinking about something completely different. He was a sort of "flight attendant".' Agnes made a sign for quotation marks with her fingers.

'Flight attendant?'

'Vilhjálmur calls them that, the sports teacher. He's from the Westman Islands.'

Sigurdur Óli gave her a blank look.

'The children who are last to leave after gym.'

'You moved him to a different seat?' Sigurdur Óli said, at a complete loss about flight attendants and the Westman Islands.

'It's not uncommon,' Agnes said. 'We do it for various reasons. I only did it indirectly because of him. Elías was good at maths. He was way ahead of his classmates, even of the rest of his year, but the boy who sat beside him, poor old Birgir – or Biggi, as he's known – has trouble puzzling out how two and two could possibly make four.'

Agnes looked Sigurdur Óli in the eye.

'I know I shouldn't say things like that,' she said sheepishly. 'Anyway, Biggi's mother came to see me and told me how he was always complaining about being stupid, and when she wheedled out of him what it was all about he said that Elías was much better than him at everything. His mother was really quite embarrassed about it. It's not uncommon and there's often a simple solution. I made Elías sit somewhere else. I put him next to a lovely girl who's another excellent pupil.'

Agnes inhaled the smoke, then blew it out of the window.

'What about Elías? Didn't he have any problems?'

'Yes,' Agnes said. 'He found Icelandic quite difficult. He and his brother used to speak Thai to each other. It's what they spoke at home. Kids can get confused by that.'

She stubbed out her cigarette.

'So Elías was a bit late this morning?' Sigurdur Óli said.

Holding the cigarette butt between her fingers, Agnes nodded.

'I'd started taking the register when Elías finally showed up. The whole class watched him sit down. His hair was ruffled and he was sleepy, as if he hadn't fully woken up yet. I asked him if he was all right and he just nodded. But he was very dreamy. He sat there with his bag on the desk, looking out of the window at the playground, and seemed to be in a world of his own. He didn't hear me when I started teaching. Just sat staring out of the window. I went over and asked what he was thinking about.

'"About the bird," he said. "What bird?" "The one I dreamed about," he said. "The bird that died."'

Agnes put the cigarette butt in her pocket and shut the window. It was cold indoors by now and she shivered when she stood up. A storm was forecast for that evening and night.

'I didn't ask him any more about it,' she said. 'Children often say things like that. I didn't see him again until lunchtime. In the break and at mealtime. I didn't notice him in particular. They had an art lesson that morning, maybe you should talk to Brynhildur too. Then they had a double period with me after lunch. The last lesson was gym with Vilhjálmur. He was Elías's last teacher today.'

'He's next on the list,' Sigurdur Óli said. 'Can you tell me anything about . . .' He browsed through his notebook looking for the name that the principal had given him. 'Kjartan, the Icelandic teacher?'

'Kjartan's not exactly a barrel of laughs,' Agnes said, 'as you'll soon discover for yourself. He doesn't keep his views to himself. Quite a pain in the neck really. A former sports star. He used to play handball, then something happened to him. I don't know exactly what. He's not stupid though. He mainly teaches the older children.'

With a nod, Sigurdur Óli put his notebook in his jacket and then said goodbye to Agnes. On his way out to the car, his mobile rang. It was his wife Bergthóra. She had seen the news on television and knew he would be late home.

'It's awful,' she said. 'Was he really stabbed?'

'Yes,' Sigurdur Óli said. 'I have a lot to do and we don't know where to begin. Don't wait up for me.'

'Do you have any idea who did it?'

'No. His brother's gone missing. His elder brother. He might know something. Erlendur thinks so anyway.'

'That he did it?'

'No, but—'

'Isn't it more likely that he's been attacked too? Has Erlendur considered that?'

'I'll pass that on to him,' Sigurdur Óli said drily. Sometimes Bergthóra inadvertently revealed that she had more faith in Erlendur than in her husband when it came to criminal investigations. Sigurdur Óli knew that she meant well, but it got on his nerves.

He grimaced. A response like that risked provoking Bergthóra's wrath but he was tired and peevish and knew that she wanted him to come home as soon as possible. They had to talk things over. Bergthóra's suggestion. A few days before she had proposed that they should look into the possibility of adopting a child from abroad. They could not have children together. Sigurdur Óli had been unenthusiastic about the idea. Hesitantly, he suggested that they put up with the status quo for the time being. Their attempts to have a baby had put a strain on their relationship. Sigurdur Óli wanted them to have a year free of worries about children or adoption. Bergthóra was more impatient. She yearned to have a baby.

'Oh, of course I shouldn't go sticking my nose in,' she said over the phone.

'It's perfectly feasible that his brother was attacked too,' Sigurdur Óli said. 'We're examining all the possibilities.'

There was silence on the line.

'Has Erlendur found that woman?' Bergthóra eventually asked.

'No. She's still missing.'

'Do you know any more about that case?'

'Not really.'

'If I'm asleep, will you wake me up when you get home?'

'I'll do that,' Sigurdur Óli said, and they rang off.

8

The boys were playing indoor football with great zeal. They fought over every single ball and did not flinch from playing dirty. Sigurdur Óli saw one of them go in for a sliding tackle that could have broken his opponent's leg. When the victim crashed to the floor he yelled at the top of his voice and clutched his ankle.

'Watch out, lads!' the coach shouted into the pitch. 'None of that, Geiri! Come on, Raggi,' he called to the boy who was climbing to his feet after the tackle.

He sent on a substitute for Raggi and the game continued just as violently as before. There were far more boys at football practice than could play at once, so the coach made frequent substitutions. Sigurdur Óli watched from the sidelines. The coach was Vilhjálmur, Elías's sports teacher. He had an extra part-time job as a boys' football trainer, as his wife had told Sigurdur Óli when he stood on their doorstep. She had directed him to the sports hall.

The practice was coming to an end. Vilhjálmur blew the whistle that hung around his neck and a boy who seemed unhappy with the result gave the ball an almighty kick, hitting one of his teammates on the back of the head. After some commotion, Vilhjálmur blew his whistle again and called out to the boys to stop that nonsense and get along to the showers. The two boys stopped their brawling.

'Isn't that a bit rough?' Sigurdur Óli asked as he walked over to Vilhjálmur. The boys stared at the policeman. They had never seen such a well-dressed man in the hall before.

'They get quite boisterous sometimes,' Vilhjálmur said, shaking Sigurdur Óli's hand. A short, chubby man aged about thirty, he gathered up the goalpost cones and balls and threw them into a storeroom that he then locked. 'These kids need toughening up. They come here fat and lazy from pizza and computer games and I get them to take some exercise. Are you here about Elías?' he said.

'You were his last teacher today, I understand,' Sigurdur Óli said.

Vilhjálmur had heard about the murder and said he could hardly believe the news.

'You feel completely thrown by something like this,' he said. 'Elías was a great kid – dedicated to sport. I think he really enjoyed playing football. I don't know what to say.'

'Did you notice anything special or unusual about him today?'

'It was just a normal day. I made them run a bit and vault over the box, then we split them up into teams. They enjoy football most. Handball too.'

'Did Elías go straight home from school, do you think?'

'I have no idea where he went,' Vilhjálmur said.

'Was he the last to leave?'

'Elías was always the last to leave,' Vilhjálmur said.

'Was he a "flight attendant"?'

'Are you from the Westman Islands too?'

'No. Not exactly. You're . . . ?'

'We moved here when I was twelve.'

'Was Elías hanging around then, or . . . ?'

'That's just the way he was,' Vilhjálmur said. 'He took a long time to leave. He was slow at changing his clothes. He sort of dithered about and you had to chivvy him along.'

'What was he doing then?'

'Just preoccupied, in a world of his own.'

'Today too?'

'Probably, though I didn't particularly notice. I had to rush off to a meeting.'

'Did you see anyone waiting for him outside? Notice if he met anyone? Did he seem afraid to go home? Could you sense anything like that about him?'

'No, nothing. I didn't see anything unusual outside. The kids were heading off home. I don't think anyone was waiting for him. But then, I wasn't thinking along those lines. You don't think about that sort of thing.'

'Not until afterwards,' Sigurdur Óli said.

'Yes, of course. But as I say, I didn't notice anything unusual. He displayed no signs of fear during the lesson. Didn't say anything to me. He was just the same as always. After all, nothing of that kind has ever happened here before. Never. I can't understand anyone wanting to attack Elías, simply can't understand it. It's horrific.'

'Do you know the Icelandic teacher at the school, a man by the name of Kjartan?'

'Yes.'

'Apparently he has certain views about immigrants.'

'That's putting it mildly.'

'Do you agree with him?'

'Me? No, he strikes me as a nutjob. He . . .'

'He what?'

'He's rather bitter,' Vilhjálmur said. 'Have you met him?'

'No.'

'He's an old sporting hero,' Vilhjálmur said. 'I remember him well from handball. Damn good player. Then something happened, he was badly injured and had to quit. Just as he was turning professional. He'd been signed up by a Spanish club. I think that festers. He's not a likeable sort of character.'

Shouts and cries came from the boys' changing rooms along the corridor. Vilhjálmur set off in that direction to calm the boys down.

'Do you know what happened?' he said over his shoulder.

'Not yet,' Sigurdur Óli said.

'Hope you catch the bastard. Was it racially motivated?'

'We don't know anything.'

Kjartan's wife was in her early thirties, slightly younger than the Icelandic teacher himself, and rather scruffily dressed in jogging pants that detracted unnecessarily from her looks. Two children stood behind her. Sigurdur Óli cast a glance inside the dim flat. The couple did not appear particularly house-proud. Instinctively, he thought about his own flat where everything was spick and span. The thought sent a warm feeling through him as he stood outside in the cold, pierced by the bitter wind. This flat was one of four in the building, on the ground floor.

The woman called her husband and he came to the door, also wearing jogging pants and a vest that looked two sizes too small and emphasised its owner's expanding paunch. He seemed to make do with shaving once a week and there was a bad-tempered look on his face that Sigurdur Óli could not quite fathom, something about his eyes that expressed antipathy and anger. He remembered having seen that expression before, that face, and recalled Vilhjálmur's words about the fallen sports star.

A face from the past, Erlendur would have said. He sometimes made remarks that Sigurdur Óli disliked because he did not understand them, snatches from those old tales that were Erlendur's only apparent interest in life. The two men were poles apart in their thinking. While Erlendur sat at home reading old Icelandic folklore or fiction, Sigurdur Óli would sit in front of the television watching American cop shows with a bowl of popcorn in his lap and a bottle of Coke on the table. When he joined the police force he modelled himself on such programmes. He was not alone in thinking that a job with the police could sharpen one's image. Recruits still occasionally turned up for work dressed like American TV cops, in jeans and back-to-front baseball cap.

'Is it about the boy?' Kjartan said, making no move to invite Sigurdur Óli in out of the cold.

'About Elías, yes.'

'It was only a matter of time,' Kjartan said with an intolerant ring to his voice. 'They shouldn't let those people into the country,' he went on. 'It only causes conflict. This had to happen sooner or later. Whether it was this boy in this school in this district at this time or someone else at some other time . . . it makes no difference. It would have happened and will happen again. You can bet.'

Sigurdur Óli began to recall more of Kjartan's story as the man stood in front of him, feet apart, with one hand on the doorframe and the other on the door, his gut hanging out under his vest. Sigurdur Óli was a keen follower of sports, although he was more interested in American football and baseball than

Icelandic sports. But he remembered this man as the great hope of Icelandic handball, recalled how he had already been in the national team when he was injured during a game in his early twenties and had to quit. The media made a big deal of him for a while, then Kjartan disappeared from the scene as quickly as he had been swept into it.

'So you think the attack was racially motivated?' Sigurdur Óli said, thinking how difficult it must have been for the man to say goodbye to professional handball. He might have been coming to the end of a star-studded career now had he not been injured, instead he was teaching at a secondary school.

'Is there any other possibility?' Kjartan asked.

'You've taught Elías.'

'Yes, as a substitute teacher.'

'What kind of a boy was he?'

'I don't know him in the slightest. I heard he'd been stabbed. I don't know any more than that. There's no point asking me. It's not my job to take care of those kids. I'm not working at a kids' playground!'

Sigurdur Óli gave him a searching look.

'There are three like him in his class,' Kjartan continued. 'More than thirty in the school as a whole. I've stopped noticing when new ones enrol. They're everywhere. Have you been to the flea market? It's like Hong Kong! No one pays any attention to it. No one pays any attention to what's becoming of our country.'

'I—'

'Do you think it's okay?'

'That's none of your business,' Sigurdur Óli said.

'I can't help you,' Kjartan said, preparing to shut the door.

'Do you think it's too much to ask you to answer a few

questions?' Sigurdur Óli said. 'We could deal with it down at the station otherwise. You're welcome to come with me. It's more comfortable there too.'

'Don't you go threatening me,' Kjartan said, undaunted. 'I'm telling you I know nothing about this matter.'

'He might have been afraid of you,' Sigurdur Óli said. 'You don't exactly seem to have been friendly towards him. Or to any of the other children you teach.'

'Hey,' Kjartan protested. 'I didn't do anything to the boy. I don't keep an eye out for the kids after school. They're not my responsibility.'

'If I find out you threatened him in some way because you regarded him as a foreigner, we'll be having another chat.'

'Wow . . . I'm scared shitless,' Kjartan said. 'Leave me alone! I don't know what happened to the boy; it's nothing to do with me.'

'What about this clash you had with a teacher called Finnur?' Sigurdur Óli asked.

'Clash?'

'In the staff room,' Sigurdur Óli said. 'What happened?'

'There was no clash,' Kjartan said. 'We had a bit of an argument. He seems to think it's all right: the more foreigners that pour into this country the better. He never produces anything but that old left-wing bollocks. I told him so. He got a bit angry.'

'You think that's acceptable, do you?' Sigurdur Óli asked.

'What?'

'Talking that way about people? Are you sure you're in the right line of work?'

'What bloody business is it of yours? Are you in the right line of work, sniffing around people who are none of your business?'

'Maybe not,' Sigurdur Óli said. 'Weren't you in handball in the old days?' he asked. 'A bit of a star?'

Kjartan hesitated for a second. He seemed poised to say something, an insult to show that he did not care what Sigurdur Óli said or thought of him. But nothing occurred to him and he shut the door without saying a word.

'Great role model you would have made,' Sigurdur Óli said to the door.

Later that evening Erlendur drove back to the block of flats. The search for Niran had proved fruitless. Sunee and her brother had returned home. The police were still looking for the boy and the public had been asked to help by telephoning in information and even taking a walk around their neighbourhoods to look for a South East Asian teenager, a fairly small fifteen-year-old boy in a blue anorak and black woolly hat.

Ódinn, Elías's father, took an active part in the search. He met Sunee and they had a long talk in private. That evening he had told Erlendur more about their marriage, how he had wanted to keep Elías after the divorce but the boy had wanted to be with his mother, so he had let the matter rest. He could not give Erlendur any details about the new man in Sunee's life. Nor had she mentioned any boyfriend to the police. Perhaps the relationship had broken down. Ódinn knew nothing about it.

Erlendur stopped in front of the block of flats. He drove a Ford Falcon, more than thirty years old, which he had acquired that autumn, black with white interior fittings. He left the engine running and lit a cigarette. It was the last one in the pack. He crumpled the packet and was about to throw it onto the back seat as he used to do in his old car, but refrained and put the empty packet in his overcoat pocket. He treated the Ford with a certain amount of respect.

Erlendur inhaled the blue smoke. Trust, he thought to himself. He had to trust people. His thoughts turned to the woman he had been searching for over the past weeks. Cases piled up on his desk and one of the most serious was connected with marital infidelity, or at least so he thought. It involved a missing person and Erlendur's theory was that it stemmed from unfaithfulness. Not everyone agreed with him.

The woman, Ellen, had walked out of her home shortly before Christmas and had not been seen since. Before the boy was discovered behind the block of flats, Erlendur had been so absorbed in the case that Sigurdur Óli and Elínborg talked among themselves about the return of his old obsession. Everyone knew that Erlendur could not stand unsolved cases on his desk, especially if they involved missing persons. Where others shook their heads and convinced themselves they had done their best, Erlendur went on delving deeper, refusing to give up.

The woman's husband was understandably very worried about her. They were both aged around forty and had got married two years before, but both had been married to other people when they met. His former wife was a departmental manager in the civil service and they had three children aged between three and fourteen. Ellen had been married to a banker and had two teenage children with him. Both apparently lived happy lives and lacked for nothing. He had a good job with an ambitious computer company. She worked in tourism, arranging safaris through the Icelandic wilderness. They had first met when he took a small group of Swedish clients on a mystery tour to the Vatnajökull glacier. She arranged the trip and saw him at meetings, and then they both went with the group to the glacier. It resulted in an affair that they kept secret for a year and a half.

At first it was merely an exciting digression from the routine, according to the husband. It was easy for them to meet. She was in the habit of travelling and he could always make up excuses, such as playing golf, which his wife was not interested in. Occasionally he even bought a cup and had it engraved with an inscription such as 'Borgarholt Tournament, 3rd prize', to show to his wife. He found it amusingly ironic. He played golf a lot but rarely won anything.

Erlendur stubbed out his cigarette. He remembered the trophies at the man's house. He had not thrown them away, and Erlendur wondered why not. They had only been the props for a lie and as such were now superfluous. Unless he kept on lying and told willing listeners that he had won them. Perhaps he kept them as mementos of a successful affair. If he was capable of lying to his wife and having an imaginary triumph engraved on a prize cup, could there be any limit to his lies?

This was the question Erlendur had been wrestling with ever since the man telephoned to report his wife missing. What had begun as a kind of yearning for adventure or change, or even blind love, had ended in tragedy.

Erlendur was startled from his speculations by a knock on the car window. He could not see who was there for the condensation that had built up on the glass, so he opened the door. It was Elínborg.

'I must be getting home,' she said.

'Just get in for a minute,' Erlendur said.

'Mad bugger,' she groaned as she walked round the front of the car and got into the passenger seat.

'What are you doing alone out here in your car?' she asked after a silence.

'I was thinking about the woman who went missing,' Erlendur said.

'You know she committed suicide,' Elínborg said. 'We only have to find the body. It'll be discovered on the beach in Reykjanes next spring. She's been missing for more than three weeks. No one knows where she is. No one's hiding her. She hasn't been in touch with anyone. She had no money on her and we can't see any card transactions anywhere. She definitely didn't leave the country. The only trail leads down to the sea.'

Elínborg paused.

'Unless you think her new husband killed her.'

'He had fake trophies made,' Erlendur said. 'He knew his ex-wife wasn't interested in golf, never read about any kind of sports and never talked about golf to anyone. She told me so. And he didn't show the cups to anyone but her, because he needed to make up an alibi. Not until afterwards. Once he was divorced he started showing them off. If that isn't being amoral . . .'

'Are you concentrating on him now?'

'We always come back to the same thing,' Erlendur said.

'Missing persons and crimes,' said Elínborg, who had often heard Erlendur describe disappearances as a 'distinctively Icelandic crime'. His theory was that Icelanders were indifferent about people who went missing. In the great majority of cases they believed there were 'natural' explanations, in a country with a fairly high suicide rate. Erlendur went further and linked the nonchalance about disappearances to a certain popular understanding, extending back for centuries, about conditions in Iceland, the harsh climate in which people died of exposure and vanished as if the earth had swallowed them up. Nobody was better acquainted than Erlendur with stories of people who had frozen to death in bad weather. His theory was that crimes were easy to commit under the cover of this indifference. At his meetings with Elínborg and Sigurdur Óli and other detectives he had tried to fit the woman's disappearance to his theory, but his words fell on deaf ears.

'Get yourself home,' Erlendur said. 'Take care of your little girl. Has Sunee come back?'

'Yes, they've just got here,' Elínborg said. 'Ódinn was with them but I think he's left again. Niran is still missing. Oh God, I hope nothing has happened to him.'

'I think he'll turn up,' Erlendur said.

'You and your missing persons,' Elínborg said, opening the door. 'Are you in contact with your daughter these days?'

'Get yourself home,' Erlendur said.

'I was talking to Gudný, the interpreter. She says Sunee emphasised that her boys should be brought up, as she was, to show respect for older people. That's one of the fundamentals in the Thai upbringing and remains part of them all their lives. Responsibility is another point. The old people, the grand-parents and great-grandparents, are the heads of the extended family. Older people pass on their experience to the younger ones, who are supposed to ensure their security in old age. It's not an obligation but something they take for granted. And the children are . . .' Elínborg sighed heavily as she thought of Elías.

'She says that in Thailand, grown-ups stand up for children on buses and give them their seats.'

They were silent.

'This is all so new to us. Immigrants, racial issues . . . we know so little about it,' Erlendur said eventually.

'That's true. But I do think we're trying our best.'

'Doubtless. Now get yourself home.'

'See you tomorrow,' Elínborg said, then stepped out of the car and slammed the door behind her.

Erlendur wished he had another cigarette. He dreaded having to go back to see Sunee. He thought about his daughter, Eva Lind. She had dropped in at Christmas but he had not seen her since. The man she was with had been sent to prison just before the Christmas holidays and she thought Erlendur could do something about it. Her partner supplied her with dope. He was given three years for smuggling cocaine and ecstasy into the country and Eva foresaw hard times while he was in confinement.

Eva and Erlendur's relationship had gone from bad to worse recently. Erlendur could not really see why. For a long time, Eva had shown no willingness to cut back on her drug habit and had distanced herself from him. She had been in rehab, but not of her own accord, and when that was over she immediately slipped back into her old ways. Sindri, her brother, tried to help her, but to no avail. The siblings' relationship had always been close. But it was up and down between Erlendur and Eva, generally depending on Eva's mood. Sometimes she was fine, talked to her father and let him know how she was coping. At other times she had no contact and did not want anything to do with him.

Erlendur locked the Ford and looked up to the top of the six-storey block of flats that towered menacingly into the darkness. He made a mental note to talk to the landlord in case he could shed any light on Sunee and the boys' circumstances. Yet again he delayed going up to her, and instead walked round to the back of the block and into the garden. The search of the crime scene had been completed. Forensics had packed up their equipment and everything was as before, as if nothing had ever happened at the site.

He walked out to the swings. The frost bit his face and he thrust his hands deep into his pockets and stood motionless for a long time. Earlier that day he had heard that his old boss from the Reykjavík CID, Marion Briem, had been admitted to the terminal ward of the National Hospital. It was many years since Marion had retired, and now the life was slowly ebbing from his old colleague. Their relationship could hardly be described as friendship. Erlendur had always been rather irritated by Marion, probably because Marion was almost the only person in his life who did not tire of asking questions and forcing Erlendur to justify himself. Marion was also one of the most inquisitive creatures ever to walk the earth, a living database of Icelandic crime, and had often proved useful to Erlendur, even in retirement. Marion had no relatives. Erlendur came closest to being at once friend, colleague and family.

A freezing wind pierced Erlendur's clothes as he stood by the swings where Elías had died, and his mind roamed over the mountains and moors to another child who had once slipped from his grasp and now followed him through life like a sad shadow.

Erlendur looked up. He knew that he could not postpone sitting down with Sunee any longer. Turning round, he strode out of the garden. When he reached the entrance to the flats he noticed that the door to the rubbish store was open. Not wide open, just ajar. He had not noticed the rubbish store before. The door was set into the wall by the entrance and painted the same colour as the block of flats itself. Although the door had come open, that need not mean anything. Anyone could have gone there to empty their rubbish into the bins. The policeman who was guarding the door was standing inside the hallway, warming himself.

After a moment's pause Erlendur went over to the rubbish store and threw the door wide open. It was pitch dark inside and he searched for the switch to turn on the lights. A naked bulb hung from the ceiling. Dustbins stood in rows along the walls, and beneath the chute was a bin chock-a-block with rubbish. It was cold and there was a sour stench of old food and other refuse. Erlendur hesitated. Then he turned off the light and pulled the door to.

It was then that he heard the whimpering.

It took him a while to work out what the sound was. Perhaps he was mistaken. Perhaps he had not interpreted it correctly. He tore open the door and switched the light back on.

'Is there anyone in there?' he called.

Receiving no answer, he went inside the storage room, shifting dustbins about and searching between them. He pushed the bin away from beneath the chute and behind it discovered a black-haired boy sitting huddled up with his head buried between his knees, as if trying to make himself invisible.

'Niran?' Erlendur said.

The boy did not move.

'Is that you, Niran?'

The boy did not answer him. Erlendur knelt down and tried to make him look up, but the boy buried his head even deeper between his knees. He was clasping his legs together in a locked position that could not be budged.

'Come along out of here,' Erlendur said, but the boy behaved as if he was not there.

'Your mother's looking for you.'

Erlendur took hold of the boy's hand. It was as cold as an icicle. The boy bowed his head down to his chest. It was as if he thought Erlendur would just go away and leave him be.

After a while Erlendur felt he had tried everything, so he stood up slowly and walked backwards out of the rubbish store. He rang Sunee's entryphone. The interpreter answered. Erlendur said he thought he had found Niran. He was safe but his mother would have to come down and talk to him. Sunee, her brother and mother-in-law and the interpreter soon came running down the stairs. Erlendur met them at the door and showed Sunee alone the way into the storage room.

The moment she saw the boy hunched up beneath the chute she gave a little shriek, ran over to him and hugged him. Then for the first time the boy released his grip on himself, and burrowed into his mother's arms.

Some time later that evening Erlendur returned home to his lair, as Eva Lind had once called his flat when he thought that their relationship was improving. She said that he crawled into it to celebrate his misery. Those were not the words she used; Eva had a very limited and monotonous vocabulary, but that was the gist of it. He did not switch on the light. The illumination from the street cast a pale glow into the living room where his books were and he sat down in his armchair. He had often sat alone in the dark, looking out of the large living-room window. When he sat like that, looking out, there was nothing in the window but the endless sky. Occasional stars glittered in the winter stillness. Sometimes he watched the moon riding past his window in all its cold and distant glory. Sometimes the sky was dark and overcast, like now, and Erlendur stared into the blackness as if wanting to be able to disperse his weary thoughts out into the void.

He pictured Elías lying in the back garden of the flats, and once again an old image entered his mind, of another boy who all those years ago, that unfathomable eternity, had died in a raging blizzard. It was his brother, eight years old. He did not realise until he was sitting at home in his own living room, alone in the calm of night, how profound an effect the discovery of the boy's body by the block of flats had had on him. Erlendur could not help thinking about his own brother. The wound that his death left behind had never healed. Guilt had gnawed at Erlendur ever since, because he felt that he was to blame for his younger brother's fate. He was supposed to take care of him, and he had failed. No one but Erlendur himself made this unfair judgement. No one had ever mentioned that he could have done better. If he had not lost his grip on his brother in the blizzard, they would have been found together when the search party was sent out and Erlendur was dug out of the snowdrift in remarkably good shape.

He thought back to Niran when Sunee led him in tears out of the rubbish store. Did he feel that he should have been his brother's keeper?

Erlendur heaved a sigh and closed his eyes. All those endless thoughts that cut into his mind like shards of glass on his descent into a dreamless sleep.

He thinks about Elínborg snuggling up exhausted against her little daughter, as if to protect her from all harm.

He sees a worried-looking Sigurdur Óli creeping into his house, taking care not to wake Bergthóra.

Elías lies in the back garden of the flats in a ripped anorak, his broken eyes watching the snow drifting past.

Ódinn paces the floor on Snorrabraut.

Niran lies in his room, his lips trembling in silent anguish.

Sunee sits alone on the sofa, weeping quietly beneath the yellow dragon.

The woman he is searching for bobs gently in the lapping waves.

His eight-year-old brother lies frozen in a blizzard that will last for ever.

In a sun-drenched dream, a little bird flicks its tail in its new bird-house and sings for its friend.

9

When Erlendur arrived at the school the following morning with Elínborg and Sigurdur Óli, the bell had just rung for break. The children were walking quietly along the corridors. Teachers and assistants were controlling the flood and all the exits stood wide open. It had snowed towards morning. The younger children intended to use every second of the break to play outside. The older ones were more blasé, huddling by the walls or strolling in small groups down to the shop.

Erlendur knew that trauma counselling was available for the children in Elías's class and that some of the parents had taken advantage of it. They had accompanied their children to school and told the teachers of their concerns. The principal had decided to gather all the pupils and staff in the assembly hall at lunchtime for a period of quiet reflection in memory of Elías. The local clergyman was going to address the pupils and a representative from the police would ask anyone who knew about Elías's movements, or had any information that might prove useful in the investigation into his death, to notify a teacher, the principal or the police. An emergency telephone number would be given for anonymous callers. All leads would be investigated, however trivial they might seem. Sigurdur Óli and Elínborg were going to ask Elías's classmates about his last day alive, although this process was complicated by the fact that parental permission was required before a child could be questioned. Agnes, Elías's form teacher, had been very helpful and telephoned the parents first thing, and had received permission from most of them to allow the police, in cooperation with the Reykjavík Child Welfare Agency, to gather important information. She emphasised that this would not involve proper questioning, only information collection. Some parents wanted to be present when their children were interviewed and stood in the corridor with anxious expressions on their faces. Sigurdur Óli and Elínborg were already sitting down with the children, one at a time, in an empty classroom they had been allocated for the purpose.

Erlendur met the principal and asked specifically about the woodwork teacher. He understood that, like the Icelandic teacher, Egill had expressed some antipathy towards Asian women who immigrated to Iceland. The principal, who was rather stressed about preparing for the lunchtime meeting with the police representative, showed Erlendur to the woodwork room. No one was there. Erlendur returned to the staff room and was told that the woodwork teacher was probably sitting in his car out in the car park. This was a long break and he had the habit of going out to his car sometimes to smoke a cigarette or two, Erlendur was told.

The police investigation was still focusing on the immediate vicinity, the school and the estate. It transpired that a repeat offender lived in a block of flats not far from Elías's. He had been brought in for questioning that night but, paralytic with drink, he had assaulted the officers and was detained in custody. Towards morning a search warrant was obtained for his flat, but so far nothing had been found that could be linked to Elías's murder. The police also investigated several of the usual suspects, who might conceivably be connected with stabbings – debt collectors and people who had been picked up by the police due to clashes with immigrants or even tourists.

Niran had not spoken a word since he was found. A child psychologist had been called in that night and a social worker from the Child Welfare Agency, but Niran remained wrapped in a blanket and said nothing, no matter how they pressed him. He was repeatedly asked where he had been that day and whether he knew about his brother's fate, whether he knew what had happened, who could have committed the deed, when he had last seen his brother, what they had talked about. While all these questions rained down on him, especially from his mother, Niran never opened his mouth, sitting instead in silence in his blanket and staring into space. It was as if he had withdrawn into a closed world; into a sanctuary that he alone knew.

Eventually Erlendur told the experts to leave and went home himself, leaving Sunee and Niran in peace. Sigrídur had left by then and the interpreter had also gone home, but Sunee's brother stayed behind with the mother and son in the flat.

It did not seem to be common knowledge that Sunee had a lover. Gudný told Erlendur that she had no idea what he was talking about; she had never heard any mention of the man. Sunee's ex-mother-in-law was equally in the dark. It was not until Erlendur asked Sunee's brother Virote that he received a positive response. He knew about a man in his sister's life but the relationship had not been going on for long, and he said he had never met the man and did not know who he was. Not wanting to disturb Sunee now that she had reclaimed Niran, Erlendur told Virote to ask her for details about the man and then get in touch. He had not done so as yet.

Erlendur soon found the woodwork teacher's silver-grey car. He knocked on the driver's window and the man wound it down. A cloud of cigarette smoke escaped into the winter air.

'Can I join you?' Erlendur asked. 'I'm from the police.'

The woodwork teacher grunted. He gave a reluctant nod, as if doubting that he could avoid having to talk to Erlendur. He clearly disliked being disturbed during his smoking break. Unruffled, Erlendur sat down in the passenger seat and took out a pack of cigarettes.

'Egill, isn't it?'

'Yes.'

'Do you mind if I smoke too?' Erlendur asked, waving a cigarette.

A grimace formed on Egill's face, which Erlendur found difficult to interpret.

'No peace anywhere,' the woodwork teacher said.

Erlendur lit up and the two men sat in silence for a little while, enjoying their tobacco.

'You're here about the boy, of course,' Egill said at last. He was a large, fat man aged about fifty, who did not fit particularly comfortably into the driver's seat. Big-boned, bald as a coot, he had a large nose, high, protruding cheekbones and a beard. When his huge hand raised the cigarette to his mouth it almost disappeared inside. On top of his bald head, towards the front, was a large, pink lump that Erlendur stole occasional glances at when he thought Egill would not notice. He did not know why, but the lump fascinated him.

'Was he good at woodwork?' Erlendur asked.

'Yes, reasonably,' Egill said, stretching out his big paw to stub out his cigarette in the ashtray. It creaked under the strain. 'Do you have any idea what happened?'

'No, none,' Erlendur said, 'except that he was stabbed close to the school here.'

'This society's going to the dogs,' Egill grunted. 'And you lot can't do a thing about it. Is it a distinctively Icelandic trait, being so lax towards criminals? Can you tell me that?'

Erlendur was not sure what the teacher was getting at.

'I read in the papers the other day,' Egill went on, 'that some jerks had broken into someone's house to collect a minor debt, smashed the place to pieces and mutilated the owner. They were caught in the act but the whole gang were released after questioning! What kind of bollocks is that anyway?'

'I—'

Erlendur could not get his answer in.

'They ought to take those men and throw them straight into jail,' Egill continued. 'When they're caught or confess, they ought to be sentenced immediately. They shouldn't see the light of day until they've spent at least ten years inside. But you let them go as if nothing had happened. Is it surprising that everything here's going to hell? Why do repeat offenders always get such ridiculously light sentences? What is it in our society that produces such a submissive attitude towards criminal scum?'

'It's the law,' Erlendur said. 'It always operates in that lot's favour.'

'Change it then,' Egill said, agitated.

'I understand you're against immigrants too,' Erlendur said, accustomed to hearing tirades against Iceland's lenient sentencing and peculiarly soft treatment of criminals.

'Who says I'm against immigrants?' Egill asked in a surprised voice.

'No one in particular,' Erlendur said.

'Is it because of the meeting the other day?'

'What meeting?'

'I took the liberty of siding with Jónas Hallgrímsson. At a parents' meeting for one of the years here someone proposed singing a few lines of his poem "Iceland, Prosperous Land" with the children. They'd been learning about the poet. Sometimes they teach a bit of sense in this school. A couple of parents started finding fault with the idea, saying that the school was a multicultural society. Like it was racist to sing Icelandic songs. There was a bit of a debate and I spoke up to ask if these people were soft in the head. I think I might have used those very words. Of course, some of them complained to the principal about me. Felt I was being rude. The poor old sod was shaking in his shoes when he talked to me about it. I told him to go ahead and fire me. I've taught here for more than a quarter of a century and I'd welcome it if someone would be kind enough to kick me out. I don't have the balls to get myself out of here.'

Another cigarette appeared in Egill's huge hand and when Erlendur darted a glance at the lump on his bald head it seemed to be turning red. He took it as a sign that Egill was becoming angry at the very thought of the parents' meeting. Or perhaps it was the quarter century that he felt he had wasted teaching woodwork at the school.

'I've got nothing against immigrants,' Egill said, lighting his cigarette. 'But I'm against changing everything that's traditional and Icelandic just to pander to something called multiculturalism, when I don't even know what it means. I'm against the conservatives too. I'm also against having to sit out here in this wreck of a car to smoke. But what say do I have?'

'It was more than just poetry, I'm led to believe,' Erlendur said. 'You made remarks about Asian women that upset people.

If I understand correctly you expressed strong antipathy against these women coming to Iceland.'

The bell rang to signal the end of break and the children started to file back into the school. Instead of making a move, Egill sat tight, inhaling the toxic fumes of his cigarette.

'Strong antipathy!' he mimicked Erlendur. 'I've got nothing against immigrants! Those buggers started arguing with me and I told them what I thought. We're still allowed to have opinions at least. I said I thought it was terrible, the circumstances under which many of those women come to Iceland. They generally appear to be fleeing appalling poverty and think they can find a better life here. I said something along those lines. I didn't criticise those women. I respect self-reliance in any form and I think they've got on very well in Iceland.'

Clearing his throat, Egill reached forward to the ashtray with difficulty and stubbed out his cigarette.

'I think that applies to all these races who come to settle in Iceland,' he went on. 'But that doesn't mean we shouldn't honour Icelandic culture and promote it everywhere, especially in schools. On the contrary, I think the more immigrants there are in this country, the more effort we should make to introduce them to our heritage, and encourage anyone who actually wants to come and live here in the cold not to reject it out of hand. We ought to support religious instruction, not shoot it down like something we're embarrassed about. I told that to the people who were glorifying the multicultural society. In my opinion, people who want to live here ought to be allowed to and we should help them in every way we can, but that doesn't mean we have to lose our Icelandic language and culture.'

'Shouldn't you have—'

'Surely, as an absolute minimum we should be allowed to

foster our own culture, even if people of other nationalities move here.'

'Shouldn't you have gone back to your class ages ago?' Erlendur asked when he finally got a word in edgeways. Egill did not appear to have noticed that the break had ended long ago.

'I have a free period now,' Egill said, making ruminatory noises. 'I totally agree that society is changing and we have to respond right from the start in a positive fashion. It's important to step in and eradicate prejudice. Everyone should have the same opportunities and if children of foreign parents have more trouble in achieving at school and entering further education, then that needs to be put right. Start right away in kindergarten. Anyway, I don't think you should waste your time on me just because I wrangle a bit at meetings. There are plenty of more obvious things to consider here when children get stabbed.'

'I'm gathering information, that's my job. Did you have any particular dealings with the brothers, Elías or Niran?'

'No, nothing special. They hadn't been at the school long. I believe they moved to this part of town in the spring and ended up at this school in the autumn. I taught Elías; I suppose the last time would have been the day before yesterday. The lad was clever with his hands. We don't do complicated tasks with that age group, just sawing and that sort of thing.'

'Was he well liked in his class?'

'As far as I could see. He was just one of the kids.'

'Are you ever aware of clashes between the immigrant pupils and the others?' Erlendur asked.

'There's not much of that sort of thing,' Egill said, stroking his beard. 'Though you do get certain cliques forming. I don't like that Icelandic teacher of ours, Kjartan. I think he causes friction in that respect. Half-bonkers, the poor sod. Had to give up a career in handball just when he was reaching the top. That sort of thing can unbalance people. But you ought to talk to him about these issues. He knows more about them than I do.'

They fell silent. The playground was quiet.

'So everything's going to hell?' Erlendur said eventually.

'I'm afraid it is.'

They sat for a while in the smoke-filled car and then Erlendur started thinking about Sigurdur Óli, who had once been a pupil at the school. It occurred to him to ask Egill. The woodwork teacher needed to think hard before he remembered a boy who had been there all those years ago, a terribly flashy sort.

'It's amazing what you can and can't remember about those kids,' Egill said. 'I think his dad was a plumber.'

'A plumber?' Erlendur said. He knew nothing about Sigurdur Óli apart from what he saw of him at work, even though they had been investigating crimes together for years. They never discussed their private lives, were both content not to. That, at least, they had in common.

'And a rabid communist,' Egill added. 'He attracted quite a bit of attention in those days, because it was always him who came to parents' meetings and school events. It was exceptional then for fathers to be seen with their children at school. He always turned up, the old bugger, and delivered thundering speeches about the bloody conservatives.'

'What about the mother?'

'I never saw her,' Egill said. 'They used to call him something, the old man. Some plumbing term. My brother's a plumber and recognised him immediately. What was it again that they used to call him?'

Erlendur glanced sideways at the red lump. It was turning paler again.

'Why can't I remember that?' Egill said.

'I don't need to know,' Erlendur said.

'Yes. Now I remember. They called him Permaflush.'

Finnur, the third-form teacher, was sitting in the staff room. His class was having a music lesson and he was marking papers when Elínborg disturbed him. The school secretary had told her where to find him.

'I understand you've been involved in a dispute with another teacher here by the name of Kjartan,' Elínborg said after introducing herself.

'There's certainly no love lost between Kjartan and me,' Finnur said. He was in his early thirties, thin, with a mop of dark hair and wearing a fleece jacket and jeans.

'What happened?'

'Have you spoken to him?'

'Yes. My colleague did.'

'And?'

'And nothing. What happened?'

'Kjartan's an idiot,' Finnur said. 'He shouldn't be allowed to teach. But that's just my opinion.'

'Did he make some kind of remark?'

'He always does. But he makes sure he doesn't go too far, because then he'd risk losing his job at this school. He's not such a coward one-to-one.'

'What did he say?'

'It was about immigrants, the children of immigrants. I don't think it has anything to do with this tragic incident.' Finnur hesitated. 'I knew he was trying to wind me up. I think it's fine for people from other countries to move here and I don't care in the slightest why they come, as long as they're not outright criminals. It doesn't matter whether they're from Europe or Asia. We need them and they enrich our culture. Kjartan wants to close the country to immigrants. We argued about that as usual, but he was exceptionally tetchy.'

'When was this?'

'Yesterday morning. But we're always arguing. We can hardly see each other these days without flaring up.'

'Have you often clashed?'

Finnur nodded.

'As a rule, teachers are very egalitarian and don't want or understand anything else. They look after the children, make sure there's no discrimination of any kind. We take a pride in it, it's sacrosanct really.'

'But Kjartan's an exception?'

'He's totally unbearable. I ought to lodge a complaint against him with the Education Board. We have no business employing teachers like him.'

'Is—?' Elínborg began.

'It's probably because of my brother,' Finnur interrupted. 'His wife's from Thailand. That's why Kjartan is always having a go at me. My brother met a woman in Thailand eight years ago. They have two daughters. They're the best people I've ever met. So maybe I have a vested interest. I can't stand the way he talks and he knows that.'

10

Erlendur's mobile rang as he got out of Egill's car. It was Gudný, the interpreter, who was back at Sunee's flat. Erlendur had asked her to be at Sunee's beck and call, day and night, and to contact him if anything happened. Niran had woken up after a rough night, she reported. His condition was unchanged. He refused to talk to anyone. Sunee insisted that he be left alone. She did not want any experts around him. She did not want any such visitors, or police officers, roaming in and out of the flat. Erlendur said he would drop in on them shortly, and they rang off.

Elínborg and Sigurdur Óli were still gathering information from Elías's classmates when Erlendur returned to the school. He watched them for a while. The children appeared to be making all manner of complaints about each other, but these rarely involved Elías directly. Someone had teased two girls, someone else had been kept out of a game of football, someone else had thrown a snowball so viciously at a boy's leg that it made him cry, but not Elías. Sigurdur Óli looked over to Erlendur and made a gesture to say that it would all take its time. The children were appalled at Elías's death and some of them were crying.

Erlendur phoned the head of the narcotics squad and asked

him to investigate any drug offences that had occurred in the neighbourhood and might conceivably be linked to the school playground.

The principal looked rough and haggard, as if he had not slept well that night. Waiting in front of his office were people from the church and parents' association, as well as representatives from the police who were going to address the children in the assembly hall at lunchtime. They all crowded round the principal, who seemed to have no control over the situation whatsoever. The matter seemed too much for him to handle. His secretary appeared and informed him of some urgent telephone calls that he had to take, but the principal waved her away. Erlendur looked at the group and backed away. He followed the secretary and found out where he could locate Niran's form teacher.

The secretary looked at Erlendur dithering in front of her.

'Was there anything else?' she asked.

'Would you call this a multicultural school?' Erlendur asked finally.

'You could say that,' the secretary said. 'Just over ten per cent of the pupils are not of Icelandic origin.'

'And are people happy with that arrangement, as a rule?'

'It works very well.'

'No particular problems on that account?'

'None worth mentioning, I don't think,' she added as if in apology.

Niran's form teacher, a woman of about thirty, was clearly shocked at the news about Elías like everyone else. A media debate had already begun about the situation of immigrants and the responsibility of society, and endless experts were called in to testify to all the gains that had been made and what must be done to prevent such an episode repeating itself. They were trying to pin the blame somewhere: had the system failed the immigrants, was this merely the thin end of the wedge? There was talk of underlying racial tensions that had flared up, and the need to respond through public debate and education – make better use of the school system to publicise, to inform and to eradicate prejudice.

Teaching was under way in Niran's class when Erlendur knocked on the door. He apologised for the disturbance. The teacher gave him a weak smile and, catching on immediately, asked him to wait just a moment. Shortly afterwards she followed him out into the corridor. She introduced herself as Edda Brá and her petite hand vanished in Erlendur's palm when they exchanged greetings. She had cropped hair, wore a thick pullover and jeans, and had a serious expression on her face.

'I hardly know what to say about Niran,' she said without preamble, as if she had been expecting the police sooner or later. Or perhaps she was simply in a hurry. Her form was waiting for her.

'Niran can be difficult and I sometimes need to pay him special attention,' she continued. 'He can hardly write Icelandic and doesn't speak the language that well, so he's difficult to communicate with. He does little or no homework and seems to have absolutely no interest in studying. I never taught his brother but I understand he was very sweet. Niran's different. He can get the other boys' backs up. Gets into fights. The last one was the day before yesterday. I know it's difficult for children to change schools and he's had a rough time right from the beginning.'

'He came to this country at the age of nine and never managed to fit in properly,' Erlendur said.

'He's not alone in that,' the teacher said. 'It can be difficult for the older kids who come here and can't relate to anything.'

'What happened?' Erlendur asked. 'The day before yesterday?'

'Maybe you should talk to the other boy.'

'Is it a boy in his class?'

'The children were talking about it this morning,' Edda said. 'This particular boy comes from a difficult home and he's been getting into trouble in the playground. He and some of the others had it in for Niran and his friends. Talk to him, find out what he says, he never tells me anything. His name's Gudmundur, Gummi for short.'

Edda went back into the classroom and came out soon afterwards with a boy whom she made to stand in front of Erlendur. Erlendur was impressed by her firmness. She wasted no time on idle chatter, was on the ball and knew how best to assist.

'You told me I'd get my mobile back,' the boy moaned, looking at Erlendur.

'It's the only thing these kids understand,' Edda Brá told Erlendur. 'I didn't want to blare out in front of the whole class that he had to talk to the police. All hell would have broken loose in the present situation. Let me know if you need anything else,' she added, then went back into the classroom.

'Gummi?' Erlendur said.

The boy looked up at him. His upper lip was slightly swollen and his nose was scratched. He was big for his age, fair-haired, and his eyes radiated deep suspicion.

'Are you a cop?' he asked.

Erlendur nodded and showed the boy behind a screen that served to partition off several computers on a long desk. Erlendur propped himself on the edge of the desk and the boy sat down on a chair in front of him.

'Have you got a cop's badge?' Gummi asked. 'Can I see it?'

'I don't have a badge,' Erlendur said. 'I expect you're talking about what the cops carry in films. Of course they're not real cops. They're just Hollywood wimps.'

Gummi stared at Erlendur as if his hearing had failed for a moment.

'What happened between you and Niran the day before yesterday?' Erlendur asked.

'What business of yours—' Gummi began, his voice full of the same suspicion that shone from his eyes.

'I'm just curious,' Erlendur interrupted him. 'It's nothing serious. Don't worry about it.'

Gummi continued to prevaricate.

'He just attacked me,' he said eventually.

'Why?'

'I don't know.'

'Did he attack anyone else?'

'I don't know. He just suddenly went for me.'

'Why?'

'I don't know,' Gummi repeated.

Erlendur pondered. He stood up and peered over the partition. Then he sat back down. He did not want to be detained by Gummi for too long.

'Do you know what happens to kids who lie to the cops?' he said.

'I'm not lying,' Gummi said, his eyes growing to twice the size.

'We call their parents in straight away and explain to them that their child has been lying to the police, then we ask the parents to take the child down to the police station to give a statement, and we decide where to go from there. So if you're free after school we can fetch you and your mum and dad and—'

'He just went berserk when I called him that.'

'Called him what?'

Gummi still prevaricated. Then he seemed to steel himself.

'I called him shit face. He's called me far worse names,' he added quickly.

Erlendur grimaced.

'And are you surprised he went for you?'

'He's a twat!'

'And you're not?'

'They never leave you alone.'

'They who?'

'His Thai and Filipino friends. They hang around behind the chemist's.'

Erlendur recalled Elínborg mentioning a group of boys by the chemist's shop when she was going over the details of the case in his car the previous evening.

'Is it a gang?'

Gummi hesitated. Erlendur waited. He knew that Gummi was pondering whether to tell things the way they were and get Erlendur on his side, or to pretend to know nothing, just say no and hope the police officer would leave it at that.

'It wasn't like that,' Gummi said in the end. 'They started it.'

'Started what?'

'Dissing us.'

'Dissing you?'

'They think they're better than us. More important. More important than us Icelanders. Because they come from Thailand and the Philippines and Vietnam. They say everything's much better there, it's superior.'

'And did you fight?'

Instead of replying, Gummi stared down at the floor.

'Do you know what happened to Elías, Niran's brother?' Erlendur asked.

'No,' Gummi said, his head still bowed. 'He wasn't with them.'

'How did you explain to your parents about the injuries to your face?'

Gummi looked up.

'They don't give a shit.'

Sigurdur Óli and Elínborg appeared in the corridor and Erlendur signalled to Gummi that he could go. They watched him close the classroom door behind him.

'Getting anywhere?' Erlendur asked.

'Nowhere,' Elínborg said. 'Though one of the boys did say that Kjartan, that Icelandic teacher, was "a bastard headcase". I had the impression he was always causing trouble but I didn't find out exactly how.'

'Everything's just hunky dory with me,' Sigurdur Óli said.

'Hunky dory?' Erlendur growled. 'Do you always have to talk like an idiot?'

'What . . . ?'

'There's nothing *hunky dory* about any of this!'

The medical equipment bleeped at regular intervals in one of the wards but it was quiet in the room where Marion Briem lay on the brink of death. Erlendur stood at the foot of the bed, looking at the patient. Marion seemed to be asleep. Face nothing but bones, eyes sunken, skin pale and withered. On top of the duvet lay hands with long, slender fingers and long nails, untrimmed. The fingers were yellow from smoking and the nails black. No one had come to visit Marion, who had been lying in the terminal ward for several days. Erlendur had particularly asked about that. Probably no one will come to the funeral either, he thought. Marion lived alone, always had, and never wanted it otherwise. Sometimes when Erlendur saw Marion his thoughts turned to his own future of loneliness and solitude.

For a long time Marion seemed to adopt the role of Erlendur's conscience, never tiring of asking about his private life, especially the divorce and his relationship with the two children he had left behind and took no care of. Erlendur, who bore a certain respect for Marion, was annoyed by this prying and their dealings had often ended with big words and raised voices. Marion laid claim to a part of Erlendur, claimed to have shaped him after he joined the Reykjavík CID. Marion was Erlendur's boss and had given him a tough schooling during his first years.

'Aren't you going to do anything about your children?' Marion had asked once in a moralising tone.

They were standing in a dark basement flat. Three fishermen on a week-long bender had got into a fight. One had pulled out a knife and stabbed his companion three times after the latter had made disparaging remarks about his girlfriend. The man was rushed to hospital but died of his wounds. His two companions were taken into custody. The scene of the crime was awash with blood. The man had virtually bled to death while the other two carried on drinking. A woman delivering newspapers had seen a man lying in his own blood through the basement window and called the police. The two other men had both passed out drunk by then and had no idea what had happened when they were woken up.

'I'm working on it,' Erlendur had said, looking at the pool of blood on the floor. 'Don't you worry yourself about it.'

'Someone has to,' Marion said. 'You can't feel too good, the way things are at the moment.'

'It's none of your business how I feel,' Erlendur said.

'It is my business if it's affecting your work.'

'It's not affecting my work. I'll solve it. Don't fret about it.'

'Do you think they'll ever amount to anything?'

'Who?'

'Your children.'

'Please just let it go,' Erlendur said, staring at the blood on the floor.

'You ought to stop and think about that: what it's like to grow up without a father.'

The bloodstained knife lay on the table.

'This isn't much of a murder mystery,' Marion said.

'It rarely is in this city,' Erlendur said.

Now Erlendur stood and looked at the shrunken body in the bed and knew what he had not known then: that Marion was trying to help him. Erlendur himself lacked a satisfactory explanation for why he had walked out on his two children when he was divorced and had done almost nothing to demand access to them afterwards. His ex-wife developed a hatred for him and swore that he would never have the children, not for a single day, and he did not put up much of a fight for that right. There was nothing in his life that he regretted as much, when later he discovered the state his two children were in once they reached adulthood.

Marion's eyes slowly opened and saw Erlendur standing at the foot of the bed.

Erlendur suddenly recalled his mother's words about an old relative of theirs from the East Fjords on his deathbed. She had been to visit him and sat by his bedside, and when she returned she said he had 'looked so shrivelled up and odd'.

'Would you . . . read to me . . . Erlendur?'

'Of course.'

'Your story,' Marion said. 'And . . . your brother's.'

Erlendur said nothing.

'You told me . . . once that it was in . . . one of those books of ordeals you're always reading.'

'It is,' Erlendur said.

'Will you . . . read it . . . to me?'

At that moment Erlendur's mobile rang. Marion watched him. The ringtone had been set by Elínborg one rainy day when they were sitting in a police car behind the District Court, escorting prisoners in custody. She had changed the ringtone to Beethoven's Ninth.

'The Ode to Joy' filled the little room at the hospital.

'What's that music?' Marion asked, in a stupor from the strong painkillers.

Erlendur finally managed to fish his mobile out of his jacket pocket and answer. 'The Ode' fell silent.

'Hello,' Erlendur said.

He could hear that there was someone at the other end, but no one answered.

'Hello,' he said again in a louder voice.

No answer.

'Who is that?'

He was about to ring off when the caller hung up.

'I'll do that,' Erlendur said, putting his mobile back in his jacket pocket. 'I'll read that story to you.'

'I hope . . . that this . . . will be over soon,' Marion said. The patient's voice was hoarse and trembled slightly, as if it took a particular effort to produce it. 'It's . . . no fun . . . going through this.'

Erlendur smiled. His mobile began ringing again. 'The Ode to Joy'.

'Yes,' he said.

No one answered.

'Bloody messing about,' Erlendur snarled. 'Who is that?' he said roughly.

Still the line was silent.

'Who is that?' Erlendur repeated.

'I . . .'

'Yes? Hello!'

'Oh, God, I can't do it,' a weak female voice whispered in his ear.

Erlendur was startled by the despair in the voice. At first he thought it was his daughter calling. She had called him before in terrible straits, crying out for help. But this was not Eva.

'Who is that?' Erlendur said, his tone much gentler when he heard the woman on the other end weeping.

'Oh, God . . .' she said, as if incapable of stringing a sentence together.

A moment passed in silence.

'It can't go on like this,' she said, and rang off.

'What? Hello?'

Erlendur shouted down the mobile but heard only the dialling tone in his ear. He checked the caller ID but it was blank. He noticed that Marion had fallen asleep again. He looked back at his mobile and suddenly in his mind's eye he saw a woman's bluish-white face rippling in the waves and looking up at him with dead eyes.

11

Erlendur sat in the interview room, his thoughts focused on the telephone call he had received at the hospital. *Oh God, I can't do it*, the weak voice groaned over and over in his mind, and he could not avoid the thought that the woman who had disappeared before Christmas might have just got in touch for the first time. She could have obtained his mobile number from the police switchboard without difficulty. It was his work number. His name had sometimes appeared in the papers in connection with police investigations. It had appeared in connection with the missing woman and now because of Elías's death. Not knowing the woman's voice, Erlendur could not tell whether it actually was her, but he intended to talk to her husband as soon as the opportunity arose.

He recalled having once read that only five per cent of marriages or relationships that began with infidelity lasted for life. That did not strike him as a high proportion and he wondered whether it was, in fact, difficult to build up a trusting relationship after betraying others. Or maybe it was too harsh to talk of betrayal. Perhaps the prior relationships had been changing and evolving and new love was kindled at a sensitive moment. That happened and was always happening. The woman who vanished felt that she had found true love, judging by her friends' remarks. She loved her new husband with all her heart.

The friends with whom she stayed in contact after the divorce stressed that point when Erlendur was seeking explanations for her disappearance. She had left her first husband and married for the second time with due ceremony. She was said to be very down-to-earth and realistic, then suddenly it was as if she had been transformed. Her friends did not doubt that her love for her new husband was genuine, and she always implied that her former marriage had run its course and she herself was 'completely different', as one of her friends put it. When Erlendur asked her to elaborate, it transpired that the woman had been elated after her divorce, talking about a new life and that she had never felt better. A grand wedding was held. They were married by a popular vicar. A huge crowd of guests celebrated with the couple on a lovely summer's day. They took a three-week honeymoon in Tuscany. When they returned they were relaxed, tanned and radiant.

All that was missing from the beautiful wedding was her children. Her ex refused to let them take part in 'that circus'.

It was not long before the expectation and excitement faded and turned into their opposite. Her friends described how, over time, the woman had been overwhelmed by sadness and regret, and ultimately by guilt at how she had treated her family. It did not help that her new husband's ex accused her constantly of destroying their family. His children moved in with them while she was fighting for custody of her own kids, a constant reminder of her culpability. All this was accompanied by crippling depression.

It was not the first time her new husband had been divorced following an affair. Erlendur found out that he had been married three times. He traced his first wife, who lived in Hafnarfjördur and had long since remarried and had a child. Exactly the same process had taken place in that case. The husband excused his absences from home on the grounds of long meetings, travelling around the country for work, golf trips. Then one day, quite unexpectedly, he announced that it was all over, they had grown apart and he was planning to move out. All this struck his wife like a bolt from the blue. She had not been aware of any fatigue in their relationship, only of his absence.

Erlendur also spoke to wife number two. She had not remarried and he sensed that she had not yet recovered from the divorce. She described the process in detail, accusing herself of not being wary enough. Trying to take her side, Erlendur said she was probably lucky to be rid of him. She gave a thin smile. 'I'm mainly thinking about the children,' she said. She had been unaware that he was married when he first began courting her. It was not until their relationship was several months old that he had said rather sheepishly that he had something to tell her. They were at a small hotel in the countryside where he had invited her to spend the night, and as they were sitting in the dining room that evening he announced that he had a wife. She stared at him in disbelief, but he was quick to add that his marriage was in ruins, it was only a question of time as to when he would leave her and he had told her so. She gave him an earful for not telling her he was married, but he managed to calm her down and win her over.

After hearing this testimony and others from friends of the missing woman, Erlendur began to detest the man. He knew that the more time that elapsed, the more likely it was that she had committed suicide, and the accounts of her depression supported that theory. But the unexpected telephone call had kindled a hope within him that this was not the case. It kindled the hope that she had moved out from her marital home and did not want her husband to discover her whereabouts; that she was hiding from him and did not know where to turn.

Only two years had passed since the fairytale wedding when the woman started whispering to a close friend of hers that her husband had begun to take part in weekend golf tournaments that she had never heard of.

Erlendur broke away from his thoughts and nodded to Sigurdur Óli, who sat down beside him in the interview room. Now the interrogation could begin. The man sitting in front of them was in his mid-forties. Since the age of twenty he had repeatedly been involved with the police for offences of varying degrees of seriousness: burglary, robbery and assault, in some cases very brutal. He lived two blocks away from Sunee and the boys. The police had compiled a list of repeat offenders who could possibly have crossed Elías's path on his way home from school. This man was top of that list.

The police had obtained a search warrant for his flat when they brought him in for questioning earlier that morning and had discovered large quantities of pornography, including child pornography. It was enough to bring charges against him yet again.

His name was Andrés and he looked at Erlendur and Sigurdur Óli in turn, prepared for the worst. A lifelong alcoholic who showed all the signs: his expression drowsy and bleary, his little eyes shifty and questioning. He was a fairly short man, stocky and strongly built.

Erlendur knew him. He had arrested Andrés more than once.

'What are you hassling me for?' Andrés asked, rough and ragged from persistent drinking, his eyes darting from one officer to the other. 'What's going on?' He tried to make this sound manly, but it ended in a little squeak.

'Do you know a boy by the name of Elías who lives in your neighbourhood?' Erlendur asked. 'Dark-skinned, of Thai descent. Ten years old.'

A tape recorder lay on the table between them, whirring softly. Given Andrés's state of intoxication when he was taken into custody, he could well claim not to have heard about Elías's murder. However, there was no believing a word he said.

'I don't know anything about any Elías,' Andrés said. 'Are you going to charge me? What are you going to charge me with? I haven't done a thing. Why are you picking on me?'

'Don't worry,' Sigurdur Óli said.

'What Elías are you talking about?' Andrés said, looking at Erlendur.

'Do you remember where you were yesterday afternoon?'

'At home,' Andrés said. 'I was at home. I was home all day, all yesterday I mean. What boy are you talking about?'

'A ten-year-old boy was stabbed to death two blocks away from you,' Erlendur said. 'Was anyone with you yesterday? Can anyone confirm your alibi?'

'A boy killed?' Andrés said, shocked. 'Who . . . ? Stabbed?'

'Do you even know what day it is today?' Erlendur asked.

Andrés shook his head.

'Please speak into the tape recorder,' Sigurdur Óli said.

'I don't know. I didn't attack any boy. I don't know about any attack. I don't know anything. I haven't done anything wrong. Why can't you leave me alone?'

'Do you know the boy?' Erlendur asked.

Andrés shook his head. Sigurdur Óli pointed a finger at the tape recorder.

'I don't know what you're talking about.'

'He has a brother, five years older,' Erlendur said. 'They moved into the neighbourhood last spring. You've lived there for more than five years. You must notice the locals. You must keep up with what's going on. Don't turn this into a pantomime.'

'A pantomime? I haven't done anything.'

'Do you know this boy?' Erlendur asked, taking a photograph of Elías from his coat pocket and handing it to Andrés.

He pored over the child's face.

'I don't know him,' he said.

'You've never bumped into him?' Erlendur asked.

Before Erlendur entered the interview room he had been told that a detailed search of the man's flat had not provided any indication of whether Elías or Niran had ever been there. However, Andrés had behaved very strangely when the police finally managed to break into his flat. He had not answered when they knocked on the door. When the police broke it down they were greeted by wretched squalor and an appalling stench. The door was double-locked and Andrés was found hiding under his bed. He screamed for help as he was dragged out. He thrashed around, apparently unaware that he was in the hands of the police but under the impression he was wrestling with an imaginary adversary to whom he repeatedly pleaded for mercy.

'I might have seen him in the neighbourhood some time but I don't know him,' Andrés said. 'I haven't done anything to him.'

His eyes darted back and forth, as if he had to make a decision but was hesitant. Perhaps he thought that he needed to bargain to get off. Sigurdur Óli was poised to speak, but Erlendur tugged at him and gestured to him to keep quiet. Andrés seemed to approve of that.

'Would you leave me alone then?' he eventually said.

'If what?' Erlendur said.

'Would you let me go home then?'

'Your flat was crammed with child pornography,' Sigurdur Óli said, not concealing the disgust in his voice. Erlendur had urged him to try not to show disrespect to criminals, as Sigurdur Óli had a tendency of doing. Nothing annoyed him more than middle-aged repeat offenders who were always in the same mess.

'If what?' Erlendur repeated.

'If I tell you.'

'I told you not to turn this into a bloody pantomime,' Erlendur said. 'Say what you want to tell us. Stop beating about the bush.'

'I guess it's a year since he moved into the area,' Andrés said.

'Elías moved in the spring, like I said.'

'I'm not talking about that boy,' Andrés said and looked at each of them in turn.

'Who then?'

'He's showing his age, the old git. That was the first thing I noticed.'

'What are you talking about?' Sigurdur Óli snapped.

'A man I reckon has more porn in his possession than I do,' Andrés said.

Sigurdur Óli and Erlendur exchanged glances.

'I've never killed anyone,' Andrés said. 'You know that. You have to believe me, Erlendur. I've never killed anyone.'

'Don't try and turn me into your confidant,' Erlendur said.

'I've never killed anyone,' Andrés repeated.

Erlendur watched him in silence.

'I've never killed anyone,' Andrés said yet again.

'You kill everything you touch,' Erlendur said.

'What man are you talking about?' Sigurdur Óli asked. 'What man moved to the area?'

Instead of answering him, Andrés focused his glare on Erlendur.

'What man is this, Andrés?' Erlendur asked.

Andrés leaned forward over the table and inclined his head slightly, like an elderly aunt giving a kindly greeting to a little child.

'He's the nightmare I can never shake off.'

12

Elínborg was waiting to meet Elías's teacher at the school the boy and his brother had attended before they moved from Snorrabraut. Having been told that a meeting was just finishing, she sat outside the closed classroom and thought about her youngest child, a daughter, who was still at home with gastric flu. Her husband, a car mechanic, would spend the first part of the day with her, then Elínborg would take over.

The classroom door opened and a middle-aged woman greeted her. During the meeting, she had been passed a note that the police wanted to talk to her. Elínborg shook the woman's hand, introduced herself and said she needed to talk to her in connection with Elías's murder, which she had doubtless heard about. The woman gave a sad nod.

'We were talking about that at the meeting,' she said in a low voice. 'Words can't describe that, that sort of . . . outrage. Who would do something like that? Who on earth would be capable of attacking a child?'

'We intend to find out,' Elínborg said, looking all around in search of a place where they could talk together without being disturbed.

The woman, whose name was Emilía, was petite with long, dark hair in a ponytail, just beginning to turn grey. She said that they could sit inside the classroom: the children were at a music lesson and it was empty. Elínborg followed her. Pupils' drawings were pinned up on all the walls and displayed different stages of maturity, from matchstick men to proper portraits. Elínborg noticed a few traditional pictures: Icelandic farmhouses, at the foot of a mountain with a bright blue sky, wisps of cloud and a brilliant sun. She remembered that classic theme from her own schooldays and was silently surprised at its longevity.

'This one's by Elías,' Emilía said, taking out a picture from a drawer in the teacher's desk. 'They never came to fetch his artwork when he left this school and I didn't want to throw this one away. It shows how genuinely talented he was at drawing, at such a young age.'

Elínborg took the picture. The teacher was right, it showed that Elías had an exceptional command of drawing. He had drawn a female face with unnaturally large brown eyes, dark hair and a broad smile, bathed in bright colours.

'It's supposed to be his mother,' Emilía smiled. 'Those poor people, having to go through all this.'

'Did you teach him from the time he started school?' Elínborg asked.

'Yes, from the age of six, I guess, only four years back. He was such a nice, sweet boy. A bit of a dreamer. Sometimes he had trouble concentrating on his schoolwork and it took some effort on my part to get him to apply himself. He could stare into space for hours on end and be off in a world of his own.'

Emilía stopped talking and turned pensive.

'It must be difficult for Sunee,' she said.

'Yes, of course, really difficult,' Elínborg said.

'She always showed the boys such love,' the teacher said, pointing at the drawing. 'I taught them both, Elías's brother

Niran too. He didn't speak Icelandic well at all. I'm told they mainly spoke Thai at home and I discussed the fact with Sunee, how it could cause them problems. Her Icelandic was so-so and she preferred to have an interpreter with her at parents' meetings.'

'What about the father? Did you get to know him?' Elínborg asked.

'No, not at all. He never attended any events here, not the Christmas party or anything of that sort. Never came to parents' meetings, for example. She always came by herself.'

'Moving to a new part of town and a new school might have been tough for Elías,' Elínborg said. 'It's not certain that he adapted to the new school. He hadn't made any friends and he spent a lot of time alone.'

'I can believe that,' Emilía said. 'I remember what he was like when he started at this school. I thought he would never let go of his mother. It took me and the class welfare officer ages to get him to relax and realise that everything would be fine even if Sunee went.'

'What about Niran?'

'The brothers are so different,' Emilía said. 'Niran is tough. He'd survive anywhere. There's not a hint of the whiner about him.'

'Did they get on well together, the brothers?'

'As far as I could see, Niran took very good care of his brother and I know Elías worshipped him. He made a lot of drawings of Niran. The difference between them was that Elías wanted to fit in, to be part of the class. Niran was more of a rebel, against the class, the teachers, the school authorities, the older pupils. There was a group of immigrant kids here, five or six boys that Niran went around with a lot. They kept themselves to themselves and did little schoolwork, because they had absolutely no interest in Icelandic history or anything like that. Once they fought with some Icelanders. This was outside school hours. It was in the evening and the gangs fought with sticks and broke windows. You hear about that sort of thing sometimes. You must be familiar with it.'

'Yes, we are,' Elínborg said. 'Generally it's to do with girls.'

'The two ringleaders moved away from this part of town in the last school year and it died down. It only takes a tiny minority. Then Elías and Niran changed schools. I haven't seen either of them since. And then you hear this on the news and can't understand what's going on.'

Emilía spoke quickly, almost gabbling. Elínborg refused to be drawn and dodged all her questions about how the boys had been doing since they left the area and about Sunee's personal circumstances. Emilía was an inquisitive woman and not afraid to show it. Elínborg liked her but did not want to reveal any details of the case. She merely said that it was at a very early stage. Emilía's curiosity was understandable. Elías's murder dominated the media. The police had probably talked to almost a hundred people in the neighbourhood, the surrounding blocks of flats, the school and nearby shops. Photographs of Elías were being circulated and attempts made to trace his precise movements on the fateful day. Witnesses who might have seen him on his way back from school were asked to come forward. Nothing concrete had come out of it yet. The only solid evidence the police had was that Elías had left school alone and was going home when he was stopped on the way.

Elínborg smiled and looked at the clock. She thanked Emilía for her comprehensive answers and the teacher accompanied her down the corridor to one of the exits. They shook hands.

'So you're no closer?' Emilía said.

'No,' Elínborg said. 'No closer.'

'Well,' Emilía said, 'as it happens I . . . Is Sunee still with that man of hers?'

'No . . . ?'

'That was one of Elías's drawings,' Emilía hurried to say. 'It showed his mother, who he often drew, with a man beside her. This was in the spring, after they'd moved away but while the boys were still at this school. I remember asking Elías who it was. It just sort of slipped out.'

Didn't it just? Elínborg thought to herself. It was as if Emilía was aware herself of how inquisitive she was.

'And he said the man was his mother's friend.'

'Really?' Elínborg said. 'Did you ask the boy his name?'

'Actually, I did.' Emilía smiled. 'Elías said he didn't know. Or he didn't tell me anyway.'

'And the man on the drawing, what . . . ?'

'He could well have been Icelandic.'

'Icelandic?'

'Yes. I didn't want to be nosy but I had the feeling that Elías liked him a lot.'

Andrés leaned back in his chair in the interview room. A click was heard as the tape came to an end and stopped recording. Sigurdur Óli reached out, turned the tape over and started the recording again. Erlendur stared at Andrés all the time.

'What's that about the nightmare you can never shake off?' he asked. 'What's that supposed to mean?'

'I doubt you'd want to hear it,' Andrés said. 'I doubt anyone would want to hear about such evil.'

'Who is this man?' Sigurdur Óli asked.

'Do you mean he did something to you?'

Andrés said nothing.

'Are you saying he's a paedophile?' Erlendur asked.

Andrés sat in silence, looking at Erlendur.

'I haven't seen him for years,' he said eventually. 'Years on end. Not until suddenly . . . I guess it was a year ago.' Andrés stopped talking.

'And?'

'It was like meeting your executioner,' Andrés said. 'He didn't see me. He doesn't know that I know about him. I know where he lives.'

'Where's that? Where does he live? Who is this man?' Sigurdur Óli showered Andrés with questions but he sat completely unmoved, looking at Sigurdur Óli as if he were absolutely irrelevant to him.

'I might well pay him a visit one day,' Andrés said. 'To say hello. I reckon I could handle him now. I reckon I could get the better of him.'

'But first you needed some Dutch courage,' Erlendur said.

Andrés did not answer.

'You had to run off and hide first?'

'I always hid. You should know how good I was at concealing myself. I found new hiding places all the time and tried to make myself as small as I could.'

'Do you think he hurt the boy?' Erlendur asked.

'Maybe he gave up ages ago. I don't know. Like I say, I haven't seen him all these years and suddenly he's my neighbour. Suddenly, after all these years, he walks past on the other side of the street from where I live. You can't imagine what I really saw when he walked past. I mean up here,' Andrés said, tapping his index finger against his temple.

'Do you think he's on our paedophile register?' Erlendur asked.

'I doubt it.'

'Are you going to tell us how to find him?' Sigurdur Óli asked. Andrés did not reply.

'Who is he?' Sigurdur Óli asked, trying a new approach. 'We can help you to get him. If you want to charge him. We can lock him up with your help. Is that what you want? Will you tell us who he is so we can throw him in the nick?'

Andrés started to laugh in his face.

'This guy's the dog's bollocks,' he said with a look at Erlendur.

Then suddenly he stopped laughing. He leaned forward in Sigurdur Óli's direction.

'Who's going to believe a scumbag like me?'

Erlendur's mobile phone started to ring. 'The Ode to Joy' filled the interview room and Erlendur tried to dig out his phone as fast as he could. He hated that ringtone. He pressed the answer button. Sigurdur Óli watched him. Andrés had clammed up. Erlendur listened and his face darkened. He rang off without saying goodbye and cursed as he leaped to his feet.

'Can this bloody mess get any worse?' he hissed through clenched teeth and rushed out of the room.

The police officer had second thoughts on his way back to the block of flats. The interpreter had popped out in her car but on the way she had asked him to fetch some bread and milk for the Thai woman and her son, who were alone in the flat. He had been in the force for two years and didn't find this job worse than any other. He had been caught up in the downtown mêlées when the weekend celebrations reached their peak. He had been called out to terrible road accidents. None of them affected him much. They described him as promising. He aimed for promotion within the police. Now he had been given the job of standing guard at the home of the Thai woman and her son. All morning, a series of experts from various agencies had trooped up the stairs to her flat, and he had stood there, asking their names, occupations and business. He let them all in. They came straight back down. The Thai woman wanted to be left alone with her child. He could understand that. What a tragedy she had suffered.

Then the interpreter came hurrying downstairs, handed him some money and a small shopping list and asked him to buy the items for the mother and son upstairs. He refused politely, shaking his head with a smile and saying he was not allowed to leave. Unfortunately, he just couldn't. He was a policeman. Not an errand boy.

'It'll only take five minutes,' the interpreter said. 'I'd do it myself but I'm in a rush.'

Then she ran over to her car and drove off.

He was left standing there with the shopping list and the banknote and a conscience that he struggled with, but only for a moment. Then he hurried off too. He wasn't long at all, as he told that Erlendur bloke who tore him off such a strip that he almost burst into tears. Perhaps he should have called for assistance. Perhaps he should not have gone on that ridiculous errand, which reminded him of when he was a child and his mother was always sending him out to the shop. Perhaps that was the point: he had acted instinctively and forgot himself for a moment. He had flicked through a trashy magazine containing stories of celebrity divorces, but did not dare to tell the inspector about that part of his journey. The old man was so worked up that he thought he would knock him senseless.

Sigurdur Óli, whom he knew slightly, had to step in to restrain the inspector.

When he came back from the shop he ran up the stairs and rang the bell. Then he knocked on the door but there was no reply. Eventually he opened it and called in, 'Hello!' The door was not locked. No one answered him. He walked around the flat, calling out in all directions. He received no reply. The flat was empty.

He stood like an idiot with a plastic shopping bag in his hand and could hardly muster the courage to inform the station that Sunee and her boy had gone missing.

13

Erlendur did not blame the officer for Sunee and Niran's disappearance although the man had showed incredible and incomprehensible neglect in the course of duty. He was convinced that the interpreter, who was the last to leave the mother and her son, had helped them to go into hiding. She had persuaded the officer to leave for a moment and then drove them off to a place that she would not name. After grilling the officer Erlendur sent for the interpreter. In the meantime the police looked for clues as to where Sunee could have taken her son. Her telephone did not have a caller ID, but Elínborg applied to the District Court to be given a list of Sunee's incoming and outgoing calls during the previous month.

Elínborg called Erlendur and told him about her conversation with the teacher from Elías's old school.

'Don't you think she's trying to protect him by running away?' she asked Erlendur when he told her that the mother and son had gone missing.

'The explanation is obviously something like that,' Erlendur said. 'The question is who she thinks she's protecting him from.'

'Maybe he's told her something.'

Erlendur had just finished talking to Elínborg when his mobile rang again. The head of narcotics told him that they had located a girl at the school who had been trying to sell drugs in the playground. She had not been involved with the narcotics squad before but her older sister was well known to the police, a hardened addict with a string of arrests for drug offences. The two sisters had an elder brother who was in prison for manslaughter; he had attacked a passer-by in the centre of Reykjavík, inflicting wounds that led to his death.

'A classy family, then,' Erlendur said.

'The crème de la crème,' the head of narcotics said. 'Do you want to talk to the girls?'

'Yes, bring them in,' Erlendur said.

At that moment Gudný appeared in the flat. Erlendur cut off his call and put his mobile in the pocket of his overcoat.

'Where are they?' he said in a determined voice, walking over to Gudný. 'Why did they run away and where did you take them?'

'Are you seriously blaming me for this?' she said.

'You deceived a police officer,' Erlendur said, 'then came back to collect them. We want to know what you've done with them. I could lock you up for obstructing the police in the execution of their duty. I wouldn't hesitate to do it.'

'I had nothing to do with this,' Gudný said. 'I didn't come back to collect them. And don't you go threatening me. If you want to "lock me up", then go right ahead.'

'We need answers from you,' Sigurdur Óli said, walking in from the corridor to the bedrooms after hearing the conversation. 'You were the last person to talk to them. Why have they disappeared?'

'I have no idea,' Gudný said with a sigh. 'I was as shocked as you when the police contacted me. When I left them about, what –' she said with a look at her watch '– three-quarters of an hour ago, there was nothing to suggest that Sunee was planning to do a disappearing act. She said she needed some shopping. I was late for a meeting. The officer was so kind as to help them. I didn't suspect that she was plotting something. She told me nothing about that. I don't care whether you believe me or not. I knew nothing about it.'

'Do you know where they could have gone?' Sigurdur Óli asked.

'No, I don't have the faintest idea. I don't even know if they are hiding. She might come straight back. Maybe she just popped out somewhere. Maybe she's not hiding at all. Have you considered that?'

'Did she contact anyone this morning?' Sigurdur Óli asked.

Gudný told them that she had visited Sunee early that morning. There had been a police officer at the door and a patrol car with another two policemen in it in the car park in front of the block. Then the patrol car was called away. Sunee had told her straight away that she wanted to be left alone with Niran. He was in a very difficult state. She had not managed to make him talk to her, and if she could not do so, then neither could a police officer or an expert of any kind. What she needed was time alone with Niran to draw him back out of himself. His brother's death had clearly been a great shock to him and she was trying to help him as best she could. That was her number-one priority under the circumstances. Gudný had sat down with them and offered her assistance, but when Sunee found out that she had to go to a meeting, she started talking about some things she needed from the shop.

'Did she know then that the police car had gone?' Erlendur asked.

'Yes, she saw it leave.'

'What happened to that bloody car?' Erlendur asked Sigurdur Óli, who had a ready answer. The car had been called out to a serious accident on a busy junction a few streets away. It was the nearest patrol car. They had not foreseen any problem in sending it on a quick call-out.

Erlendur shook his head in resignation.

'Who is Sunee's boyfriend?' he asked Gudný.

'I've told you I know nothing about any boyfriend,' Gudný said warily.

'Could she have gone to him?' Erlendur said.

'She doesn't seem to have many places to go,' Sigurdur Óli said.

'Who is this man?' Erlendur said with an angry look at Sigurdur Óli. He had a habit of interrupting, which got on Erlendur's nerves.

'I don't know about any boyfriend,' Gudný repeated. 'She might be with her mother-in-law. Have you checked that? Or her brother?'

'That's the first place we'll look,' Erlendur said.

At that point Elínborg arrived.

'How can they be missing?' she asked. 'Weren't they under supervision?'

'She's scared,' Gudný said. 'Who wouldn't be scared in her position? If she's run off, it's to protect her only surviving son. That's all she can think of at the moment. She doesn't trust you. That's obvious. She trusts herself. She always has.'

'Why shouldn't she trust us?' Elínborg said. 'Has she any reason not to?'

Gudný looked at her.

'I don't know,' she said. 'I don't have answers to all your questions.'

'Who is her boyfriend?' Erlendur asked. 'What kind of relationship do he and Sunee have? When did they meet? Was he the reason Sunee and her husband divorced? Did he know the boys well? How did he get along with them?'

Gudný looked at each of them in turn.

'She met a man recently,' she said at last.

'Yes, and . . .?' Erlendur said impatiently.

'I don't think she's with him. I don't know anything about Sunee's divorce from Ódinn. I don't know exactly when this man entered the picture.'

'And who is he?'

'Sunee's friend.'

'What kind of friend?' Erlendur asked.

Gudný looked over at Elínborg, then at Sigurdur Óli and finally back at Erlendur, and shrugged.

'Does he work? Do you know where he lives?'

'Sunee has never talked about him. I don't even know his name.'

'Why don't you think she's gone to him? You said she wouldn't go to him, why do you think that?'

'That's just my feeling,' Gudný said.

Erlendur recalled the words of Sunee's ex-husband, who had said that she had a boyfriend but he knew little about him. Virote knew about him. Gudný had finally acknowledged his existence. Emilía, Elías's former teacher, thought he was Icelandic.

'Is he an Icelander?' Erlendur asked.

'Yes,' Gudný said.

'And has this relationship been going on for long?'

'I don't know exactly.'

'There's another thing, since you mentioned trust,' Erlendur said. 'I know you don't have answers to all our questions. But there's one question we can't ignore, however much we would like to, and that's the question of Niran. Now that Sunee's fled with him, that question has become all the more pressing.'

'What are you talking about?' the interpreter asked.

Sigurdur Óli and Elínborg exchanged glances as if they had no idea what Erlendur was driving at.

'Why did she run off with Niran?' Erlendur asked, lowering his voice.

'I don't know,' Gudný said.

'Could she be trying to get him out of the country?'

'Out of the country?'

'Why not?'

'I think she's trying to protect him, not that I know anything about it. No, I don't think she's trying to get him out of the country. In the first place, I don't think she'd have a clue how to go about it.'

'She might know someone.'

'That's absurd!'

'I agree that she's trying to protect Niran,' Erlendur said. 'I think she's gone into hiding because he's told her something at last. He knows what happened.'

'I can't believe you're claiming he was involved in murdering his own brother!' Gudný said, outraged.

'We have to examine all the possibilities and Sunee disappearing with the boy doesn't help. She may well want to protect him by doing so but she may also know something that we don't. I expect he told her something important.'

'If Niran has done something wrong, Sunee would tell us. I know her. She wouldn't cover up for the boy.'

'We have to keep all our options open.'

'But it's out of the question!' the interpreter shouted.

'Don't tell me what's out of the question and what isn't,' Erlendur said.

'You can't keep them imprisoned here at least,' Gudný said. 'You can't lock them up in this flat! They must be free to go where they please.'

'I don't want anything else to happen to them,' Erlendur said. 'They need to let us know where they're going.'

'That's crap,' Gudný said.

'There she is!'

Sigurdur Óli stared out through the door into the corridor where Sunee was standing. Her brother was with her, but there was no sign of Niran.

Gudný went over to them and said something in Thai. Virote answered her. Sunee looked apprehensively at Erlendur.

'Niran not do nothing,' she said.

'Where is he?' Erlendur asked.

Sunee spoke to Gudný for a long while.

'She's not certain that she can look after him,' Gudný said. 'He's safe where he is. Sunee knows you want to question him, but says it's unnecessary. He hasn't done anything and doesn't know anything. He came home by himself yesterday and saw the police and his brother and went into a state of shock. He hid and couldn't speak to his mother until this morning. He assured Sunee that he has no idea what happened to his brother. He had no part in it himself and didn't see or meet Elías that day. He was scared.'

'Scared of what?'

'That the same thing would happen to him,' Gudný said.

'Will you tell Sunee that it's not right to conceal the boy. It's suspicious behaviour and even dangerous as long as we don't know any more about the case. We don't know what happened

138

to Elías and if she thinks Niran's in danger she'll have to trust us to look after him. She's just making things worse.'

Gudný translated Erlendur's words as he spoke but Sunee started shaking her head before she managed to finish.

'Niran not do nothing,' she said again, glaring at Erlendur.

'Please ask her to tell us where her son is,' Erlendur asked.

'She says you needn't worry about him,' Gudný said. 'She asks you to find Elías's murderer instead. Are there any new developments on that front?'

'No,' Erlendur said, trying to imagine what he himself would do in Sunee's shoes. Perhaps she was doing the right thing. He could not tell.

'We hear you've met a man – an Icelander,' Erlendur said. 'I haven't had the opportunity to ask you about him yet.'

Gudný interpreted between them.

'He's nothing to do with this,' Sunee said.

'Who is this man?' Sigurdur Óli asked. 'What can you tell us about him?'

'Nothing,' Sunee said.

'Do you know where we can reach him?'

'No,' Sunee replied.

'Is he at work? Do you know where he works?'

'He's none of your business,' Sunee said.

'What kind of relationship do you have?' Erlendur asked.

'He's my friend.'

'What kind of friend?'

'I don't understand the question.'

'Is he more than just a friend?'

'No, nothing more.'

'Do you think this man was involved in the murder of your son?' Sigurdur Óli asked.

'No,' Sunee said.

'Isn't that enough for now?' Gudný asked.

Erlendur nodded.

'We'll talk to her again later today. And try to make her understand that she's not helping at all by hiding Niran.'

'Except helping to save his life perhaps,' Gudný said. 'Try to put yourself in her position. Try to understand what she's going through.'

They walked downstairs and got into Erlendur's car.

'Who is this woman who's such a good interpreter?' Erlendur asked, taking out a pack of cigarettes.

'Are you going to smoke?' said Sigurdur Óli, who was sitting in the back seat.

'Gudný?' Elínborg said. 'She lived in Thailand for years. Goes there regularly, worships the place and the people, and works as a tourist guide during the summer. I think she's done a great job under difficult circumstances. I like her.'

'She can't stand you,' Sigurdur Óli said to Erlendur.

Erlendur lit his cigarette and tried to blow the smoke into the back seat.

'Did you get anything else out of Andrés?' he asked.

Sigurdur Óli had stayed behind in the interview room when Erlendur had leaped to his feet and run out. He told him how he had tried to get Andrés to name the man who had recently moved to the neighbourhood, but to no avail. Sigurdur described the interview to Elínborg; he thought Andrés was spinning a cock-and-bull story to shift the attention away from himself. It was a tired old ruse.

'He refused to describe the man to me,' Sigurdur Óli said, 'or to provide any details about him.'

'If he harmed Andrés when he was a child, then at least he must be quite a bit older,' Erlendur said. 'I don't know, he might be in his sixties by now. Actually, I don't think it was a paedophile. They're not murderers. Not in the literal sense anyway.'

The investigation was into its second day and they still lacked sufficient information to be able to draw any conclusions. No one had come forward who had seen Elías's movements that day. At the place where he was stabbed – the substation – there was an open path that narrowed to accommodate garages on one side. The scene was overlooked by the top flats of the nearby blocks but none of the residents had seen anything unusual or suspicious. Very few people were home at the time of day when Elías was attacked.

Erlendur's interest focused on the school. Elínborg told them how, at the boys' previous school, Niran had been a member of a gang of immigrant children who were involved in fights. She wondered if he had imported the influences that he came under there to the new school. Erlendur pointed out that he was a member of a gang which, one pupil had told him, hung around the local chemist's shop and sometimes clashed with other pupils from the school.

'And then we have a paedophile and a repeat offender and an Icelandic boyfriend,' Sigurdur Óli said. 'Not forgetting a teacher who patently hates all immigrants and foments bad feeling at the school. Nice bunch.'

Niran obviously had to be a key witness in the case, and the fact that he had disappeared or fled or gone into hiding with his mother underlined his importance. They had let him slip out of their grasp in the clumsiest way imaginable. Erlendur had plenty of strong words to say about that. He blamed himself for the way it had all turned out. No one else.

'How could we have foreseen this?' Elínborg protested at his overreaction. 'Sunee was very cooperative. There was nothing to suggest that she would go and do something stupid.'

'We need to talk to the boy's father and Sunee's mother-in-law and brother straight away,' Sigurdur Óli said. 'They're the people closest to her. They're the people who would want to help her.'

Erlendur looked at them.

'I think that woman called me today,' he said after a pause.

'The missing woman?' Elínborg said.

'I think so,' Erlendur said, then told them about the call he had received while he was visiting Marion in hospital.

'She said: "It can't go on like this", then rang off.'

' "It can't go on like this"?' Elínborg repeated after him. ' "It can't go on like this." What does she mean?'

'If it is the woman,' Erlendur said. 'Not that I know who else it could be. Now I need to go and see her husband and tell him that she's conceivably still alive. He hasn't heard from her all this time and then she goes and phones me. Unless he already knows everything that's going on. What does it mean, "It can't go on like this"? It's as if they're plotting something together. Could they be involved in a scam?'

'Had she taken out a big life assurance policy?' Sigurdur Óli asked.

'No,' Erlendur said. 'There's nothing like that in the picture. This isn't a Hollywood movie.'

'Were you beginning to suspect that he'd killed her?' Elínborg asked.

'That woman shouldn't still be alive,' Erlendur said. 'All the indications are that she's committed suicide. The phone call was completely at odds with the whole scenario up to now, with every aspect of it.'

'What are you going to tell her husband?' Elínborg asked.

Erlendur had been grappling with that question ever since he received the call. He had a pretty low opinion of the man, which deteriorated the clearer his past became. This was a man who seemed driven by an insatiable urge to cheat. That was the only way to describe it. Adultery appeared to be an obsession with him. The man's colleagues and friends whom Erlendur had spoken to described him in quite favourable terms. Several said that he had always been a ladies' man, even a philanderer, a married man who had no scruples about trying to ensnare other women. One of his colleagues described how a group from work had gone out for a drink and the man had flirted with a woman who had shown an interest in him. He had surreptitiously taken off his wedding ring and thrust it deep inside a handy flower pot. The following day he had had to go back to the club to dig up the ring.

This was before he met the woman who had now gone missing. Erlendur did not think she was the type to have an affair. The man had laid a trap for her, naturally concealing the fact that he was married, then the affair had gone further and further, much further than she could ever have imagined at first, until there was no turning back. They were stuck with each other and she was beset by profound guilt, depression and loneliness. The man refused to acknowledge any of this when Erlendur had asked about her state of mind before she disappeared. She was in good spirits, he said. 'She never said anything to me about feeling bad.' When Erlendur pressed him by asking about the woman's suspicions that he was having another affair only two years after they had married, he shrugged as if it were none of Erlendur's business and quite irrelevant. When Erlendur pressed him further the man had said that it was his private business and no one else's.

There were no witnesses to the woman's disappearance. She had phoned in sick to work and was at home alone during the day. Her husband's children were with their mother. When he returned at around six, she was not there. He had not had any contact with her during the day. As the evening passed with no word from her he became uneasy and was unable to sleep that night. He went to work the following morning and telephoned home regularly but there was no answer. He called their friends, her colleagues and various places where he thought she might be, but could not find her anywhere. The day went by and he baulked at contacting the police. When she had still not turned up the following morning he finally called to report her missing. He did not even know what she had been wearing when she left home. The neighbours had not noticed her and it transpired that none of their friends or her old friends knew her whereabouts. They owned two cars and hers was still parked in front of the house. She had not ordered a taxi.

Erlendur visualised her leaving her home and heading out alone and abandoned into the dark winter's day. When he first called at their house the neighbourhood was lit up with Christmas decorations and he had thought to himself that she had probably never noticed them.

'There can never be any bloody trust between people who start a relationship against that sort of background,' Elínborg said, the disapproving tone entering her voice as always when she discussed this case.

'And then there's the question of the fourth woman,' Sigurdur Óli said. 'Does she exist?'

'The husband flatly denies having an affair and I haven't found any evidence that he did,' Erlendur said. 'We have only his wife's word about how she thought he was meeting another woman and her distress at the whole business. She appears to have deeply regretted her actions.'

'And then she calls up one day when she sees your name in the papers because of the murder,' Elínborg said.

'As if from the grave,' Erlendur said.

They sat in silence and thought about the woman who had gone missing and about Sunee and little Elías in the garden behind the block of flats.

'Do you seriously believe it?' Elínborg asked. 'About Niran? That he's to blame for his brother's death?'

'No,' Erlendur said. 'Not at all.'

'But she does seem to be trying to get the boy out of the way, otherwise she'd have stayed at home,' Sigurdur Óli said.

'Perhaps he's afraid,' Erlendur said. 'Perhaps they're both afraid.'

'Niran could have had an altercation with someone who threatened him,' Elínborg said.

'Possibly,' Sigurdur Óli said.

'At least he must have said something to arouse such a strong reaction from Sunee,' Elínborg said.

'How's Marion doing, by the way?' Sigurdur Óli asked.

'It'll soon be over,' Erlendur said.

He stood by the window of his office at the police station on Hverfisgata, smoking and watching the drifting snow swirl along the street. The light was fading and the cold continued to tighten its grip on the city as it slowed down towards evening before descending into sleep.

The intercom on his desk crackled and he was informed that a young man was asking for him at the front desk. He gave his name as Sindri Snaer. Erlendur had him shown in immediately and his son soon appeared at the door.

'I thought I'd drop in on you on my way to the meeting,' he said.

'Come in,' Erlendur said. 'What meeting?'

'AA,' Sindri said. 'It's down the road here on Hverfisgata.'

'Aren't you cold, dressed like that?' Erlendur pointed at Sindri's thin summer jacket.

'Not really,' Sindri said.

'Have a seat. Would you like a coffee?'

'No, thanks. I heard about the murder. Are you handling it?'

'With others.'

'Do you know anything?'

'No.'

Some time earlier, Sindri had moved to Reykjavík from the East Fjords where he had been working in a fish factory. He knew the story of how Erlendur and his brother had been caught in a snowstorm on the moors above Eskifjördur, and how Erlendur went there every couple of years to visit the moors where he almost froze to death as a child. Sindri was not as angry with his father as Eva Lind was; until very recently, he had not wanted anything to do with him. Now, however, he was in the habit of dropping in on him unexpectedly, at home or at work. His visits were generally brief, just long enough for one cigarette.

'Heard anything from Eva?' he asked.

'She phoned. Asked about Valgerdur.'

'Your woman?'

'She's not my woman,' Erlendur said.

'That's not what Eva says. She says she's virtually moved in with you.'

'Is she upset about Valgerdur?'

Sindri nodded and produced a pack of cigarettes.

'I don't know. Maybe she thinks you'll put her first.'

'Put her first? Over whom?'

Sindri inhaled the smoke and blew it out through his nose.

'Over her?' Erlendur asked.

Sindri shrugged.

'Has she said anything to you?'

'No,' Sindri said.

'Eva hasn't been in touch with me for weeks. Apart from that call yesterday. Do you think that's the reason?'

'Could be. I think she's getting back on her feet. She's left that dealer and told me she's going to get a job again.'

'Isn't that the same old story?'

'Sure.'

'What about you? How are you doing?'

'Fine,' Sindri said, standing up. He stubbed out his cigarette in the ashtray on the desk. 'Are you thinking of going out east this summer?'

'I haven't thought about it. Why?'

'Just wondered. I went to take a look at the house once when I was working out there. I don't know if I told you.'

'It's derelict now.'

'A pretty depressing place. Probably because I know why you moved away.'

Sindri opened the door to the corridor.

'Maybe you could let me know,' he said. 'If you do go out east.'

He closed the door quietly behind him without waiting for an answer. Erlendur sat in his chair, staring at the door. For an instant he was back home on the farm where he was born and brought up. The farmhouse still stood up on the moor, abandoned. He had slept in it when he visited his childhood haunts for a purpose that was not entirely clear. Perhaps to hear again the voices of his family and recall what he had once had and loved.

It was in this house, which now stood naked and lifeless and exposed to the elements, that he had first heard that unfamiliar, repulsive word which had become etched in his mind.

Murder.

14

The girl reminded him slightly of Eva Lind, apart from being younger and considerably fatter; Eva had always been painfully thin. The girl was wearing a short leather jacket over a thin green T-shirt, and dirty camouflage trousers, and had a metal piercing through one eyebrow. She had on black lipstick and one of her eyes was circled with black. Sitting down opposite Erlendur, she looked like a real tough cookie. The expression on her face betrayed an obstinate revulsion towards everything that the police could possibly represent. Beside him, Elínborg gave the girl a look that suggested she wanted to stuff her in a washing machine and switch it to rinse.

They had already questioned her elder sister, who seemed to be more or less the role model for the younger one. She was all mouth, a hardened character with a string of convictions for handling and selling drugs. Because she had never been caught with large amounts on her at any one time, she had only received short suspended sentences. As was customary, she refused to reveal the names of the dealers she sold for, and when asked whether she realised what she was doing to her sister by dragging her into the world of drugs, she laughed in their faces and said: 'Get a life.'

Erlendur tried to make the younger sister understand that he did not care what she was up to at the school. Drug-dealing was not his department and she would not be in any trouble with him, but if she did not give satisfactory answers to his questions he would have her sent to a smallholding in the middle of nowhere for the next two years.

'Smallholding?' the girl snorted. 'What the hell's that?'

'It's where milk comes from,' Elínborg said.

'I don't drink milk,' the girl said, wide-eyed, as if that could be to her advantage.

Looking at her, Erlendur could not help smiling in spite of everything. In front of him sat an example of the most wretched depths that a human life could descend to, a young girl who knew nothing but neglect and squalor. The girl could do little about the state she was in. She was from a typical problem home and had largely been left to bring herself up. Her elder sister, her role model and possibly one of the people who were supposed to look after her, had talked her into selling drugs and naturally into taking them as well. But that was probably not the worst of it. He knew from his own daughter how the debts were paid, what it cost to buy a gram, what they sometimes had to do to buy their bliss, the kind of life this young girl lived.

She was nicknamed Heddý and appeared to fit the profile that the police had of playground dealers. She was finishing compulsory schooling, lived in the neighbourhood and hung around with twenty-year-old men, her big sister's friends. She was the go-between and they had heard various unsavoury details about her at the school.

'Did you know Elías? The boy who died?' Erlendur asked.

They were sitting in the interview room. With the girl was a child welfare officer. Her parents could not be reached. She knew why she had been called in. The welfare officer spoke to her and told her they were only gathering information.

'No,' Heddý said, 'I didn't know him at all. I don't know who killed him. It wasn't me.'

'No one's saying it was you,' Erlendur said.

'It wasn't me.'

'Do you know of any . . . ?' Erlendur paused. He was going to ask if there had been any altercations between Elías and anyone in particular at the school, but was uncertain whether she would understand the word 'altercation'. So he began again: 'Do you know if Elías had any particular enemies at the school?'

'No,' the girl said. 'I don't know. I don't know anything about this Elías kid. I'm not dealing there. That's just bullshit!'

'Did you try to sell him dope?' Elínborg asked.

'What sort of cunt are you?' the girl snarled. 'I don't talk to cunts like you.'

Elínborg smiled.

'Did you sell him dope?' she asked again. 'We've heard that you force the younger kids to give you money. You even force them to buy dope from you. Maybe your sister's taught you how to go about it, because she's experienced and knows how to make the kids scared of her. Maybe you're scared of big sister too. We don't give a damn about that. We couldn't care less about a girl like you—'

'Hey, listen . . .' the child welfare officer objected.

'You heard what she called me,' Elínborg said, slowly turning her head to the welfare officer, a woman of about thirty. 'You kept your mouth shut then and you should keep it shut now as well. We want to know if Elías was scared of you,' she continued, looking back at Heddý. 'If you chased him to frighten him and stabbed him with a knife. We know that you like preying on smaller kids, because that's the only thing you're any good at in this miserable existence of yours. Did you attack Elías too?'

Heddý stared at Elínborg.

'No,' she said after a long silence. 'I never went near him.'

'Do you know his brother?' Erlendur asked.

'I know Niran,' she said.

'How do you know Niran? Are you friends?'

'No way,' she said, 'we're not friends. I hate gooks. Never go near them. Not that Elías either. I never went near him and I don't know who attacked him.'

'Why did you say that you know Niran?'

The girl smiled, revealing adult teeth that were completely out of proportion with her small mouth and childlike face.

'They're the ones who sell,' she said. 'They sell the fucking dope. The fucking gooks!'

Marion Briem was asleep when Erlendur visited the hospital towards evening. Peace reigned in the terminal ward. A radio was switched on somewhere, broadcasting the weather report. The temperature had dropped to ten degrees below, exacerbated by the dry northerly wind. Few people went out in such cold. They stayed at home, switched on all the lights and turned up the central heating. The television showed sunny films from Spain and Italy featuring blue skies, Mediterranean warmth and vibrant colours.

Marion's eyes opened when Erlendur had been standing at the foot of the bed for several minutes. One hand lay on the duvet and lifted up excruciatingly slowly. After a moment's hesitation Erlendur moved closer, took hold of the hand and sat down by the bedside.

'How are you feeling?' he asked.

Marion's eyes closed and that big head shook as if it did not matter any more. The moment of departure was approaching. There was not much time left. Erlendur noticed a small hand-held mirror on the table by Marion's bedside and wondered what it was doing there. He had never known Marion to care for appearances.

'The case?' Marion said. 'What's happening in the case?'

Erlendur knew precisely what was expected of him. Even at death's door, Marion was absorbed in the latest investigation. From the weary eyes that rested on him, Erlendur read the question that he had been asking himself, sleeping and waking: who could do such a thing? How could something like this happen?

Erlendur began to report the progress of the investigation. Marion listened with eyes closed again. Erlendur did not know whether his old boss was asleep. He had slight pangs of conscience about not necessarily visiting Marion for purely compassionate reasons. He longed to ask the dying patient about something he knew he would never find in the police records. Erlendur took his time. It helped him, too, to go through the case slowly. Once during the account, Marion's eyes opened and Erlendur thought he should stop, only to be given a sign to continue.

'There's one point I need to ask you about,' Erlendur said when he had finally completed his story about the visit to Andrés. Marion seemed to be sleeping, with eyes closed and breathing barely perceptible. The hand that Erlendur held was limp. But it was as if Marion realised that Erlendur was not merely making a courtesy call. Those tired eyes opened a fraction and the grip on Erlendur's hand tightened, as a signal to go on.

'It's about Andrés,' Erlendur said.

Marion squeezed his hand.

'He told us about a man he knew and implied that he was a paedophile, but would not reveal his identity. He did something to Andrés when he was a child. All we know is that this man lives in the neighbourhood where the murder was committed. We have no name and no description. I don't think he's on our register. Andrés told us he was too clever for that. I was wondering if you could help us. The investigation is all over the place at the moment and we have to examine anything we find suspicious. I don't have to tell you that. You know it. We're in a hurry as usual. But more than ever this time. I thought you might be able to help us with a shortcut.'

A long silence followed Erlendur's words. He thought that Marion had dozed off. The hand he was holding had gone slack and peace had descended over his former boss's face.

'Andrés . . . ?' Marion said at last. It was more like a groan or a sigh.

'I checked,' Erlendur said. 'He was born and bred in the capital. If anything happened it was most likely here in Reykjavík. We don't know. Andrés is silent as the grave.'

Marion said nothing. Erlendur thought the situation was hopeless. He had not really expected anything, but felt it was worth a try. He knew Marion Briem's capacities, that memory and the talent for making the most unlikely connections in an instant. Perhaps he was taking advantage of his ex-boss. Perhaps this was going too far. He decided to forget it. Marion should be allowed to die in peace.

'He had . . .' Marion strained to say, and the grip on Erlendur's hand tightened.

'What? What did he have?'

Erlendur thought he could discern a hint of a smile playing

across Marion's face. At first he thought he was imagining this, but became convinced that Marion was actually smiling.

'. . . stepfather,' Marion gasped.

Silence again.

'Erlendur,' Marion said after a long while. The patient's eyes remained closed but a grimace slowly appeared.

'Yes,' Erlendur said.

'There's . . . no . . . time . . .' Marion whispered.

'I know,' Erlendur said. 'I . . .'

He was lost for words. He did not know how to say goodbye, could not find a way to express a last farewell. What was there to say? Marion was still holding his hand. Erlendur struggled for words, for something he thought Marion would want to hear. When he found nothing he sat in silence holding that old hand with its yellow nicotine stains and long nails.

'Read to . . . me,' Marion said.

Marion's final ounce of strength went into those words. Erlendur leaned forward to hear better.

'Read . . .'

Marion groped helplessly for the mirror on the bedside table.

Erlendur picked up the mirror and put it into Marion's hands to prop up and confront the face of death.

Erlendur took out a book he had brought with him. It was dog-eared and tattered. He opened it at a page he had often consulted and began to read.

For centuries a mountain path lay from Eskifjördur to Fljótsdalshérad across Eskifjördur moor. It was an old horse-track skirting north of the Eskifjördur River, inland along the ridge Langihryggur, up the river Innri-Steinsá through Vínárdalur valley and over Vínárbrekkur slopes to

Midheidarendi, and from there up to the Urdarflöt plateau and along the cliffs of Urdarklettur to the boundary of the Eskifjördur district. Thverárdalur valley bisects the mountains Andri and Hardskafi to the north, and Hólafjall and Selheidi even further north.

Bakkasel was once a tenant croft near the head of the Eskifjördur valley, on the old mountain path to Fljótsdalshérad. It is now abandoned, but in the middle of the century Sveinn Erlendsson farmed there with his wife Áslaug Bergsdóttir and their two sons, of eight and ten years old. Sveinn kept a few sheep . . .

Erlendur stopped reading.

'Marion?' he whispered.

A deep silence spread over the ward. The early darkness of winter had descended upon the city, which was transforming into a glittering sea of lights. Erlendur saw his own reflection in the window overlooking the hospital garden. The large pane of glass was like a muted painting, a still-life portraying them at the final moment. He stared into the window until he confronted his own face, and the image became like the closing lines of a poem that crept into his mind.

. . . Am I the one, who lives on, or the other, who died?

Erlendur returned to his senses when the little mirror fell to the floor and broke. He clasped the limp hand and checked the pulse. Marion had departed from this world.

Erlendur drove the Ford Falcon into a parking space in front of the block of flats where he lived. He left the engine running for a while before switching it off. Although old, the car ran like clockwork and purred cosily in low gear. Erlendur was very fond of his Ford and sometimes, when he had nothing else to do, he would go for a drive outside the city. He had never done that before. Once he had invited Marion out for a drive, to Lake Kleifarvatn. Erlendur drove Marion down to the lakeside and told him about the conclusion to a case he had been investigating. A skeleton had been discovered on the bed of the lake and was linked to a group of Icelanders who had studied in the former East Germany in the 1960s. Marion took a particular interest in that. Erlendur wanted to do something for Marion in his ex-boss's illness. He knew that when the moment of death drew near, there was no one else that the cancer victim could depend upon.

Pulling a face at the recollection, he stroked the thin, ivory-coloured steering wheel. He would never see Marion again. All that remained were memories, fairly mixed ones at that. He thought about his own time on this earth, how brief it was before new generations took over, to be swept even further into the future. His time had gone by without his noticing it, lacking as he did all contact with anything but work. Before he knew it he would be lying in a ward like Marion Briem, staring death in the face.

Erlendur was not aware of any claims to the body. Marion had once asked him to handle the funeral arrangements. He had discussed the next steps with a nurse.

On his way home from the hospital Erlendur had called on Sunee. Her brother was with her, and the interpreter Gudný, who was leaving when Erlendur arrived. He accepted her offer to stay.

'Is it anything special?' Gudný asked. 'Any news?'

'No, not yet,' Erlendur said, and Gudný conveyed the fact to Sunee.

'Does she want to tell me where Niran is?' he asked.

Gudný spoke to Sunee who shook her head, staring obstinately at Erlendur.

'She thinks he's better off where he is. She wants to know when she can have Elías's body.'

'Very soon,' Erlendur said. 'This case is top priority and his earthly remains will only be kept while the investigation is ongoing.'

Erlendur sat in an armchair beneath the yellow dragon. The atmosphere in the flat was calmer than before. The brother and sister sat side by side on the sofa. They both smoked. Erlendur had not seen Sunee smoke before. She did not look well, with bags under her eyes, at once grief-stricken and anxious.

'How have you liked living in this neighbourhood?' Erlendur asked.

'It's a good place to live,' Sunee said through Gudný. 'It's a very quiet area.'

'Have you got to know your neighbours, in the other flats?'

'A little.'

'Have you run into trouble with anyone because you're from Thailand? Been aware of any racial prejudice or hostility?'

'A tiny bit if I go out to a bar.'

'What about your boys?'

'Elías never complained. But there was one teacher he didn't like.'

'Kjartan?'

'Yes.'

'Why not?'

'He liked school but didn't like the Icelandic lessons when Kjartan taught him.'

'And what about Niran?'

'He wants to go home.'

'Home to Thailand?'

'Yes. I want him with me. It was difficult for him to come here but I want him with me.'

'Ódinn wasn't pleased to find out about Niran so long after you had got married.'

'No.'

'Was that the reason for your divorce?'

Sunee listened to Gudný translate the question. Then she looked at Erlendur.

'Maybe,' she said. 'Maybe that was one reason. They never got on together.'

'I'd like to find out about your boyfriend,' Erlendur said. 'What can you tell me about him? Did he come between you and Ódinn?'

'No,' Sunee said. 'It was all over between Ódinn and me when he entered the picture.'

'Who is he?'

'He's my good friend.'

'Why won't you tell us anything about him?'

Sunee did not reply.

'Is it because he doesn't want you to?'

Sunee said nothing.

'Is he shy about this relationship in some way?'

Sunee looked at him. She seemed poised to answer him, then stopped.

'Is Niran with him?'

'Don't ask about him,' she said. 'He's got nothing to do with this.'

'It's important for us to talk to Niran,' Erlendur said. 'Not because we think he did anything wrong, but because he might know something useful to us. Will you think about it until tomorrow?'

Gudný passed on this request but Sunee did not reply.

'Do you ever miss Thailand?' Erlendur asked.

'I've been there twice since Elías was born,' Sunee said. 'My family will come over for the funeral. It will be nice to see them again but I don't miss Thailand.'

'Are you going to have Elías buried here?'

'Of course.'

Sunee went quiet.

'I just want to live here in peace,' she said after a long pause. 'I came here in hope of a better life. I thought I'd found it. I knew nothing about Iceland before I came here. I didn't even know it existed. It was the country of my dreams. Then this happens, this horrible thing. Maybe I will go back. Niran and I. Maybe we don't belong here.'

'We've heard from a very unreliable source, so we're not attaching much importance to it, that Niran goes around with boys who are involved with drugs.'

'That's absurd.'

'Do you know what a debt collector is?'

Sunee nodded.

'Has Niran been in any trouble with them?'

'No,' Gudný said after Sunee had spoken. 'Niran never goes near drugs. Whoever said that is lying.'

Erlendur switched off the car engine outside the block of flats where he lived and stepped out into the chill winter. He pulled his overcoat tightly around him and walked slowly over to the block. Inside the dark flat, he turned on a lamp. Now there was no moon riding past the window, the sky was overcast and the wind howled past the walls of the building.

He did not know how long he had been sitting thinking about Marion when he heard a tap at his door. He thought he had fallen asleep, but could not be sure. He stood up and opened the door. A figure stepped quietly out of the shadowy corridor and greeted him. It was Eva Lind.

Erlendur was flustered. He had not seen his daughter for quite some time. Their relationship had been at rock bottom for so long that he had actually expected never to see her again. He had decided to stop running after her, to stop rescuing her from drug dens; to stop involving himself if she was named in police reports; to stop trying to make her stay with him, and looking after her; to stop trying to send her away to detox. None of this had changed anything, except for the worse. The more they saw of each other, the worse they got on together. Eva Lind had sunk into depression after a miscarriage and he was helpless to act. All his efforts had the opposite effect on her and she accused him of interfering and being overbearing. His last attempt had been to persuade her to enter rehab for alcohol and drug addiction. When that did not work he gave up. He was familiar with instances of this from his work. In the end, many parents gave up on children who were taking drugs and sinking deeper and deeper without seeing sense or showing the slightest willingness to cooperate.

He had decided to leave her to her own devices, and the feeling was mutual. He realised that he was rarely dealing with his daughter herself. He hardly knew her. What he was continuously wrestling with was the poison that turned her into a different person. It was a hopeless battle. The poison was not Eva Lind. He knew this even though she had never stooped so low as to use it as an excuse for anything. The poison was one thing. Eva Lind was another. Generally it was hard to distinguish between the two, but it could be done. And while this was no consolation as such, he was aware of the fact.

'Can I come in?' Eva Lind asked.

He was more pleased to see her than he would ever have admitted. She was no longer wearing her ugly black leather jacket but a long red coat. Her hair was clean and tied up in a ponytail, her make-up was moderate and he could not see any piercings in her face. Instead of black lipstick, she wore none. She was dressed in a thick green sweater against the cold, jeans and black, almost knee-length, leather boots.

'Of course,' he said, opening the door for her.

'It's always so horribly dark in here,' she said, walking into the living room. He closed the door and followed her. Pushing a pile of newspapers aside on the sofa, she sat down, took out a pack of cigarettes and thrust it at him with a questioning look. He made a gesture to say that she was free to smoke in his flat but declined the offer himself.

'So, what's new?' he asked and sat down in his armchair. It was as if nothing had changed, as if she had simply left him the day before yesterday and just happened to be passing by again.

'Same old,' Eva said in English.

'Isn't Icelandic good enough for you then?' he asked.

'You never change, do you?' Eva looked around the bookshelves and stacks of books, and into the kitchen where there were two stools at the table, a saucepan on the cooker and a coffee maker.

'What about you? Do you change?'

Eva Lind shrugged instead of answering him. Perhaps she did not want to talk about herself. As a rule that ended in arguments and bad feeling. He did not want to provoke her by asking where she had been all this time and what kind of state she was in. She had told him so often that it was none of his business what she got up to. It had never been any of his business, and he was to blame for that.

'Sindri dropped in on me,' he said, looking his daughter in the face. Sometimes her features reminded Erlendur of his mother, she had her eyes and high cheekbones.

'I talked to him a week or so ago. He's selling timber. Works in Kópavogur. What did you talk about?'

'Nothing special,' Erlendur said. 'He was on his way to an AA meeting.'

'We were talking about you.'

'Me?'

'We always do when we meet. He told me he's in touch with you.'

'He phones sometimes,' Erlendur said. 'Sometimes he comes to see me. What do you say about me? Why do you talk about me?'

'This and that,' Eva said. 'What a weirdo you are. You're our dad. There's nothing odd about us talking about you. Sindri speaks well of you. Better than I thought.'

'Sindri's all right,' Erlendur said. 'At least he's got a job.'

This remark was not meant in approbation. He had not meant to pass any judgements but the words slipped out and he saw that they affected Eva. He did not even know whether she had a job or not.

'I didn't come here to argue with you,' she said.

'No, I know,' he said. 'Anyway, arguing with you is pointless. That's been proven time and again. It's like shouting into the wind. I don't know what you're doing or have been doing for a long time and that's fine with me. It's nothing to do with me. You were right. It's none of my business. Do you want some coffee?'

'Okay,' Eva said.

She stubbed out her cigarette and immediately took out another, but did not light it. Erlendur went to the kitchen and put the coffee and water in the coffee maker. Soon it began belching and the brown liquid dripped down into the jug. He found some biscuits. They were a month past their sell-by date, so he threw them away. He dug out two mugs and took them into the living room.

'How's the investigation going?'

'So so,' Erlendur said.

'Do you have any idea what happened?'

'No,' Erlendur said. 'Dealers might be operating close to the school, even in the playground,' he added, and named the two sisters but Eva had never heard of them. Nonetheless, she was familiar with playground dealing. She had briefly done it herself some years before.

Erlendur fetched the coffee and filled the mugs. Then he sat back down in his armchair. Over the coffee, he watched his daughter. He had the impression that she looked older since the last time they had met, older and possibly more mature. He did not realise immediately what had changed. It was as if Eva was no longer the loud-mouthed girl who was in constant rebellion against him and would give him a piece of her mind if she felt so inclined. In that coat she looked more like a young woman. The teenage behaviour that had so long been part of her character was there no longer.

'Me and Sindri also talked a lot about your brother who died,' Eva Lind said, lighting her cigarette.

She came right out with it, as if it had no more personal bearing on her than a story in a newspaper. For an instant Erlendur was angry with his daughter. What damn business of hers is that! More than a generation had passed since his brother had died, but Erlendur was still highly sensitive about it. He had not discussed his brother's death with anyone until Eva wheedled the story out of him one day, and sometimes he regretted having bared his soul to her.

'What were you saying about him?'

'Sindri told me how he heard all about it when he was in a fish factory out east. They remembered you and your brother and our grandparents, people neither of us had ever heard of.'

Sindri had told Erlendur this too. His son had turned up one day, newly arrived in the city, and told him what he had heard about Erlendur and his brother and their father, and their fateful journey up onto the moors when the blizzard struck without warning.

'We talked about the stories he heard,' Eva Lind said.

'The stories he heard?' Erlendur parroted. 'What are you and Sindri—?'

'Maybe that was the reason for my dream,' Eva Lind interrupted him. 'Because we were talking about him. Your brother.'

'What did you dream?'

'Did you know some people keep diaries about what they dream? I don't, but my friend writes down everything she dreams. I never dream anything. Or at least I never remember my dreams. I've heard that everyone has dreams but only some people can remember them.'

'So tell me what you and Sindri were saying.'

'What was your brother's name?' Eva asked, ignoring his question.

'Bergur,' Erlendur said. 'My brother was called Bergur. What did Sindri hear about us in the east?'

'Shouldn't he have been found?'

'They did everything they could to find him,' Erlendur said. 'Rescue teams and the local farmers, everyone who was able searched for us. I was found. We became separated in the blizzard. He was never found.'

'Yes, but what I mean is, shouldn't he have been found later on?' Eva said, with the obstinate tone in her voice that Erlendur knew from his own mother. 'Body parts, bones?'

Erlendur was perfectly aware what Eva was talking about although he pretended not to be. Sindri had probably heard this story in the east, where people were still talking about the boys who were lost in a blizzard with their father so many years ago. Erlendur had heard many theories before he moved to Reykjavík with his parents. Now his daughter, who knew nothing of the matter apart from the little that Erlendur had told her, was sitting in front of him eager to discuss the theories about his brother's disappearance. All of a sudden she had turned up at his flat and wanted to discuss his brother, the memories that had tormented him since the age of ten.

'Not necessarily,' Erlendur said. 'Do you mind if we talk about something else?'

'Why don't you want to discuss it? Why is it so difficult?'

'Was that why you came?' Erlendur asked. 'To tell me what you dreamed?'

'Why was he never found?' Eva said.

He could not understand his daughter's obstinacy. As time passed it had caused interest that his brother's remains were never found, not even a hat or glove or scarf. Nothing. People had various theories as to why. He avoided brooding on them too much.

'I don't want to talk about it,' he said. 'Another time maybe. Tell me about yourself. We haven't seen each other for ages. What have you been up to?'

'You were there,' Eva said, refusing to leave him alone. 'You were in my dream. I've never dreamed anything as clear as that. I haven't dreamed about you since I was little and I didn't even know what you looked like then.'

Erlendur said nothing. His mother had tried to teach him to interpret dreams, but he had always been reluctant and uninterested. It was only in recent years that his attitude had softened and his interest became roused, in spite of everything. Eva told him that she never had dreams or remembered them, and his mother had said the same. It was not until the age of thirty that his mother started dreaming to any extent, when she suddenly developed the gift of foretelling deaths, births, visitors and many other events with uncanny accuracy. But she did not foresee her son's death in a dream and he visited her in her sleep only once afterwards. She had described the dream to Erlendur.

It was summer and her boy was standing at the door of the farmhouse, leaning up against the doorpost. His back was turned to her and she could only discern his outline. The image persisted for a long while but it was impossible for her to approach him. She felt she was stretching her arms towards him without his noticing her. Then he stood up straight, bowed his head and thrust his hands into his pockets the way he sometimes did, walked out into the summer's day . . . and disappeared.

That was six years after it had happened. They had moved to Reykjavík by then.

Erlendur seldom recalled the world of his dreams unless he became too emotionally involved in a case he happened to be investigating. Then he might have bad dreams, although he would not necessarily remember their substance. It took him a long time to digest the fact that Eva had come to see him after all this time to tell him about a dream she had had, involving him and his brother.

'What did you dream, Eva?' he asked falteringly. 'What happened in your dream?'

'First tell me how he died.'

'You know that,' Erlendur said. 'He froze to death on the moors. A storm blew up and we were buried in a snowdrift.'

'Why was he never found?'

'Where are you heading with all this, Eva?'

'You haven't told me the whole story, have you?'

'What story?'

'Sindri told me what could have happened.'

'What are they blathering on about out there in the east?' Erlendur said. 'What do they reckon they know?'

'In my dream he didn't die of exposure, you see. And that fits in with what Sindri said.'

'Please drop the subject,' Erlendur said. 'Let's stop. I don't want to talk about it. Not now. Later, Eva. I promise.'

'But—'

'Surely you can tell,' he interrupted her. 'I don't want to. Maybe you ought to leave. I . . . I'm very busy. It's been a rough day. Let's discuss it better another time.'

He stood up. Eva watched him without saying a word. She could not comprehend his reaction. It was as if the event had just as much effect on Erlendur now as it did at the time; as if he had proved completely incapable of dealing with it for all those years.

'Don't you want to hear my dream?'

'Not now.'

'Okay,' she said as she stood up.

'Say hello to Sindri from me if you see him,' Erlendur said, running his fingers through his hair.

'I will,' Eva said.

'It was nice seeing you,' he said awkwardly.

'Same here.'

When she had left he stood facing the bookshelves for a long time, as if in another world. Eva had a knack of riling him. No one else could do it in quite the same way. He was not ready to embark on accounts of his brother's disappearance. Once he had promised to tell Eva the whole story, but nothing had come of it. She could not burst into his life now, insisting on answers whenever she had the urge.

The book he had read aloud from for Marion Briem was lying on the table in the living room and he picked it up. Like so many of his books, it dealt with fatal accidents, but what distinguished it from all the others was that it contained a short narrative of events that had taken place many years before, when a father and his two sons were caught in a violent storm on the moors above Eskifjördur.

Erlendur looked up the story as he had done so often before. The accounts varied in length but most were structured in the same way. First came a heading and a subheading or source reference. The story generally opened with a topographical description, followed by the narrative proper and a short postscript. He had read this account more often than anything else in his life and knew it off by heart, word for word. It was impartial and impersonal, despite telling of the lonely death of an eight-year-old boy. It made no mention of the devastation that the incident had left behind in the hearts of those who experienced it. That story would never be written.

16

The police attached the highest priority to locating Niran, who had not been heard of since the previous day. With the help of the school staff, they gathered information about his friends, boys he knew and spent most of his time with at school. A lower-profile and more personal search was also in progress, known only to Erlendur and based on Marion Briem's memory of Andrés's stepfather. He wanted to keep that line of inquiry quiet because he had the feeling Andrés was lying to them. He had done as much in the past.

When word spread that Sunee, the victim's mother, had spirited her older son away to a safe haven, it became headline news and a talking point all over Iceland. The police were heavily criticised for their ineptitude. Either they had let a key witness slip through their hands or, even worse, they had driven him to flight through their own sheer incompetence. After suspicions were raised that the police had tried to conceal this information, like so much else connected with the investigation, a furore broke out about the information act and lack of cooperation with the media.

Erlendur despised nothing more than having to inform journalists and reporters about 'the progress of the investigation', as it was called. He had long maintained that police investigations had nothing to do with the media and that it could be downright damaging to give constant updates about the latest developments. Sigurdur Óli disagreed. He considered it a matter of course to give information, provided it did not jeopardise the interests of the investigation.

'Interests of the investigation?' Erlendur fumed. 'Who invents phrases like that? That lot can stick it where the sun don't shine. We shouldn't be releasing any bloody information until we ourselves know what's happened. It serves no purpose whatsoever.'

They were sitting in Erlendur's office, with Elínborg. A press conference was to be held later that day in response to demands by the media, but Erlendur had refused to attend. This created quite a rumpus between him and his immediate superiors. The outcome was that Sigurdur Óli would be police spokesman and media liaison, along with the deputy head of Reykjavík CID. Erlendur considered it stupid to waste manpower on such pointless exercises.

He had met Ódinn, Elías's father, the previous day when it transpired that Niran had gone missing again and Sunee refused to disclose his whereabouts. Erlendur went to visit him in the flat on Snorrabraut. Ódinn had taken several days off work. He did not look as if he had slept well that night, he was unkempt and in bad shape.

Sigrídur, Sunee's mother-in-law, had also taken leave from work and Sigurdur Óli visited her at her home. She said she had been on her way to see Sunee when she heard the news, and really could not understand what was going on. She had offered to sleep at their flat that night, but Sunee had declined. Sigrídur had no idea of her movements and could not imagine what had become of Niran. She wondered why Sunee should take such drastic action. Sigurdur Óli hinted that she might have something to hide from the police, but Sigrídur dismissed that as absurd. Rather Sunee was trying to protect the boy, she thought.

The most likely scenario was that Sunee had approached someone within the Thai community in the city. Elínborg spent a long time with her brother Virote. She could not tell whether he was lying when he claimed to know nothing. He was deeply anxious about his sister and Niran and reproached the police for allowing such a thing to happen. Elínborg visited the brother on her own, although he could not speak much more Icelandic than Sunee. She repeatedly asked him about Niran, but Virote stood firm.

'I can well understand if you don't want to tell me where Niran is,' Elínborg said, 'but you have to believe that it's in his best interests to come out of hiding.'

'I not know about Niran,' Virote said. 'Sunee not tell me nothing.'

'You must help us,' Elínborg said.

'I not know nothing.'

'Why did Sunee do this?' Elínborg asked.

'I not know what she do. She afraid. Afraid for Niran.'

'Why?'

'I not know nothing.'

The brother stuck to his guns until Elínborg gave up and left.

'We have to find Niran and tell him he can trust us,' Erlendur said. 'Sunee has to understand that.'

'He can hardly spend long in hiding,' Elínborg said. 'Surely Sunee will want him to attend Elías's funeral. Anything else would be out of the question.'

'She could be getting the boy out of the way,' Sigurdur Óli

said. 'This bizarre twist has turned the spotlight on Niran, on what he knows and what he did. We can't ignore that.'

'I can't imagine that he attacked his brother,' Elínborg said. 'I just can't picture it. Maybe he does know something and he's afraid, but I don't believe he played any part in what happened.'

'If only we could go by what you can imagine, Elínborg,' Sigurdur Óli said. 'Wouldn't everything be just dandy?'

'There's nothing bloody "dandy" about it,' Erlendur snapped.

Sigurdur Óli grinned.

'I told Sunee we couldn't be sure when the body would be released because of the investigation,' Erlendur said. 'One possibility is that she's trying to win time. But time for what?'

'Is she waiting for us to solve the case?' Sigurdur Óli asked. 'However we're supposed to do that.'

'There are some small-scale racial clashes in or around the school,' Erlendur said. 'Niran's mixed up in them somehow. There's a minor altercation. Elías isn't necessarily involved but Niran is. When Elías is attacked, Niran disappears or doesn't come home. When he finally does show up he's obviously had a major shock. Maybe he saw what happened. Maybe he only heard about it. He was in a state of shock when I found him in the rubbish store. He'd locked himself away in some private place in his mind where he felt safe. Anyway, Niran tells his mother what he knows and she responds by bundling him off into hiding. What does that tell us?'

'That they know what happened,' Sigurdur Óli said. 'Niran knows and he's told his mother.'

Erlendur looked at Elínborg.

'Something happened when Niran was alone with his mother,' she said. 'That's all we can be sure of. Anything else is conjecture. They don't necessarily know anything. She's already lost one son and she's not prepared to lose the only one she has left.'

'What about that little dealer's claim that Niran and his friends were selling dope?' Erlendur asked.

'You can't trust a word that girl says,' Elínborg said.

'Could it be that Sunee no longer feels safe among us?' Erlendur said. 'Here in Iceland? Could that explain why she's hidden her son? We can't begin to understand what it's really like for immigrants in this country. We can't begin to understand what it's like for someone from the other side of the globe to move over here, settle, start a family and try to integrate into Icelandic society. It's bound to be tough and I think it's very hard for us to put ourselves in their shoes. Racism may not be an everyday occurrence here but we know that not everyone's happy with the way society is going.'

'According to surveys, the majority of young Icelanders feel things have gone far enough,' Sigurdur Óli chipped in. 'Which shows they're not exactly keen on multiculturalism.'

'We want foreigners to come here and do shitty jobs at power stations, fish factories and as cleaners, then pack up and leave again when we don't need them any more,' Elínborg said. ' "Thanks for the help, don't hurry back!" God forbid that we might get stuck with these people. But if they do insist on coming here, they can stay away from us. Like the Yanks on the Base who've always been kept safely behind fences. Wasn't it official policy for years that no black people were allowed on the Base? I reckon that's still a common attitude: that foreigners ought to be kept behind fences.'

'You can't rule out the possibility that they erect the fences themselves,' Sigurdur Óli said. 'It's not a one-way street. I think you're oversimplifying. There are also cases of immigrants not wanting to integrate, only marrying within their own group and so on. Wanting to close ranks and ignore what goes on in the wider community.'

'From what I hear, it's worked out best in the West Fjords,' Elínborg said, 'where a variety of nationalities, people from literally dozens of countries, live in a small area and respect each other's cultural differences and backgrounds while trying to make a life for themselves in Iceland.'

'If I can continue,' Erlendur said, 'what I think may have happened is that Sunee sought refuge among her own kind. She doesn't trust us, so she's taken Niran somewhere where she thinks he'll be safer. I reckon we ought to organise our search on that basis. She's turned to the people she trusts best for protection, her own kind.'

Elínborg nodded.

'Very probably,' she said. 'So it's not necessarily a question of what Niran knows or has done.'

'Only time will tell,' Erlendur said.

By midday the school staff had supplied them with the names of the boys who Niran was believed to spend most of his time with at school and in the neighbourhood. Sigurdur Óli and Elínborg took the list and set off. It contained four names, all of them boys from immigrant families who lived in the school's catchment area: one of Thai origin, two from the Philippines and one from Vietnam. All except the Thai boy had been born in Asia, moved to Iceland after the age of ten, and had problems adapting to Icelandic society.

Erlendur spent the rest of the morning making the arrangements for Marion Briem's funeral. He contacted the funeral director's, who told him to leave it to them. A date was set and he placed an announcement of the death and funeral in the papers. He was not expecting a large turn-out and didn't entertain the idea of a reception for long. Marion had left instructions for the funeral, including the name of a minister and a choice of hymns, and Erlendur followed them to the letter.

Once he had completed the preparations as best he could, he began his search for the stepfather that Marion had mentioned in connection with Andrés, who might be the man that Andrés had spotted by chance in the area. Erlendur traced the name of Andrés's mother and found his date of birth, then searched the register of Reykjavík residents for the period when he was growing up. According to the records Erlendur examined, the boy had been four years old when he lost his father. After that his mother was registered as living alone with her son. From what Erlendur could discover, Andrés was her only child. If she had lived with anyone for any length of time, he or they were not registered at her home, apart from one man who turned out to have died thirteen years ago. Erlendur found the street names and numbers where the woman had lived. She had moved constantly, even within the same area, living in the city centre, in Skuggahverfi, in the suburb of Breidholt when it was under construction, and moved from there to Vogar and finally to Grafarvogur. She died early in the 1990s. At first glance, Erlendur could find no trace of the stepfather Marion had mentioned before dying.

Since he was digging through the police archives anyway, he decided to examine any reports of incidents linked to racial prejudice or hate crimes. Erlendur knew that other members of the CID had been detailed to look into that aspect of the case but he did not let this deter him. He generally did as he pleased, ignoring his place in the precise hierarchy of the investigation. In all, more than twenty detectives were working on Elías's case, each assigned a specific task relating to the collection of information, surveillance of comings and goings from the country, or examination of transactions at car-rental companies and hotels in the city and surrounding area. They had also contacted the Bangkok police and enquired about any possible movements to or from the country by Sunee's relatives. The Reykjavík CID were inundated with tip-offs every day, most of which were recorded and followed up, although this was a time-consuming process. Members of the public called in after watching the news or reading the papers, claiming to have important information about the case. Some of it was absurd and irrelevant: drunks claiming to have solved the case using nothing but their own ingenuity and even giving the names of relatives or acquaintances who were 'a bunch of arseholes'. Every lead was investigated.

As far as Erlendur knew, there were not many individuals in the police files who were considered actively dangerous or likely to commit serious crimes from racist motives. A few violent thugs had been arrested, at their own homes in a couple of instances, and a variety of offensive weapons – clubs, knives and knuckledusters – had been removed, along with propaganda that could be described as neo-Nazi: material from the Internet, pamphlets, books, photocopies, flags and other racist para-phernalia. Much of it had been confiscated. This was no organised circulation of hate propaganda, and few people had been picked up by the police specifically for showing hostility towards immigrants. Most complaints about racial prejudice were the result of random, one-off incidents.

Erlendur rooted around in the boxes. In one he found a

carefully folded Confederate flag and another bearing a swastika. There were also a variety of publications in English, which, judging from the titles, seemed to write off the holocaust as a Zionist conspiracy, and racist pamphlets featuring pictures of primitive African tribes. He unearthed articles from American and British magazines inciting hatred, and finally an old book of minutes from an association calling itself 'Fathers of Iceland'.

The book recorded several meetings that took place in 1990, where the issues discussed included Hitler's contribution to the reconstruction of post-Weimar Germany. At one point there was a passage referring to the problem of immigration in Iceland and discussing how to stem the tide. It predicted that the Nordic race would face extinction in Iceland within a hundred years if miscegenation continued. Among the measures to oppose this it advocated passing tougher laws on eligibility for citizenship, and even closing the borders to foreigners, regardless of whether they came to the country to work, for family reasons or as asylum seekers. The entries stopped abruptly. Apparently the association had disbanded without warning. Erlendur registered that the handwriting was elegant, the style terse and to the point, with no unnecessary digressions.

Although no list of members was appended, the minutes contained a name that seemed familiar to Erlendur. He was sitting racking his brains about where he had heard it before when his mobile rang. He recognised the voice immediately.

'I know I mustn't call but I don't know what . . .'

The woman began to sob.

'. . . I don't know what to do.'

'Come and talk to me,' Erlendur said.

'I can't. I can't do it. It's so terrible how . . .'

'What?' Erlendur said.

'I want to,' the voice said. 'I do want to, but it's impossible.'

'Where are you?'

'I . . .'

The woman abandoned what she had been going to say and there was silence.

'I can help you,' Erlendur said. 'Tell me where you are and I'll help you.'

'I can't,' the voice said, and he could hear the woman crying down the phone. 'I can't . . . live like this . . .' She trailed off again.

'But you keep calling,' Erlendur said. 'You can't be in a good way if you're phoning me like this. I'll help you. Are you hiding because of him? Is it because of him that you're in hiding?'

'I'd do anything for him, that's why—' The woman broke off.

'We need to talk to you,' Erlendur said.

Silence.

'We can help you. I know it must be difficult but . . .'

'It should never have happened. Never . . .'

'Tell me where you are and we'll talk,' Erlendur said. 'It'll be all right. I promise.'

He waited with bated breath. All he could hear over the phone was the woman's sobbing. A long moment passed. Erlendur did not dare to speak. The woman was weighing up her options. His mind racing, he tried to find something to say to her to clinch the matter. Something about her husband. Her family. Her two children.

'Your children will certainly want to know—'

Erlendur got no further.

'Oh God!' the woman cried, and hung up.

Erlendur stared at the phone in his hand. The caller ID was

blank like last time. He assumed the woman had called from a public payphone; the background noise had suggested as much. When he had her first call traced, it turned out to have been made from the Smáralind shopping mall. Information of this kind had little bearing as a rule. People who called the police from public payphones did so for a reason and avoided using phones near their home or workplace. The location would tell the police nothing.

Pensively, he shoved the phone back in his pocket. Why was the woman calling him? She disclosed no information. She did not tell him why she was in hiding. She did not mention her husband or reveal anything about what she was thinking. Maybe she felt it was enough to let him know that she was alive. She might even be trying to prevent him from looking for her. What was she concealing? Why had she left him?

He had got little response when he put the same questions to her husband. The man shook his head as if he had no idea what was going on. It was almost his sole reaction to the disappearance. It was not until after New Year that Erlendur met his ex-wives and asked them what they thought could have happened. One received him at her home in Hafnarfjördur; her husband was abroad on business. The woman was eager to help Erlendur with his inquiries, eager to tell him what a shit her ex-husband was. He listened to the diatribe, then asked her if she thought her ex was capable of harming his new wife. The answer came instantly.

'No question,' she said. 'I'm certain of it.'

'Why?'

'Men like him,' she said contemptuously, 'they're capable of anything.'

'Have you any proof of what you say?'

'No,' the woman said, 'I just know. He's the type. I bet he's started sleeping around again. Men like that never give up. It's like a disease. It's like a disease with those bastards.'

The other woman was more informative when she came, at her own request, to see Erlendur down at the station. She did not want him to come to her house. He described the case to her and she listened attentively, especially when he began to hint at the possibility that her ex-husband might be involved in his new wife's disappearance.

'Have you no idea what happened to her?' she asked, her eyes wandering around the office.

'Do you think he could have done something to her?' Erlendur asked.

'Is that what you think?'

'We don't think anything,' Erlendur said.

'Yes you do or you wouldn't be asking.'

'It's simply a routine inquiry,' Erlendur said. 'We try to consider every angle. It has no bearing on what we do or don't think.'

'You think he killed her,' the woman said, seeming to perk up.

'I don't think anything,' Erlendur said, more firmly this time.

'He's capable of anything,' the woman said.

'Why do you say that?'

'He once threatened me,' she said. 'Threatened to kill me. I refused to divorce him so he could get married for a third time to that bitch you're looking for. I said I'd never give him a divorce and he'd never be able to marry again. I was very angry, maybe even hysterical. A friend of mine told me about the affair, she'd heard people gossiping about it at work and told me. Everyone knew but me. Do you know how humiliating it is when everyone knows except the person who's being cheated on? I went berserk. He hit me. Then he said he'd kill me if I put up any fucking obstacles.'

'He threatened to kill you?'

'He said he'd throttle me nice and slow till I was dead.'

Erlendur started out of his musings. He looked down at the book he had been perusing and his thoughts returned to the name recorded under the minutes. He remembered who it might be. Sigurdur Óli had mentioned the name and how bad-tempered and unpleasant he had been. If it was the same man, Erlendur would have to bring forward the interview he had scheduled with Kjartan, the school's Icelandic teacher.

His mobile rang. It was Elínborg. She had a printout listing Sunee's incoming calls over the last month. Some were from her ex-mother-in-law, others from the chocolate factory or friends, and twice she had been called from the school.

'Then the same number crops up eight times.'

'Whose is it?'

'It's a business number. An insurance company. It's the only unexpected number on this list, as far as I can see. There aren't many numbers.'

'Have you asked Sunee about it?'

'She claims not to recognise it. Says she vaguely remembers someone trying to sell insurance.'

'Do you think it's the boyfriend?'

'We'll soon find out.'

17

Ever since news of Elías's murder had passed like wildfire round the country, a steady trickle of people had been coming to the block of flats to lay flowers and cards on the spot where his body was found. Toys, teddy bears and model cars could be glimpsed among the bouquets. A memorial service was to be held for Elías in the garden that evening.

Elínborg and Sigurdur Óli were busy in the area. Twice they drove past and saw people laying flowers on the spot. Most of their day was spent interviewing Niran's friends individually. Their accounts tallied in all the main details; none of them admitted to knowing Niran's movements on the afternoon Elías was attacked, nor could they say where Sunee might have taken him. They flatly denied selling drugs at the school, dismissing it as a lie, and although they admitted that they had once come to blows in the school playground, they insisted that it had not been their fault. None of them had seen Elías that day. Two of them had hung around with Niran for a while after school but parted from him at about the time Elías was found. They had been by the chemist's. The two of them had spent the rest of the day together and seen no more of Niran. None was aware that Elías had any particular problems at school. They claimed they'd had no contact with Niran since Elías was found. As far as they knew, the brothers had a very good relationship.

The most talkative and helpful of the boys was called Kári. He seemed genuinely willing to help the police, whereas the other three were very reluctant, gave curt answers and volunteered nothing unless specifically asked. Kári's manner was different. Sigurdur Óli saw him last and was prepared for a fairly brief interview but it turned out to be quite the opposite. The boy was accompanied by his parents; his mother was from Thailand and his father from Iceland. They knew Sunee and her brother and talked of the tragic, incomprehensible event.

'Mostly people just go on about having nothing against immigrants,' the man said. He was an engineer and had taken time off work to provide moral support for his son. He sat at the kitchen table, a tallish, rather overweight figure, with his wife who was small and petite with a friendly, smiling face. The police had contacted them and both were clearly very concerned. The woman had also cut short her day at work as departmental manager at a pharmaceuticals company. The man was talking about his experience of Icelanders, as the husband of a foreigner.

Sigurdur Óli nodded. He was alone. Elínborg had been called away to deal with another matter.

'We say we have nothing against Asian immigrants, nothing against people coming over from Asia and settling here. It's exciting to eat out at Thai restaurants and experience an exotic culture, listen to different music. But when it comes to the crunch people always say that we shouldn't let in "too many" of those people,' the man said, making a sign for quotation marks with his fingers.

'We've discussed it so often,' the woman said, looking at her husband. 'I suppose it's understandable in a way. There are so few Icelanders; they're proud of their heritage and want to preserve it. Their tiny population makes them vulnerable to change. Then along come the immigrants and spoil everything. Many of the people who move here become isolated, whether they're from Asia or wherever, they never learn the language properly and remain outsiders. Others do a better job of fitting in; they realise how important it is and really work at it. Learning the language is absolutely key.'

Her husband nodded. Kári sat looking down at the floor, awaiting his turn.

'Wasn't there something about that on the news the other day?' the man said. 'Some problem with the Icelanders living in Denmark. Their children refused to learn Danish. That's no different, is it?'

'Of course immigration can cause problems,' the woman continued, her eyes on her husband. 'That's nothing new. It happens all over the world. The crucial thing is to help people adapt, though of course they have to show a willingness to adapt themselves if they really want a future in Iceland.'

'What's the worst sort of thing you hear?' Sigurdur Óli asked.

'Fuck off home, Thai bitch.'

She came right out with it, without the slightest hesitation or sign of the impact such words might have on her. As if she had been asked this before and had developed a thick skin to such abuse. As if it was just another fact of life. Kári darted a glance at his mother.

'Do you get the impression that prejudice is on the rise?'

'I don't know,' the man said.

'Do you experience prejudice at school?' Sigurdur Óli asked the boy.

Kári hesitated.

'No-o,' he said uncertainly.

'I don't think you can really expect him to admit to that sort of thing,' the man said. 'No one likes telling tales. Especially not after such a terrible thing has happened.'

'Some other kids have claimed that Kári and his friends are peddling dope at the school. They said it without hesitation.'

'Who said that?' the woman asked.

'It's just something we've heard,' Sigurdur Óli said. 'There's probably no need to take it too seriously at this stage. And I can tell you that the witness was not very reliable.'

'I've never sold any drugs,' Kári said.

'What about your friends?' Sigurdur Óli asked.

'No, they haven't either.'

'And Niran?'

'None of us have,' Kári said. 'It's a lie. We've never sold any drugs. They're lying.'

'Kári doesn't do drugs,' his father said. 'It's out of the question. He doesn't sell drugs either.'

'You would know, would you?' Sigurdur Óli asked.

'Yes, we would,' the man replied.

'Tell us about the trouble at school that we've been hearing about,' Sigurdur Óli said. 'What's really going on?'

Kári stared down at the floor.

'Tell them what you know,' his mother said. 'He hasn't been very happy at school this winter. Some days he hasn't wanted to go in. He thinks people are lying in wait for him, that some of the boys have got it in for him and want to attack him.'

'Mum!' Kári protested, looking at his mother as if she was giving away embarrassing secrets.

'One of Kári's friends was beaten up,' her husband said. 'The school authorities can't seem to do a thing. When there's trouble it seems they're powerless to act. A boy was suspended for a few days, that was it.'

'The school claims there's no overt racism or tension,' Sigurdur Óli said. 'No trouble or fighting beyond what you'd usually expect in a large school. I take it you wouldn't agree with that, judging from what Kári has told you?'

The man shrugged.

'What about Niran?'

'They often have a tough time, boys like Niran,' the woman said. 'It's not easy for them to adjust to a totally alien and remote culture, learn a difficult language, face open hostility, and so on.'

'They can get into trouble,' her husband added.

'Can you tell us anything about that, Kári?'

Kári cleared his throat awkwardly. Sigurdur Óli thought, not for the first time, that it was often better to talk to kids without their parents present.

'I don't know if you understand the seriousness of the matter,' Sigurdur Óli said.

'I think he understands perfectly well what's at stake,' the man said.

'I would be very grateful if you could help us.'

Kári looked from his parents to Sigurdur Óli.

'I don't know how he died,' he said. 'I didn't know Elías at all. He didn't spend much time with Niran. Niran didn't want him tagging along. He was much younger as well. But Niran looked after Elías. Made sure no one bullied him. I have no idea how he died. I don't know who attacked him. None of us know. No one knows what happened. And we haven't a clue what became of Niran that day.'

'How did you get to know Niran?'

Kári sighed. He described his first meeting with the new boy at school. Niran was put in his form and they soon got to know each other as both were the sons of immigrants. Kári had moved to the neighbourhood fairly recently himself and although he had made some good friends who were not from ethnic minorities, he also knew two boys of Filipino origin and one from Vietnam. They in turn were acquainted with Niran's mates from his old school. Niran quickly became the leader of the gang and fed them various facts about what he called their status as the children of immigrants. They were neither nor. They weren't Icelandic. Couldn't be even if they wanted to. To the majority of people they were foreigners, even if they were born in Iceland. Most had experienced prejudice directed at themselves or their families: stares, name-calling, even outright hostility.

Niran was not an Icelander and had no interest in becoming one, but living up here in the Arctic meant that he could hardly call himself Thai either. He realised that he was neither. He belonged to neither country, belonged nowhere except in some invisible, intangible no man's land. Previously he had never had to think about where he came from. He was a Thai, born in Thailand. Now he drew strength from the company of other immigrant children with similar backgrounds and made his best friends among them. He became fascinated with his heritage, with the history of Thailand and the story of his ancestors. The feeling had only intensified when he got to know other, older immigrant children at his last school.

'We gather that he didn't have a very good relationship with his stepfather,' Sigurdur Óli said.

'That's right,' Kári said.

'Any idea why?'

Kári shrugged.

'Niran said he was glad about the divorce because then he wouldn't have to see him any more.'

'Do you know anything about a man Sunee knows, possibly a boyfriend?' Sigurdur Óli asked.

'No.'

'Did Niran never mention that she was seeing someone?'

'No, I don't think so. I don't know anything about that.'

'Where did you last see Niran?'

'I've been ill, so I haven't been to school. I haven't talked to the lads. I last saw Niran a few days ago. We hung out together for a bit after school, then went home.'

'By the chemist's?'

'Yes.'

'Why are you always hanging out by the chemist's?'

'You know, we just meet there sometimes. We don't do anything.'

'What do you usually get up to during the day?' Sigurdur Óli asked.

'Just chill out, mess around, rent a video, play football, whatever we feel like, really. Go to the movies.'

'Do you think Niran did something to his brother?'

'You can't expect him to answer a question like that,' Kári's father interrupted. 'That's outrageous.'

'No way,' Kári said. 'He'd never hurt Elías. I'm certain of it. He always took care of Elías, he was always nice about him.'

'You got into fights at school and here in the neighbourhood, can you tell me about that?' Sigurdur Óli asked. 'And one of your friends was beaten up, you say? Were you afraid of going to school?'

'It wasn't anything serious,' Kári said. 'It's just . . . sometimes there's a bit of aggro and I don't want to get involved. I just want to be left alone.'

'Did you tell that to Niran and the lads?'

'No.'

'Who's head of the other gang?' Sigurdur Óli asked. 'If Niran's your leader?'

Kári did not reply.

'Don't you want to tell us?'

He shook his head.

'There are no leaders,' he said. 'Niran wasn't our leader. We're just a bunch of mates.'

'Who bugs your gang most?' Sigurdur Óli asked.

'He's called Raggi,' Kári said. 'He's the main one.'

'Was it him who attacked one of you?'

'Yes.'

Sigurdur Óli noted down the name. The parents exchanged glances as if they felt this had gone on long enough.

'You asked if I'm aware of any prejudice at school,' Kári said, suddenly breaking the silence.

'Yes,' Sigurdur Óli said.

'It's not just . . . we say stuff too,' Kári said. 'It's not just them. It's us too. I don't know how it started. Niran got into a punch-up with Gummi because of something somebody said. It's all so stupid.'

'What about the teachers?'

Kári nodded hesitantly.

'They're all right, though there is one who hates immigrants.'

'Who's that?'

Kári glanced at his father.

'Kjartan.'

'And what does he do?'

'He can't stand us,' Kári said.

'In what way? Is it something he says or something he does?'

'He says things when no one else can hear.'

'Like what?'

'"You stink of shit."'

'Are you kidding?' Kári's father gasped. 'Why didn't you tell us?'

'They had an argument,' Kári said.

'Who?'

'Kjartan and Niran. I don't know what it was about but I think they almost had a scrap or something. Niran didn't want to talk about it.'

'When was this?'

'The day Elías died.'

The insurance company's public relations officer sat opposite Elínborg, impeccably dressed and sporting a flamboyant tie. There was nothing on his desk but a keyboard and a flat-screen computer, and on the shelves behind him were a few cardboard boxes containing papers, though most were empty. He didn't seem to have much to do, unless it was his first day at work. Elínborg explained the purpose of her visit; someone from the company had phoned a specific number; she mentioned Sunee's name. The police needed to know the identity of the caller, but the list did not show which extension the calls had been made from, only the company's main switchboard number.

'Is this about the boy who died?' the smart PR man asked.

'That's right,' Elínborg said.

'And you want to know . . . ?'

'Whether someone from this office has been phoning his home,' Elínborg said.

'I see,' the PR man said. 'You want to know which extension the calls were made from.'

As she had already explained this, Elínborg wondered whether he was being abnormally reluctant or was simply so pleased at finally having something to do that he was determined to spin it out.

She nodded.

'Firstly, we need to know if the woman holds an insurance policy with the company.'

'What's her name?' the PR man asked, placing beautifully manicured hands on the keyboard.

Elínborg told him.

'No one here by that name,' he said.

'Have you had a sales campaign, cold-calling people or the like, during the last month?'

'No, the last campaign was three months ago. There's been nothing since then.'

'Then I'll have to ask you to keep your ear to the ground for us and find out if any employee of this office knows the woman. How will you go about that?'

'I'll ask around,' the PR man said, leaning back in his chair.

'Keep it low-key, though,' Elínborg said. 'We only want to talk to the individual concerned. That's all. He's not under suspicion. He could be a friend of Sunee's, possibly her boy-friend. Do you think you could make some discreet enquiries for me?'

'Shouldn't be a problem,' the PR man said.

Erlendur rang the doorbell. He heard a squeaking noise from inside the flat as he pressed the bell. Time passed and he rang again. The same squeaking noise. He listened hard. Soon he heard a rustling from inside and finally the door opened. Erlendur had obviously woken the man, although it was midday, but since he appeared to be an old-age pensioner, he could presumably sleep whenever he liked.

Erlendur introduced himself but the man was not yet properly awake, so he was forced to repeat that he was from the police and wanted to know if the man could help him with a minor matter. The man stood at the door and stared at him. Evidently he was not accustomed to receiving a stream of visitors. The bell probably squeaked like that from lack of use.

'Huuhh . . . eh . . . ?' the man said hoarsely, peering at him. His jaw was covered in white stubble.

Erlendur repeated his spiel and the man finally grasped the fact that he had a visitor. Opening the door wider, he invited Erlendur in. He was rather dishevelled, his white hair sticking up in all directions, and his flat was a tip, the air a stale fug. They went into the sitting room where the man sat down on the sofa and leaned forwards. Erlendur took a seat facing him. He noticed that the man had enormous eyebrows; when he moved them they looked like two small furry animals squirming above his eyes.

'I haven't quite grasped what's going on,' the man said. His name, it transpired, was Helgi. 'What do the police want with me?'

The flat was one of several in an old building near a busy road in the eastern part of town. The rumble of traffic was clearly audible. The house was showing its age both outside and inside. It had not been particularly well maintained and large patches of concrete had flaked off the façade; not that any of the residents seemed to care. The stairs were narrow and squalid, the carpet full of holes, and it was dark in the flat, despite the daylight outside, the windows grimy from exhaust fumes.

'You've lived in this house a long time,' Erlendur commented, watching the small furry animals above the man's eyes. 'I wanted to ask you if you remember some neighbours of yours from many years ago. A woman with one child, a boy. She may have lived with a man, who would have been the boy's stepfather. It was a long time ago. We're talking – what? – thirty-five years.'

The man looked at Erlendur without speaking. A long moment passed and Erlendur thought perhaps he had nodded off with his eyes open.

'They lived on the ground floor,' he added.

'What about them?' the man said. So he had not been asleep after all, merely trying to recall the family.

'Nothing,' Erlendur said. 'There's some information we need to pass on to the stepfather, that's all. The woman died some time ago.'

'And the child?'

'It was the child who asked us to trace the man,' Erlendur lied. 'Do you remember these people, by any chance? They lived on the ground floor.'

The man continued to stare at Erlendur without saying a word.

'A woman with one son?' he asked at last.

'And a stepfather.'

'It's a hell of a long time ago,' the man said, beginning to wake up properly from his nap.

'I know,' Erlendur said.

'And what, wasn't he registered as living there with her?'

'No, there's no one registered at the flat during the time she lived there apart from her and her son. But we know this man was living with her.'

Erlendur waited.

'We need the name of the stepfather,' he added, when it became apparent that Helgi was not going to volunteer anything else, merely sit there motionless, staring vacantly at the coffee table.

'Doesn't the child know?' Helgi asked after a pause.

Ah, so he is awake after all, Erlendur thought.

'The child was young,' he said, hoping that this answer would satisfy the man.

'There's a bunch of riff-raff living downstairs now,' Helgi said, continuing to stare absent-mindedly at the table in front of him. 'A pack of yobbos, up all hours making a racket. Doesn't matter how many times I phone you lot, it's not the blindest bit of use. One of those hooligans owns the flat, so it's impossible to turf him out.'

'One's not always lucky with one's neighbours,' Erlendur said, for the sake of saying something. 'Can you help us out at all with this man?'

'What was the woman called?'

'Sigurveig. The child's name was Andrés. I'm trying to cut corners; it would be tricky and time-consuming to trace the man through the system.'

'I remember her,' the man said, looking up. 'Sigurveig, that's right. But hang on a minute, that boy wasn't too young to remember the man who lived with them.'

Helgi gave Erlendur a long speculative look.

'Maybe you're not telling me the whole truth?' he said.

'No,' Erlendur said. 'I'm not.'

A faint smile touched Helgi's lips.

'He's a ruddy menace, that chap downstairs,' he said.

'You never know, it might just be possible to do something about that,' Erlendur said.

'That man you're asking about lived with the woman for several years,' Helgi said. 'I hardly got to know him at all, he seemed to be away a lot. Was he at sea?'

'I haven't the foggiest,' Erlendur said. 'He could well have been. Can you remember his name?'

'Not for the life of me, I'm afraid,' Helgi said. 'I'd forgotten Sigurveig's name too, and it only came to me just now that the boy was called Andrés. It all goes in one ear and out the other, and seldom stops for long in between.'

'And of course a lot of people have come and gone since then,' Erlendur added.

'You can't imagine,' Helgi said, now more or less recovered from the shrill interruption of his afternoon rest and pleased that someone had come round to talk to him and, what's more, seemed to take a greater interest in what he had to say than anyone else had for years. 'But I'm afraid I can't remember much about those people,' he added. 'Hardly a thing, to be honest.'

'It's a general rule in my profession that everything helps, however trivial,' Erlendur said. He had once heard a cop say this on TV and thought it might come in handy.

'Is he supposed to have done something wrong? This man?'

'No,' Erlendur said. 'Andrés approached us. We shouldn't really be wasting our time on this but . . .'

Erlendur shrugged. He saw that Helgi was smiling. By now they were almost bosom buddies.

'If I remember correctly, that fellow came from somewhere in the countryside,' Helgi said. 'He came along with her to a house meeting once, in the days when they still had house meetings. Now you just get a bill, if anyone can be bothered to do anything, which is once in a blue moon. It was one of the few occasions that I met him.'

'Can you describe him to me?'

'Not really. Quite tall. Strongly built. Made a good impression. Quite pleasant, if I remember correctly. He moved out, as far as I can recall. They split up, didn't they? I don't know why. You should talk to Emma. She used to live opposite them.'

'Emma?'

'Wonderful person, Emma. Moved out about twenty years ago but still keeps in touch, sends Christmas cards and so on. She lives in Kópavogur now. She's sure to remember more than me. Talk to her. I just can't remember those people well enough.'

'Do you remember anything in particular about the boy?'

'The boy? No . . . except . . .' Helgi paused.

'Yes?' Erlendur said.

'I seem to recall that he was always rather hangdog, poor little wretch. A sad little chap, a bit scruffy, as if no one took proper care of him. The few times I tried to talk to him I got the feeling he wanted to avoid me.'

Andrés was standing out in the cold, a short distance from a corrugated-iron-clad house on Grettisgata, his eyes fixed on a basement window. He could not see inside and did not dare to risk going any closer. About six months ago he had trailed the man he had mentioned to the police to this house and seen him disappear into the basement flat. He had followed him, keeping a little way behind, from the block of flats and onto a bus. The man did not notice him. They had got out at the Hlemmur bus station and Andrés had followed him to this house.

Now he was standing at a safe distance, trying to protect himself from the bitter north wind. He had walked the short way from Hlemmur several times since then and ascertained that the man had a second home on Grettisgata.

Andrés dug his hands into his pockets.

He sniffed, his eyes wet from the cold, and stamped his feet before walking away.

18

Kjartan was not at home but the detectives said that they would wait. The woman regarded them in astonishment.

'Out here?' she asked, her features stretching in surprise.

Erlendur shrugged.

'Why do you keep wanting to talk to Kjartan?' she asked.

'It's in connection with the incident at the school,' Elínborg said. 'Routine procedure. We're interviewing teachers and pupils.'

'I thought you'd already talked to him.'

'We need to talk to him again,' Elínborg said.

The woman looked from one of them to the other and they sensed that she would have preferred to shut the door in their faces and never see them again.

'Wouldn't you rather come in?' she asked after an awkward pause.

'Thank you,' Erlendur said and ushered Elínborg inside before him. Two children, a boy and a girl, watched them enter the living room and take a seat. Erlendur would rather have talked to Kjartan down at the station or at the school but he had been avoiding them. He failed to turn up for a meeting at the station and when they went to pick him up from the school he was not there. As he was not answering his phone either,

Elínborg suggested they pay him a visit at home and Erlendur had agreed.

'He took the car to the garage to get it looked at,' the woman said.

'I see,' Erlendur said.

It was evening and the woman had been making supper in the kitchen when they knocked on the door. She did not elaborate on the business with the car. She said she had heard from Kjartan that afternoon but not since then. Sensing her apprehension at the visit from the police, Erlendur tried to reassure her, repeating Elínborg's words about routine procedure.

The woman was not entirely convinced, however, and when she went back into the kitchen she took her mobile with her. The two children followed, turning round in the kitchen doorway to stare wide-eyed at the detectives. Elínborg smiled at them. The woman's voice carried into the living room. They heard her voice rise sharply at one point, then fall silent. Some time passed before she emerged. By then she was calmer.

'Kjartan's been slightly held up,' she said, trying to smile. 'He'll be here in five minutes.'

'Thank you,' Elínborg said.

'Can I offer you anything?' the woman asked.

'Coffee, please, if there's any in the pot,' Erlendur said.

The woman disappeared back into the kitchen. The children were still standing in the doorway, staring at them.

'Maybe this wasn't such a good idea,' Elínborg murmured to Erlendur after a long silence. She didn't take her eyes off the children.

'It was your idea,' Erlendur said.

'I know, but isn't it a bit OTT?'

'OTT?'

'We could make up some lie about a call-out. I had no idea it would be so awkward. If he comes, we could nab him outside.'

'Maybe you should never have quit geology,' Erlendur said.

'Geology?'

'Bits of rock don't give you this sort of bother,' Erlendur said.

'Oh, ha ha!' Elínborg replied.

She had managed to irritate him in the car on the way over. Started quizzing him about Valgerdur and their future plans, and Erlendur had instantly retreated into silence. Elínborg was not daunted, however, even when he told her not to keep asking those infernal bloody questions. She asked if Valgerdur was still involved in some way with her former husband, a question that Erlendur would have had to answer in the affirmative, if he had answered at all, and if she ever intended to move in with him, a matter that he had still not confronted himself. Elínborg's tendency to pry into his private life got on his nerves at times; questions about Eva Lind and Sindri Snaer, about himself. She seemed incapable of leaving well alone.

'Are you conducting a distance relationship, by any chance?' she asked. 'Lots of people prefer it to living together.'

'Will you give me a break?' Erlendur said. 'I don't know what you mean by a distance relationship.'

Elínborg shut up temporarily, then began to hum the tune to a well-known poem by Steinn Steinarr: *Cadet Jón Kristófer, the Sally Army meeting's at seven, when Lieutenant Valgerdur will show you the way to heaven . . .*'

She kept up her humming until Erlendur lost patience.

'I don't know how things'll work out,' he said. 'And it's none of your business anyway.'

'All right,' Elínborg said, still humming.

'*Lieutenant Valgerdur*...!' Erlendur snapped.

'What?'

'The things you come out with!'

Kjartan's wife emerged from the kitchen with some coffee cups. Her face wore a look of acute anxiety. The children followed and were left standing in the middle of the room at something of a loss when their mother returned to the kitchen to fetch the coffee. At that moment the door opened and Kjartan came in. Elínborg and Erlendur rose to their feet.

'Is this really necessary?' Kjartan said, clearly agitated.

'We've been trying to get hold of you all day,' Elínborg pointed out.

Kjartan's wife came in with a coffee pot.

'What's going on?' she asked her husband.

'Nothing,' Kjartan said, immediately calming down. He spoke reassuringly to his wife. 'I told you on the phone, it's because of the attack on the boy at school.'

'What about it? It doesn't have anything to do with you, does it?'

'No,' Kjartan said, looking at the detectives as if for help.

'We're talking to all the teachers at the school, as I've already told you,' Elínborg said. 'Could we maybe sit down somewhere where we won't be disturbed?'

She addressed her words to Kjartan, who hesitated. He looked at the three of them in turn and they all waited for him to speak. At last he nodded.

'I have a study down in the basement,' he said reluctantly. 'We can go in there. Is that all right?' he asked his wife.

'Take the coffee with you,' she said.

Kjartan smiled.

'Thanks, love, I'll be up as soon as they've gone.'

Picking up his younger child he kissed her, then stroked the elder child's hair.

'Daddy'll be right back,' he said. 'He just needs to talk to these people, then he'll be back.'

Kjartan showed them down to the basement. He had set up a study for himself in a little storeroom with a desk, computer and printer, books and papers. There was only one chair, which he occupied himself. The two detectives stood by the door. Kjartan had led them down to the basement in silence but now his anger seemed to erupt.

'What do you mean by persecuting me in my own home like this?' he snarled. 'In front of my family! Did you see the look on my children's faces? Do you really think this is an acceptable way to behave?'

Erlendur did not respond. Elínborg was poised to speak but Kjartan pre-empted her.

'Am I some sort of criminal? What have I done to deserve this kind of treatment?'

'We've been trying to get hold of you all day,' Erlendur said again. 'You haven't been answering your phone. We decided to check if you were at home. Your wife was kind enough to invite us in and make coffee. Then you turned up. Is that any reason to get excited? We only came round to try to catch you at home. Luckily, we did. Do you want to make a complaint?'

Kjartan looked at them in turn.

'What do you want with me?' he asked.

'Perhaps we could begin with something that calls or called itself "Fathers of Iceland",' Erlendur said.

Kjartan smirked. 'And with that you think you've solved the case, do you?'

'I don't think anything,' Erlendur said.

'I was eighteen years old,' Kjartan said. 'It was kids' stuff. You can imagine. Fathers of Iceland! Only kids come up with that sort of crap. Teenagers trying to sound big.'

'I know plenty of eighteen year olds who couldn't even spell Weimar Republic.'

'Look, we were a bunch of college boys,' Kjartan said. 'It was a joke. It was fifteen years ago. I can't believe you're going to try and smear me as some kind of racist because of what happened to that boy.'

Kjartan said this sneeringly, as if any connection to the case was so far-fetched that it was a joke, and Elínborg and Erlendur were jokes as well; dumb cops barking up the wrong tree. There was something inexpressibly arrogant about the way he lounged in his chair, legs splayed, grinning at their stupidity. As if he pitied them for not having the same watertight view of life as him. Elías's fate did not seem to have touched him in the slightest.

'What did you mean when you said that an attack like the one on Elías was only a matter of time?' Elínborg asked.

'I think it's self-explanatory. What do people expect when they let those people in? Everything's supposed to be just fine, is it? We aren't prepared for it. People pour into this country from all over the world to do menial jobs and we turn a blind eye. We're all supposed to be one big, happy family. Well, it doesn't work like that and it never will. The Asian lot create their own little ghetto, cling to their customs and traditions and make sure they don't marry outside their own community. They don't bother to learn the language, so of course they underachieve at school – how many of them make it to university? Most drop out of education once they've finished compulsory schooling, grateful not to have to waste any more time on crappy Icelandic history, the crappy Icelandic language!'

'I see you haven't entirely given up on Fathers of Iceland,' Erlendur remarked drily.

'Yeah, right, the moment anyone says anything they're branded a bloody racist. No one's allowed to open their mouth. Everyone has to be so diplomatic. A positive addition to Icelandic culture and all that crap. Fucking bollocks!'

'Do you think Elías's attacker was of Asian origin?'

'Of course you lot have ruled that out entirely, haven't you?' Kjartan said contemptuously.

'Do you talk like that to your pupils?' Elínborg asked. 'Do you talk about immigrants like that to your pupils?'

'I don't see what that's got to do with you,' Kjartan retorted.

'Do you stir up trouble between the kids at school?' Elínborg continued.

Kjartan looked from one of them to the other.

'Who have you been talking to? Where did you get hold of that stuff about Fathers of Iceland? What have you been digging up?'

'Answer the question,' Erlendur said.

'I haven't done anything of the sort,' Kjartan said. 'If anyone says I have, they're lying.'

'It's what we've been told,' Elínborg said.

'Well, it's a lie. I haven't been inciting anyone to do anything. Who says I have?'

The detectives did not answer.

'Don't I have a right to know?' Kjartan asked.

Erlendur stared at him without saying a word. He had looked Kjartan up in the police records and found nothing but a speeding fine. He had never been in any trouble with the law.

Kjartan was a respectable citizen, an upstanding family man and a good father, from what Erlendur could tell.

'How did you arrive at the conclusion that you're somehow better than other people?'

'I'm not saying I am.'

'It seems blindingly obvious from everything you say and do.'

'Is that any of your business?'

Erlendur looked at him.

'No, none at all.'

Ragnar, nicknamed Raggi at school, sat face to face with Sigurdur Óli at home in his living room. His mother sat beside him, looking anxious. She was divorced; Ragnar was the eldest of her three children and she struggled to make ends meet as the sole breadwinner. She'd had a chat with Sigurdur Óli before Raggi came home. 'It's not easy to provide for three children,' she'd said, as if excusing herself in advance. Yet Sigurdur Óli had done nothing but trot out the usual cliché about routine inquiries due to the incident at the school; the police were speaking to a number of pupils from different forms. The woman listened with apparent understanding, but since the police had come round to the little basement flat she rented for an extortionate amount from the rich old lady upstairs, who owned the whole house and at least three fur coats, it seemed a good opportunity to pour out her troubles. The mother was very overweight and short of breath; she smoked almost incessantly. The air in the flat was stifling. Sigurdur Óli never saw the other two children during his visit. The flat was littered with dirty laundry, junk mail and newspapers. The mother stubbed out her cigarette and he gave a despairing thought to his clothes. They would reek of smoke for days.

Raggi was initially alarmed to see a police officer in his home but quickly recovered. He was tall for his age with a shock of jet-black hair and acne, especially round his mouth. He seemed on edge. Sigurdur Óli began by asking him general questions about the school, the atmosphere there, the teachers and older kids, before gradually bringing the conversation round to immigrants and Niran. Raggi answered mainly in monosyllables. He was polite. His mother stayed out of the conversation and just sat there lighting one cigarette from another and drinking coffee. She had only just come home from work when Sigurdur Óli rang the doorbell. The coffee she made was good and strong, and he waited for her to offer him another cup. He used to be a tea drinker but Bergthóra had taught him to appreciate coffee through her connoisseurship of different types of beans and roasts.

'How do you get on with Kjartan who teaches Icelandic?' he asked.

'He's all right,' Raggi said.

'He's not keen on coloured people, is he?'

'Maybe not,' Raggi said.

'How does it show? In something he says or something he does?'

'No, just, you know.'

'Just what?'

'Nothing.'

'Did you know Elías?'

'No.'

'What about his brother, Niran?'

Raggi hesitated.

'Yes.'

Sigurdur Óli was on the point of mentioning Kári but

refrained. He did not want to give Raggi any reason to suspect that he had just come from visiting the other boy.

'How?'

'You know,' Raggi said.

'You know what?'

'He thinks he's special.'

'In what way?'

'He calls us Eskimos.'

'What do you call him?'

'A dickhead.'

'Do you know what happened to his brother?'

'No.'

'Can you tell me where you were when he was attacked?'

Raggi stopped and thought. He had clearly not considered the question before and it occurred to Sigurdur Óli that he must be a bloody hardened case if he could act that well. Finally the answer came.

'We were at the Kringlan shopping mall, me, Ingvar and Danni.'

It was consistent with the accounts given by his friends Ingvar and Danni whom Sigurdur Óli had already questioned. Both flatly denied any involvement in the attack on Elías, claimed ignorance about drug-dealing at the school and talked of minor scraps with pupils from ethnic minorities. The three friends were known troublemakers at the school and no one could wait for them to finish their compulsory education that spring and leave for good. They went in for bullying, and had caused a major stir at New Year when two of them had been suspended for a week for setting off explosions in and around the school, using fireworks left over from New Year's Eve, big firecrackers and powerful rockets that they had tampered with to make them even more potent. One of them had let off the largest make of rocket in a corridor and the explosion had shattered two large panes of glass. The whole school rocked and it was only by a miracle that no one was around because teaching was in full swing.

'When did you last see Elías?' Sigurdur Óli asked.

'Elías? I don't know. I don't know him at all. I never see him.'

'Have there been serious clashes at school between your gang and Niran's lot?'

'No, just, you know, that lot are always showing off.'

Raggi paused.

'The immigrants?' Sigurdur Óli prompted.

'Iceland should be for us. For the Icelanders. Not for a load of foreigners.'

'We know there have been clashes between gangs,' Sigurdur Óli said. 'We know these can be serious at times. Not just in this part of town. But we're also aware that few of them run very deep. Would you agree?'

'I . . . I don't know.'

'Then this incident with Elías happens.'

'Yeah.'

'Do you think it's connected to the fights between your gangs?'

'I don't know. Probably not. I mean, we wouldn't do anything like that. We'd never kill anyone. That's ridiculous. We don't do that kind of thing. It's not like that.'

'Are you sure?'

The mother had sat silently smoking throughout their conversation. Now she intervened.

'You think my Raggi attacked that boy?' she said, as if it had finally dawned on her why a policeman had entered her home and started asking a series of questions about racial tension at the school.

'I don't think anything,' Sigurdur Óli said. 'Do you know anything about drug-dealing at the school?' he asked Raggi.

'My Raggi's not involved in drugs,' the mother said instantly.

'That's not what I asked,' Sigurdur Óli said.

'I don't know anything about any drugs at the school,' Raggi said.

'No, that's right, you just let off fireworks in the corridors,' Sigurdur Óli said.

'I—' Raggi began, but his mother interrupted.

'He's been punished for that,' she said. 'And it wasn't even him that did the worst damage.'

'Is it possible that someone is dealing drugs and someone else owes him money and the debt could have resulted in the sort of thing that happened to Elías?' Sigurdur Óli asked, suddenly realising how the mother justified her son's behaviour to herself.

Raggi stopped to think for the second time in their conversation.

'No one from the school's dealing drugs,' he said after a pause. 'Sometimes people hang around the school gates, selling something. Or at the school discos. That's all. I don't know about any other cases. No one's tried to sell me anything.'

'Do you know what happened to Elías?'

'No.'

'Do you know who attacked him?'

'No.'

'Do you know where Niran was the day his brother was attacked?'

'No. I just saw when Kjartan knocked him down in the road.'

'Kjartan the Icelandic teacher?'

'Niran scratched his car. Right down the side. Kjartan went mental.'

Sigurdur Óli stared at Raggi. He remembered what Kári had said about Kjartan and Niran.

'Will you say that again?'

Raggi sensed that he had said something important and immediately began to backtrack.

'I didn't see it, I only heard about it,' he said. 'Someone said he had attacked Niran because Niran scratched the side of his car.'

'When? When was this?'

'The morning of the day the boy died.'

'More coffee?' his mother asked, exhaling smoke.

'Thanks, maybe I'll have a drop,' Sigurdur Óli said, taking out his phone. He selected Erlendur's number.

'What else?' he asked.

'I don't know,' Raggi said. 'That's all I heard.'

19

The search for Niran had still yielded no results by the evening of Elías's memorial service. A large crowd joined the torchlit procession that filed in silence to the block of flats, led by the local vicar. Sunee, present with Ódinn, Virote and Sigrídur, was deeply touched by this show of warmth and solidarity.

It was not enough, however, to persuade her to entrust her son to the police. She stubbornly refused to reveal where she was hiding him, and neither her brother nor anyone connected to them would provide any information on that score.

Erlendur and Elínborg attended the memorial service and watched the procession moving slowly towards the flats. Elínborg held a small handkerchief concealed in her hand and raised it unobtrusively to her eyes from time to time.

Erlendur phoned Valgerdur when he got back to the office. He knew it was her shift at the hospital. While waiting for her to come to the phone, he had begun, quite oblivious to the fact, to whistle Elínborg's tune about Cadet Jón Kristófer of the Sally Army, and Lieutenant Valgerdur, who showed him the way to heaven. When he realised what he was doing, he cursed Elínborg.

'Hello,' Valgerdur answered.

'Just thought I'd give you a call,' Erlendur said. 'I'm about to call it a day.'

'I'm going to have to work all night,' Valgerdur said. 'A little boy came in for a blood test and it's a clear case of domestic violence. He's only seven. We've notified the police and the Child Welfare—'

'Please don't tell me any more,' Erlendur said.

'Sorry . . . I . . .' Valgerdur faltered. It wasn't the first time this had happened. She wanted to share something that she'd experienced at work but he forestalled her. He rarely spoke to her about the sordid side of life that he encountered in his job as a detective. In his opinion it had nothing to do with the two of them. As if he wanted to protect their relationship from all the squalor. It was not so much an escape from all the ugliness and injustice of the world, more a brief respite.

'It's just . . . when you work with that stuff, day in, day out, you long to hear about something different,' he said now. 'You want to know that there's more to life than endless bloody filth.'

'Are you getting anywhere with the case of the boy?'

'We're not making any progress.'

'We saw the procession on television. You haven't found his brother yet?'

'His mother's afraid,' Erlendur said. 'She'll talk to us once she's got over her fear.'

Neither of them spoke. Erlendur liked talking to Valgerdur. The mere sound of her voice on the phone was enough for him. She had a beautiful voice, low and mellow, which automatically made him feel better. He couldn't quite put his finger on it, but sometimes he just longed to hear her speak. Like now.

'An old colleague of mine has just died,' he said at last. 'I've mentioned Marion Briem to you.'

'Yes, I recognise the name. Unusual.'

'Marion died yesterday after a long illness. It probably came as a relief but it was rather a lonely death. Marion had no family. Was my boss for donkey's years, but retired a while back. I didn't visit often enough. It didn't occur to me until too late. Marion didn't have many visitors. I was one of the few. Perhaps the only one, I don't know. Sometimes I had the feeling I was the only one.'

Erlendur fell silent and Valgerdur waited for him to continue. She didn't want to disturb his train of thought, sensing that he needed to talk to her, but the pause became so prolonged that she began to wonder if Erlendur was still there.

'Erlendur?' she said when she could no longer bear the silence.

'Yes, sorry, I was just thinking about it all. Marion asked me to handle the funeral arrangements. It's all been set in motion. That's how it ends. Life. All that long life, only to end up alone and abandoned in a hospital bed.'

'What are you talking about, Erlendur?'

'I don't know. Death . . .' He trailed off again.

'Eva Lind came round,' he said eventually.

'Wasn't that nice?'

'I suppose so, I'm not sure. She looks better. I haven't seen her for weeks and then she turns up out of the blue. Typical. It's . . . She's become a woman. It suddenly struck me. There was something about her, something different. More mature, I think, calmer. Maybe the whole thing's blowing over. Maybe she's had enough.'

'We all grow older.'

'True.'

'What did she want?'

'I think she wanted to tell me about a dream she had.'

'You think?'

'She left before she could tell me. I suppose I told her to go. I think I know what she wants. She was asking what happened when Bergur died. She thought her dream was somehow connected. I didn't want to hear it.'

'It was only a dream,' Valgerdur said.

'The thing is, I haven't told her everything. I haven't told her why he was never found. There were various theories. She seemed to know about them.'

'Theories?'

'He should have been found,' Erlendur said.

'But . . . ?'

'He never was.'

'What sort of theories?'

'The moor. Or the river.'

'But you don't want to talk about it?'

'It has nothing to do with anyone else,' Erlendur said. 'It's an old story that has nothing to do with anyone else.'

'And you want to keep it to yourself.'

Erlendur did not reply.

'Eva's your daughter,' Valgerdur said. 'You spoke to her about this once.'

'That's the headache,' Erlendur said.

'Find out what she has to say. Listen to her.'

'I suppose I'll have to,' Erlendur said.

Again he paused.

'I keep thinking about that boy lying alone and abandoned in the snow behind the block of flats. I don't understand what could have happened. I can't fathom it, not for the life of me.'

'Of course, it's too horrific for words.'

'I . . . it made me think about my brother. He was the same

age as Elías, a little younger. All alone. I started thinking about all those lonely deaths. About Marion Briem.'

'Erlendur, it's not as if you could ever have put it right. You could never have done anything. It was never your responsibility. You have to understand that.'

Erlendur did not speak.

'I'll be stuck here all night,' Valgerdur repeated in an apologetic tone. She had already spent too long on the phone.

'That's what you get for being a biotechnician,' Erlendur said.

'We're not biotechnicians any more,' Valgerdur said.

'Really? What are you then?'

'We're biomedical scientists.'

'What?'

'Times change.'

'What'll become of the biotechnicians then?'

'We're not going anywhere, we've just changed our name.'

'Biotechnician's a perfectly good name.'

'You've heard the last of it.'

'Shame.'

A silence developed.

'Sorry to offload on you like this,' Erlendur said. 'We'll talk properly later.'

'You're not offloading on me,' Valgerdur said. 'Don't talk like that. I'm free tomorrow evening.'

'Maybe I'll see you then,' Erlendur said.

'Listen to Eva,' Valgerdur repeated.

Erlendur went out into the corridor and down to the interview room where Sigurdur Óli and Elínborg were questioning Kjartan about the scratch on his car and reports that he had blamed Niran for it and assaulted him. Kjartan was not under arrest. When Sigurdur Óli phoned Erlendur with the information and Erlendur confronted Kjartan with it, he had lost his temper and started hurling abuse at them. But after ranting about lies and conspiracies for a while, he finally admitted that he had held Niran responsible for the scratch. He had not so much as harmed a hair on his head, however; stories of his attacking Niran were completely unfounded.

He accompanied them down to the station without protest. Sigurdur Óli was given the job of interviewing him. The car was a newish Volvo that Kjartan said he had owned for less than a year. It was already undergoing repairs at his cousin's garage. On further questioning it transpired that the scratch had already been repaired and the car was waiting to be resprayed. Photos of the damage taken for Kjartan's insurance company showed a narrow scratch running from the rear lights, over the wing and doors to the front lights. The cost of repairing such a scratch was high and Kjartan was involved in a row with his insurance company who were trying to exploit a loophole. The photos could not provide conclusive evidence of the type of instrument used to make the scratch but a knife seemed likely, though it could have been a screwdriver, or even a key.

It was uncertain as yet whether Kjartan would be detained in custody. He was vehement that it was utterly absurd to link the vandalism to the attack on Elías later that day. He had not noticed the scratch when he left for work that morning. It had been pitch dark outside and when pressed he was unable to say with any certainty whether the car had been vandalised in the school car park. He lived in a different neighbourhood, but it was only half an hour's walk from the school. He had noticed the scratch when he went out to run a quick errand into town at lunchtime. Spotting Niran and a friend loitering near the car park, he had asked if they knew anything about the scratch but Niran had jeered at him. He never hit the boy. They had an exchange of words which were not exactly polite, as Kjartan admitted, but he did not knock the boy down in the street. The police need only talk to the other boy, who witnessed the incident.

Erlendur opened the door and entered the interview room.

'Why didn't you tell us about this?' Sigurdur Óli asked. 'Why did we have to find out from someone else?'

'I didn't think it was relevant,' Kjartan said, looking at Erlendur who leaned against the wall with arms folded. 'It's absurd to try and link it to the attack on the boy. I don't understand how you can connect the two incidents. I asked Niran if he had damaged my car and he just laughed in my face. I got nothing out of him.'

'So you lost your temper,' Sigurdur Óli said.

'Of course I did,' Kjartan said, his voice rising. 'You'd have lost your temper too. How would you like to get reaction like that?'

'From what we hear, you were unusually touchy at school that morning.'

'You mean the business with Finnur?'

Sigurdur Óli nodded.

'That was nothing. We're always arguing.'

'Was Niran carrying a sharp object or did he say something that implied he had vandalised your car?'

'I wanted to know if he had a knife or screwdriver on him,' Kjartan said. 'So I grabbed at him and he struggled. I didn't throw him in the street. He tore himself away from me and fell. I left him alone after that. I never did find out if he had a knife or anything. Are you going to arrest me for that?'

Sigurdur Óli glanced at Erlendur whose expression was unreadable.

'I didn't do anything to that boy,' Kjartan said. 'If you arrest me it's tantamount to branding me a murderer. Maybe only for one day but that's all it takes. What if you never find the person who did it? I'll be branded for life! And I haven't done anything!'

'You express antipathy to immigrants,' Erlendur said. 'Not just resentment, but out-and-out hatred. You don't deny it. You admit it. You're proud of it. You show it in a variety of ways. Surely you don't think it's our job to clean up your image?'

'You have no right to insult me just because you don't share my views!'

'No one's insulting you,' Sigurdur Óli said.

Erlendur asked Sigurdur Óli to step outside for a moment. Kjartan watched them go. 'I haven't done anything!' he yelled as the door of the interview room closed.

'He's got a point,' Sigurdur Óli remarked when they were outside in the corridor.

'Of course,' Erlendur said. 'It's the most pathetic motive I've ever heard for a murder. Kjartan's all bark and no bite. He has no record of violence, has never been in trouble with the police. We'll let him go. But hold him as long as possible.'

'Erlendur, we can't—'

'Oh, all right,' Erlendur said huffily and stalked off down the corridor. 'Let him go now, then.'

Bergthóra was still up when Sigurdur Óli came home late that evening. She was waiting for him. He had not been home much recently, not only because of Elías's murder but for other reasons. She thought he was avoiding her. The way she saw it, and had put it to him, their relationship was at a crossroads.

Since there was no question of their having a child together, they had to decide where to go from there.

Sigurdur Óli went into the kitchen and poured himself a glass of fruit juice. He had visited the gym on the way home and been the last to leave. He had pounded the treadmill and pumped iron until the sweat poured off him.

'Any news of the case?' Bergthóra asked, coming into the kitchen in her dressing gown.

'No,' Sigurdur Óli said. 'Nothing. We don't have a clue what happened.'

'Wasn't it racially motivated?'

'No idea. We'll just have to see.'

'Poor child. And the mother. She must be going through sheer hell.'

'Yes. How are you?'

Sigurdur Óli wanted to tell her that Elías had attended his old school, and how odd it had felt to revisit his old haunts and see a photo of himself from the disco era. But he refrained. He didn't know why. Perhaps he was tired.

'Not too tired to skip your workout,' Bergthóra would have retorted.

Once he would have been happy to share the details of his day with her.

'I'm fine,' Bergthóra said now.

'I think I'll go straight to bed,' Sigurdur Óli said, putting his glass in the sink.

'We need to talk,' Bergthóra said.

'Can't we do it tomorrow?'

'It's tomorrow now,' she said. 'I keep wanting to talk to you but you're never home. I've started to think you're avoiding me.'

'Work's frantic at the moment. Your job's frantic too sometimes. We both work a lot. I'm not avoiding anything.'

'What do you want to do?'

'I don't know, Begga,' Sigurdur Óli said. 'It just seems rather a drastic step to me.'

'People adopt children every day of the year,' Bergthóra said. 'Why shouldn't we do it?'

'I'm not saying . . . I just want to be careful.'

'What are you scared of?'

'I've just never imagined that I would adopt a child. I've never needed to give the matter any thought. It's a completely new and alien concept for me. I understand that it isn't for you, but it is for me.'

'I know it's a big step.'

'Maybe too big,' Sigurdur Óli said.

'What do you mean by that?'

'Maybe it's not for everyone. Adoption.'

'You mean maybe it's not for you?'

'I don't know. Can't we sleep on it?'

'That's what you always say.'

'I know.'

'Go to bed then!'

'Look, we've been quarrelling about this for far too long. Babies, adoption . . . '

'I know.'

'I go around with a knot in my stomach all day long.'

'I know.'

'Can't we just forget it?'

'No,' Bergthóra said, 'we can't.'

20

The block of flats was still under police guard. Erlendur spoke briefly to the officer on duty on the staircase. He had nothing to report. The residents had trickled home from work towards evening and a variety of cooking smells began to permeate the landing. Sunee had been at home all day. Her brother was with her.

It was late. Erlendur was on his way home but still had a few calls to make. The first was to the morgue on Barónsstígur. He saw at once that something terrible had happened. Two bodies covered in white sheets were carried into the building on stretchers. People were gathering, Erlendur did not know why, until he was informed that a serious accident had occurred on the main road out of town, near Mosfellsbaer. He had not heard the news. Three people had lost their lives in a five-car pile-up, an elderly woman and two teenage boys, one of whom had only recently passed his driving test. An ambulance pulled up, bringing the last body. The families of the deceased were standing around in a state of shock. There was blood on the floor. Someone threw up.

Erlendur was about to make his escape when he ran into the pathologist. He was acquainted with him through work. The man sometimes indulged in gallows humour, which Erlendur guessed was his method of coping in a pretty grim profession. He was in no mood for jokes now, however, as he stared at Erlendur in momentary confusion. Erlendur said he would call back another time.

'Your boy's in there,' the pathologist said, nodding towards a closed door.

'I'll come back later,' Erlendur repeated.

'I haven't found anything,' the pathologist said.

'It's all right, I—'

'There was dirt under his fingernails but I don't think that's anything out of the ordinary. Two of his nails were broken. We found traces of fibres. There must have been a struggle. That's obvious from the bad rip in his anorak too. Didn't the mother say it had been in good condition? I assume you'll be able to make some kind of connection if you can trace the article of clothing. Your forensics team is analysing the fibres to find out what type of material they come from, though of course they could be from his own clothes.'

'And the stab wound?'

'Nothing new there,' the pathologist said, opening the door. 'The wound penetrated the liver and the boy would have bled to death relatively quickly. The incision is not particularly large, the instrument that inflicted it would have been fairly broad but needn't have been especially long. I simply can't work out what kind of instrument it was.'

'A screwdriver?'

The pathologist frowned. He paused in the doorway. He was needed elsewhere.

'I hardly think so. Something sharper. It's really a very neat incision.'

'He wasn't stabbed through his anorak?'

'No, his anorak was unzipped. He was stabbed through a cheap sweater and vest. They were the only obstacles, his only protection.'

'Would there have been splashes of blood?'

'Not necessarily. It's a single straightforward stab wound which caused massive internal haemorrhaging. The blood wouldn't necessarily have splashed his assailant, but he might have had to clean himself up.'

The pathologist closed the door. Erlendur walked over to the body and lifted the sheet that covered it. Looking at the neat little stab wound, he pondered the possibility which had occurred to him earlier that day: that the same instrument had been used to stab the boy as the one used to scratch Kjartan's car. The incision in his side was so small as to be barely visible but it was in precisely the right place to inflict irreversible damage. A few centimetres either way and Elías might have survived the attack. Erlendur had already discussed this detail with the pathologist who would not commit himself but admitted that it was conceivable the attacker knew what he was doing.

As he draped the sheet over Elías's body again, he wondered how Sunee must feel, knowing that her son was in this grim place. Surely she must start cooperating with the police soon; the alternative was unthinkable. Maybe she believed her son was in danger. Maybe she was protecting Niran from the furore that had raged in society since his brother's death. Maybe she did not want pictures of him in the press and on television. Maybe she did not want all that attention. And maybe, just maybe, Niran knew something that had forced Sunee to send him into hiding.

The cold had intensified by the time Erlendur drove away, his eyes reflecting the frozen grief at the morgue.

Sunee met him at the door. She assumed that he was bringing news of the investigation but Erlendur said straight away that nothing new had emerged. She was still up; her brother Virote was asleep in her room and he sensed that she was glad of the company. He had not spoken to her before without the presence of either her brother or the interpreter. She invited him into the living room, then went into the kitchen to make tea. When she returned she sat down on the sofa and poured out two cups.

'All people come outside,' she said.

'We don't want that kind of violence,' Erlendur said. 'Nobody does.'

'I thank everything,' Sunee said. 'It was so beautiful.'

'Will you trust me with your son?' Erlendur asked.

Sunee shook her head.

'You can't hide him for ever.'

'You find murderer,' she said. 'I look after Niran.'

'All right.'

'Elías good boy. Not do nothing.'

'I don't believe he was attacked because of anything he did. But it's possible he was attacked because of what he was. Do you understand?'

Sunee nodded.

'Have you any idea who might have wanted to attack him?'

'No,' Sunee said.

'Are you quite sure?'

'Yes.'

'The kids at school?'

'No.'

'One of the teachers?'

'No. No one. All good to Elías.'

'What about Niran? He doesn't seem very happy.'

'Niran good boy. Just angry. Not want to live in Iceland.'

'Where is he?'

She didn't answer.

'All right,' Erlendur said. 'It's up to you. Think about it. Maybe you'll tell me tomorrow. We need to talk to him. It's very important.'

Sunee looked at him in silence.

'I know it's difficult for you and that you want to do what you feel is right. I understand that. But you must also understand that this is a sensitive murder investigation.'

Sunee remained mute.

'Did Niran mention anything about the Icelandic teacher, Kjartan?'

'No.'

'Nothing about a quarrel between them?'

'No.'

'What did he say to you?'

'Not much. He just scared. Me too.'

Sunee glanced over at the small corridor leading to the bedrooms, where her brother now appeared. She held out her hand to him.

'Do you mind if I take a quick look in Elías's room?' Erlendur asked, rising to his feet.

'Okay,' Sunee said.

She met his eye.

'I want to help,' she said. 'But I look after Niran too.'

Erlendur smiled and went through the little corridor to the boys' room. He switched on a small desk lamp that cast a feeble glow over the room.

He didn't know exactly what he was looking for. The police had already searched the room without finding any clues as to where Niran might be hiding. He sat down on a chair and recalled that he and his brother Bergur had shared a room like this in the old days at home in the east.

As Erlendur examined the room, he reflected on the brutal act that had cut short Elías's life. He tried to fit it into the criminal landscape that he knew so well but was completely at a loss. No mercy had been shown to Elías when he fell wounded on the path. No one had been there to help him in his pathetic struggle to reach home. No one had been there to warm him when he froze to the icy ground behind the block of flats.

He looked around. Model dinosaurs of every shape and size trooped round the room. Two pictures of dinosaurs were Blu-Tacked to the wall above the bunks. In one a menacing tyrannosaurus bared its teeth above its prey.

He noticed an exercise book on Elías's bunk and reached for it. On the cover was written 'Story Book' and Elías's name. It contained creative-writing exercises and drawings. Elías had written about 'Space' and illustrated it with a colour drawing of Saturn. He had also written about 'A Trip to the Shopping Mall' that he had made with his mother. And one piece was entitled 'My Favourite Movie', about a recent fantasy film that Erlendur had not heard of. He read the stories, which were written in an attractive, childish hand, and turned the pages to the point Elías had reached in the book. He had written the title of the most recent exercise at the top of the page but had got no further.

Closing the exercise book, Erlendur replaced it on Elías's bed and stood up. What had he wanted to be? A doctor, maybe. A bus driver. Or a cop. The possibilities were infinite, the world a new and exciting place. His life had barely begun.

He went back to join Sunee in the living room. Her brother was in the kitchen.

'Do you know what he wanted to be when he grew up?' Erlendur asked.

'Yes,' Sunee said. 'He say often. Big word, I learn it.'

'What was it?'

'Palaeontologist.'

Erlendur smiled.

'It used to be a cop,' he said, 'or a bus driver.'

On his way out he again asked the police officer on the staircase if he had been aware of any suspicious comings and goings on or near the landing but the answer was negative. He asked about the neighbour, Gestur, who lived in the flat opposite Sunee's, but the officer had not been aware of him.

'No one's had any reason to come up here,' the officer said, and Erlendur said goodbye and left.

Although it was fairly late by now, Erlendur still had one last visit to make. He had phoned the man that afternoon and arranged to go round to his house. The man answered the door promptly when Erlendur rang the bell, and invited him in. Erlendur had felt uneasy during his previous visit; he could not put his finger on the exact reason. It was something about the atmosphere, something about the owner of the house.

The man had been watching television but he switched it off and offered him coffee. Erlendur declined, looked at his watch and said he would not stay long. He did not apologise for the lateness of his visit. His gaze fell on a photo of the couple on the table. They were both smiling. They had gone to a photographer before the wedding reception and had their picture taken in all their finery. She was holding a small bouquet.

'Not very popular with your exes, are you?' Erlendur said. 'I've been hearing what they have to say.'

'Tell me something I don't know,' the man said.

Erlendur could see why women fell for him if they happened to like the type. He was a slim, neat man with a friendly face, dark hair, brown eyes, an attractive, olive complexion and elegant hands. He dressed with a good taste that was completely foreign to Erlendur. His home was furnished with handsome, trendy furniture, a magnificent kitchen and expensive flooring. Graphic prints decorated the walls. All that was lacking was the faintest sign that anyone actually lived there.

Erlendur wondered if he should tell him about the phone calls he had received, which were in all probability from his wife. The man had a right to know about them. If Erlendur's suspicions were correct, his wife was alive and the news would surely bring him joy. Erlendur did not really know why he didn't tell him everything. There was something ugly about this case that he could not quite fathom.

'No, of course,' Erlendur said. 'One of them claimed you threatened to kill her.'

He said it matter-of-factly, as if remarking on the weather, but the man did not bat an eyelid. Perhaps he was expecting it.

'Silla's not right in the head,' he said after a moment's pause. 'She never has been.'

'So you know the episode I'm referring to?'

'It's just something you say, you've probably said it yourself some time. You don't mean anything by it.'

'That's not what she says.'

'Are you focusing your investigation on me now? You think I've done something to her? To my own wife?'

'I don't kn—'

'She's gone missing!' the man interrupted. 'I didn't touch her. It's just a normal missing-person case!'

'I've never heard of a "normal missing-person case" before,' Erlendur said.

'You know perfectly well what I mean. Stop twisting everything I say.'

Erlendur did know what he meant. A normal missing-person case. He wondered if there was any other country in the world where they talked about 'a normal missing-person case'. Perhaps history had taught the Icelanders not to make too much of a fuss when people went missing.

'There's nothing normal about her disappearance,' Erlendur said.

He paused a moment. The case was heading in a direction from which there would be no turning back. From now on the nature of the inquiry would be different and more serious.

'Did you threaten to kill her?' Erlendur asked.

The man glared at him.

'Are you investigating it as a murder now?' he asked.

'Why did she leave home?'

'I've told you over and over again, I don't have a clue what happened. I came home and she wasn't here! That's all I know. You have to believe me. I've done nothing to hurt her and I find it abhorrent that you should imply anything else!'

He took a step towards Erlendur.

'I mean it,' he said. 'Abhorrent!'

'We have to examine all the possibilities,' Erlendur said. 'You must understand that. We've carried out a very thorough search for her, combed the beaches, advertised in the papers and on television. She's not going to come forward. She may be dead. When people disappear like this it's generally a sign that they're unhappy, so unhappy that they're capable of doing something stupid. Was your wife unhappy? Why? Was it something you did to her? Did she reproach herself? Did she regret the whole thing? Did she regret the affair, the divorce, the marriage? Did she regret losing her children? Was the whole thing a fatal mistake?'

'You've been talking to her friends, haven't you?' the man said.

Erlendur did not answer. Up to now he had spared the man the third degree, but the phone calls had changed that.

'They're crazy!' the man continued. 'I've never liked them. They've never liked me. What do you expect?'

'She was depressed,' Erlendur said. 'She regretted losing her family and she believed you had started cheating on her.'

'Bullshit!'

'Found a new one, have you?'

'A new one? What are you talking about?'

'Had you started cheating on her?'

'I don't know what you're talking about.'

'Her friends say she suspected there was another woman,' Erlendur said. 'Is that true?'

'It's all a pack of lies! There is no "other woman".'

Erlendur vacillated a moment.

'Over the past couple of days I've been receiving phone calls from a woman who won't reveal her name,' he said after a pause. 'She's distraught; she knows I'm handling the case but doesn't trust herself to come forward. I don't know whether that's because she doesn't dare or can't. What she says doesn't help much either because she's always in such a state when she phones; she's probably had to steel herself to make the call, but when it comes to the crunch she backs off and hangs up on me.'

'You mean it's her?' the man asked, stunned. 'She's been in touch with you? Is . . . is she *alive*? Is she all right?'

'If it is her,' Erlendur said, instantly regretting having mentioned the phone calls. He ought to have waited, waited until he had heard from the woman at least once more and persuaded her to meet him and tell him the truth.

'If?' the man said. '*If* it's her? You mean you're not sure?'

'I'm as sure as I can be,' Erlendur said. 'But that's not saying much.'

'My God! What's she thinking of? And what . . . what does she say? Why is she doing this?'

'Is this some sort of scam you two are cooking up?' Erlendur asked.

'Scam? No. Is that what she's saying, that it's a scam? Is that what she's saying?'

'No,' Erlendur said, trying to damp the man's eagerness. 'As a matter of fact, she doesn't say much. She . . .'

He was about to say that all she did was sob down the phone, but stopped himself.

'What . . . what does she say? Why is she calling you?'

'She's in distress,' Erlendur said. 'That's obvious from talking to her. But she won't tell me anything. Can you enlighten me? Do you know more than you're letting on?'

'Why doesn't she talk to me?' the man said.

Instead of answering, Erlendur simply stared at the man as if to throw the question back at him. Why doesn't she talk to you?

'I haven't done anything to her!' the man shouted. 'It's a lie! I'm not cheating on her. Okay, okay, I have done, but not now. I haven't been cheating on her. You have to understand that! You have to believe me!'

'I have no idea what to believe,' Erlendur said.

'You have to believe me,' the man repeated, with all the sincerity he was capable of.

'Then again it could be the new woman you're seeing,' Erlendur said. 'You have affairs. That's no lie. Time passes. You revert to your old habits, meet another woman. You have this little secret together. Then your wife finds out and disappears.'

'That's rubbish,' the man said.

'The new mistress gets cold feet. Her conscience is killing her. She calls me and . . .'

'What are you doing?' the man groaned.

'Isn't it rather a question of what you've done?'

'I've never threatened to kill anyone,' the man said. 'It's a lie!'

'Were you cheating on your wife?' Erlendur asked. 'Is that why she left you?'

The man stared at him for a long time without saying anything. Erlendur had not taken a seat and they stood eyeball to eyeball in the living room like two bulls, neither prepared to back down. Erlendur saw the rage seething in the man. He had succeeded in goading him to fury.

'Did your mistress call her?' Erlendur asked.

'You have no idea what you're talking about,' the man said through gritted teeth.

'It has been known to happen.'

'It's bullshit!'

'Was that how your wife found out that you were cheating on her?'

'I think you should leave now,' the man said.

'It's not just a simple missing-person case, is it?' Erlendur said.

'Get out,' the man said.

'You must see that something doesn't fit.'

'I have nothing more to say to you. Get out!'

'Oh, I can leave,' Erlendur said, 'but this case is not going anywhere. 'You can't drive it away. Sooner or later the truth will out.'

'It is the truth,' the man yelled. 'I don't know what's happened. Try to understand that. For God's sake, try to understand! I don't know what's happened!'

When Erlendur finally got home he sat down in his armchair without turning on the lights in the flat and lay back, grateful for the rest. He looked out of the window and his thoughts went to Eva Lind and the dream that she wanted to tell him.

His mind conjured up an image of a horse struggling in a bog, with eyes bulging and nostrils flaring. He heard the sucking noise when it managed to free a foreleg before sinking even deeper.

He longed to be at peace. He longed to see the stars that were obscured behind the clouds. He wanted to seek solace in them: the awareness of something greater and more important than his own consciousness, the awareness of vast tracts of time and space where he could lose himself for a while.

The family had lived in rather cramped conditions in the little house that now stood derelict. The brothers had to share a bedroom. Their parents had the other bedroom, and apart from that there was a big kitchen with a pantry opening off it, and a little parlour containing old furniture and family photographs, some of which now hung in the sitting room of Erlendur's flat. He took a trip out east every few years to sleep in the ruins of what had once been his home. From there he would walk or ride up onto the moors, and even sleep under the open sky. He enjoyed travelling alone; the gradual sensation of being overwhelmed by the profound solitude of his childhood haunts, surrounded by places and incidents from a past that was still so vivid to him, that filled him with nostalgia. He knew it only existed in his memory. When he was gone there would be nothing left. When he was gone it would be as if none of it had ever existed.

Like the evening when he and Bergur were lying in the darkness of their room, too over-excited to sleep, and heard a car drive into the yard. They heard the front door open and their parents' voices inviting someone in. They heard but did not recognise the visitor's deep voice. Visitors were rare at this time of night. The brothers did not dare to leave their room but Erlendur opened the door a crack and they lay and eavesdropped. They could see the kitchen, the visitor's feet, solid black shoes and black trousers, his crossed legs. They could see one of his hands resting on the kitchen table, big, with thick fingers and a gold ring sunk into the flesh. They could not hear what was said. Their mother stood by the table, half turned away from them, and they could see one of their father's shoulders where he sat diagonally opposite the visitor. Erlendur went to the window and peered out at the car. He did not know the make, had never seen the car before.

He decided to tiptoe into the passage. He meant to go alone but Bergur threatened to tell, so he allowed him to come too. They opened the door with extreme caution and crept out. Their mother did not notice them, their father and the visitor were hidden from sight. Erlendur began to make out what they were saying. The visitor's deep voice became clearer, the words more distinct, whole sentences took shape. He spoke calmly and clearly, as if to ensure that what he said would have the right impact. Erlendur noticed the smell the visitor brought with him, a strangely sweet fragrance hung in the air. He crept closer, Bergur on his heels, making such an effort to be silent that he had got down on all fours in his stripy pyjamas.

Erlendur was seven years old. It was the first time he heard mention of the vilest crime of all.

'. . . which means it could well be,' the visitor said.

'When was this?' their mother asked.

'Around dinnertime. The murder was probably committed in the afternoon. It was a gruesome scene. He must have gone off his head. Gone completely off his head and run amok in the room.'

'With a filleting knife?' their father whispered.

'You never know with these incomers,' the visitor said. 'He'd been working at the fish factory for two months. They say he was very quiet. Taciturn and withdrawn.'

'The poor girl,' their mother groaned.

'As I say, we haven't noticed anyone out this way today,' their father said.

'Could he be hiding nearby?' their mother asked and Erlendur could hear the anxiety in her voice.

'If he means to cross on foot, he may pass this way. There's a possibility that he will. We wanted to let you know. He was spotted heading in this direction. We're watching the roads but I don't know what good that will do.'

'What should we do?' their father asked.

'Oh my God,' Erlendur heard his mother whisper under her breath. He looked at Bergur behind him and gestured to him not to make a sound.

'We'll catch him,' the visitor said from behind the kitchen door. Erlendur stared at the solid black shoes. 'It's only a question of time. There's back-up on the way from Reykjavík.

They'll help us. But you're right, of course; it's horrific to have something like this happen here in the East Fjords.'

'At least you know who it is,' their father said.

'You'd better lock your doors tonight and keep tuned to the news,' the visitor said. 'I don't want to alarm you unnecessarily but better safe than sorry. The murderer may still be armed. With a knife, that is. We don't know what he's capable of.'

'And the girl?' their mother asked falteringly.

The visitor was silent for a space before answering.

'Sigga and Leifi's daughter,' he said eventually.

'No!' their mother gasped. 'You can't mean it? Dagga? Little Dagga?'

Erlendur saw his mother sink slowly onto the kitchen bench, staring at the stranger in horror.

'We can't find Leifi,' the visitor said. 'He's out there somewhere with a shotgun. He may come this way too. If you see him, try to talk him out of it. He'll only make matters worse by going after this man. Sigga said he was beside himself.'

'Oh, the poor man!' Erlendur heard his mother whisper.

'I can understand him only too well,' their father said.

Erlendur didn't know what to do as he stood rooted to the spot by the kitchen door. Bergur was on his feet beside him. He did not understand the seriousness of the matter, but he wanted to hold his brother's hand and slipped his little paw into Erlendur's. Erlendur looked down at him and again gave him a sign not to make a sound. He heard their father put the question that had begun to prey on his own mind.

'Are we in any danger?'

'I don't think so,' the stranger said. 'But all the same it makes sense to take care. You never know when something like this happens. I wanted you to know. I've still got one more place to visit, then—'

A chair scraped on the kitchen floor, the visitor was standing up. Erlendur squeezed his brother's hand and they fled back down the passage to their room and shut the door behind them. They heard their parents say goodbye to the man at the front door and when they looked out of the window they saw a shadowy figure stride swiftly to the car and climb inside. The engine started, the headlights came on and the car drove off and disappeared down the drive.

Erlendur opened the door a crack and peered out. He saw his parents talking quietly by the front door, then his father did something he had never done before: he thoroughly locked both the front door and the back door to the laundry. His mother checked the windows and firmly closed those that were open. When he saw her heading his way, he and Bergur leaped into bed just before the door opened and she appeared in the gap to check on them. She came into the room and made sure that the window was locked. Then she tiptoed out again and shut the door.

Erlendur could not sleep. He heard his parents whispering in the kitchen but did not dare go out to them. His brother, who understood nothing, soon dozed off but Erlendur lay wide awake in the darkness, dwelling on thoughts about the murderer who might be heading towards their house, about the girl's father, hunting for him with a shotgun, beside himself with rage and hatred and grief. He listened as the night sounds magnified around him. What had previously been the friendly creaking of a loose sheet of corrugated iron out in the sheepsheds now became blood-curdling proof that someone was lurking outside. If he heard the bleating of a ewe he was sure it was the murderer on the prowl. A gust of wind against the house made his stomach lurch.

He pictured Dagga and the filleting knife, visualising the grisly scene until he thought his heart would burst. They knew the girl well. She was from a neighbouring fjord, the daughter of friends, and had babysat for the brothers on several occasions when their parents had to go out.

Erlendur had never before heard of the existence of crime, let alone murder, but in an instant that evening this changed and his world became a different and more pitiless place. There was some destructive force in humans whose existence he had never suspected before, a force he feared and could not comprehend. The following day his parents talked to him and Bergur about what had happened but spared them the details. They stayed inside all day. Erlendur asked why men did such things but his parents had no answers. He kept up an endless stream of questions; he wanted to understand what had happened even though it was incomprehensible, but his parents could not give him the answers he was looking for. He discovered that the man with the gold ring and black shoes was the local magistrate. The radio news reported the murder and the exhaustive hunt that was now under way for the man who had committed the atrocity. As the family sat in the kitchen listening, Erlendur saw the anxiety on his parents' faces, sensed the horror and grief and devastation and knew that from now on nothing would ever be the same again.

The murderer was apprehended two days later in the northern town of Akureyri. He had never been anywhere near them. People were certain that if the girl's father had found him first he would have shot the killer dead. The father had roamed around with his gun all night and half the next day before he was picked up by the police, a broken man.

It was then that Erlendur learned of the existence of something called murder. Later he had stood face to face with murderers and although he did not show it, he sometimes felt deep down just as he had done that evening when the magistrate came on his unexpected visit and warned them about the man with the filleting knife.

21

Erlendur heard the phone through his sleep. It took him a long time to surface. He had nodded off in his chair and his whole body ached. Glancing at his watch, he saw that it was well past nine. He looked out of the window and for a moment did not know if it was night or day. The ringing persisted and he got laboriously to his feet to answer.

'Were you asleep?'

Sigurdur Óli was a famous early bird who generally arrived at work long before anyone else, after an energetic swim in one of the city's many pools and a hearty breakfast.

'What now?' Erlendur grunted, still half asleep.

'I should put you onto the new granola I had this morning, it sets you up for the day.'

'Sigurdur.'

'Yes?'

'Is there something you want to tell me before I—?'

'It's the scratch,' Sigurdur Óli said hurriedly.

'What about it?'

'Three other cars were vandalised in the vicinity of the school over the preceding few days,' Sigurdur Óli said. 'It emerged this morning at a meeting where your presence was sorely missed.'

'Was it the same sort of damage?'

'Yes. Scratches all along the bodywork.'

'Do we know who did it?'

'No, not yet. Forensics are examining the other cars, if they haven't been resprayed already. It's conceivable that the same instrument was used. And another thing: Kjartan has given us permission to examine his Volvo. He claims that Elías never set foot in his car but I thought it would be better to make sure.'

'Is he being cooperative?' Erlendur asked.

'Well, a bit better,' Sigurdur Óli said. 'And there's one more thing.'

'You've been very busy. Is it the granular?'

'Granola,' Sigurdur Óli corrected him. 'Maybe we should take a closer look at Niran's relationship with his stepfather.'

'In what way?'

Erlendur was waking up. He should not have been caught napping at home like this and knew he deserved Sigurdur Óli's teasing.

'Elínborg thinks we should have another chat with Ódinn. I'm going to drop round and see him. To ask about Niran.'

'Do you think he'll be home?'

'Yes. I phoned just now.'

'See you there, then.'

Ódinn was looking unkempt, his eyes were bloodshot and his voice hoarse. He had been granted compassionate leave from work and dropped round to see Sunee from time to time with his mother but mostly stayed at home waiting for news. He invited Erlendur and Sigurdur Óli into his living room and put on some coffee.

'Tell us a bit about Niran,' Erlendur said when Ódinn sat down with them in the living room.

'What about Niran?'

'What kind of boy is he?'

'A very ordinary boy,' Óðinn said. 'Should he be some-how...? What do you mean?'

'Did you have a good relationship?'

'You couldn't really say that. I had nothing to do with him.'

'Do you know if the boy has been in any trouble recently?'

'I haven't had any real contact with him,' Óðinn said.

'Did Niran have any reason to be hostile towards you?' Erlendur said. He did not know how to express the question any better.

Óðinn looked from one of them to the other.

'He wasn't hostile to me,' he said. 'Things were okay between us. He had nothing to do with me and I had nothing to do with him.'

'Do you think he's gone into hiding because of you?' Erlendur asked. 'Because of something he thought you might do?'

'No, I can't imagine that,' Óðinn said. 'Of course, it came as a bit of a shock when she told me about him. I stayed out of it when she sent for him.'

'Why did you get divorced?' Sigurdur Óli asked.

'It was over.'

'Was it because of anything in particular?'

'Maybe. This and that. Like in any normal marriage. People break up and start again. That's how it goes. Sunee's an independent woman. She knows what she wants. We quarrelled about the boys sometimes, especially Elías. She wanted him to speak Thai but I said it would only confuse him. It was more important for him to speak Icelandic.'

'You weren't afraid of not being able to understand them? Of losing control of the home? Being left out?'

Ódinn shook his head.

'She likes living in Iceland, except perhaps the weather sometimes. It gives her a chance to support her family in Thailand, and she stays in close contact with them. She wants to keep in touch with her roots.'

'Don't we all?' Erlendur said.

No one spoke.

'You don't think that Niran could be hiding because of you?' Erlendur repeated.

'Definitely not,' Ódinn said. 'I've never done anything to him.'

The mobile rang in Erlendur's pocket. It took him a little while to work out who the man on the phone was. He said his name was Egill and that they had spoken together in his car the other day; the woodwork teacher.

'Oh yes, hello,' Erlendur said, when he finally clicked who it was.

'It, you see, the thing is, it's always happening,' Egill said, and Erlendur pictured him with his beard, sitting in his car, smoking. 'So I don't know if it's significant at all,' Egill continued. 'But I wanted to talk to you anyway.'

'What is it?' Erlendur asked. 'What's always happening?'

'Those knives are always being stolen,' Egill said.

'What knives?'

'Er, the wood-carving knives,' Egill said. 'So I don't know if it'll help you at all.'

'What is it? What's happened?'

'But I keep a close eye on them,' Egill continued, as if he had not heard the question. 'I always try to keep a close eye on the knives. They're not cheap. I counted them the other day, maybe two weeks ago, but just now I noticed that one of them is missing. One of the carving knives has gone from the box. That's all I wanted to tell you.'

'And?'

'And nothing. I haven't found the thief or anything. I just wanted to inform you that there's a knife missing. I thought you'd want to know.'

'Of course,' Erlendur said, 'thank you for telling me. Who steals these knives?'

'Oh, the pupils probably.'

'Yes, but do you know which ones in particular? Have you caught anyone? Is it the same pupils again and again or . . .?'

'Why don't you just come and take a look for yourself?' Egill asked. 'I'll be here all day.'

Twenty minutes later Erlendur and Sigurdur Óli parked in front of the school. Teaching was under way and there was not a soul to be seen in the playground.

Egill was in the woodwork room. Nine teenage kids were busy with assignments at the carpentry tables, armed with chisels and small saws, but stopped what they were doing when the two detectives entered the classroom. Egill looked at his watch and informed the kids that they could finish ten minutes early. They gazed at him in astonishment as if such an offer from him was unthinkable, then jumped into action and started tidying away. The workshop emptied in a matter of minutes.

Egill closed the door behind the kids. He took a good long look at Sigurdur Óli.

'Didn't I teach you once?' he asked, then walked over to a cupboard in the corner, bent down, took out a wooden box and laid it on the table.

'I was at school here years ago,' Sigurdur Óli said. 'I don't know if you remember me.'

'I remember you all right,' Egill said. 'You were mixed up in those riots in 'seventy-nine.'

Sigurdur Óli darted a glance at Erlendur who pretended to be oblivious.

'I keep the carving knives here,' Egill said, taking them out of the box one at a time and laying them on the table. 'There should be thirteen of them. It didn't occur to me to check them after the attack.'

'Nor us,' Erlendur said, with a glance at Sigurdur Óli.

'It isn't necessarily significant,' Sigurdur Óli said, as if to excuse himself. 'Even if something is missing.'

'Then this morning,' Egill continued, 'when we needed to use them, one of the pupils came to me and said he didn't have a knife to work with. There were thirteen of them in the group and I knew there should be exactly the right number of knives. I counted them. There were twelve. So I collected them, put them back in the box in the cupboard, double-checked the workshop, then called you. I know there were thirteen about two weeks ago, no longer.'

'Is this cupboard kept locked?' Erlendur asked.

'No, that is, not during lessons. But apart from that, yes, these cupboards are kept locked.'

'And all the pupils have access to them?'

'Yes, in reality. We haven't regarded woodwork knives as potential murder weapons until now.'

'But people steal them?' Sigurdur Óli said.

'That's nothing new,' Egill said, stroking his beard. 'Things go missing. Chisels. Screwdrivers. Even saws. Always something every year.'

'Wouldn't it be a good idea to lock the cupboards then?' Erlendur said. 'Hand out the tools under some sort of supervision?'

Egill glared at him.

'Is that any of your business?' he asked.

'They're knives,' Erlendur said. 'Carving knives, what's more.'

'The classroom is kept locked, isn't it?' Sigurdur Óli said hurriedly.

'Wood-carving knives are only a weapon in the hands of morons,' Egill said, ignoring Sigurdur Óli. 'Why should the rest of us always have to suffer because of a few morons?'

'What about—' Sigurdur Óli began, but got no further.

'In addition to which,' Egill persisted, 'the kids use these tools in here and can stab themselves or slip them into their school-bags whenever they like. It's difficult to keep them under constant supervision.'

'And presumably all the kids in the school will have attended woodwork lessons since you last counted the knives,' Erlendur pointed out.

'Yes,' Egill said, his face flushing an angry red. 'The workshop is locked between classes. I don't leave until the last kid has gone, for safety reasons. I always lock up after myself and I'm the one who opens the door when I arrive in the morning and after all the breaks. No one else. Ever.'

'What about the cleaners?' Sigurdur Óli asked.

'Oh, and them, of course,' Egill said. 'But I haven't been aware that any of the cupboards have been broken into.'

'So in your view the most likely scenario is that the knife was taken during a lesson?' Sigurdur Óli said.

'Don't start blaming me for that!' Egill almost shouted, beside himself with indignation. 'I can't possibly be expected to keep an eye on everything that goes on here! If some stupid kids want to steal from the workshop it wouldn't exactly be difficult. And, yes, I reckon it must have been during a lesson. I can't see how else it could have happened.'

Erlendur picked up one of the knives and tried to recall what the pathologist had said about the instrument used to stab Elías. A broad but not very long blade, he remembered. The carving knife had a very sharp point, a short blade and a broad reverse by the wooden handle. It was razor sharp. Erlendur imagined that it would not require much force to push it deep into someone's flesh. It struck him that it would also be possible to produce satisfying scratches on cars with a tool like a carving knife.

'How many kids do you think we're talking about?' he asked. 'If we assume that the knife was stolen during a lesson?'

Egill considered.

'Most of the kids in the school, I expect,' he said.

'We'll have to get a photo of one of these knives and circulate it,' Erlendur said.

'Is this the boy you were asking me about in the car?' Egill asked Erlendur, his eyes fixed on Sigurdur Óli.

A faint smile twisted Erlendur's lips. He had riled the woodwork teacher and now Egill was after revenge.

'We should get moving,' Erlendur said to Sigurdur Óli.

'Has he told you what happened here in 'seventy-nine?' Egill continued. 'About the riot?'

They had reached the door. Sigurdur Óli opened it and stepped out into the corridor.

'Thanks for your help,' Erlendur said, half turning back to Egill. 'This knife business could be very important. You never know what may come out of it.'

Erlendur looked at Sigurdur Óli, who didn't seem to know what was happening, then closed the door in Egill's face.

'The old bugger,' he said as they walked down the corridor. 'What's this riot he was referring to?'

'It was nothing,' Sigurdur Óli said.

'What happened?'

'Nothing, it was just a stupid prank.'

They had emerged into the open air and were heading towards the car.

'I find it hard to imagine you involved in a stupid prank,' Erlendur said. 'You weren't at this school very long. Did you get into some sort of trouble?'

Sigurdur Óli sighed heavily. He opened the car door and got behind the wheel. Erlendur took the passenger seat.

'Me and three others,' Sigurdur Óli said. 'We refused to go outside during the break. It was all very innocent. The weather was terrible and we said we weren't going outside.'

'Bloody silly of you,' Erlendur said.

'We chose the wrong teacher,' Sigurdur Óli continued in a serious tone. 'He was a temporary supply teacher and we didn't know him but he managed to get on our nerves. That was probably how it started. Some of the boys had tried to disrupt his lessons by taking the piss out of him and so on. Things got out of hand. He started hurling abuse at us and we answered him back insolently. He got angrier and angrier, and starting trying to drag us outside but we fought back. Then some other teachers and pupils joined in and it ended up in a massive brawl throughout the building. People were injured. It was like everyone was venting their rage at once, pupils on teachers and teachers on pupils. When all attempts to calm the situation failed, someone called the police. It ended up in the papers.'

'And it was all your fault,' Erlendur said.

'I was involved and got suspended for two weeks,' Sigurdur Óli said. 'All four of us were suspended, along with some others who'd got a bit carried away in the fight. My father went ballistic.'

Erlendur had never heard Sigurdur Óli talk about his father before, never heard him so much as mention his name, and wondered if he should take the opportunity to find out more. The whole thing was completely novel to him. He couldn't imagine Sigurdur Óli being suspended from school.

'It . . . I . . .' Sigurdur Óli wanted to say more but floundered in his attempt to find the words. 'It wasn't like me at all. I'd never been mixed up in anything like that before and I've never lost control of myself since.'

Erlendur said nothing.

'I injured the teacher really badly,' Sigurdur Óli said.

'What happened?'

'That's why everyone remembers it. He was taken to hospital.'

'Why?'

'He fell and cracked his head on the floor,' Sigurdur Óli said. 'I knocked him down and he landed on his head. At first I didn't think he was going to pull through.'

'You can't have been very happy with that on your conscience.'

'I . . . I wasn't very happy at the time. There were various things that . . .'

'You don't have to tell me.'

'They got divorced,' Sigurdur Óli said. 'My parents. That summer.'

'Ah,' Erlendur said.

'I moved out with my mother. We'd only been here two years.'

'It's always rough on the kids. When their parents split up.'

'Were you discussing me with that woodwork teacher?' Sigurdur Óli asked.

'No, he recognised you,' Erlendur said. 'Remembered the riot.'

'Did he mention my dad at all?' Sigurdur Óli said.

'He may have done,' Erlendur said guardedly.

'Dad was always working. I don't think he ever realised why she left him.'

'Had it been on the cards for a long time?' Erlendur asked, amazed that Sigurdur Óli was willing to discuss this with him.

'I didn't know the background. Still don't really know what happened. My mother didn't much like talking about it.'

'You're an only child, aren't you?'

Erlendur recalled that Sigurdur Óli had once alluded to the fact.

'I spent a lot of time alone at home,' Sigurdur Óli said, nodding. 'Especially after the divorce, when we moved house. Then we moved again. After that we were always moving.'

Neither of them spoke.

'It's weird coming back here after all this time,' Sigurdur Óli said.

'Small world, this town.'

'What did he say about Dad?'

'Nothing.'

'Dad was a plumber. He was known as Permaflush.'

'Really?' Erlendur said, feigning ignorance.

'Egill remembered me clearly. I could tell at once. I remember him too. We were all a bit scared of him.'

'Well, he's not exactly Mr Nice Guy,' Erlendur said.

'I know people used to call Dad that, he was the type. You

252

could make fun of him. Some people are like that. He didn't mind but I couldn't stand it.'

Sigurdur Óli looked at Erlendur.

'I've tried to be everything he wasn't.'

She greeted Erlendur at the door with a smile, a small woman in her sixties with thick, brown, shoulder-length hair and friendly eyes that radiated complete ignorance about the purpose of his visit. Erlendur was alone. He had popped over at lunchtime on the off-chance that he would find her at home. The woman lived in Kópavogur and was called Emma, that was all he knew.

He introduced himself and when she heard that he was a detective she invited him into an overheated sitting room. He hastily removed his coat and unbuttoned his jacket. It was minus nine outside. They sat down. Everywhere there were signs that she lived alone. She had an aura of extraordinary calm, a serenity that suggested a solitary existence.

'Have you always lived alone?' he asked to break the ice and help her relax, only realising too late what a personal question it was. She seemed to think so too.

'Is that something the police need to know?' she asked, her manner so deadpan that he wasn't sure if she was teasing him.

'No,' Erlendur said sheepishly. 'Of course not.'

'What do the police want with me?' the woman asked.

'We're looking for a man,' he said. 'He was once a neighbour of yours. You lived in the flat opposite him. It's rather a long time ago, so I don't know if you'll remember him, but I thought it was worth a try.'

'Does it have something to do with that terrible case in the news, with that boy?'

'No,' Erlendur said, telling himself that this was not strictly a lie. He didn't know exactly what he was looking for or why he was intruding on this woman.

'It's dreadful knowing that something like that can happen,' the woman said. 'That a child should be attacked like that, it's quite incomprehensible, an incomprehensible outrage.'

'Yes, it is,' Erlendur said.

'I've only lived in three places in my life,' the woman added. 'The place where I was born, the block of flats you're talking about and here in Kópavogur. That's it. What year was this?'

'I'm not absolutely certain, but we're probably talking about the end of the sixties or beginning of the seventies. It was a small family. A mother and son. She may possibly have been living with a man at the time she was resident in the block. It's him I'm looking for. He wasn't the boy's father.'

'Why are you looking for him?'

'It's a police matter,' Erlendur said and smiled. 'Nothing serious. We just need to have a word with him. The woman's name was Sigurveig. The boy was called Andrés.'

Emma hesitated.

'What?' Erlendur said.

'I remember them well,' she said slowly. 'I remember that man. And the boy. The mother, Sigurveig, was an alcoholic. I used to see her coming home late at night, drunk. I don't think she looked after the boy properly. I don't think he was very happy.'

'What can you tell me about the man she lived with?'

'His name was Rögnvaldur. I don't know his patronymic, I never heard it. He was at sea, wasn't he? Anyway, he wasn't home much. I don't think he drank, at least not like her. I didn't really understand what they saw in each other, they were such different types.'

'Do you mean they didn't seem fond of each other or . . . ?'

'I never understood that relationship. I used to hear them quarrelling, I could hear it through their door if I was on the landing—'

She abruptly broke off her account as if she felt it necessary to clarify.

'I wasn't eavesdropping,' she said, with a faint smile. 'They used to argue pretty loudly. The laundry was in the basement and I'd be on my way down there or coming home . . .'

'I see,' Erlendur said, picturing her standing on the landing with ears pricked outside her neighbours' door.

'He spoke to her as if she was worthless. Always denigrating her, mocking and humiliating her. I didn't like him, from what little I had to do with him, not that that was much. But I heard what he was like. Nasty. A nasty piece of work.'

'What about the boy?' Erlendur asked.

'Quiet as a mouse, poor little thing. He avoided the man completely. I had the impression he wasn't happy. I don't know what it was, he was somehow so forlorn. Oh, those poor little dears, some of them are just so vulnerable . . .'

'Can you describe this Rögnvaldur for me?' Erlendur asked when she trailed off in mid-sentence.

'I can do better than that,' Emma said. 'I believe I have a photo of him somewhere.'

'You do?'

'Where he's walking past the block of flats. My friend took a picture of me standing outside the front door and it turned out that he was in the background.'

She stood up and went over to a cabinet. Inside were a number of photograph albums, one of which she removed. Erlendur looked around the flat. Everything was spotlessly

255

tidy. He guessed that she put her photos in an album the moment she had them developed. Probably numbered them and labelled them with the date and a short caption. What else was one to do alone in a flat like this during the long, dark winter evenings?

'One of his forefingers was missing,' Emma said as she brought the album over. 'I noticed it once. He must have had an accident.'

'I see,' Erlendur said.

'Maybe he was doing some carpentry. It was only a stump. On his left hand.'

Emma sat down with the album and turned the pages until she found the picture. Erlendur was right, the photos were carefully arranged in chronological order and clearly labelled. He suspected that every single one had a place in her memory.

'I simply adore looking through these albums,' Emma said, inadvertently confirming Erlendur's guess.

'They can be precious,' he said. 'Memories.'

'Here it is,' she said. 'It's actually not a bad picture of him.'

She handed Erlendur the album and pointed to the photo. There was Emma, more than thirty years younger, smiling at the camera, a slender figure wearing a headscarf, a pretty little cardigan and Capri pants. The picture was in black and white. Behind her he saw the man she referred to as Rögnvaldur. He was also looking at the camera but had raised a hand as if to shield his face, as if it had dawned on him too late that he might be caught in the shot. He was thin with a receding hairline, fairly large protruding eyes and delicate eyebrows below a high, intelligent forehead.

Erlendur stared at the man's face and a shiver ran down his spine when he realised that he had seen him before, very recently. He had changed extraordinarily little despite the passage of time.

'What's the matter?' Emma asked.

'It's him!' Erlendur groaned.

'Him?' Emma said. 'Who?'

'That man! Is it possible? What did you say his name was?'

'Rögnvaldur.'

'No, his name's not Rögnvaldur.'

'Oh, then I must be mistaken. Do you know him?'

Erlendur looked up from the album.

'Is it possible?' he whispered.

He looked again at the man in the picture. He didn't know anything about him but he had been inside his home and knew who he was.

'Did he call himself Rögnvaldur?'

'Yes, that was his name,' Emma said. 'I don't think I'm making it up.'

'I don't believe it,' Erlendur said.

'Why? What's the matter?'

'He wasn't called Rögnvaldur when I met him,' Erlendur said.

'You've met him?'

'Yes, I've met that man.'

'So? If he wasn't called Rögnvaldur, what was his name?'

Erlendur didn't answer immediately.

'What was he called?' Emma repeated.

'He was called Gestur,' Erlendur said absently, staring at the picture of Sunee's neighbour from across the landing, the man who had invited him in, the man who knew both Elías and Niran.

22

Erlendur was present when they entered Gestur's flat across the landing from Sunee's. Elínborg was with him. The Reykjavík District Court had issued them with a search warrant that afternoon. According to the police officers who had been guarding the staircase since the boy's body was found, Sunee's neighbour from the top floor but one had not shown his face at all. Erlendur was the only person to have met and spoken to him. He had not been seen since.

In the end there was no need to break down the door. Gestur rented his flat like the other residents on the staircase, and Erlendur had managed to obtain a spare key. When all the necessary documents were in place and their ringing and knocking had elicited no response, Erlendur put the key in the lock and opened the door. He knew that he had only Andrés's intimation that there was a paedophile in the area, and Andrés was an accomplished liar, but Erlendur was disposed to believe him this time. There was something about Andrés's manner when he spoke of this man. Some old fear that still haunted him.

The flat was unchanged since Erlendur's last visit, apart from the fact that someone seemed to have gone over the whole place with a cloth and disinfectant. The smell of cleaning fluid hung in the air. The kitchen shone like a mirror, as did the bathroom.

The living-room carpet had obviously been recently vacuumed, and Gestur's bedroom looked as if no one had ever slept there. Erlendur was more aware this time of how sparsely furnished the flat was. When he first entered he'd had the impression that it was larger than Sunee's place, although they were, in fact, identical. Standing in the middle of the living room, he thought he knew why: there was very little furniture in Gestur's flat. Erlendur had entered it on a dark winter's evening and Gestur had only turned on one lamp but even so he had sensed the emptiness. There were no pictures on the walls. The living room contained only two armchairs and a coffee table, besides a small dining table with three chairs, and a bookcase containing foreign paperbacks. There was nothing in the bedroom but a bed and an empty bedside table. The kitchen contained three plates, three glasses and three sets of cutlery, a small frying pan and two saucepans of different sizes. Everything had been thoroughly cleaned and put away.

Erlendur looked round the flat. It contained nothing new. The tables and chairs were probably second-hand, the bedside table too. The single bed in the bedroom had an old spring mattress. He wondered if Gestur had set to work immediately after their talk, obliterating all traces of himself in the flat. There were no shaving things or toothbrush in the bathroom. The flat was completely devoid of personal belongings. The man did not even have a computer, and no bills or letters of any sort were found in the drawers, no papers or magazines, no sign that anyone had ever lived there.

The head of forensics came over to Erlendur. He had two assistants with him.

'What did you say we were looking for?' he asked.

'A child abuser,' Erlendur said.

'He hasn't exactly left much behind,' the head of forensics pointed out.

'Maybe he was prepared to have to leave at short notice,' Erlendur said.

'I doubt we'll find so much as a fingerprint.'

'No, but do your best anyway.'

Elínborg was walking silently around the flat when her mobile rang. She spoke into it for a good while before replacing it in her pocket and going over to Erlendur.

'I wish my flat would look like this for once,' she said. 'Do you think this Gestur attacked Elías?'

'It's a possibility like any other.'

'He seems to have done a runner, doesn't he?'

'Perhaps he got out the cleaning things the moment I left,' Erlendur said.

'It couldn't just be that he's terribly house-proud and has gone away for a few days?'

'I don't know,' Erlendur said.

'Sigurdur Óli can't find anything on this man,' Elínborg said. 'There's no one of either name on our paedophile register, which goes back decades. He's running a match of the photo with our visual database. He sent his best regards.'

'Visual database,' Erlendur said. 'I hate these clunking terms. Why not just "our picture files"? What's wrong with that?'

'Oh . . . let people talk how they like.'

'I suppose I'm tilting at windmills anyway,' Erlendur said.

'It's not as if he brought children here,' Elínborg remarked.

This was not intended to be ironic. Erlendur knew what she meant. They had entered the homes of paedophiles that looked like a children's fairytale come true. There was nothing like that here. Not a single sweet wrapper. Not a single computer game.

'Gestur knew Elías, assuming he wasn't lying,' Erlendur said. 'Our search should focus on that. But as you say, if Elías did come in here, Gestur has obliterated all sign of it.'

'He may have some other bolthole where he keeps the chocolate and cakes.'

'It wouldn't be the first time.'

'Should we talk to Andrés again?' Elínborg asked.

'Yes, we'll have to,' Erlendur said, without much enthusiasm.

They had tried to gather more information on Gestur while waiting for the search warrant to come through. Erlendur and Elínborg drove over to meet the landlord who owned most of the flats on the staircase at his office in the centre of town. He was a rather manic individual in his thirties who had sold the fishing quota he inherited up north and gone into property dealing in Reykjavík, apparently with some success. He told them he planned to sell off the flats on the staircase, the lettings business was far too stressful, the rental market attracted all sorts. He also rented out flats in another part of town and was involved in constant legal wrangles, evictions and debt collection.

'This Gestur, did he keep up with his payments?' Elínborg asked.

'Always. He's rented the place for a year and a half and I've never had a moment's trouble with him.'

'Does he pay into an account?'

The landlord hesitated.

'Is it cash in hand?' Erlendur asked. 'Does he come here and pay you in person?'

The landlord nodded.

'That's how he wanted it,' he said. 'He was the one who insisted on it. In fact, he made it a condition.'

'You didn't check his ID number when you took him on as a tenant?' Elínborg asked.

'I must have forgotten.'

'You mean it's black?' Erlendur asked. 'The rent he pays you?'

The landlord did not answer. He cleared his throat.

'Er, does this have to go any further?' he asked hesitantly. They had not told him why the police were asking questions about this particular tenant. 'Does the taxman have to find out?'

'Only if you're a lying scumbag,' Erlendur said.

'It's . . . ,' the landlord said awkwardly. 'I do all sorts of deals, okay. This man came in wanting to know if we could come to an arrangement. He didn't mind paying the full amount but he didn't want any paperwork. I told him I would need him to fill in a tenancy agreement but the old guy was very convincing. He said he would pay six months in advance and I could keep three months' payment as a deposit. He paid in cash. Said he was too old for all that electronic nonsense. I believed him. He's one of the best tenants I've ever had. Never late with a single payment.'

'Did you see him at all?' Elínborg asked.

'I've met him maybe a couple of times since then. That's all. Are you going to the tax authorities with this?'

'So the flat wasn't registered in anyone's name?'

'No,' the landlord said with a shrug, as if confessing to a minor oversight.

'Tell me something else. Sunee who lives opposite him, does she always pay on time?' Erlendur asked.

'You mean the Thai?' the landlord asked. 'Always pays.'

'Cash in hand?' Elínborg asked.

'No, no,' the landlord said. 'It's all above-board. They're all above-board except for that bloke.'

He paused.

'Well, and maybe two or three others. But no more. And I told her that I'd kick her out double quick if she didn't pay. I don't like letting to her sort but the market's a nightmare, the types you get renting! I'm going to call it a day. Sell the flats. I can't be doing with it any more.'

That was all they had to go on when they entered the flat. They stood in the living room of the man who called himself either Gestur or Rögnvaldur, utterly perplexed. They had no idea where to look for him, did not know who he was. In fact, they had nothing whatsoever to go on but the word of a known criminal.

'Strange how people keep vanishing in this case,' Elínborg said. 'First Niran, now this guy.'

'I'm afraid it'll prove a harder job to track this man down than Niran,' Erlendur said. 'It's as if he's done the same thing before. As if he's been forced to do a disappearing act at short notice before.'

'You mean, if he is what Andrés says he is?'

'It's too well prepared somehow,' Erlendur said, 'too premeditated. He probably has some other bolthole where he can lie low if something happens to draw attention to him.'

'He doesn't even keep any personal belongings here,' Elínborg said. 'He's left nothing behind. As if he doesn't exist – as if he never existed.'

The landlord had told them when handing over the spare key that he himself owned the few bits and pieces that were in the flat. Even the paperbacks in the bookcase were his property. There was an old television in the living room and an ancient radio-cassette player in the kitchen. The television was licensed to the landlord as well.

'We need to talk to his neighbours on the staircase,' Erlendur said with a sigh. 'Ask about his movements. Whether he showed any particular interest in the kids in the block or in the neighbourhood. That sort of thing. Would you mind seeing to it?'

Elínborg nodded.

'Do you think Sunee hid Niran because of this man?' she asked.

'I don't know,' Erlendur said. 'It's all so hazy still.'

'Why doesn't she just tell us what she's afraid of so that we can help her?'

'Search me.'

Erlendur walked across the landing to Sunee's flat once Gudný had arrived. He had called her over to assist. He did not know exactly how to express the questions to find out what he wanted to know without distressing Sunee. He sat down with her and Gudný under the yellow dragon and told her about her next-door neighbour and their suspicions as to what kind of offender he might be. Sunee listened attentively, asked questions and answered without hesitation, and by the time they stood up again Erlendur was convinced that the man had never behaved in an inappropriate way towards her boys.

'I'm sure,' Sunee said firmly. 'It never happen.'

'He seemed to know Niran and Elías.'

'They knew him because he lives right opposite,' Gudný translated. 'It's out of the question that they ever went into his flat. Elías went to the shop for him a couple of times, that's all.'

The other residents on the staircase had had little to do with the man; he came and went without anyone paying much attention. There was never any noise from his flat. 'He crept around here like a mouse,' Fanney said.

Elínborg noticed that Erlendur seemed preoccupied when he returned from Sunee's flat.

'Has Sigurdur Óli ever talked to you about his father?' he asked as they walked downstairs. 'Do you know anything about him?'

'Sigurdur Óli? No. Not that I remember. He never talks about himself. Why do you ask? What about his father?'

'Oh, nothing. I was talking to Sigurdur Óli today and it suddenly occurred to me that I don't know anything about him.'

'I don't know anyone who does,' Elínborg said.

It was intended as a joke but she sensed that Erlendur was being serious and regretted her words. She often made snide comments at Sigurdur Óli's expense, but then he asked for it by being so inflexible in his views, so pedantic and lacking in empathy. He never let his job get to him, whatever happened. He seemed completely thick-skinned. Elínborg knew that this was the difference between Erlendur and Sigurdur Óli; the source of the friction, almost amounting to antipathy, that existed between them.

'Oh, I don't know,' Erlendur said. 'He's not a bad cop. And he's not as bad as you think.'

'I never said he was,' Elínborg answered. 'I just don't feel like spending much time with him.'

'It suddenly struck me as odd when I was talking to him today that I don't know him at all. I know nothing about him, any more than I ever really knew Marion Briem. You know Marion's passed away?'

Elínborg nodded. The news had spread around the force. Few people remembered Marion, apart from the oldest members. No one had stayed in touch except Erlendur, who had been wondering ever since Marion died just what their working partnership and friendship had been based on. His thoughts had turned to Sigurdur Óli and Elínborg, his closest colleagues. He barely knew them and recognised that this was not least his own fault. He was well aware that he was not a sociable man.

'Do you miss Marion?' Elínborg asked.

They stepped outside into the bitter cold. Erlendur stopped and pulled his coat tight around him. He had not had time to consider the question until suddenly confronted by it now. Did he miss Marion?

'I do,' he said. 'I miss Marion. I'll miss—'

'What?' Elínborg said when Erlendur broke off in mid-sentence.

'I don't know why I'm burdening you with this,' he said and walked towards his car.

'You're not burdening me,' Elínborg said. 'You never do,' she added, in the belief that Erlendur would not hear.

'Elínborg,' Erlendur said, turning.

'Yes.'

'How's your daughter? Is her gastric flu any better?'

'She's perking up,' Elínborg said. 'Thanks for asking.'

They arrived at Andrés's place shortly after dinnertime. He was at home, rather the worse for wear but not too drunk to hold a conversation. The police had released him after the initial interview; they did not have sufficient grounds to detain him any longer. He let them in with a grin that immediately got on Erlendur's nerves. Sigurdur Óli closed the door behind them. He had spent the best part of the day looking for leads that might help them trace Gestur but had found nothing on him in the police records and was feeling tired. Elínborg had gone home. It was dark in Andrés's flat and there was a suffocating odour of cooking, almost a stench, as if he had been eating putrefied skate with dripping. They stood in the living room. Andrés sat down in front of the television. Beer cans littered the table beside him and empty schnapps bottles lay overturned on the floor. He sat with his back to them, glued to the television as if they did not exist. The sole illumination was the flickering glow of the screen. Only the top of his head was visible over the high back of the chair.

'How's it going?' Andrés asked. He picked up a beer can, took a swig and belched.

'We found him,' Erlendur said. 'Your old stepfather.'

Andrés slowly replaced the beer can.

'You're taking the piss.'

'He calls himself Gestur. Lives in the same block of flats as the boy who was attacked.'

'So what?'

'You tell us.'

'What do you mean?'

'Where is he?'

'Hang on a minute, didn't you just find him?'

'We found his flat,' Erlendur said.

Andrés reached out for the beer again.

'But not him?'

'No,' Erlendur said.

There was a silence.

'You'll never find him,' Andrés said.

'Do you know where he is?' Erlendur asked.

'What if I do?'

'Then tell us,' Sigurdur Óli said angrily.

'Did you go inside his place?' Andrés asked.

'None of your business,' Erlendur said.

'What was his flat like? Was it anything like mine?' he asked, extending the hand with the beer can, as if to invite them to admire the dump that was his home.

'We can bang you up for obstruction,' Sigurdur Óli said.

'Can you now?'

'And for refusing to testify,' Sigurdur Óli said.

'Ooh, I'm shitting myself,' Andrés said.

'Do you know who he is?' Sigurdur Óli asked.

'You've drawn a blank, and now you expect little Andy to save your bacon,' he said. 'Is that it? Is that what you expect? Cop wankers. When have you ever helped anyone?'

Erlendur looked at Sigurdur Óli. He mouthed the words 'little Andy' and shook his head, as though mystified.

'What name was he using when you knew him?' Erlendur asked.

'He called himself Rögnvaldur,' Andrés said. 'He was known as Rögnvaldur in those days. You've been in his flat, haven't you? You won't find anything. You won't find out anything about him. You don't know who that man is. Only little Andy can help you. But let me tell you something: Andy's not going to help you. Little Andy's not going to lift so much as a little finger. Do you know why?'

'Why?' Erlendur asked.

'What's all this "little Andy" crap?' Sigurdur Óli asked, seizing Andrés's chair and dragging it round from the television. Erlendur grabbed at Sigurdur Óli to prevent him but it was too late. The chair swivelled slowly round until Andrés was staring up at them.

'You bloody idiot!' Erlendur yelled at Sigurdur Óli.

'You tell him, mate!' Andrés cackled.

'Wait outside,' Erlendur ordered.

'What?' Sigurdur Óli began to object but shut up at once.

After staring first at Erlendur, then at Andrés, he walked out without another word. Andrés jeered.

'Yeah, get out of here,' he called after him.

'Why won't you help us?' Erlendur asked when Sigurdur Óli had gone.

'It's none of your business what I do,' Andrés said, turning back to the glare of the television.

'Are you lying to us, Andrés?'

The glow from the screen flickered over the little flat, illuminating the squalor and neglect. Erlendur felt uncomfortable. There was nothing here but self-destruction.

'I'm not lying,' Andrés said.

'What kind of man is he, this bloke who calls himself Rögnvaldur?' Erlendur asked. 'Who is he?'

Andrés did not answer.

'You told us you had seen him again recently. Do you know where he is?'

'I haven't a clue,' Andrés said. 'I'm not going to help you with this. Do you understand?'

'When did you first notice him in the neighbourhood?'

'A year ago.'

'And you've been watching him ever since?'

'I'm not going to help you.'

'Do you know where he works? What he does during the day? What he does for a living? Does he work?'

Andrés did not answer.

Erlendur reached into his pocket and took out the photograph of the man who had gone by the name of Rögnvaldur when he lived with Andrés's mother. He took another brief glance at the face of the man he was looking for, then held the picture over the high back of the TV chair. Andrés took it.

'Is that him?' Erlendur asked.

Andrés did not answer.

'Do you recognise the man in the photograph?'

'That's him,' Andrés said at last.

'Did he look like that when you knew him?'

'Yes, that's him.'

'What kind of man is he?' Erlendur repeated. 'What can you tell me about him?'

Andrés did not reply. Erlendur could see nothing but the top of his head over the chair but guessed that he was holding the picture in front of him.

'Is he capable of killing a child?' Erlendur asked.

Some time passed, then the chair began to swivel round from the television again and Andrés reappeared. He was no longer grinning. His face wore a drawn, sober expression as he met Erlendur's eye. He handed back the picture.

'I believe he's capable,' Andrés said. 'Maybe he already did. Years ago.'

'What do you mean? Maybe he did what?'

'Fuck off. You're not getting any more out of me. Get out of here. This is my affair. I'll sort it out.'

'What did he do?'

'Fuck off and leave me alone,' Andrés said.

'Are you saying he's a murderer?'

Andrés turned back to the television and, despite all his attempts, Erlendur could not extract another word from him about the man who lived on Sunee's landing.

23

One of the younger employees at the recycling depot was feeling quite satisfied with his day. He had found two vinyl records that were well worth keeping. Of course, he was supposed to hand them in to the market at which useful goods from the recycling depot were sold, instead of taking them home with him. But no one kept tabs on what people salvaged from the dump. In fact, anybody could wander round the depot and have a rummage. Sometimes record collectors almost ended up in the crusher. Book collectors too. All sorts. Later he would take the two records to a collectors' shop and get a good price for them. He was not especially interested in records or music but after working for two years at the depot he knew what was valuable. One day he had come across a whole set of golf clubs by the scrap-metal container, which someone had forgotten to put back in the car after throwing away their rubbish. The bag was rather tatty but otherwise the set was in excellent condition and he sold it later for a tidy sum. He got an especially good deal on the 'driver'. Two days after he found the set the owner came looking for it but the poor man was easily fobbed off with the lie that unfortunately the clubs had probably ended up in the rubbish.

During his time at the depot he had learned to keep an eye out for useful objects, things he might be able to sell or use himself. He knew some of the collectors complained that not everything ended up on the second-hand market according to the rules but he did not give a toss about those weirdos. He had a nice little sideline in watching what people threw out, and, after all, it was not as if the company was generous with its wages. It was shitty pay for a shitty job.

He never ceased to be surprised by what people threw away. They would chuck out literally anything. He was not much of a reader himself but he saw vans bringing whole libraries that people wanted to clear out, as well as apparently intact furniture, perfectly good clothes, kitchen appliances, even relatively new audio equipment.

It had been quite busy that day, despite the cold and the northerly gale that ripped and tore at his blue overalls. People threw out rubbish all day long, all year round, whatever the weather. Vans brought the personal effects of the recently deceased, someone was getting rid of a bath, others were replacing their kitchen units. And then there was the drink-can gang. Receiving cans and bottles was his least favourite job. They were always trying to lie about the number. Sometimes when he could be bothered to count out the contents of the bags (nice clean job that was), their estimate would turn out to be wildly different from his calculation. And they were not even abashed. Just grinned and acted all surprised.

A car drove up to the gate and halted by the large sign that directed everyone to stop and await instructions. Most obeyed. When he saw that no one else was going to attend to the driver, he slouched over.

'I've got an old bed here,' the man said as he lowered the window.

He was in a large jeep and had broken up the bed to fit it in the back. No use to anyone then.

'Does it come with the mattress and everything?' he asked.

'Yes, the lot,' the man said.

'Straight on, mattress on the right, planks on the left, okay?'

The man wound up his window. The employee watched him go, then put his head round the door of the staff hut by the gate. The seven o'clock news was just beginning and he wondered if he should step into the warmth for a minute. He could not hear the television but could see the screen: crowds throwing stones in the Middle East, the American president giving a speech, Icelandic sheep, a knife on a table, an Icelandic cabinet minister cutting a ribbon, the president of Iceland receiving guests . . .

Another car pulled up at the gate. Window down.

'I've got a fridge,' the man said.

'Does it work?' he asked. He always checked on the refrigerators to see if they were in working order as he could use a decent one himself.

'Completely caput, I'm afraid,' the man said with a smile.

He noticed out of the corner of his eye that the knife had reappeared on the TV screen and all of a sudden he had the feeling that he had seen it before.

'Where do I go with the fridge?' the driver asked.

'Over there, to the right,' he said, pointing to where kitchen appliances stood around, forlorn and abandoned in the howling gale.

He hurried into the hut and sat down in front of the little television set. The newsreader was saying that the murder weapon could possibly look like this; it was a wood-carving knife of the type used in school carpentry workshops. He knew

273

what murder they were talking about: the Asian boy by the block of flats. He had seen the news footage.

He took the knife out of its sheath and examined it. It was identical to the knife on TV. He had found it in the scrap-metal container and made a sheath for it. Then he had found a belt which he now wore over his overalls, with the sheath fixed to it and the knife in the sheath. It made an excellent tool for cutting string, opening bags of drink-cans, or simply whittling bits of wood in the hut when business was slow. He stared at the knife in his hand as gradually it dawned on him that he might be holding a murder weapon.

A car drove up to the gate and stopped.

He would probably have to hand in the knife, let the cops know. Or would he? What did it have to do with him? It was a bloody good knife.

The driver spotted him loitering in the hut and hooted.

He did not hear the car horn. He was thinking that the cops might jump to the conclusion that he had killed the boy if he had the knife on him. Would they believe him that he had found the knife in the scrap-metal bin? Had crawled inside because he glimpsed the little wooden handle and was well trained in spotting handy objects? They emptied the container every few days and it had been only about half full. Someone had come to the depot and thrown the knife in the container.

The murderer?

The newsreader had said that the murder weapon might possibly be a knife of this type, and if so the attacker might be connected in some way to the school.

The driver, who was growing extremely impatient, hooted again, this time for longer.

The employee jumped and looked outside.

Maybe they wouldn't believe him. He had been called a racist once when he described how the Asians brought in bags of cans and lied about the number.

But then again, he might become famous.

He might become famous.

He looked at the driver who glared angrily back at him and beckoned him to come out and attend to him.

He smiled.

The driver emitted a shout of rage when the employee gave him an idiotic grin, then picked up the phone right in front of his eyes and started making a call.

He dialled the emergency number, 112.

He could be famous.

Sigurdur Óli was waiting for Erlendur in the corridor outside Andrés's flat.

'How did it go?' he asked as they walked down the stairs.

'I don't know,' Erlendur said, preoccupied. 'I reckon Andrés has really lost the plot.'

'Did you get anything useful out of him? Did he say anything?'

'Nothing about Elías.'

'What then? What did he say?'

'Firstly, he knew the man in the photo,' Erlendur said. 'It is his stepfather. He implied that the man had committed a murder a long time ago.'

'What?'

'I don't know,' Erlendur said. 'I don't know what to believe.'

'What murder?'

'I don't know.'

'Isn't it just a wind-up?'

'Probably,' Erlendur said. 'But the little he's said so far has proved accurate.'

'Yes, but that's not saying much.'

'Then he said he was going to sort it out himself, whatever that means. We should have Andrés watched over the next few days.'

'Yes. Anyway, they think they've found the knife,' Sigurdur Óli said.

'Really?'

'They just called. Someone disposed of it in a rubbish container. We still have to check whether it's the same knife but it seems likely. I gather it's identical. They showed it on the news and some boy turned out to have retrieved it from the tip. We may find some trace elements, though the boy who found it had been using the knife at work and would have given it a good clean first. But forensics always manage to find something with that fancy equipment of theirs.'

They drove to the recycling depot. The forensics team had closed the place to traffic and a yellow police cordon flapped in the wind. The technicians were searching for clues as to who had thrown the knife away, but only for form's sake. Two days had elapsed since the employee found the knife. Countless people and cars had passed through the depot since the murder was committed and none of the employees had spotted anything out of the ordinary. No one had been seen sneaking around the container. There was no CCTV on the gate. The police had nothing to go on.

They had contacted the woodwork teacher Egill about the discovery. He was shown the knife and judged that it could well have come from the carpentry knife store. He pointed out, however, that similar knives could probably be found in every school workshop in the country.

Erlendur went to question the young employee who had found the knife and soon established that he was telling the truth. He asked Erlendur if he could sell his story to the papers; did Erlendur know whether the tabloids would pay for it and, if so, how much. He had been carrying the knife and using it, you see, ever since he found it.

Prat, Erlendur thought.

He came home some time later. It was late and he had stopped off at a twenty-four-hour convenience store to buy a ready-meal of Icelandic stew. He stuck it in the microwave and set the timer to three minutes. Valgerdur phoned and they talked; he told her the latest on the investigation without divulging too much. She asked if he had been in touch with Eva Lind. Valgerdur told him she had to take an extra shift and would not be able to see him tonight after all, so they decided to meet the following evening when she was free.

'Come over to mine,' she insisted.

'All right,' he said. 'I'll come. I may be late though.'

'It doesn't matter,' she said.

They rang off.

He took the stew out of the microwave, fetched a spoon and sat peacefully slurping it out of the plastic tray at the kitchen table. He tried not to brood on the cases he was handling, but his thoughts kept slipping back to Elías in the garden behind the block of flats. He wondered about the men who brought as many as three or four women like Sunee into the country, married them, then dumped them when the fun was over or when the women walked out on them because they were only really interested in acquiring residency and a work permit. How did such things happen? He thought about Niran whom Sunee had summoned after many years' separation, but who could not find his feet in the new country, so ended up an outsider, seeking out the company of kids with the same kind of background and experience, kids who could not come to terms with their fate, could not understand the country or its language and history, and anyway had little interest in understanding any of it. He sympathised with them.

He thought about Sunee and her grief.

When his mobile started ringing he assumed it must be Sigurdur Óli calling so late but the voice was a woman's, whispering as if she was using the phone in secret. Erlendur could not hear what she was saying.

'What?' he said. 'Sorry . . . ?'

'. . . and take . . . But he won't. He absolutely refuses. I've tried to talk to him. It's hopeless.'

'I've had enough of this,' Erlendur said when he realised who it was. He decided to try a new approach with this woman who he had been searching for since before Christmas. 'Either come and see me or forget it. I can't be doing with this sort of nonsense!'

'I'm telling you, he won't—'

'I think . . . ,' Erlendur said.

'I just need more time.'

'I think you should stop messing me about like this.'

'I'm sorry,' the voice said. 'It's just so hard. I don't want it to be like this.'

'What's the point of all this?' Erlendur asked. 'What are you both up to? What nonsense is this?'

The woman did not answer.

'Come and talk to me.'

'I keep trying to make him. But he won't.'

'Stop being so silly,' Erlendur said. 'You should go home to him and stop bothering me. It's getting ridiculous!'

There was silence on the other end.

'I went and saw your husband,' Erlendur said.

Still the woman said nothing.

'Yes, I went and saw him. I don't know what you're both plotting and it's nothing to do with me. Just stop making these calls. Stop bothering me with this stupid nonsense.'

There was a long silence.

Then the woman hung up.

Erlendur stared at the phone in his hand. He had no idea what he had done. He half expected the woman to call straight back but when nothing happened he put the phone down on the kitchen table and stood up. Taking the book he had read aloud to Marion Briem at the hospital, he settled down in his armchair. It contained stories of travellers' ordeals and fatal accidents in the East Fjords. He weighed the book in his hands as he had done so often before and opened it at the account he knew so well, but which contained only a fragment of the true story.

TRAGEDY ON ESKIFJÖRDUR MOOR

He began to read it for the umpteenth time but was soon interrupted by a quiet tap on the door. Putting down the book, he got up and went to answer it. Eva Lind stood out on the landing. Sindri Snaer was with her.

'Do you two never sleep?' he asked as he let them in.

'No more than you,' Eva said, slipping past him. 'Were you eating stew?' she asked, sniffing the air.

'From the microwave,' Erlendur said. 'Can't really call it food.'

'I'm sure you could cook yourself a proper meal if you could be arsed,' Eva said and sat down on the sofa in the living room. 'What are you reading?' she asked when she saw the open book on the desk by his chair. Sindri sat down beside her. It was a year and a day since they had last visited him together.

'Travel stories,' Erlendur said. 'What are you two up to?'

'Oh, you know, we just felt like seeing how it's hanging with you.'

'How it's hanging?'

'Are they about people lost in the wilderness?' Sindri asked.

'Yes.'

'You told me once that there was a story like that about your brother,' Eva said.

'That's right, there is.'

'But you won't show it to me?'

He didn't know why he didn't hand Eva Lind the book. It lay open on the desk between them and although it didn't contain the whole truth, it would be enough to give her and Sindri a reasonably good idea of what happened. Erlendur had only told them the bare facts about the brothers' ordeal. The account did not really add much more. He no longer knew what it was that he was clinging on to so stubbornly. If he ever had known. Sindri had heard about the events when he was living out east; it wasn't as if they were a secret.

'I dreamed about him,' Eva said. 'I told you. I'm sure it was your brother.'

'You're not going to start on about that again? I don't know what tales you've been filling her head with, Sindri.'

'I didn't tell her anything,' Sindri said, taking out a packet of cigarettes.

'It's only a dream. Why are you so afraid of dreams? I can't imagine you taking them seriously.'

'I don't, I just find it hard to rake up the memory of what happened.'

'Yeah, right,' Eva Lind said, nodding towards the book on the table. 'You're forever reading about it or stuff like it. It's not like you've just forgotten about it!'

'I don't want to rake up the memories with other people,' Erlendur corrected.

'Ah,' Eva said. 'So you want to keep it all to yourself. Is that it?'

'I don't know what *it* is.'

'You don't want anyone to take it away from you?'

'I don't think even you know what you're talking about,' Erlendur said.

'I just want to tell you my dream. I never had a dream like it before. I don't know why you refuse to hear it. Anyway, it was hardly even a dream. More like waking up with a picture in my head.'

'How do you know it was my brother?'

'I couldn't think of anyone else,' Eva said.

'Dreams don't mean anything, you know that,' Sindri said.

'That's exactly what I'm trying to tell him,' Eva said.

There was a silence.

'How did he die?' Eva asked.

'I've told you. Bergur died of exposure. He was eight years old. We got separated. I was found. His body was never found. Maybe you did dream about him. It doesn't matter, don't get all excited about it. Tell me about yourselves instead. What are you both up to these days?'

'Could he have drowned?' Eva Lind asked.

Erlendur stared at his daughter. She knew he didn't want to

discuss the matter any further but she did not let that deter her. She stared back defiantly. Sindri looked down at the table between them.

'Sindri told me it was one of the theories,' she added, 'that he heard when he was out east.'

Sindri raised his eyes. 'Loads of people know the story out there,' he said. 'People who remember the whole thing.'

Erlendur did not respond.

'What do you think happened?' Eva Lind asked.

Erlendur still did not reply.

'It was dark,' Eva said. 'I was in water. At first I thought I was swimming but this was different. I never go swimming. Not since I was at school. But all of a sudden I was in water and it was incredibly cold . . .'

'Eva . . .' Erlendur looked pleadingly at his daughter.

'You told me I could tell you my dream another time. Have you forgotten?'

Slowly Erlendur shook his head.

'And a boy came towards me and looked at me and smiled and he immediately reminded me of you. I thought at first it *was* you. Were you alike?'

'So people said.'

'Anyway, we weren't swimming or in a swimming pool,' Eva said. 'We were just in some kind of water that changed into mud and slime. Then the boy stopped smiling and everything went black. I couldn't breathe. Like I was drowning or suffocating. I woke up gasping. No dream's ever affected me like that before. I'll never forget it. His face.'

'His face?'

'When everything went black. It was . . .'

'What?'

'It was you,' Eva Lind said.

'Me?'

'Yes. All of a sudden it was you.'

No one spoke.

'Was that after Sindri had told you about the bogs?' Erlendur asked with a glance at Sindri.

'Yes,' Eva said. 'How did your brother die? What about the bogs?'

'Did he drown?' Sindri asked.

'He may have drowned,' Erlendur said in a low voice.

'There are rivers running into the fjord,' Sindri said.

'Yes.'

'Some people say he must have fallen in one of them.'

'That's probably one hypothesis. That he fell in the Eskifjördur River.'

'But there's another, worse one, isn't there?' Eva Lind said.

Erlendur grimaced. An old memory resurfaced in his mind of men trying to save a horse that had wandered too far into the bog. A great big beast that belonged to a man from the village. The horse floundered around, sending up a spray of mud, but the more it thrashed, the deeper it sank until only its head remained above the surface, its flaring nostrils and frenzied eyes that slowly, inexorably vanished into the mire. It was a horrific sight, a horrific death. Every time he thought of Bergur the image entered his mind of the horse sinking deeper and deeper into the bog until it disappeared.

'There are boggy areas up on the moors,' Erlendur said at last. 'Quagmires that can be dangerous. They freeze over in winter, but every now and then there's a thaw. The ice may have cracked and Bergur may have fallen through and got stuck. That's one theory because we never found his remains.'

'So the ground swallowed him up?'

'We searched for weeks, months,' Erlendur said. 'Local farmers. Our friends and relatives. It was no good. We found nothing. Not a single trace. It was literally as if the ground had swallowed him up.'

Sindri contemplated his father.

'That's what people said.'

No one spoke for a long moment.

'Why is it still so hard after all these years?' Eva asked.

'I don't know,' Erlendur said. 'Because I know he's still up there somewhere lost and alone, with nothing to look forward to but death.'

They sat in silence for a long time and the only sound was the howling of the north wind. Eva Lind stood up and walked over to the living-room window.

'Poor little boy,' she said into the cold winter's night.

When they had gone, he sat down in his chair again and a sentence from Elías's exercise book came into his mind; a little comment or thought that Elías had written on its own at the bottom of a page, as if he had noted it down on the spur of the moment. Perhaps he had meant to ask his mother.

How many trees does it take to make a forest?

24

Erlendur woke from a dreamless sleep. A book about avalanches in Iceland lay open on the bedside table. More books were piled beside it: Icelandic novels, descriptions of arduous journeys over mountain tracks, folktales and legends, ghost stories and travellers' tales from days gone by, but mostly tragic accounts of death and destruction in extreme weather conditions. Valgerdur had asked if these accounts he revered so much dealt only with death and injury. Erlendur said that on the contrary many of them told of miraculous rescues, and the apparently limitless capacity and endurance of people who survived the most extraordinary ordeals. That's the point of the stories, he said. That's why they're so relevant.

He admitted that they contained few laughs, though he did find the occasional glimmer of wry amusement amidst all the trials and tribulations. Before going to sleep he had read an account in a parish register from 1847 that told of a farm labourer who went far into the mountains in search of sheep, having been warned of the danger from avalanches. When the labourer did not return at the appointed hour, two men were sent out to look for him. After searching for some time they saw that he had probably fallen over a snowy precipice into a large gully that was by now almost entirely full of snow. The men scraped away at the snow with their hands and after they had dug down about four feet they uncovered the soles of the labourer's feet. Assuming he must be dead, they ceased their digging and returned to the farm, but when they reported their discovery, there was a commotion. The farm people would not have it that the labourer's death was beyond doubt, and ordered the pair back up the mountain, this time armed with a shovel, some Hoffmann's drops and camphor oil. When they dug the man out of the snow, it transpired that he had been trapped head-down in the drift, was still very much alive in spite of everything, and 'came out talking furiously'.

Erlendur smiled to himself as he got out of bed and put on some coffee. Sigurdur Óli phoned and they had a brief conversation about the knife from the recycling depot. Anyone from the school could have removed the knife from the workshop, assuming it came from there in the first place, as there was a steady stream of pupils, teachers and other staff through the classroom. Egill was right, the carving knives used at Icelandic schools were identical, and it was uncertain whether they would be able to find any evidence to link the knife to the attack on Elías. The employee who discovered it had been using it at work and claimed that it was so shiny when he found it that someone must have cleaned it before it ended up in the scrap-metal bin.

The phone rang again. This time it was Elínborg.

'She's been found,' she announced without preamble. 'The missing woman.'

'Who?'

'The missing woman. Exactly where I said we'd find her. On Reykjanes. In the lavafield south of the aluminium plant.'

*

The police forensics team were standing over the body, well bundled up in thick down jackets. A tripod supporting two arclights lay on its side with the bulbs smashed, where it had blown over. Erlendur had driven the Ford along the old track as far as he dared before getting out and walking the last stretch. The place was known as Hraun, a short distance from the aluminium plant at Straumsvík. The lava shoreline was indented here by small coves full of sharp skerries. Snow fell in intermittent flurries and an angry sea crashed on the rocks. Erlendur was aware that this used to be a landing place for rowing boats and noted the outlines of ruined walls, which were all that remained of the old fishermen's huts and sheds.

The corpse had been washed up in one of the coves. Although the official search for the woman had been called off some time ago, a small team of voluntary rescue workers from nearby Hafnarfjörður had been on a dawn exercise, combing the beaches south of the aluminium plant, when they stumbled across the body. Elínborg was talking to members of the team in one of the patrol cars that had made it all the way down to the sea. An ambulance and two other police cars were parked a short way from the corpse, their headlights illuminating the narrow cove, the breakers on the beach and the figures stooping over the body.

Elínborg stepped out of the car when she saw Erlendur approaching.

'Has someone let the husband know?' he asked, stopping.

'I gather he's on his way.'

'Is it definitely her?'

'There's no question. We found her ID. Aren't you going to take a look at her?'

'Yes, in a minute,' Erlendur said, taking out a packet of

cigarettes and lighting one. He had dreaded this moment. It would be the first time he had seen the woman and he wished that it had not been like this, as a corpse on a Reykjanes beach. He remembered their last telephone conversation. He had been a brute. He regretted it now.

The Hafnarfjördur district medical officer had been summoned to sign the death certificate. When he had finished examining the body, he walked over to them.

'Can you see any injuries?' Erlendur asked.

'No, not at first sight,' the medical officer said.

The phone calls had been so brief, so truncated. Erlendur wondered if he could have responded differently. Could he have helped her? Ought he to have listened to her better?

'I'm only here to sign the death certificate,' the medical officer said. 'The police pathologist will have to determine the cause of death.'

They saw a jeep approaching. Erlendur flicked away his cigarette butt. The jeep stopped by the squad cars and the woman's husband jumped out and started running towards them.

'Have you found her?' he called.

Erlendur and Elínborg exchanged glances. The man's path was blocked by police officers.

'Is it her?' the man yelled, staring over towards the body. 'Oh my God! What has she done?'

He tried to push past them but the police officers held him back.

'What have you done?' he shouted in the direction of the body.

Erlendur and Elínborg stood motionless in the cold, their eyes meeting. The man turned to Erlendur.

'Look what she's done!' he shouted in utter despair. 'Why did she do this? Why?'

The officers led the man aside and tried to calm him.

Erlendur stood in the shelter of a large police vehicle with Elínborg and the medical officer. His thoughts went out to the woman's children and former husband. He knew that the more time that elapsed after her disappearance, the more their fears for the worst had grown, and now their worst nightmares had been realised.

Erlendur had told the husband about the phone calls and had no idea what to do about that now that she was dead. He felt it was probably best to maintain a discreet silence about them. He heard her voice, heard her desperation and fear and that strange hesitancy, the half-finished sentences that made it hard for him to know what she wanted of him. He sighed heavily and lit up another cigarette.

'What are you thinking?' Elínborg asked.

'Those bloody phone calls,' Erlendur said.

'From her?' Elínborg asked.

'They keep preying on my mind. The last time I spoke to her I was . . . I was a bit sharp with her.'

'Typical,' Elínborg said.

'I could tell she was suffering but I had the feeling that she was playing some kind of game with me. I didn't give her enough time. I'm such a crass idiot.'

'You couldn't have changed anything.'

'Excuse me,' the medical officer said. 'When did you talk to her?'

He was an older man with whom Erlendur was slightly acquainted.

'Yesterday evening,' Erlendur said.

'You were talking to that woman yesterday evening?'

'Yes.'

'That's strange.'

'Oh?'

'That woman hasn't been phoning anyone recently.'

'Really?'

'And certainly not yesterday.'

'I'm telling you, she's called me several times over the past few days.'

'Of course I'm just an ordinary doctor,' the medical officer said. 'I'm no expert, but it's out of the question. Forget it. She's unrecognisable.'

Erlendur ground his cigarette under his shoe and stared at the medical officer.

'What are you saying?'

'She's been in the sea for at least two weeks,' the medical officer said. 'It's out of the question that she could have been alive a couple of days ago. Totally impossible. Why do you think they haven't let her husband see her?'

Erlendur gazed at him, speechless.

'What on earth's happening?' He sighed and started to walk towards the woman's body.

'You mean it wasn't her?' Elínborg said, following on his heel. 'What . . . ?'

'Who else could it have been?'

'I don't know.'

'If it wasn't her who called, who was it?'

Erlendur looked down at the corpse with utter incomprehension. It had been badly battered during its stay in the sea.

'Who was it then?' he groaned. 'Who is this woman who's

been calling me and talking to me about . . . about . . . What was it she said? *I can't do it?*'

The man who had first complained about the scratches on his car was voluble on the subject of the indifference shown by the police when he originally reported the vandalism. They could not have been less interested, merely wrote a report for the insurance company, and he had heard nothing since. He phoned to find out what progress they were making in catching the bastards who vandalised his car but could never get to speak to anyone who had a clue what was going on.

The man ranted on in the same vein for some time and Sigurdur Óli could not be bothered to interrupt him. He was not really listening; his thoughts were preoccupied with Bergthóra and the issue of adoption. After exhaustive tests it had emerged that the problem lay with Bergthóra. She could not have children, although she yearned to with all her heart. The whole process had put a severe strain on their relationship, both before they discovered that Bergthóra could not have children – after bitter experience and countless visits to specialists – and, not least in the aftermath. Sigurdur Óli felt sure that Bergthóra had not yet recovered. He himself had come to the conclusion that 'since that's the way it is', as he put it to Bergthóra, perhaps they should accept the situation and leave it at that. The subject had raised its head again when he came home from work yesterday evening. Bergthóra had started saying that, as Sigurdur Óli was well aware, Icelandic couples mainly adopted from South East Asia, India and China.

'I don't spend as much time thinking about it as you do,' he said as carefully as he could.

'So you don't care then?' Bergthóra asked.

'Of course I care,' Sigurdur Óli said. 'I care about your feelings, about our feelings. I just . . .'

'What?'

'I don't know if you're in any state to make a snap decision about adoption. It's a pretty big step.'

Bergthóra took a deep breath.

'We'll never agree on this,' she said.

'I just feel we need more time to recover and talk it over.'

'Of course, you can have a child any time you like,' Bergthóra said cynically.

'What?'

'If you had the slightest interest, which you never have had.'

'Bergthóra . . .'

'You've never really been interested, have you?'

Sigurdur Óli did not reply.

'You can find someone else,' Bergthóra said, 'and have children with her.'

'This is exactly what I mean. You're not . . . you can't discuss it reasonably. Let's just give it time. It won't do any harm.'

'Don't keep telling me what sort of state I'm in,' Bergthóra said. 'Why do you always have to belittle me?'

'I'm not.'

'You always think you're somehow better than me.'

'I'm not prepared to adopt as matters stand,' he said.

Bergthóra stared at him for a long time without saying a word. Then she gave a wan smile.

'Is it because they're foreign?' she asked. 'Coloured? Chinese? Indian? Is that the reason?'

Sigurdur Óli stood up.

'We can't talk with things as they are,' he said.

'Is that why? You want your children to be Icelandic, do you?'

'Bergthóra. Why are you talking like this? Don't you think I've . . . ?'

'What?'

'Don't you think I've suffered? Don't you think I was upset when it didn't work, when we lost the ba—' He stopped.

'You never said anything,' Bergthóra said.

'What was I supposed to say?' Sigurdur Óli said. 'What is it that I'm always supposed to say?'

He started out of his reverie when the man raised his voice.

'Yes, er . . . no, sorry?' Sigurdur Óli said, adrift in his own thoughts.

The owner of the vandalised car glared at him.

'You aren't even listening to me,' he said in disgust. 'It's always the same story with you cops.'

'I'm sorry, I was just wondering if you saw who did this to your car.'

'I didn't see anything,' the man said. 'I just found it scratched like that.'

'Any idea who could have done it? Someone with a score to settle? Local kids?'

'I have no idea. Isn't that your job? Isn't it your job to find the bastard?'

Next Sigurdur Óli had arranged to meet the man's neighbour, a young woman who studied medicine at the university and rented a small flat in the next-door block. She sat down for a chat, and Sigurdur Óli made an effort to concentrate better than he had when he spoke to the man, who had left in something of a huff.

The woman was about twenty-five and rather fat. Sigurdur Óli had caught a brief glimpse of her kitchen where fast-food packaging predominated.

She told Sigurdur Óli that her car was nothing special but it was still awful to have it scratched like that.

'Why the sudden interest now?' she asked. 'Your lot could hardly be bothered to come round when I originally reported the damage.'

'Several other cars have been vandalised,' Sigurdur Óli said. 'One belonging to someone from the block of flats next door. We need to put a stop to it.'

'I think I saw them,' the woman said, taking out a packet of cigarettes. The flat stank of smoke.

'Really?' Sigurdur Óli said, watching her light up. He thought of the fast-food packaging in the kitchen and had to remind himself that this woman was studying medicine.

'There were two boys loitering outside,' she said, exhaling smoke. 'You see, I was at home when it happened. It was so peculiar. I had to run back inside because I'd forgotten my lunch. I left the car unlocked with the keys in the ignition, something you should never do.'

She gave Sigurdur Óli a look, as if she was giving him important advice.

'When I came out, only a few minutes later, there was this terrible scratch on my car.'

'Was it early in the morning?' Sigurdur Óli asked.

'Yes, I was on my way to lectures.'

'How long ago was this?'

'A week or so.'

'And you saw who did it?'

'I'm sure it was them,' the woman said, stubbing out her cigarette. There was a small bowl of toffees on the table. She put one in her mouth and proffered the bowl to Sigurdur Óli who declined.

'What did you see?'

'I told the police all this last week but they didn't seem very interested in the scratch at the time.'

'There have been other incidents,' Sigurdur Óli said. 'Yours is not the only car they've vandalised. We want to catch them.'

'It was about eight o'clock,' she said. 'Still pitch black, of course, but there's a light by the entrance to the block and as I was on my way upstairs I saw two boys walk past. They can't have been more than about fifteen, both carrying schoolbags. I told the police all this.'

'Did you notice which way they were going?'

'Towards the chemist's.'

'The chemist's?'

'And the school,' the woman said, chewing her toffee. 'Where the boy was murdered.'

'Why do you think those boys scratched your car?'

'Because it wasn't scratched when I ran upstairs and it was when I came back down. They were the only people I saw that morning. I'm sure they were hiding somewhere, laughing at me. What kind of people scratch cars? Tell me that. What kind of bastards are they?'

'Pathetic losers,' Sigurdur Óli said. 'Would you recognise them again if you saw them?'

'I'm not a hundred per cent sure it was them.'

'No, I know that.'

'One had long, fair hair. They were wearing anoraks. The other had a woolly hat on. They were both sort of gangling.'

'Could you recognise them from photos?'

'Maybe. You lot didn't bother to offer me the chance the other day.'

*

Erlendur shut the door when he got back to his office on Hverfisgata. He sat down at his desk with his hands in his lap and stared into space with unseeing eyes. He had made a mistake. He had broken one of the golden rules that he had always tried to obey. The first rule that Marion Briem had taught him: nothing is as you *think* it is. He had been over-confident. Arrogant. He had forgotten the caution designed to protect him from blundering when he did not know the terrain. Arrogance had led him astray. He had overlooked other obvious possibilities; something that should not have happened to him.

He tried to remember the phone calls, what the woman had said, what it had been possible to glean from her voice, what time of day she had phoned. He had misinterpreted everything she said. *It can't go on like this,* he suddenly remembered her saying in her first phone call. In the most recent call he had refused to listen to her.

He knew that the woman wanted his help. She had something to hide and it was torturing her, so she had turned to him. There was only one possible explanation. If she was not the missing woman, it could only be connected to one case. He was handling the investigation into Elías's death. The phone calls must have been linked to that. It couldn't be anything else. This woman had information that might help the investigation into the child's murder and he had told her to get lost.

Erlendur slammed his clenched fists on the desk as hard as he could, sending papers and forms flying.

He kept going over and over the question of what the woman might have been trying to tell him but simply could not work it out. He could only hope that she would call him again, although that was hardly likely after the way he had treated her the last time.

He heard a knock and Elínborg put her head round the door. She saw the papers on the floor and looked at Erlendur.

'Is everything all right?'

'Did you want something?'

'Everyone makes mistakes,' Elínborg said, shutting the door behind her.

'Any news?'

'Sigurdur Óli's going over photos of the older pupils at the school with some car owner. A couple of them were loitering outside her block of flats when her car was vandalised.'

Elínborg began to pick up the papers from the floor.

'Leave them,' Erlendur said and started to help her.

'The pathologist is examining the body,' she said. 'The woman appears to have drowned and on first impression there are no signs of anything suspicious. She's been in the sea for at least two to three weeks.'

'I should have known better,' Erlendur said.

'So?'

'I made an error of judgement.'

'Come on, you weren't to know.'

'I should have talked to her instead of being hostile. I judged her for what she had done. And it wasn't even her.'

Elínborg shook her head.

'That woman phoned me so that I would reassure her and persuade her to help us, because she knows it's the right thing to do. And I reacted by cutting her off. She knows something about Elías's murder. A woman of uncertain age with a slightly husky voice, perhaps from smoking. Now, after the event, I realise how worried and frightened and apprehensive she was. I thought the missing woman and her husband were playing some kind of game. I couldn't understand it. Couldn't work out what they were up to and it got to me. Then it turns out I'd got the wrong end of the stick entirely.'

'What was she thinking of? Why did she throw herself in the sea?'

'I think . . .' Erlendur trailed off.

'What?'

'I think she'd fallen in love. She sacrificed everything for love: family, children, friends. Everything. Someone told me she had changed, become a different person. As if she'd found a new lease of life, discovered her true self during that time.'

Erlendur stopped again, lost in thought.

'And? What happened?'

'She found out that she'd been deceived. Her husband had started cheating on her. She was humiliated. All her . . . everything she had done, everything she had sacrificed, was for nothing.'

'I've heard about men like that,' Elínborg said. 'They're addicted to the first flush of passion and when that begins to fade, they go looking for it elsewhere.'

'But her love was genuine,' Erlendur said. 'And she couldn't bear it when she found out that it wasn't reciprocated.'

25

Sigurdur Óli rang the doorbell at the entrance to a four-storey block of flats close to the school. He stood and waited, then rang the bell again. A cold wind blew about his legs in the meagre shelter by the front door and he stamped his feet. It seemed no one was home. The block, which was not unlike the one where Sunee lived with her sons, was in a poor state of repair. It had not been painted for a long time and the wall by the entrance was still stained with soot from a fire in the rubbish store. Dusk was falling. The morning's snow flurries had deteriorated into a blizzard, cars were getting stuck on the roads and the Met Office had issued a severe weather warning for that evening. Sigurdur Óli's thoughts went to Bergthóra. He had not heard from her all day. She had already left for work when he woke up at the crack of dawn and lay alone with his thoughts.

The entryphone emitted a crackle.

'Hello?' he heard a voice say.

Sigurdur Óli introduced himself, explaining that he was from the police.

There was silence on the entryphone.

'What do you want?' the voice asked eventually.

'I want you to open the door,' Sigurdur Óli said, stamping his feet.

A long moment passed before the lock clicked and Sigurdur Óli entered the hall. He climbed up to the landing where the owner of the voice lived and knocked on the door. It opened and a boy of about fifteen peered shiftily into the corridor.

'Are you Anton?' Sigurdur Óli asked.

'Yes,' the boy said.

He appeared in pretty good health considering; he was fully dressed and even had a little colour in his cheeks. Sigurdur Óli noticed a smell of pizza from inside the flat and when he peered inside he saw an anorak slung over a chair and an open pizza box with one slice missing. He had been informed that Anton was ill and had been absent from school for the last few days.

'Feeling better?' Sigurdur Óli asked, walking into the flat uninvited.

The boy retreated before him and Sigurdur Óli shut the door. He noticed that the boy had made himself comfortable in front of the television with a pizza and a fizzy drink and two or three videos. An action film was playing on the screen.

'What's going on?' the boy asked in astonishment.

'It's one thing to scratch cars, Anton, another to kill people,' Sigurdur Óli said, helping himself to a slice of pizza. 'Your mum and dad not home?'

The boy shook his head.

'Several days ago you were spotted scratching a car near here,' Sigurdur Óli said and bit into the pizza. He watched the boy while he chewed.

'I haven't scratched any cars,' Anton said.

'Where did you get the knife?' Sigurdur Óli asked. 'And don't lie to me.'

'I . . .' Anton hesitated.

'Yes?'

'Why do you say *kill* people?'

'The little Asian boy who was stabbed, I reckon you did that too.'

'I didn't do that.'

'Sure you did.'

'I haven't done anything,' Anton said.

'Where can I get hold of your mother?' Sigurdur Óli asked. 'She'll need to come down to the station with us.'

Anton stared in bewilderment at Sigurdur Óli who calmly finished his pizza slice and surveyed the flat, as if Anton were an irrelevance. The medical student had identified the boy from a recent class photograph. She believed that he was one of the two boys she had seen outside the block of flats when her car was scratched. She was not quite so sure when shown a picture of Anton's classmate Thorvaldur, though she said that he could well have been the other boy. It was all very vague so Sigurdur Óli did not have much to go on when he rang Anton's doorbell. He decided to behave as if it was an open-and-shut case, and all that remained was to take the two friends down to the station. A mere formality. This tactic seemed to work on the boy.

Sigurdur Óli did not as yet have much information on Anton and Thorvaldur. They were in the same class, spent a lot of time together and sometimes got into trouble with the teachers and school authorities; disrupting school activities, it was called. Once they had attacked a caretaker and received a two-day suspension. They were typical wasters and troublemakers who only turned up to school to ruin things for everyone else.

'I didn't stab anyone,' Anton said at Sigurdur Óli's mention of his mother and the police station.

'Call your mother,' Sigurdur Óli said. 'Tell her to meet us down at the station.'

Anton saw that Sigurdur Óli was in deadly earnest. This cop actually believed that he had stabbed the Asian boy. He tried to grasp the situation in which he suddenly found himself but could not quite take it in. They had vandalised a few cars, Doddi had done most of them, he himself maybe one, and now they had been caught. But the cop was also under the impression that he had attacked and killed that boy. Anton stood dithering in front of Sigurdur Óli, examining his options. His mother would go mental – again. She had often threatened to chuck him out. He looked at the video he had rented and the congealing pizza and the strange thing was that what he regretted most was being deprived of a quiet day in front of the television.

'I didn't do anything,' he repeated.

'You can tell that to your mother,' Sigurdur Óli said. 'Your mate Thorvaldur lost no time in squealing on you. Whined and blubbered throughout. He says you scratched the cars. He says he only went along with you.'

'Doddi? He said that?'

'The biggest wimp I've ever come across,' Sigurdur Óli said, though he had not, in fact, tracked Thorvaldur down yet.

Anton vacillated in front of him.

'He's lying, he can't have said that.'

'Yeah, right,' Sigurdur Óli said. 'You two can discuss it down at the station.'

He made to grab Anton's arm and lead him out but the boy tore himself away.

'I only scratched one car,' he said. 'Doddi did the rest. He's lying!'

Sigurdur Óli drew a deep breath.

'We didn't do anything to that boy,' Anton added, as if to make it quite clear.

'You mean you and your mate?' Sigurdur Óli said.

'Doddi, yes. He's lying! It was him who scratched the cars.'

It was time to ease up the pressure a little, so Sigurdur Óli took a step back from the boy.

'How many cars was it?'

'I don't know. A few.'

'Do you know the Icelandic teacher Kjartan's car?'

'Yes.'

'Did you scratch his car? Outside the school?'

Anton hesitated before answering.

'That was Doddi. I didn't even know. He just told me about it. He can't stand Kjartan. Does Mum have to find out about this?'

'What did you make the scratches with?' Sigurdur Óli asked, ignoring his question.

'A knife,' Anton said.

'What kind of knife?'

'It was Doddi's.'

'He said it was yours,' Sigurdur Óli lied.

'It was his knife.'

'What kind of knife was it?'

'Like the one on TV,' Anton said.

'On TV?'

'The one they were showing pictures of. It was like our knife.'

Sigurdur Óli was speechless. He stared at the boy who gradually cottoned on to the fact that he had said something important. He wondered what it could have been and when it suddenly struck him, it was like a blow to the face. It had not occurred to him. Of course it was the same knife! He had seen pictures of it on television but had not made the connection with the damage that he and his mate Doddi had done to a few cars on the way to school. He began to see his situation as part of something much larger and more serious.

Sigurdur Óli took out his phone.

'I didn't do it,' Anton said. 'I swear it.'

'Do you know where the knife is now?'

'Doddi has it. Doddi had it all along.'

Sigurdur Óli watched the boy as he waited for Erlendur to answer, then glanced round the little flat, noting how Anton had made himself comfortable before the intrusion.

'Call your mother,' he said. 'You're coming with me. Tell her to meet you down at the station.'

'Yes.' Erlendur answered his phone.

'I think I'm on to something,' Sigurdur Óli said. 'Are you at the station?'

'What have you got?' Erlendur asked.

'Is the knife there?'

'Yes, what are you going to do?'

'I'm on my way,' Sigurdur Óli said.

When the police arrived to fetch Doddi an hour or so later he was not at home. A man in his early forties answered the door to the two officers and looked them up and down. Doddi's mother appeared in the doorway as well. They did not know where the boy was and demanded to be told what he had done wrong. The police officers said they did not know, they had simply been sent to bring him in to the police station on Hverfisgata along with a guardian.

'Since he's under age,' one of them elaborated.

The officers were both in uniform and driving a patrol car. The intention was to put the fear of God into Doddi. They were standing on the doorstep of the small town house where Doddi lived, explaining their business, when the man, who turned out to be the boy's stepfather, called out that there he was, there was Doddi!

'Come here!' he called. 'Doddi, get over here!'

The boy was walking round the corner of a nearby house, taking a footpath that cut through the area. He stopped dead when he heard his stepfather's call, then spotted the police car, the two officers looking in his direction and his mother's head craning from the doorway. It took him a moment to grasp the situation. He contemplated making a run for it, then decided it would be futile.

After an interrogation lasting nearly three hours, Doddi finally confessed to Sigurdur Óli that he had stolen a carving knife from the school and used it to vandalise cars that he and his friend Anton passed on their way to school. Both boys flatly denied having touched Elías, however, claiming that they did not even know him and had no idea who killed him. It was more than a week since they had scratched the car belonging to the young woman whom they had seen dashing back inside her block of flats, leaving the engine running. They did not realise that she had spotted them. At first they meant to steal the car as it had been handed to them on a plate with the engine left running and all, but when it came to the point they couldn't be bothered. Doddi walked along beside it, scraping the point of the knife along the paintwork, then they ran and hid. This was the first time they had seen the owner of one of the cars they had vandalised and it heightened the adrenalin. They waited for the woman to come out again in order to watch her reaction when she saw the scratch. She soon came dashing back out of the house and opened the car door but stopped dead when she saw the scratch along the bodywork. She bent down to take a closer look, then peered round, walked out into the car park and scanned in all directions, before taking a frantic glance at her watch, returning to her car and driving away.

The knife found at the recycling depot was in a box in the interview room and Doddi recognised it immediately. The police pathologist confirmed that it could well be the murder weapon.

Elínborg was in another interview room with Anton. The boys' statements matched in all the main details. Doddi had stolen the knife, and the initiative when it came to satisfying their destructive urge had largely been his.

'How did the knife end up in the recycling bin?' Elínborg asked Anton, who had been extremely cooperative ever since arriving at the police station.

'I don't know,' Anton replied.

'Did you use it to attack Elías?'

'No,' Anton said. 'I didn't touch him.'

'Why did you throw the knife away?'

'I didn't.'

'What about your mate, Doddi?'

'I don't know. He had the knife last.'

'He says you had it.'

'He's lying.'

'Did you know the knife was used to kill Elías?'

'No.'

'Do you know Niran, Elías's brother?'

'No, not at all, except that he's at my school. I don't know him at all.'

In the other interview room similar questions were being

flung at Doddi who claimed that Anton had had the knife last.

'How long is it since you took the knife from the carpentry workshop?' Sigurdur Óli asked.

'About ten days or . . .' Doddi thought. 'Yeah, something like that. It was straight after the Christmas holidays.'

'Where did you last see it?'

'Anton took it home with him.'

'He says you had it.'

'He's lying.'

'Do you know who Elías was?'

'Yes.'

'Did you know him?'

'No. Not at all.'

'Did you stab him to death?'

'No.'

'Did you stab him to death with the knife that you stole from the carpentry workshop?'

'No. I didn't do anything.'

'Why did you scratch those cars?'

'I don't know.'

'You don't know?'

'We were bored.'

In the other room, Elínborg stared at Anton for a long time without saying a word, then rose to her feet. She had been sitting still for too long and her whole body ached. She leaned against the wall and folded her arms.

'Where were you when Elías was attacked?' she asked.

Anton could not give a clear account of his whereabouts. At first he said he had been at home, that he had gone straight home from school. Then he suddenly remembered that he had gone to a computer-games shop with Doddi.

'You will both be charged with Elías's murder,' Elínborg said. 'You had the knife, you killed him.'

'I didn't,' Anton said.

'What about your friend?'

'There's no way he did either.'

'What's your attitude to immigrants, foreigners, coloured people?'

'I don't know.'

Doddi hesitated when asked a similar question. Sigurdur Óli repeated the question but Doddi just stared at him without answering. Sigurdur Óli asked a third time.

'I don't have any attitude to them,' Doddi said at last. 'I don't give them any thought.'

'Have you attacked any immigrant kids?'

'No, never,' Doddi said.

Neither he nor Anton had ever been in trouble with the law. Anton's mother was a single parent with two children, who struggled to make ends meet on her meagre wages. Anton had a three-year-old half-brother. He saw his father briefly once a month or so. Doddi had two full siblings and a half-sister. He told them that his father, who had little to do with him, was a foreman on the Kárahnjúkar dam project.

'Why did you attack Elías?' Sigurdur Óli asked.

'I didn't.'

'We're going to charge you with Elías's murder,' Sigurdur Óli said. 'We have no other option.'

Doddi stared at him and it was clear from his expression that he fully grasped the implications of what Sigurdur Óli was saying. He was quite a tough nut. Sigurdur Óli had often questioned teenage boys who did not give a shit about anything or anyone and answered back with jeers and even threats against the police. He sensed that there was more to Doddi. He was not yet a hardened case. The vandalism of the cars was a brainless stunt but no more than that. At least for the time-being.

'He gave away the knife,' Doddi said.

'Gave it away?'

'I stole it but Anton had it last and he gave it away. I didn't know it had been used in the murder. And I'm sure he didn't either.'

Elínborg was still leaning against the wall with arms folded when Sigurdur Óli entered the interview room. He sat down in front of Anton and stared at him for a long time without saying a word. Elínborg refrained from asking any questions. Anton became restless, squirmed in his chair and fixed his gaze on Sigurdur Óli and Elínborg in turn. He was extremely uneasy.

'Do you know a boy called Hallur?' Sigurdur Óli asked.

Elínborg was leaving the interview room shortly afterwards when her mobile rang. It took her some time to work out who was on the other end but at last she came up with an image of the flamboyant tie belonging to the PR guy from the insurance firm where someone had been making calls to Sunee.

'I've been involved in a major investigation on your behalf,' the PR man said gravely.

'Really?' Elínborg said.

'Yes, really. I've spoken to a number of people here at the firm, all in confidence of course, and none of them is in a relationship with that woman, as far as I can tell.'

'No?'

'No. At least, nothing that can be confirmed.'

'What about unconfirmed?'

'Well, there are rumours about one man.'

'Yes?'

'I don't know him. He's in his late forties and has worked in the claims department for years. The girls say he's dating an Asian woman.'

'Which girls?'

'The customer service reps. Someone spotted him at a nightclub about a month ago. He was with one of those women.'

'One of what women?'

'Thai, maybe.'

'Did you talk to him?'

'No.'

'Good. What's his name?'

'The girls want to know if he's connected in any way to the mother of the boy who died.'

'Tell them to mind their own business!'

26

Erlendur drove slowly past the house, parked several doors down and got out of the car. He walked unhurriedly back towards the house, looking around warily. He saw the junction with Stýrimannastígur and the large wooden building that had once been the Seaman's College after which the road was named. The insurance company employee lived in a pretty wooden house clad in corrugated iron. It had been lovingly restored from what Erlendur could see from where he stood in the cold, studying the house. Lights were on in two of the windows. The street was quiet and Erlendur feared that he would be too conspicuous as he strolled back and forth. He wanted to proceed with caution.

It was late. Snow was falling, the wind had picked up and a major blizzard was forecast. The radio had warned people not to leave anything unsecured outside and to avoid going out unless absolutely necessary. Roads were already closed in rural areas in the wake of the storm that was now heading towards the city.

Erlendur was still brooding over the identity of the woman who had been phoning him and what she could have wanted. He couldn't figure it out and only hoped that she would make contact with him one more time. She had to give him another chance. He was conscious that there was not much likelihood of this happening but at least he now knew how to react should he ever hear from her again.

He was about to cross the road to the house when the basement door opened and a figure appeared in the rectangle of light. It was very small and Erlendur thought that it might be Niran. He could not see its face, which seemed to be obscured by something. The figure was wearing a windcheater and a baseball cap with a large peak. It closed the door carefully and headed down the street towards the town centre. Erlendur followed a little way behind, unsure what action to take. He noticed that the figure had a scarf bound over its face so that only its eyes were visible. It was holding something but Erlendur could not see what.

The figure bowed its head and set a course straight for the town centre. It was Saturday evening, the clubs and restaurants were all open and a number of people were about. The figure unfolded what it was holding, revealing it to be a large plastic bag. It approached a litter bin and looked inside, rooted around in it briefly, then moved on. Two beer cans lying under a bench disappeared into the bag, then the figure moved on to the next litter bin. Erlendur watched this behaviour. The figure was collecting used bottles and cans. It moved silently and purposefully, as if it had done this many times before, as unobtrusively as possible, largely unmarked by passers-by.

He followed its movements around the town centre for some time. The bag soon began to fill up. Erlendur came to a corner shop, stepped inside and bought two cans of some soft drink. When he came out again he emptied the cans into the gutter, then walked up to the figure who had paused by a litter bin in a small alleyway off Austurvöllur Square.

'Here's a couple,' Erlendur said, holding out the cans.

The figure looked at him in astonishment, the scarf completely obscuring its face, the baseball cap pulled down over its eyes. The figure accepted the cans hesitantly and put them in the bag, then immediately made to move on again without saying a word.

'My name's Erlendur,' he said. 'Can I talk to you for a moment?'

The figure stopped and looked searchingly at Erlendur.

'I only want to talk to you, if that's all right,' Erlendur said.

The figure backed away, without replying.

'Don't worry,' Erlendur said, moving closer.

The figure tensed, poised to run, but apparently reluctant to abandon the bag half full of bottles and cans, and this gave Erlendur a chance to seize hold of its jacket. The figure tried to hit him with the bag and tear itself loose but Erlendur held on tight with both hands. The figure struggled in his grasp but could not get away. Erlendur spoke to it reassuringly.

'I'm trying to help you,' he said. 'I need to talk to you. Do you understand?'

He received no answer. The figure tried with all its might to break free but Erlendur was strong and it could not get away.

'Do you understand Icelandic?'

The figure did not answer.

'I don't want you to do anything stupid,' he said. 'I want to help you.'

No answer.

'I'm going to let you go,' Erlendur said. 'Don't run away. I need to talk to you.'

He gradually relaxed his hold and finally released the figure who immediately took to its heels. He chased it a few steps and saw it run across the square. As he watched it go, wondering if he had any chance of catching up with this light-footed person, his quarry began to slow down and finally stopped under the statue of the independence hero, Jón Sigurdsson. It turned and looked at Erlendur who stood motionless, waiting to see what would happen. A long time elapsed until finally the figure began to walk slowly back towards him.

On the way it removed its baseball cap, revealing thick, black hair, and when it reached him it untied the scarf from its face so that he could see who it was.

Hallur sat between his parents, insisting that he knew nothing about the wood-carving knife that Anton claimed to have given him. The police had found his full name and address in the school register. He was acquainted with Doddi and Anton, who were the same age as him but in a different class. He did not know them well, however, as he was new to this part of town. His family had moved into the area about six months ago. Hallur was an only child, quite short, with a mane of unruly dark hair covering his eyes. He repeatedly flicked his head whenever his fringe blocked his view. He was very calm and looked wide-eyed at Sigurdur Óli and Elínborg in turn.

His parents were very eager to please. They were not at all annoyed at being disturbed so late in the evening by Sigurdur Óli and Elínborg. They chatted about the crazy weather that had been forecast and the mother offered the detectives coffee. They lived in a two-storey detached house.

'I expect you're talking to lots of children from the school,' the mother said. 'On account of that ghastly business. Are you getting anywhere with your inquiries?'

The father regarded them in silence.

'We're making progress,' Elínborg said, her eyes on Hallur.

'We thought you'd probably call round,' the woman said. 'Aren't you talking to all the kids at the school? Do you know anything about this knife, Hallur dear?' she asked her son.

'No,' Hallur said a second time.

'I've never seen him with a knife,' she said. 'I can't imagine who could have told you that Hallur has this knife. I . . . it's rather shocking when you come to think of it. I mean, that people can make wild accusations like that. Don't you think?'

She looked at Elínborg as if they women should stand together.

'Still, it's not as bad as having your child stabbed to death,' Elínborg said.

'We have no reason to disbelieve the testimony of the boys who told us,' Sigurdur Óli said.

'Do you know anything about these boys, Doddi and Anton?' the woman asked her husband. 'I've never heard of them. We ought to know all Hallur's friends.'

'They're not his friends,' Sigurdur Óli said. 'Though one of them, Anton, wants to be his friend. That's why he gave Hallur the knife and delayed telling us about it for as long as possible. Isn't that right?' he asked, looking at Hallur.

'I don't really know Anton,' Hallur said. 'I don't know many people at school.'

'He's only been there since the autumn, since we moved,' his mother said.

'You moved, when, last summer?'

'Yes,' the mother answered.

'How have you settled into your new school?' Elínborg asked.

'You know,' Hallur said. 'Fine.'

'But you don't have any friends there . . . ?'

The question dangled in the air.

'He's adjusted very well,' the woman said at last, looking at her husband who had not contributed anything to the conversation as yet.

'Have you changed schools often?' Sigurdur Óli asked.

Hallur looked at his mother.

'About three times,' he said.

'But this time we're staying put,' the woman added, directing another glance at her husband.

'Anton said you were with another boy when he met you and gave you the knife,' Sigurdur Óli said. 'Anton didn't know him and said he wasn't at the school. Who was this boy?'

'He didn't give me any knife,' Hallur said. 'He's lying.'

'Are you sure?' Elínborg asked.

Anton had confessed under cross-examination to having given Hallur the knife. A boy he had never seen before had been with Hallur at the time. Hallur was new to the school and kept a fairly low profile, though Anton said that he had once been round to see him at that big house. According to Anton, Hallur had talked candidly about his parents, describing his mother as an appalling snob, who was constantly interfering, a total control freak. His parents were forever in financial difficulties; once their house had even been repossessed, yet this did not seem to prevent them from living in some luxury. Hallur had the biggest collection of computer games Anton had ever seen.

He didn't know why Hallur wanted the knife, unless perhaps because it was stolen. Hallur saw him with it and when Anton told him that Doddi had stolen it from the carpentry workshop, Hallur suddenly became very keen to acquire it. They met round at Anton's. Hallur brought along another boy the same age but Anton did not know his name.

'You went round to Anton's,' Sigurdur Óli said. 'You gave him a computer game, he gave you the knife.'

'That's a lie,' Hallur said.

'There was a boy with you at Anton's place,' Elínborg said. 'Who was he?'

'My cousin was with me.'

'What's his name?'

'Gústi.'

'When was this?'

'I don't remember, several days ago.'

'His name's Ágúst, he's my brother's son,' the woman said. 'He and Hallur spend a lot of time together.'

Sigurdur Óli noted down the name.

'I don't know why Anton's claiming he gave me the knife,' Hallur said. 'He's lying. It's his knife. He's just trying to frame me.'

'Why?'

'I don't know.'

'Can you tell us where you were last Tuesday afternoon when Elías was stabbed?' Elínborg asked.

'Is this really necessary?' Hallur's father asked. 'You're talking to him as if he's done something wrong.'

'We're just checking the reliability of the witness statement we've taken, nothing more,' Elínborg said, without removing her eyes from Hallur. 'Where were you?'

'He was at home,' the woman said. 'He was asleep in his room. He finished school at one and slept till four. I was at home.'

'Is that right?' Elínborg asked the boy.

'Yes,' he said.

'Sleep a lot during the day, do you?'

'Sometimes.'

'We can never get him to bed in the evening,' his mother said. 'He's up all night. It's hardly surprising he sleeps during the day.'

'Don't you go out to work?' Elínborg asked, addressing the mother.

'I only work half days,' she said. 'In the mornings.'

When the figure removed the muffling scarf, Erlendur found himself face to face with Sunee's brother Virote. He was still holding the bag of drink-cans.

'You?' Erlendur said.

'How you find me?' Virote asked.

'I . . . what are you doing out in this weather?'

'You follow me?'

'Yes,' Erlendur said. 'Do you collect cans?'

'It pay little money.'

'Where's Niran?' Erlendur asked. 'Do you know?'

'Niran okay,' Virote said.

'Do you know where he is?'

Virote was mute.

'Do you know Niran's whereabouts?'

Virote looked at Erlendur for a long time, then nodded.

'Why are you hiding him?' Erlendur asked. 'You're only making matters worse. We're starting to think he must have attacked his brother. Your actions only support the idea. When you take him away like this, hide him.'

'It not like that,' Virote said. 'He not do nothing to Elías.'

'We have to talk to him,' Erlendur said. 'I know you're trying to protect him but this has gone too far. You won't gain anything by keeping him hidden.'

'He not attack Elías.'

'Then what? What do you mean by hiding him like this?'

Virote did not speak.

'Answer me,' Erlendur ordered. 'What were you doing at your sister's friend's house?'

'I visit him.'

'Is Niran with him?' Erlendur asked.

Virote did not answer. Erlendur repeated his question. An icy wind whipped about them in the alleyway and it occurred to Erlendur that Virote must be freezing. His light trainers were wet through, and he was only wearing jeans, a thin windcheater, a scarf and a baseball cap besides. Sensing that Virote was wavering, Erlendur put the question a third time.

'You have to trust us,' Erlendur said. 'We'll make sure nothing happens to Niran.'

Virote looked at him for a long time, as if pondering what to do, whether to trust him. Finally he seemed to make up his mind.

'Come. You come with me.'

27

The mobile rang in Erlendur's pocket. It was Elínborg to tell him about the meeting with Hallur and his parents. Erlendur asked her to call back later. Elínborg said that next she and Sigurdur Óli were going to visit Hallur's cousin, Ágúst, who might possibly be able to give them some answers about the knife. They rang off.

Erlendur replaced the phone in his coat pocket.

'Where's Niran now?' he asked.

'He with Jóhann,' Virote said.

'Where you were?'

'Yes.'

'Is Jóhann with him?'

'Yes.'

On the way Virote told him about Jóhann whom Sunee had met last spring. They had been seeing each other ever since but Jóhann was very hesitant and wanted to take things slowly. He was divorced, with no children of his own.

'Do they plan to live together, Sunee and Jóhann?' Erlendur asked.

'Maybe. I think they get married.'

'And Niran?'

'Jóhann help Niran. Sunee take to him.'

'Why?'

'Jóhann help Niran. He very angry. Very difficult. Then this happen.'

The parents of Hallur's cousin Ágúst looked on as Elínborg grilled their son. The mother gasped and the father leaped to his feet in agitation when Elínborg asked the boy straight out if he had murdered Elías. Ágúst answered every question very much as Hallur had and their stories tallied in all the main details. Neither he nor Hallur had received a knife from Anton. Ágúst said he had only met Anton on that one occasion at his place and couldn't explain why the boy was claiming that he had intended to swap a computer game for the wood-carving knife. He didn't know him at all.

Ágúst attended a different school from his cousin Hallur but their circumstances were very similar. Ágúst's parents seemed to have no shortage of money; they lived in an attractive detached house with two cars parked outside the garage.

'Do you know a boy by the name of Niran at your cousin's school?' Sigurdur Óli asked.

Ágúst shook his head. Like Hallur he seemed quite unperturbed by the visit from the police, and gave the impression of being polite and well brought up. He was an only child and it emerged that he and Hallur were almost like brothers and were always messing about together. A quick check revealed that neither had ever been in trouble with the law.

'Did you know his brother Elías?'

Again Ágúst shook his head.

'Where were you when the murder was committed?'

'He was with his father up at Hafravatn,' the mother said. 'We have a summer cottage by the lake.'

'Do you often go there midweek, in the middle of the day?' Elínborg asked, looking at the father.

'We go there whenever we like,' he said.

'And you were both there all day?'

'Till evening,' the father said. 'We're doing up an old range at the cottage. Are you telling me that on the basis of a pack of lies told by a couple of youths, you come here late at night, in the middle of a blizzard, to ask a string of preposterous questions?'

'That's what's so odd,' Sigurdur Óli said. 'Why should they lie about Hallur and Ágúst, boys they don't even know?'

'Isn't that something you should be looking into? It's bloody outrageous to come here and pester the boy in the middle of the night with nonsensical questions based on information from some youths who sound to me as if they're trying to get themselves out of trouble.'

'Maybe,' Elínborg said. 'We're only doing our job. You're welcome to complain to our superiors.'

'I might just do that.'

'Do you want me to call for you?'

'Stop it, Óttar,' the woman said.

'No, I'm serious,' the man said. 'This conduct is bloody outrageous.'

Elínborg had taken out her mobile phone. It had been a long day and she would have given anything to be at home. She could have had a word with Sigurdur Óli and agreed to come back in the morning, apologising yet again for the intrusion, but this man was seriously aggravating her. Everything he said was correct but he was being deliberately provocative and getting on her nerves. Before she knew what she was doing she had selected Erlendur's number and handed the man the phone.

'This is the man you want to talk to,' she said.

Erlendur approached the house with Virote. It had taken them ten minutes to walk up from the town centre. Virote pressed the bell, the door opened and a man whom Erlendur assumed was Jóhann appeared, clearly upset, and started talking in a rush to Virote. He did not notice Erlendur at first but when he stepped forwards the man started back and stared at them both in turn.

'Are you from the police?' he asked, looking suspiciously at Erlendur.

Erlendur nodded.

'You're Jóhann, aren't you?'

'Yes.'

'What's going on here?'

'Sunee wanted it this way. I'm trying to help her.'

'Where Niran?' Virote asked.

'Niran's disappeared,' Jóhann said.

'Do you know where he's gone?' Erlendur asked.

'No.'

'Home, maybe?' Erlendur suggested.

'No, I called Sunee,' Jóhann said. 'She's desperately worried.'

'Where can he have gone?'

'Impossible to say. He's been more agitated than usual today. He's in a bad way. He feels he should have looked after Elías better.'

'When did he leave?'

'I didn't hear him go out.'

Jóhann showed Erlendur into the kitchen.

'Not more than fifteen, twenty minutes ago. I had to pop out to the shop and when I came back he was gone.'

There was no mistaking Jóhann's anxiety. He was of medium height, fair-haired and lean, dressed in a blue denim shirt and

323

black trousers, and had a neat beard that he kept stroking down from his mouth.

'I heard at work that the police have been asking questions about me,' he said.

'You and Sunee must have known each other for some time if she trusts you with Niran.'

'Yes, nine months, more or less.'

'But you've been keeping it pretty hush-hush.'

'No, I don't know. Hush-hush. We wanted to be cautious. I got divorced four years back and have lived alone since. Sunee's the first woman I've met since my divorce who I really like. She's special.'

'Are you planning to live together?'

'We've talked about my moving into her place in the summer.'

'You've been to her place?'

'Yes, several times. I couldn't believe what happened to poor little Elías. I didn't hear about it till the day afterwards because I was in the West Fjords on business and didn't see the news. When people started talking about the murder, I immediately thought of Sunee. Then her brother, Virote here, called me from his mobile and Sunee came on the phone and told me what had happened. She told me about Niran, that he was in shock and in a terrible state and could he stay with me for a few days. He was frightened and knocked sideways by the whole affair as you might expect, and she was afraid for him, afraid that something might happen to him too or that he might do something stupid. I got back to town at lunchtime and found them waiting outside my house. Niran was a terrible sight. Totally destroyed. Sunee asked me to look after him and there was no way I could refuse, no way I could argue with her. It was just something I had to do.'

Jóhann looked at Erlendur.

'Niran wasn't hostile to me as Sunee had expected,' he explained. 'I hit it off with Elías straight away but she was worried about how Niran would react if we started living together. But Niran didn't take against me. He may not exactly have welcomed me with open arms but he didn't take against me. He didn't take much notice of me the few times I visited them at the flat, though I managed to chat to him a bit about football. I was going to sort out a new computer for them so that they could get online. He was very enthusiastic about that.'

'And you talked about football?'

'We both support the same English team,' Jóhann said with a shrug.

'You didn't want to get in touch with the police?'

'No, I did it for Sunee, for her and myself and Niran.'

'It didn't occur to you that they might have anything to hide?'

'Niran could never have harmed a hair on Elías's head. The very idea is absurd. Ludicrous. You'd know that if you'd only met them for a few minutes. Their relationship was special. I think that's why Niran reacted so badly. They used to play together and Niran read Thai comics or books to Elías in the evenings. I told Sunee that I wished I'd had such a kind big brother when I was young.'

'How did you and Sunee meet?'

'At a nightclub. She was with her friends from the chocolate factory. I'd been at my company's annual do. I didn't know her at all. She invited me to dance and we danced and talked. She told me about Thailand. Then I got in touch with her a couple of days later and asked if she remembered me. We met again. She was completely open about everything, about Óðinn and her boys and her work at the chocolate factory.'

'What then?'

'We started seeing each other regularly. It's . . . Sunee . . . she's positive and happy and sincere and fun, always sees the bright side of everything. Maybe it's the Thai mentality, I don't know. Then this happens, this horrific crime.'

'But you were a bit coy about the relationship?'

'We both were, actually. We didn't want to rush into anything and I admit I needed to think about it. It was completely new and unexpected for me.'

'You didn't tell anyone at work?'

'Only my closest friends, and recently my family, after Sunee and I decided to move in together. But the grapevine has obviously been buzzing because it didn't take you long to track me down. I've asked Sunee to marry me. We've discussed getting married as early as this summer but I don't know . . . then this nightmare happens.'

'Can you guess where Niran might have gone?'

'No. As I say, he's been very restless all day.'

'Did he mention anyone in particular? Anyone he suspected of committing the crime?'

Jóhann looked at Erlendur.

'He talked of revenge. He'd been involved in a scuffle at school with a teacher who threatened him. Niran didn't want to say who it was but that was one of the reasons why Sunee hid him. She was afraid for him. He's her only child now.'

At that moment Virote came into the kitchen holding a scrap of paper. He handed it to Erlendur.

'I find in Niran room,' Virote said.

The paper had been torn out of the telephone directory at Kjartan's name.

The phone began to ring in Erlendur's pocket.

He took it out and pressed the answer button.

'Hello,' he said.

'. . . *I'm sorry, he doesn't want to. He doesn't need to make a complaint . . .*' he heard a familiar voice say, then the caller hung up.

Erlendur looked up in disbelief. He stared at the phone in his hand. He recognised the voice immediately. He had heard it before.

A woman of uncertain age with a slightly husky voice, perhaps from smoking.

He knew he would never forget that voice. It haunted him waking and sleeping because he had not listened to it properly. In his mind it would always be the voice of the guilt-stricken woman who had run away from her husband and turned up dead on Reykjanes beach.

28

Ágúst's mother intervened and snatched the phone as Elínborg was handing it to the husband so that he could complain to Erlendur about the conduct of his junior officers.

Passing the phone back to Elínborg, she asked her to excuse her husband's outburst. He had no reason to criticise the police for doing their job, especially not in such a sensitive case.

'It's all right,' she said. 'I'm sorry, he doesn't want to. He doesn't need to make a complaint.'

Elínborg took the phone and cut the connection, staring from husband to wife. Then she replaced the phone in her bag. Shortly afterwards it started ringing. She looked at the number display. It was Erlendur.

Kjartan took a taxi home. He had been at a pub in the city centre with some old mates who used to get together from time to time for a few beers. He had left his car at home. Three of them shared a taxi and his was the last stop. The weather had deteriorated dramatically during the evening and visibility was virtually nil. The taxi's windscreen wipers struggled to cope with the snow and the car narrowly avoided getting bogged down in a drift on the way.

Kjartan was a little unsteady on his feet when he stepped out of the taxi, which slowly moved off. He straightened up. He'd had one too many, although they had called it a night earlier than usual because of the weather.

A wild blizzard had blown up. Erlendur drove the Ford as fast as he dared in the conditions. Virote and Jóhann were with him. The radio reported that whole suburbs of Reykjavík were being cut off due to the severe weather. Erlendur had ordered out a couple of squad cars to go to Kjartan's house. He only hoped they would arrive in time.

'The woman you're with is the one who's been calling me ever since Elías was attacked,' he informed Elínborg the moment she answered her phone. 'She's the one I mistook for the woman who committed suicide.'

'Really?' Elínborg said.

'Is she the mother of the boy you're with?'

'Yes.'

'Keep her talking, I'm going to try to get to you.'

'All right,' Elínborg said. 'Where are you?'

'I'm on my way,' Erlendur said and hung up.

Kjartan fumbled in his pocket for the keys; his wife liked to keep the house locked at all times, but he was not as worried about burglars. He found the keys but as he was about to pull them out of his pocket, he noticed a figure emerge from the shadow of the house and block his path.

'Who are you?' Kjartan asked.

He heard police sirens in the distance.

Erlendur saw the flashing blue lights of the police cars through the blizzard. They were turning into Kjartan's road. He glanced at Virote who was sitting beside him. In the rear-view mirror he could see Jóhann's anxious face.

'Who are you?' Kjartan repeated.

The figure did not answer. He could not see its face. The sirens grew louder and Kjartan turned his head in their direction. In that very instant the figure lunged, and Kjartan felt a piercing pain as he looked back at his assailant. In the glow of the streetlights he saw that the figure was wearing a basketball cap on its head and had a scarf over its face.

He fell to his knees, aware of something hot flowing from his belly, and saw the snow at his feet turn dark with blood.

Raising a hand, he reached out for his attacker, grabbed hold of the scarf and snatched it from its face.

The two police cars skidded in the snow as they stopped in front of the house. Four officers piled out and ran over to Kjartan as he sank slowly onto his side, still clutching the scarf in his cramped fist. Erlendur's car drew up and he leaped out with Virote and Jóhann. Virote ran past the police officers who were cautiously picking their way towards the figure in the shadows.

'Niran!' Virote yelled.

Niran looked up when he heard his name.

Virote saw Kjartan lying in a pool of blood.

He shouted something in Thai at Niran who stood as if turned to stone over Kjartan's body and dropped his knife into the snow.

Half an hour later the doorbell rang at the house where Sigurdur Óli and Elínborg were sitting with Ágúst and his parents. An awkward silence had prevailed for a good while now. Elínborg and Sigurdur Óli had tried to fill the time until Erlendur's arrival with questions and remarks but the conversation had gradually petered out. When it came to a complete standstill, they announced that they were expecting another detective who wanted to speak to the family, although they could not say what he wanted to talk about. The atmosphere in the living room grew increasingly tense. When the doorbell finally rang, they all jumped out of their skins.

The father went to let Erlendur in and they entered the living room together. The mother who was sitting beside her son on the sofa had become very uneasy and rose to her feet when she saw Erlendur. Smiling apologetically, she said she would make some more coffee. She was on her way to the kitchen when Erlendur asked her to wait a moment.

He walked over to her and she retreated a couple of steps.

'It's all right. It's nearly over,' Erlendur said.

'What? Over?' the woman said, looking to her husband for help. He stood very still and did not say a word.

Ágúst got up from the sofa.

'I recognised your voice immediately,' Erlendur said. 'You've been phoning me over the last few days and I can understand why. It's no joke finding yourself in a situation like this.'

'In a situation like this?' the woman prevaricated. 'I don't know what you're talking about.'

Sigurdur Óli and Elínborg exchanged glances.

'I thought you were someone else at first,' Erlendur said. 'I'm glad I've found you.'

'Mum?' Ágúst said, staring at his mother.

'I think I understand now what you meant when you said that you couldn't live like this,' Erlendur said. 'What I don't understand is how you ever dreamed you could get away with pretending nothing had happened.'

The woman's eyes were fixed on Erlendur.

'You wanted help,' he said. 'That's why you called. Well, that help is here. So you can start behaving like a decent human being. You can do what you wanted to do all along.'

The woman looked at her husband who had still not moved a muscle. Then she looked at Elínborg and Sigurdur Óli who had no idea what was going on. Finally she looked at her son who had started to cry. When she saw this, her own eyes filled with tears.

'It was never a good idea,' Erlendur said.

Tears rolled down the woman's cheeks.

'Mum!' her son whispered.

'We did it for them,' she said in a low voice. 'For our boys. What they did could never be undone, disgusting and horrible though it was. We had to think of the future. We had to think of their future.'

'But there was no future, was there?' Erlendur said. 'Only this dreadful crime.'

The woman looked back at her son.

'They didn't mean to do it,' she said. 'They were just messing about.'

'I want to speak to a lawyer,' her husband said. 'Don't say another word.'

'They behaved like bloody fools,' the woman groaned, hiding her face in her hands.

All of a sudden the tension seemed to leave her, as if everything she had had to bottle up inside her for all those long days since the murder of Elías could at last be released.

'Why?' she yelled, taking a step towards her son. 'Why do you always have to behave like bloody fools? Just look what you've done!'

Her husband ran to her and tried to calm her down.

'Look what you've done!' she yelled at her son.

She fell into her husband's arms.

'God help us!' she moaned and slumped in a heap on the floor.

29

Hallur and Ágúst were taken straight in for questioning and later that night committed to the care of the Reykjavík Child Welfare Agency. The police interviewed both sets of parents as well and ordered that they be detained in custody. They blamed each other for the idea of covering up the boys' crime and both they and their sons gave conflicting accounts as to who had actually wielded the knife. After three days of interrogation Hallur finally confessed and the detectives were gradually able to piece together a picture of how Elías died.

The boys had all lied to the police. Hallur saw Anton with the knife that Doddi had stolen and offered to swap a recent computer game for it. All four met at Anton's house, where he tried out the computer game Hallur had brought along. They discussed doing a swap but nothing came of it. Thorvaldur and Anton admitted that they had scratched Kjartan's car on the morning of the day Elías was attacked and afterwards decided to get rid of the knife. Meeting Hallur in the school playground, they decided to hand it over to him.

Hallur had arranged to meet Ágúst straight after school. They were in the mood for trouble and went into a supermarket where they shoplifted some CDs and sweets. It was something they did from time to time, although they received plenty of pocket money from their parents. This was different. 'For the kicks,' Ágúst said, and could not give any better explanation. They were a bit high on adrenalin when they came out of the supermarket and saw Elías ahead of them with the large schoolbag on his back and the anorak askew on his little shoulders.

Perhaps he caught their attention because he was dark-skinned. Perhaps that was irrelevant. Ágúst said during questioning that of course they would have done the same if he had been a white boy. Hallur shrugged and could not answer the same question. He could not really explain what sort of state they were in. They were buzzing, he said. Excited after the shoplifting. Up for anything. They didn't know the boy who caught their eye. Didn't know his name was Elías. Hallur couldn't remember seeing him before, even though he attended the same school. They had no score to settle with him. Elías had never crossed their path before. He had never done anything to them.

They were buzzing.

They caught up with Elías where the path was at its narrowest and the concealing bushes rose highest. Dusk was falling and it was cold but they were feverish with excitement. They asked his name and if he had any money and what he was doing in Iceland anyway.

Elías said that he did not have any money. He tried to tear himself free but Ágúst held on to him. Hallur took out the knife to frighten him. They didn't mean to hurt him, they were just messing about. Hallur threatened him with the knife. Brandished it in his face.

Elías struggled even more frantically when he saw the knife. He began to call for help and Ágúst put a hand over his mouth.

Elías fought for all he was worth. Ágúst shouted to warn Hallur that he was going to let him go when Elías bit his hand, hurting him so badly that he yelled out.

Hallur had hold of Elías's anorak and before he knew what he was doing he had stabbed him with the knife. Elías stopped struggling. He fell silent, clutched his stomach and crumpled onto the path.

Hallur and Ágúst looked at one another, then set off at a run down the path, back the way they had come.

They took the bus to Ágúst's house. They were in shock. Ágúst's father was home and without a moment's hesitation they poured out the whole story. Hallur's hand was covered in blood. He had thrown away the knife on the way home. They said that they had stabbed a boy on the path by the school. They didn't mean to. It was an accident. They never meant to hurt the boy. It just happened. Ágúst's father stared at them, stunned.

Ágúst's mother came home at that point and immediately saw that something serious had happened. When she heard what the boys had done she wanted to call the police straight away. Her husband prevaricated.

'Did anyone see you?' he asked the boys.

They shook their heads.

'No, no one,' Hallur said.

'Are you sure?'

'Yes.'

'Where's the knife?'

Hallur described the place.

'Wait here,' Ágúst's father said. 'Don't do anything till I get back.'

'What are you doing?' his wife moaned.

He took her aside, out of earshot of the boys.

'Think about it,' he said. 'Think about the boys' future while I'm away. Call my sister. Tell her to come round and bring Dóri with her.'

He went out and returned three-quarters of an hour later with the knife. He announced that the boy was not on the path and they breathed easier. Maybe he was all right.

At that moment Hallur's parents arrived and were told what had happened. They couldn't believe their ears at first until they saw the boys' expressions and sensed Ágúst's parents' helplessness in the face of the unthinkable. They looked at their son, and all of a sudden they knew that it was true. Something horrific and incomprehensible had happened and nothing would ever be the same again.

'We didn't mean to do it,' Hallur said.

'It just happened,' Ágúst added.

They had nothing else to say.

'So it wasn't Ágúst who stabbed him?' his mother asked.

'They were both involved,' Hallur's father said firmly. 'Your son was holding him.'

'Your son stabbed him.'

A row broke out and the boys looked on. The brother and sister, Hallur's mother and Ágúst's father, eventually managed to calm down their spouses. Ágúst's father proposed that they should not go to the police yet.

They quarrelled again. In the end, the fathers went out looking for Elías. If he had disappeared from the path it might mean that he was all right. As they drove through the neighbourhood they noticed police cars parked by a block of flats. Cruising slowly past they saw uniformed officers in the garden of the block and a number of squad cars, their blue lights reflecting off the surrounding buildings in the winter dusk.

They drove away.

They waited at Ágúst's house for the news, caught between hope and fear. The radio reported that Elías had been found dead. The police were refusing to release any details but the attack seemed to have been entirely unprovoked and might conceivably have had a racist motive. It was not known who was behind the deed and no witness to the incident had yet come forward.

In the end they agreed to wait. Hallur's father would dispose of the knife. The cousins were not to meet for a while. They would behave as if nothing had happened. The damage had been done, their boys had killed another boy, but surely it was an accident rather than premeditated murder. It had started out as a harmless prank. They hadn't meant to hurt the boy. Of course they would never be able to forget what had happened but they had to think about their sons' future, at least for the time being. Wait and see.

Erlendur took part in cross-examining Ágúst's mother. She had been seeing a psychiatrist since the arrest and was on tranquillisers.

'Of course we should never have done it,' she said. 'But we weren't thinking of ourselves, we were thinking of the boys.'

'Of course you were thinking of yourselves,' Erlendur said.

'No,' she said. 'It wasn't like that.'

'Did you really think you'd be able to live with that on your conscience?' Erlendur asked.

'No,' she said. 'Not me. I . . .'

'You called me,' Erlendur said. 'You were the weakest link.'

'I can't describe it,' she said, rocking in her seat. 'I was suicidal. It was a mistake. Not a minute has passed since it happened when I haven't thought about that poor little boy and his family. Of course it was an error of judgement on our parts, a moral lapse but—' She broke off.

'I know we shouldn't have done it. I know it was wrong and I tried to tell you. But you . . . you reacted so strangely.'

'I know,' Erlendur said. 'I thought you were somebody else.'

'We believed them when they said it was an accident. Things like that can happen. We wouldn't have done it otherwise. We would never have tried to cover up a murder. My husband said that every parent would understand what we did. Understand our reaction.'

'I don't believe that,' Erlendur said. 'You wanted it to go away, to disappear as if it had nothing to do with you. You added outrage to an already terrible crime.'

When it was all over, the police had obtained their confessions and the case was officially deemed to be closed, Erlendur sat down with Hallur in an interview room at the place where he was being held by the Child Welfare Agency. They talked over the incident at length and Erlendur asked why they had decided to attack Elías. What had given them the idea.

'Just, you know,' Hallur said.

'You know what?'

'He was there.'

'That was the only reason?'

'We were bored.'

30

Erlendur held the urn in his hand, a plain, green ceramic pot with a decorated lid, containing the ashes of Marion Briem. It had been delivered to him in a brown paper bag. He looked down into the small grave, then stooped and lowered the urn into it. The minister looked on, making the sign of the cross. They were the only two people in the cemetery on that raw January afternoon.

The snow that had fallen in the blizzard the night Niran attacked Kjartan had mostly thawed during the two days of rain that followed. After that the mercury had plummeted again, the ground was frozen hard and a bitter north wind chilled them to the bone.

Erlendur stood over the grave in the freezing cold, searching for a purpose to the whole business of life and death. As usual he could find no answers. There were no final answers to explain the life-long solitude of the person in the urn, or the death of his brother all those years ago, or why Erlendur was the way he was, and why Elías was stabbed to death. Life was a random mass of unforeseeable coincidences that governed men's fates like a storm that strikes without warning, causing injury and death.

Erlendur thought about Marion Briem and their shared story, which was now at an end. He felt a sense of loss and regret.

He had not realised until he was standing there alone with the urn in his hands that it was over. He thought about their relationship, the experiences they had shared, the story that was part of him, that he could not and would not have done without. It was him.

Before coming to the cemetery, Erlendur had gone to see Andrés and had tried yet again to persuade him to disclose more details about his stepfather. Andrés was obdurate.

'What are you going to do?' Erlendur asked.

'I don't know if I'll do anything,' Andrés said.

He stood at the door of his flat, staring bleakly at Erlendur.

'What are you lot going to do?' he asked.

'We have no reason to do anything unless you want us to,' Erlendur said. 'We have nothing on him. We know nothing about this man. If you know where he lives, why won't you tell me?'

'What for?' Andrés said.

Erlendur regarded him in silence.

'Were you referring to yourself?' he asked. 'When you said he was a murderer?'

Andrés did not answer.

'Was it you he killed?'

Andrés finally nodded.

'Are you going to do anything about it?' Erlendur asked.

Andrés stared at Erlendur for a long moment without answering, then shut the door on him.

Kjartan survived the attack, although he lost a lot of blood and his life hung in the balance for a while. The knife had missed his cardiac muscle by millimetres but thanks to quick action by the police he had reached a doctor before it was too late. Niran was

341

in the care of the Child Welfare Agency. He had been convinced that Kjartan had killed his brother and as time passed his head became filled with nothing but thoughts of revenge. He had talked of revenge to Jóhann who had tried to persuade him that it was pointless. Niran had told his mother that he had been threatened but would not reveal by whom. Kjartan had been beside himself with rage and, convinced that Niran had been involved in vandalising his car, threatened to kill him. Sunee was afraid for Niran and to be on the safe side had asked Jóhann to look after him for a few days.

Several days after Elías's funeral Erlendur went to visit Sunee. They sat in the boys' room while Virote, who was staying with his sister, made tea. Elínborg took a seat in the kitchen and talked to him about the service. Óðinn and his family had stood with Sunee's family who had come over from Thailand to follow Elías to the grave. His body had been cremated and the ashes given to Sunee in an urn.

'You didn't cry,' Erlendur said. Gudný, who was sitting with them, interpreted.

'I've cried enough,' she said.

Gudný translated Sunee's words, her eyes on Erlendur.

'I don't want to worry him too much,' Sunee said. 'It will make it harder for him to get to heaven. It will be harder if he has to swim through my tears.'

They talked of the future. Niran had expressed a wish to return home to Thailand after he had served his sentence but Sunee was not sure he meant it. She herself intended to remain in Iceland, as did her brother. And of course there was Jóhann. Sunee said that he was a good man. He had been hesitant to go public about his relationship with her at first because she was from Thailand; he was new to this sort of thing and wasn't sure how his family would react, so he wanted to take it slowly. All that was past now.

Erlendur told Sunee about the two boys who had been messing about after school, carrying a knife; how Elías had crossed their path by chance and they had attacked him for no real reason. They had intended to play with him, frighten him. 'You never know what brainless idiots like that are capable of,' he said. 'Elías was unlucky to bump into them.'

Sunee's face was unreadable. She listened to Erlendur's explanation of why she had lost her son and her face displayed blank incomprehension.

'Why Elías?' she said.

'Because he was there,' Erlendur said. 'No other reason.'

They sat in silence for a long time until eventually Erlendur mentioned the sentence that he had found in Elías's exercise book about the trees and the forest. Did she know what had been on his mind when he asked how many trees it took to make a forest?

Sunee did not know what he was talking about. The exercise book was on the desk and he showed her what Elías had written. How many trees does it take to make a forest?

Sunee smiled for the first time in ages.

'His Thai name Aran,' she said.

'Yes, Gudný told me. What does Aran mean?'

'Forest,' Sunee said. 'Aran mean forest.'

Erlendur made the sign of the cross over Marion Briem's grave. Then he turned into the wind that bit his face, tore at his hair and pierced his clothes. His thoughts flew home to his books about torment and death in merciless winter storms. Those were stories that he could understand; they kept alight the embers of old feelings in his breast, of regret and grief and loss. He bowed his head into the wind. As so often before at this darkest time of the year he wondered how people had survived for hundreds of years in a country with such a harsh climate.

The frost tightened its grip as evening fell, whipped up by the chill Arctic wind that blasted in from the sea and south over the desolate winter landscape. It plunged down from Mount Skardsheidi, past Mount Esja and ravaged its way over the lowlands where the settlement spread out, a glittering winter city on the northernmost shores of the world. The wind howled and shrieked between the buildings and down the empty streets. The city lay lifeless, as if in the grip of a plague. People stayed inside their houses. They locked their doors, closed their windows and pulled the curtains, hoping against hope that the cold spell would soon be over.